He yelped as he moved.

A force yanked at his wrapper and sent him landing on his buttocks. A hand emerged from the darkness and clamped over his mouth, pressing so hard and high into his nose that he couldn't breathe. Cold, sharp iron landed on his larynx. Something—someone—breathed hard and fast on his neck. The person barked something under their breath, a language Danso did not know.

"Mmhn!" He shook his head vigorously.

The person smacked his mouth, repeated the command, and pressed the blade harder.

He struggled, panic beating drums in his chest. *I don't understand!*

Smack. Again, in the mouth.

I get it, I get it! I won't scream! He stopped moving, his only motion the heaving of his shoulders. After what seemed like eternity, the hand grudgingly withdrew from his mouth.

Danso screamed.

Something hit his head, heavy, and then darkness embraced him.

By Suyi Davies Okungbowa

THE NAMELESS REPUBLIC
Son of the Storm

David Mogo, Godhunter

SON
OF THE
STORM

THE NAMELESS REPUBLIC: BOOK ONE

SUYI DAVIES
OKUNGBOWA

orbitbooks.net

Copyright © 2021 by Suyi Davies Okungbowa
Excerpt from *The Bone Shard Daughter* copyright © 2020 by Andrea Stewart
Excerpt from *The Jasmine Throne* copyright © 2021 by Natasha Suri

Cover design by Lauren Panepinto
Cover illustration by Dan Dos Santos
Cover copyright © 2021 by Hachette Book Group, Inc.
Map by Tim Paul
Author photograph by Manuel Ruiz

Orbit
Hachette Book Group
1290 Avenue of the Americas
New York, NY 10104
orbitbooks.net

First Edition: May 2021
Simultaneously published in Great Britain by Orbit

Orbit is an imprint of Hachette Book Group.
The Orbit name and logo are trademarks of Little, Brown Book Group Limited.

The publisher is not responsible for websites (or their content) that are not owned by the publisher.

The Hachette Speakers Bureau provides a wide range of authors for speaking events. To find out more, go to www.hachettespeakersbureau.com or call (866) 376-6591.

Library of Congress Cataloging-in-Publication Data
Names: Okungbowa, Suyi Davies, author.
Title: Son of the storm / Suyi Davies Okungbowa.
Description: First edition. | New York, NY : Orbit, 2021. | Series: The nameless republic ; book 1
Identifiers: LCCN 2020042815 | ISBN 9780316428941 (trade paperback) | ISBN 9780316540384
Subjects: GSAFD: Fantasy fiction.
Classification: LCC PR9387.9.O394327 S66 2021 | DDC 823/.92—dc23
LC record available at https://lccn.loc.gov/2020042815

ISBNs: 978-0-316-42894-1 (trade paperback), 978-0-316-54039-1 (ebook)

Printed in the United States of America

LSC-C

Printing 1, 2021

For everyone fighting for space in a world designed to spit you out:
You are seen, you are heard, you are loved.

THE CONTINENT OF
OON

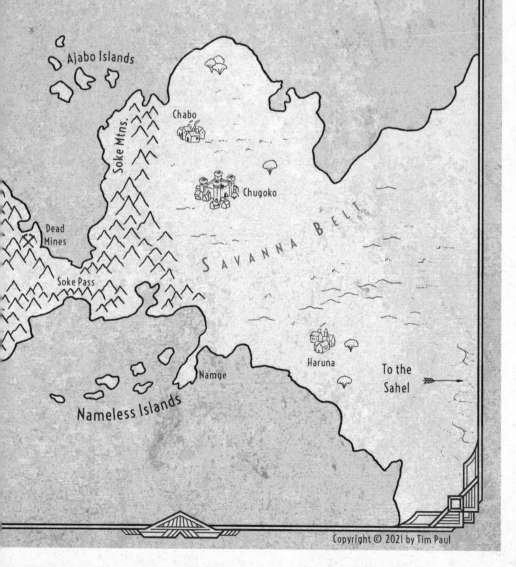

Ajabo Islands

Chabo

Soke Mtns.

Chugoko

Dead Mines

S A V A N N A   B E L T

Soke Pass

Haruna

To the Sahel

Namge

Nameless Islands

Prologue

Oke

THE WEARY SOJOURNER CARAVANSARY stood at the corner of three worlds.

For a multitude of seasons before Oke was born, the travelhouse had offered food, wine, board, and music—and for those who had been on the road too long, companionship—to many a traveller across the Savanna Belt. Its patronage consisted solely of those who lugged loads of gold, bronze, nuts, produce, textile, and craftwork from Bassa into the Savanna Belt or, for the even more daring, to the Idjama desert across Lake Vezha. On their way back, they would stop at the caravansary again, the banana and yam and rice loads on their camels gone and now replaced with tablets of salt, wool, and beaded ornaments.

But there was another set of people for whom the caravansary stood, those whose sights were set on discovering the storied isthmus that connected the Savanna Belt to the yet-to-be-sighted seven islands of the archipelago. For people like these, the Weary Sojourner stood as something else: a vantage point. And for people like Oke who had a leg in all three worlds, walking into the Weary Sojourner called for an intensified level of alertness.

Especially when the fate of the three worlds could be determined by the very meeting she was going to have.

She swung open the curtain. She did not push back her cloak.

Like many public houses in the Savanna Belt, the Weary Sojourner operated in darkness, despite it being late morning. During her time in the desertlands, Oke had learned that this was a practice carried over from the time of the Leopard Emperor when liquor was banned in its desert protectorates, and secret houses were operated under the cover of darkness. Even though that period of despotism was thankfully over, habitual practices were difficult to shake off. People still preferred to drink and smoke and fuck in the dark.

Which made this the perfect place for Oke's meeting.

She took a seat at the back and surveyed the room. It was at once obvious that her contact wasn't around. There were exactly three people here, all men who had clearly just arrived from the same caravan. Their clothes gave them away: definitely Bassai, in brightly coloured cotton wrappers, bronze jewellery—no sensible person travelled with gold jewellery—over some velvet, wool, and leatherskin boots for the desert's cold. Senior members of the merchantry guild, looking at that velvet. Definitely members of the Idu, the mainland's noble caste. Guild aside, their complexions also gave that away—high-black skin, as dark as the darkest of humuses, just the way Bassa liked it. It was the kind of complexion she hadn't seen in a long time.

Oke swept aside a nearby curtain and looked outside. Sure enough, there was their caravan, parked behind the establishment, guarded by a few private Bassai hunthands. Beside them, travelhands—hired desert immigrants to the mainland judging by their complexions, what the Bassai would refer to as *low-brown* for how light and lowly it was—unpacking busily for an overnight stay and unsaddling the camels so they could drink. There were no layers of dust on anyone yet, so clearly they were northbound.

"A drink, maa?"

Oke looked up at the housekeep, who had come over, wringing his hands in a rag. She could see little of his face, but she had been here twice before, and knew enough of what he looked like.

"Palm wine and jackalberry with ginger," she said, hiding her hands.

The housekeep stopped short. "Interesting choice of drink." He peered closer. "Have you been here before?" He enunciated the words in Savanna Common in a way that betrayed his border origins.

Oke's eyes scanned him and decided he was asking this innocently. "Why do you ask?"

"You remember things, as a housekeep," he said, leaning back on a nearby counter. "Especially drink combinations that join lands that have no place joining."

"Consider it an acquired taste," Oke said, and looked away, signalling the end of the discussion. But to her surprise, the man nodded at the group far away and asked, in clear Mainland Common:

"You with them?"

Oke froze. He had seen her complexion, then, and knew enough to know she had mainland origins. What had always been a curse for Oke back when she was a mainlander—*Too light, is she punished by Menai?* people would ask her daa—had become a gift in self-exile over the border. But there were a few people with keen eyes and ears who would, every now and then, recognise a lilt in her Savanna Common or note how her hair curled a bit too tightly for a desertlander or how she carried herself with a smidgen of mainlander confidence. There was only one way to react to that, as she always did whenever this came up.

"What?" She frowned. "Sorry, I don't understand that language."

The housekeep eyed her for another moment, then went away.

Oke breathed a sigh of relief. It was of the utmost importance that no one knew who she was and what she was doing here, living in the Savanna Belt. Because the history of the Savanna Belt was what it was, a tiny enough number of people who originated from this side of the Soke border looked just a bit like she did. Passing as one was easier once she perfected the languages. Thank moons she had studied them as a scholar in Bassa.

She drank slowly once the housekeep brought her order, and she put forward some cowries, making sure to add a few pieces to clearly signal she wanted to be left alone.

Halfway through her drink, she realised her contact was running late. She looked outside again. The sky had gone cloudy, and the sun was missing for a while. She went back to her drink and nursed it some more.

The men in the room rose and went up to be shown to their rooms. Oke peeked out of the curtain again. The travelhands were gone. One hunthand stood and guarded the caravan. One stood at the back door to the caravansary. The camels still stood there, lapping water.

Oke ordered another drink and waited. The sun came back out. It was past an hour now. She looked out again. The camels had stopped drinking and now lay in the dust, snoozing.

Something was wrong.

Oke got up without touching her new drink, put down some more cowries on the counter in front of the housekeep, and walked to the front door of the caravansary. On second thought, she turned and went back to the housekeep.

"Your alternate exit. Show me."

The man pointed without looking at her. Oke took it and went around the building, evading both the men and the animals. She eventually showed up to where she had left her own animal—a kwaga, a striped beauty with tiny horns. She untied and patted it. It snorted in return. Then she slapped its hindquarters and set it off on a run, barking as it went.

She waited for a moment or two, then dashed away herself.

Going through a secluded route on foot, while trying to stay as nondescript as possible, took a long time. Oke had to take double the usual precautions, as banditry had increased so much on the trade routes that one was more likely to get robbed and murdered than not. Back when Bassa was Bassa—not now with its heavily diluted population and generally weakening influence—no one would dare attack a Bassai caravan anywhere on the continent for fear of retaliation. These days, every caravan had to travel with private security. The Bassai Upper Council was well known for being toothless and only concerned with enriching themselves.

The clouds from earlier had disappeared, and the sun beat mercilessly on her, causing her to sweat rivers beneath her cloak, but Oke knew she had done the right thing. It was as they had agreed: If either of them got even a whiff of something off, they were to make a getaway as swiftly as possible. She was then to head straight for the place nicknamed the Forest of the Mist, the thick, uncharted woodland with often heavy fog that was storied to house secret passages to an isthmus that connected the Savanna Belt to the seven islands of the eastern archipelago.

It didn't matter any longer if that bit of desertland myth was true or not. Whether the archipelago even still existed was moot at this point. The yet undiscovered knowledge she had gleaned from her clandestine exploits in the library at the University of Bassa, coupled with the artifacts her contact was bringing her—if either made it into the wrong hands, the whole continent of Oon would pay for it. Oke wasn't ready to drop the fate of the continent in the dust just yet.

Two hours later, Oke looked back and saw in the sky the grey tip of what she knew came from thick, black smoke. Not the kind of smoke that came from a nearby kitchen, but the kind that said something far away had been destroyed. Something big.

She took a detour in her journey and headed for the closest high point she knew. She chose one that overlooked a decent portion of the savanna but also kept her on the way to the Forest of the Mist. It took a while to ascend to the top, but she soon got to a good enough vantage point to look across and see the caravansary.

The Weary Sojourner stuck out like an anthill, the one establishment for a distance where the road from the border branched into the Savanna Belt. The caravansary was up in flames. It was too far for her to see the people and animals, but she knew what those things scattering from the raging inferno were. The body language of disaster was the same everywhere.

Oke began to descend fast, her chest weightless. The Forest of the Mist was the only place on this continent where she would be safe now, and she needed to get there *immediately*. Whoever set that fire to the Weary Sojourner knew who she and her contact were. Her contact may or may not have made it out alive. It was up to her now to ensure that the continent's biggest secret was kept that way.

The alternative was simply too grave to consider.

bassa

Danso

THE RUMOURS BROKE SLOWLY but spread fast, like bushfire from a rain-cloud. Bassa's central market sparked and sizzled, as word jumped from lip to ear, lip to ear, speculating. The people responded minimally at first: a shift of the shoulders, a retying of wrappers. Then murmurs rose, until they matured into a buzzing that swept through the city, swinging from stranger to stranger and stall to stall, everyone opening conversation with whispers of *Is it true? Has the Soke Pass really been shut down?*

Danso waded through the clumps of gossipers, sweating, cursing his decision to go through the central market rather than the mainway. He darted between throngs of oblivious citizens huddled around vendors and spilling into the pathway.

"Leave way, leave way," he called, irritated, as he shouldered through bodies. He crouched, wriggling his lean frame underneath a large table that reeked of pepper seeds and fowl shit. The ground, paved with baked earth, was not supposed to be wet, since harmattan season was soon to begin. But some fool had dumped water in the wrong place, and red mud eventually found a way into Danso's sandals. Someone else had abandoned a huge stack of yam sacks right in the middle of the pathway and gone off to do moons knew what, so that Danso was forced to clamber over yet another obstacle. He found a large brown stain on his wrappers there-after. He wiped at the spot with his elbow, but the stain only spread.

Great. Now not only was he going to be the late jali novitiate, he was going to be the dirty one, too.

If only he could've ridden a kwaga through the market, Danso thought. But markets were foot traffic only, so even though jalis or their novitiates rarely moved on foot, he had to in this instance. On this day, when he needed to get to the centre of town as quickly as possible while raising zero eyebrows, he needed to brave the shortest path from home to city square, which meant going through Bassa's most motley crowd. This was the price he had to pay for missing the city crier's call three whole times, therefore setting himself up for yet another late arrival at a mandatory event—in this case, a Great Dome announcement.

Missing this impromptu meeting would be his third infraction, which could mean expulsion from the university. He'd already been given two strikes: first, for repeatedly arguing with Elder Jalis and trying to prove his superior intelligence; then more recently, for being caught poring over a restricted manuscript that was supposed to be for only two sets of eyes: emperors, back when Bassa still had them, and the archivist scholars who didn't even get to read them except while scribing. At this rate, all they needed was a reason to send him away. Expulsion would definitely lose him favour with Esheme, and if anything happened to their intendedship as a result, he could consider his life in this city officially over. He would end up exactly like his daa—a disgraced outcast—and Habba would die first before that happened.

The end of the market pathway came within sight. Danso burst out into mainway one, the smack middle of Bassa's thirty mainways that crisscrossed one another and split the city perpendicular to the Soke mountains. The midday sun shone brighter here. Though shoddy, the market's thatch roofing had saved him from some of the tropical sun, and now out of it, the humid heat came down on him unbearably. He shaded his eyes.

In the distance, the capital square stood at the end of the mainway. The Great Dome nestled prettily in its centre, against a backdrop of Bassai rounded-corner mudbrick architecture, like a god surrounded by its worshippers. Behind it, the Soke mountains stuck their raggedy heads so high into the clouds that they could be seen from every spot in Bassa, hunching protectively over the mainland's shining crown.

What took his attention, though, was the crowd in the mainway, leading up to the Great Dome. The wide street was packed full of mainlanders, from where Danso stood to the gates of the courtyard in the distance. The only times he'd seen this much of a gathering were when, every once in a while, troublemakers who called themselves the Coalition for New Bassa staged protests that mostly ended in pockets of riots and skirmishes with Bassai civic guards. This, however, seemed quite nonviolent, but that did nothing for the air of tension that permeated the crowd.

The civic guards at the gates weren't letting anyone in, obviously—only the ruling councils; government officials and ward leaders; members of select guilds, like the jali guild he belonged to; and civic guards themselves were allowed into the city centre. It was these select people who then took whatever news was disseminated back to their various wards. Only during a mooncrossing festival were regular citizens allowed into the courtyard.

Danso watched the crowd for a while to make a quick decision. The thrumming vibe was clearly one of anger, perplexity, and anxiety. He spotted a few people wailing and rolling in the dusty red earth, calling the names of their loved ones—those stuck outside the Pass, he surmised from their cries. Since First Ward was the largest commercial ward in Bassa, businesses at the sides of the mainway were hubbubs of hissed conversation, questions circulating under breaths. Danso caught some of the whispers, squeaky with tension: *The drawbridges over the moats? Rolled up. The border gates? Sealed, iron barriers driven into the earth. Only a ten-person team of earthworkers and ironworkers can open it.* The pace of their speech was frantic, fast, faster, everyone wondering what was true and what wasn't.

Danso cut back into a side street that opened up from the walls along the mainway, then cut into the corridors between private yards. Up here in First Ward, the corridors were clean, the ground was of polished earth, and beggars and rats did not populate here as they did in the outer wards. Yet they were still dark and largely unlit, so that Danso had to squint and sometimes reach out to feel before him. Navigation, however, wasn't a problem. This wasn't his first dance in the mazy corridors of Bassa, and this wasn't the first time he was taking a shortcut to the Great Dome.

Some househands passed by him on their way to errands, blending into the poor light, their red immigrant anklets clacking as they went. These narrow walkways built into the spaces between courtyards were natural terrain for their caste—Yelekuté, the lower of Bassa's two indentured immigrant castes. The nation didn't really fancy anything undesirable showing up in all the important places, including the low-brown complexion that, among other things, easily signified desertlanders. The more desired high-brown Potokin were the chosen desertlanders allowed on the mainways, but only in company of their employers.

Ordinarily, they wouldn't pay him much attention. It wasn't a rare sight to spot people of other castes dallying in one backyard escapade or another. But today, hurrying past and dripping sweat, they glanced at Danso as he went, taking in his yellow-and-maroon tie-and-dye wrappers and the fat, single plait of hair in the middle of his head, the two signs that indicated he was a jali novitiate at the university. They considered his complexion—not dark enough to be wearing that dress in the first place; hair not curled tightly enough to be pure mainlander—and concluded, *decided*, that he was not Bassai enough.

This assessment they carried out in a heartbeat, but Danso was so used to seeing the whole process happen on people's faces that he knew what they were doing even before they did. And as always, then came the next part, where they tried to put two and two together to decide what caste he belonged to. Their confused faces told the story of his life. His clothes and hair plait said *jali novitiate*, that he was a scholar-historian enrolled at the University of Bassa, and therefore had to be an Idu, the only caste allowed to attend said university. But his too-light complexion said *Shashi caste*, said he was of a poisoned union between a mainlander and an outlander and that even if the moons intervened, he would always be a disgrace to the mainland, an outcast who didn't even deserve to stand there and exist.

Perhaps it was this confusion that led the househands to go past him without offering the requisite greeting for Idu caste members. Danso snickered to himself. If belonging to both the highest and lowest castes in the land at the same time taught one anything, it was that when people had to choose where to place a person, they would always choose a spot beneath them.

He went past more households who offered the same response, but he paid little heed, spatially mapping out where he could emerge closest to the city square. He finally found the exit he was looking for. Glad to be away from the darkness, he veered into the nearest street and followed the crowd back to the mainway.

The city square had five iron pedestrian gates, all guarded. To his luck, Danso emerged just close to one, manned by four typical civic guards: tall, snarling, and bloodshot-eyed. He made for it gleefully and pushed to go in.

The nearest civic guard held the gate firmly and frowned down at Danso.

"Where you think you're going?" he asked.

"The announcement," Danso said. "Obviously."

The civic guard looked Danso over, his chest rising and falling, his low-black skin shiny with sweat in the afternoon heat. Civic guards were Emuru, the lower of the pure mainlander caste, but they still wielded a lot of power. As the caste directly below the Idu, they could be brutal if given the space, especially if one belonged to any of the castes below them.

"And you're going as what?"

Danso lifted an eyebrow. "Excuse me?"

The guard looked at him again, then shoved Danso hard, so hard that he almost fell back into the group of people standing there.

"Ah!" Danso said. "Are you okay?"

"Get away. This resemble place for ruffians?" His Mainland Common was so poor he might have been better off speaking Mainland Pidgin, but that was the curse of working within proximity of so many Idu: Speaking Mainland Pidgin around them was almost as good as a crime. Here in the inner wards, High Bassai was accepted, Mainland Common was tolerated, and Mainland Pidgin was punished.

"Look," Danso said. "Can you not see I'm a jali novi—"

"I cannot see anything," the guard said, waving him away. "How can you be novitiate? I mean, look at you."

Danso looked over himself and suddenly realised what the man meant. His tie-and-dye wrappers didn't, in fact, look like they belonged to any respectable jali novitiate. Not only had he forgotten to give them to Zaq to wash after his last guild class, the market run had only made them worse. His feet were dusty and unwashed; his arms, and probably face, were crackled, dry, and smeared with harmattan dust. One of his sandal straps had pulled off. He ran a hand over his head and sighed. Experience should have taught him by now that his sparser hair, much of it inherited from his maternal Ajabo-islander side, never stayed long in the Bassai plait, which was designed for hair that curled tighter naturally. Running around without a firm new plait had produced unintended results: Half of it had come undone, which made him look unprepared, disrespectful, and not at all like any jali anyone knew.

And of course, there had been no time to take a bath, and he had not put on any sort of decent facepaint either. He'd also arrived without a kwaga. What manner of jali novitiate *walked* to an impromptu announcement such as this, and without a Second in tow for that matter?

He should really have listened for the city crier's ring.

"Okay, wait, listen," Danso said, desperate. "I was late. So I took the corridors. But I'm really a jali novitiate."

"I will close my eye," the civic guard said. "Before I open it, I no want to see you here."

"But I'm supposed to be here." Danso's voice was suddenly squeaky, guilty. "I *have* to go in there."

"Rubbish," the man spat. "You even steal that cloth or what?"

Danso's words got stuck in his throat, panic suddenly gripping him. Not because this civic guard was an idiot—oh, no, just wait until Danso reported him—but because so many things were going to go wrong if he didn't get in there immediately.

First, there was Esheme, waiting for him in there. He could already imagine her fuming, her lips set, frown stuck in place. It was unheard of for intendeds to attend any capital square gathering alone, and it was worse that they were both novitiates—he of the scholar-historians, she of the counsel guild of mainland law. His absence would be easily noticed. She had probably already sat through most of the meeting craning her neck to glance at the entrance, hoping he would come in and ensure that she didn't have to suffer that embarrassment. He imagined Nem, her maa, and how she would cast him the same dissatisfied look as when she sometimes told Esheme, *You're really too good for that boy.* If there was anything his daa hated, it was disappointing someone as influential as Nem in any way. He might be of guild age, but his daa would readily come for him with a guava stick just for that, and his triplet uncles would be like a choir behind him going *Ehen, ehen, yes, teach him well, Habba.*

His DaaHabba name wouldn't save him this time. He could be prevented from taking guild finals, and his whole life—and that of his family—could be ruined.

"I will tell you one last time," the civic guard said, taking a step toward Danso so that he could almost smell the dirt of the man's loincloth. "If you no leave here now, I will arrest you for trying to be novitiate."

He was so tall that his chest armour was right in Danso's face, the branded official emblem of the Nation of Great Bassa—the five ragged peaks of the Soke mountains with a warrior atop each, holding a spear and runku—staring back at him.

He really couldn't leave. He'd be over, done. So instead, Danso did the first thing that came to mind. He tried to slip past the civic guard.

It was almost as if the civic guard had expected it, as if it was behaviour he'd seen often. He didn't even move his body. He just stretched out a massive arm and caught Danso's clothes. He swung him around, and Danso crumpled into a heap at the man's feet.

The other guards laughed, as did the small group of people by the gate, but the civic guard wasn't done. He feinted, like he was about to lunge and hit Danso. Danso flinched, anticipating, protecting his head. Everyone laughed even louder, boisterous.

"Ei Shashi," another civic guard said, "you miss yo way? Is over there." He pointed west, toward Whudasha, toward the coast and the bight and the seas beyond them, and everyone laughed at the joke.

Every peal was another sting in Danso's chest as the word pricked him all over his body. *Shashi. Shashi. Shashi.*

It shouldn't have gotten to him. Not on this day, at least. Danso had been Shashi all his life, one of an almost nonexistent pinch in Bassa. He was the first Shashi to make it into a top guild since the Second Great War. Unlike every other Shashi sequestered away in Whudasha, he was allowed to sit side by side with other Idu, walk the nation's roads, go to its university, have a Second for himself, and even be joined to one of its citizens. But every day he was always reminded, in case he had forgotten, of what he really was—never enough. Almost there, but never complete. That lump should have been easy to get past his throat by now.

And yet, something hot and prideful rose in his chest at this laughter, and he picked himself up, slowly.

As the leader turned away, Danso aimed his words at the man, like arrows.

"Calling me Shashi," Danso said, "yet you *want* to be me. But you will always be less than bastards in this city. You can never be better than me."

What happened next was difficult for Danso to explain. First, the civic guard turned. Then he moved his hand to his waist where his runku, the large wooden club with a blob at one end, hung. He unclipped its buckle with a click, then moved so fast that Danso had no time to react.

There was a shout. Something hit Danso in the head. There was light, and then there was darkness.

Danso awoke to a face peering at his. It was large, and he could see faint traces left by poorly healed scars. A pain beat in his temple, and it took a while for the face to come into full focus.

Oboda. Esheme's Second.

The big man stood up, silent. Oboda was a bulky man with just as mountainous a presence. Even his shadow took up space, so much so that it shaded Danso from the sunlight. The coral pieces embedded into his neck, in a way no Second that Danso knew ever had, glinted. He didn't even wear a migrant anklet or anything else that announced that he was an immigrant. The only signifier was his complexion: just dark enough as a desertlander to be acceptably close to the Bassai Ideal's yardstick—the complexion of the humus, that which gave life to everything and made it thrive. Being high-brown while possessing the build and skills of a desert warrior put him squarely in the higher Potokin caste. Oboda, as a result, was allowed freedoms many immigrants weren't, so he ended up being not quite Esheme's or Nem's Second, but something more complex, something that didn't yet have a name.

Danso blinked some more. The capital square behind Oboda was filled, but now with a new crowd, this one pouring out of the sectioned entryway arches of the Great Dome and heading for their parked travel-wagons, kept ready by various househands and stablehands. Wrappers of various colours dotted the scene before him, each council or guild representing itself properly. He could already map out those of the Elders of the merchantry guild in their green and gold combinations, and Elders of other guilds in orange, blue, bark, violet, crimson. There were even a few from the university within sight, scholars and jalis alike, in their white robes.

Danso shrunk into Oboda's shadow, obscuring himself. It would be a disaster for them to see him like this. It would be a disaster for *anyone* to see him so. *But then*, he thought, *if Oboda is here, that means Esheme...*

"Danso," a woman's voice said.

Oh moons!

Delicately, Esheme gathered her clothes in the crook of one arm and picked her way toward him. She was dressed in tie-and-dye wrappers just like his, but hers were of different colours—violet dappled in orange, the uniform for counsel novitiates of mainland law—and a far cry from his: Hers were washed and dipped in starch so that they shone and didn't even flicker in the breeze.

As she came forward, the people who were starting to gather to watch the scene gazed at her with wide-eyed appreciation. Esheme was able to do that, elicit responses from everything and everyone by simply *being*. She knew exactly how to play to eyes, knew what to do to evoke the exact reactions she wanted from people. She did so now, swaying just the right amount yet keeping a regal posture so that she was both desirable and fearsome at once. The three plaited arches on her head gleamed in the afternoon sun, the deep-yellow cheto dye massaged into her hair illuminating her head. Her high-black complexion, dark and pure in the most desirable Bassai way, shone with superior fragrant shea oils. She had her gaze squarely on Danso's face so that he couldn't look at her, but had to look down.

She arrived where he sat, took one sweeping look at the civic guards, and said, "What happened here?"

"I was trying to attend the announcement and this one"—Danso pointed at the nearby offending civic guard—"hit me with his runku."

She didn't respond to him, not even with a glance. She just kept staring at the civic guards. The three behind the errant civic guard stepped away, leaving him in front.

"I no hit anybody, oh," the man said, his pitch rising. "The crowd had scatter, and somebody hit him with their elbow—"

Esheme silenced him with a sharp finger in the air. "Speak wisely, guard. You have this one chance."

The man gulped, suddenly looking like he couldn't make words.

"Sorry," he said, going to the ground immediately, prostrating. "Sorry, please. No send me back. No send me back."

The other civic guards joined their comrade in solidarity, all prostrating on the ground before Esheme. She turned away from them, leaned in, and examined Danso's head and clothes with light touches, as one would a child who had fallen and hurt themselves.

"Who did this to him?"

"Sorry, maa," the civic guards kept saying, offering no explanation. "Sorry, maa."

Oboda moved then, swiftly, light on his feet for someone so big. He reached over with one arm, pulled the errant guard by his loincloth, and yanked him over the low gate. The man came sprawling. His loincloth gave way, and he scrambled to cover his privates. The gathering crowd, always happy to feast their eyes and ears on unsanctioned justice, snickered.

"Beg," Oboda growled. The way he said it, it was really *Beg for your life*, but he was a man of too few words to use the whole sentence. However, the rest of the sentence was not lost on anyone standing there, the civic guard included. He hustled to his knees and put his forehead on the ground, close to Esheme's sandals. Even the crowd stepped back a foot or two.

Danso flinched. Surely this had gone past the territory of fairness, had it not? This was the point where he was supposed to jump in and prevent things from escalating, to explain that no, the man might not have hit him at all, that he was actually likelier to have fallen in the scramble. But then what good reason would he have for missing this meeting? Plus, with Esheme, silence *always* had a lower chance of backfiring than speaking up did.

He kept his lips tight together and looked down. *Why throw good food away?* as his daa would say.

"You don't know what you have brought on yourself," Esheme said to the guard quietly, then turned away. As she did, Oboda put his hand on his waist and unclipped his own runku, but Esheme laid a hand gently on his.

"Let's go," she said to no one in particular, and walked off. Oboda clipped his runku back, gave the civic guards one last long look of death, and pulled Danso up with one arm as if flicking a copper piece. Danso dusted off his shins while Oboda silently handed him a cloth to wipe his face. The civic guard stayed bowed, shaking, too scared to rise.

Danso hurried off to join Esheme in the exiting crowd, spotting her greeting a couple of councilhands. He stood far off from her for a moment, and she ignored him for as long as she could, until she turned and wordlessly walked over to him, adjusted his wrappers, re-knotted them at the shoulder, then led him by the arm.

"Let's do this," she said.

Danso

HEADING SOUTH ON MAINWAY one was a slightly downhill trip, so that people always seemed like they were rushing when leaving the city centre, their backs to the towering Soke mountains in the distance behind them, framing the border and its moats. Esheme and Danso performed their walk of intendedship with deliberate intent, so that they seemed to be in slow motion next to everything else. Esheme interlocked her fingers with his and he let her, despite the fact that he abhorred this part of the performance. Today, though, he swallowed his usual thoughts and walked hand-in-hand with her, considering it penance for his errant ways. He'd been so occupied with attending the meeting that he'd even completely forgotten about this part.

The frenzy of the announcement had yet to wear off, and First Ward, being the only ward that was nonresidential and all commercial, remained as packed as possible. Cart pushers ran their carts at a speed faster than usual, whipping their oxen, raising dust and going *hyaah* and making that loud click with their tongues. Pawpaws, watermelons, and soursops bounced in their attached barrows. Kwagas strutted and cantered past them, their striped equine coats and polished double horns shining in the midday light, massive hooves and hindquarters stomping the dust. Hitched travelwagons housing returnees hurried by amid all of the clacking. Danso and Esheme stuck to the wayside near the mainway's earthen walls, street and corridor connections opening up from them like yawns. Nighttime palm oil torches, unlit, were the only things that stood with them, silent and unhurried.

Why intendeds were expected to advertise their togetherness, Danso could never understand. He'd once read at the university library that it was a practice developed in the early days before Bassa, when the indigenous peoples of the mainland's hamlets needed to advertise that they had chosen someone, lest they be snatched up by another. But Danso found it ridiculous that such a tradition should persist until today, in the greatest city on the continent. Why should the public care about who he was being joined to? It made even less sense because they never spent time together in any other way. They attended the same university, sure, but Esheme barely spoke to him when they went past each other in the hallways.

But again, today he couldn't nag about any of these things as usual. The possibility of invoking Esheme's wrath was the beginning of wisdom. She had a way of making things happen just exactly as she wanted them, and anyone who caused that to derail would face the consequences, her intended being no exclusion.

"Is all this furore over just the Pass closure?" Danso said. "I feel like I missed something big at that announcement."

Esheme said nothing in response. She draped a wrapper over her hair to ward off dust from the disturbed earth. Her sullen expression flipped into a pleasant smile as they neared a group of passersby who chattered breathlessly about rumoured reasons for the meeting. The group eased up once they spotted the couple, and fell into yet another expression Danso was familiar with, one where they bit their lips because they couldn't disrespect two semi-outcasts since they were performing their walk. So the group paused and offered the requisite greeting.

"Your home supports you," they said.

"Outsiders cannot harm us," Danso and Esheme chorused.

Danso scratched at his neck, uncomfortable with the tightness of the wrapper crisscrossing at his collarbone. Esheme had done this too tight, hadn't she? Too late now, though. He would have to wear it like that.

"So humid," he said, as they went on. "Isn't it supposed to be harmattan yet?"

Esheme smiled at another passing greeter, and then her face returned to passive. Danso was unsure how to proceed.

"How did the meeting go, by the way?" he asked, and that was what did it.

"Shut up," she said, stopping to face him for the first time. "Shut your dirty mouth." She contorted her face in mockery. "*How did the meeting go?* Are you not a jali? Is it not your job to *know* such things, to be the documenter of our history, to be *here*, present when asked?" She made a sound at the back of her tongue. "Would it kill you not to be aloof for once? Just look at the nonsense you've put me through today."

"It wasn't my fault."

"Don't even try," she said, pointing a finger in his face. "That's market mud on you, okay? And no kwaga, no Zaq. I'm not stupid; I know you were already late."

He muttered an apology that she didn't acknowledge. She instead turned and kept walking. He jogged to keep up with her. He thought about easing his hand back into hers, but was unsure which was now the greater risk: holding her hand or not holding it at all. He stuck with the status quo.

"I said I was sorry," he muttered.

"Danso, you must remember—"

"My place, I know," he said. But she had to understand that it was this *place* that had gotten him in trouble, didn't she? If he never had to be *both* an Idu scholar and a Shashi man attending the meeting, there would've been no altercation. Whether he was late or not would've been moot. The real problem was that he was both gold and shit at once, but no one wanted to hear *that*.

"You can't keep blaming everyone else for your misfortunes," she said, as if reading his mind. "You broke the rules, and you paid for it." She ran her fingers over his plait; he was unsure if the gesture was one of intimacy or correction. "They held you because you were late and without a Second, not because you're..." She searched for a word other than the one Danso knew was at the tip of her tongue, one that she consciously avoided using to describe him, though he was unsure if it was out of respect for him or because she thought it would reflect poorly on her.

"Just because you're you," she said at last. "Besides, count your appearance as a blessing. It's how Oboda spotted you in the first place."

Another group passed by them and performed the greeting for intendeds. Danso answered noncommittally. He was never sure what to do when Esheme pretended not to see his Bassai-Ajabo heritage. As though, if not for his ability to recall every single word he read—a talent the Bassai elite considered incomparable—he wouldn't be down at Whudasha right now with the thousands of Shashi corralled there. They would never have met if he was cordoned off, in a protectorate on the coast so far out of sight that mainlanders didn't have to face the truth of his existence every day.

But she *did* understand, because she, too, knew what it was like to be disrespected for where one came from. They were together for that very reason. No one would touch the daughter of Bassa's prime fixer with a stick. It did not matter that Esheme herself was an Idu. Her maa both was a fixer for Idu nobles *and* hailed from the lower Emuru caste. That combination was enough reason to be marginalised. The reasons for hers might be a tad different from his, but the feeling in the pits of their stomachs were the same.

"They're closing the Pass," Esheme said, bringing him out of his thoughts. "Since you were wondering what the meeting was about."

Danso's eyes widened. "For real? I thought that was just a rumour."

She shot him a look. "Why won't you think like a commoner when you act like one? Of course it's not a rumour. The meeting was just more details, but it's decided. Speaker Abuso said there will only be essential import/export activities for now. No more crossing the moats, no movement into or out of the mainland until further notice."

"Well, moons," Danso said. "That's drastic. The outer wards will feel that hard. They'll protest."

"The Coalition for New Bassa will definitely whip up something in response." She seemed to have shaken off her anger, and Danso thought she sounded oddly excited about it. "This will affect immigration the most, though. Trade still remains open with the outer lands, even though only First Merchant caravans are now allowed through."

"And this closure is, what, temporary or . . . ?"

"Looks permanent. Something tells me no one will ever be allowed to enter the mainland again, which is just as well. Part of the reason for our waning influence with our hinterlands and the desertland is that we have too many immigrants anyway. Not near enough work for everyone, and fealty is increasingly unsure."

Danso's eyebrows arched. "For them to literally close the drawbridges over the moats sounds like something more than curbing immigration is going on."

She glanced at him. "What are you, a desertlander advocate?"

"Well, I mean—"

"What happens when our resources can no longer serve us? What happens when the desertlanders suddenly outnumber us and attack?"

"Attack?" Danso snorted. "There hasn't been an attack on the mainland since the Second Great War, Esheme."

"Maybe. But also . . ." She put a finger to her lip. "I shouldn't be telling you this, but, I mean, you're my intended, so." She paused again. "I think my maa wouldn't mind."

Danso fought back a scoff. Esheme and MaaNem didn't quite have the best maa-daughter relationship, but one thing he was sure of was that nothing ever got past either of them. The MaaNem household was like a sponge—things got *in* more than they got out, unless Nem was the one doing the squeezing. If anyone who was anyone in Bassa needed to get something *fixed*, in all the ways possible, Nem was the person to go to. The network of assets in her employ—hunthands, alchemists, smiths, skylookers, tinkerers, scouts, whisperers—was notorious enough to make her highly despised but extremely useful to the Bassai elite. For someone who traded daily on information, Danso thought Elder Nem would very much mind Esheme letting him in on whatever this piece of information was, but he gave her his ear anyway because he had made her angry enough for one day.

"There was an intruder, they say," Esheme said. "At the border. Rumour is they made it over the Soke Pass."

"You mean like an illegal immigrant? That happens every day."

"Yes, but not a desertlander." She paused. "An islander."

Danso jerked his head back. "Don't be silly."

"I'm not." Esheme's voice was low, conspiratorial. "Within Idu's upper circles, there's a story that a border official thought they caught a glance of—you won't believe this—*yellowskin* around some caravans that had just arrived from the Savanna Belt. They reported it to the civic guard captain on duty at the Pass. Some men were sent after the described person, but no one has found anything."

"*Yellowskin*," Danso said. "You can't be serious."

"Danso," Esheme said. "I literally overheard my maa discussing this with an Elder."

Danso's eyes watered, and the back of his throat suddenly felt parched.

Every season since birth, there was one thing Danso had been completely sure of: that there used to be three places in the world, but now there were only two—the mainland, and the sprawling desertland north of the Soke mountains, with the Soke Pass separating them. The only islands known to the continent—the Ajabo Islands to the west where his maa's people had come from, and the Nameless archipelago to the east—both went extinct hundreds of seasons ago. *Sunk into the great waters*, said the manuscripts at the university library. *Sent by Menai to a deep-sea grave*, said the jali litanies he learned in class. *Yellowskin* was the mainland slur for the people of the seven islands of the northeastern Nameless archipelago, geographically closer to the desert than the mainland. The Nameless Islands were *nameless* for the very reason that mainlanders had never interacted with anyone from there—at least not in the same way they had with the Ajabo. It was widely accepted that human life didn't exist there, wherever it was. The only tales that attempted to refute that were those of returning travellers to the desert who reported sightings of a yellowskin or two. They called them contagious, that if a yellowskin touched you, you became one. They said yellowskins were of low intelligence and unable to stay too long in the sun or see very far. They described them as having *red eyes and yellow hair up to their eyebrows*. They said if killed, their body parts could be used to cure diseases.

So basically, a bunch of drivel. The only people who believed in them were the same sects who ardently believed in lightning bats, ghost apes, and other entities no one had ever seen but many were sure plagued Bassa's rainforests.

"You don't really believe that, do you?" Danso asked her.

"Does it matter?" Esheme shrugged. "There's no such thing as too much precaution."

"I guess." They went on in silence, but Danso found that a familiar spark had been lit within him. The same kind of spark that had caused him to begin the search for the history of the Ajabo, which led him to discover the Codex of the Twenty-Third Emperor of Great Bassa, the Manic Emperor Nogowu, at the university library. Which had then, of course, put him in big trouble. He had to rein this one in. This was *really* not the time.

"My maa and the Elder were saying leadership is not making it public because they don't want to alert the intruder," Esheme was saying. "But they've put out a bounty to the hunthand guild. The Elder, I believe, wanted my maa to make a go for it with the hunthands in her employ."

"How much?"

"A hundred gold pieces, dead or alive."

Danso whistled.

"I know!" Esheme said. "Imagine that. Enough gold to buy some respect on this mainland."

"Why so high, though? I mean, for someone who could easily be spotted by anyone, I don't know..."

"Well, the Elder said the yellowskin can change their complexion and look like one of us. Apparently, that's how they escaped at the border."

Now Danso had to laugh. "You mean the skinchanging myth."

"I'm not saying it's true," Esheme said. "I'm saying if a top Elder believes it, it's worth concern."

"Seriously? They're closing our border because of *that*? So, what, how did the skinchanger do it now, by the power of ibor?"

Esheme frowned. "What do you mean, ibor?"

"Never mind, never mind." He couldn't discuss what he'd learned in the codex with anyone—that had been one of the conditions of being allowed to remain at the university. The stone-bone mineral was something that came up in stories every now and then. Like most myths and legends in Bassa, few people took to them with any manner of seriousness. But Danso had read something in the codex that, though it sounded vague at the time, he began to think might be in reference to ibor:

Know this, in the very presence of our Holinesses Ashu and Menai—
may they strike me if I lie—that the Second Great War may have been
rendered needless if the intruders had parted with their stones of sor-
cery upon joining the land.

Perhaps these *stones of sorcery* were something else entirely, who could tell? Perhaps the man was simply high on opiates. He *was* called the Manic Emperor for a reason.

They stopped to perform another greeting of intendedship. Danso wished he could prod someone with more questions. His daa and uncles rarely spoke a word about his maa and what had really happened with her or with the Ajabo, not even to discuss the pogroms against Shashi that came after, before Whudasha's Peace Treaty was agreed upon. Whenever he asked, they retreated into their shells like disturbed snails and would remain cold for a long time. The little he knew was from the sparse jali lectures and library archives, and if there was anything he'd learned from this codex business, it was that prodding in that direction had consequences.

A runner sped down the road, pushing a small wagon with a young couple in it. Esheme gazed at them and said something about how her maa would like to see them like that, once their joining ceremony was complete. Danso pretended not to see or hear. If there was one thing he was looking forward to, it was *not* that. He might not have a very clear idea of what he wanted, but he was sure it did not lie here in Bassa with its rules and confines and expectations.

He looked up to see that they had arrived at their destination. Nem's house rose with thick walls of mudbrick and mortar. To Danso's eyes each time he looked upon it, it was thrice the size of the DaaHabba abode. Nem's household was well cared for, with a hired caretaker and an army of househands, much unlike Danso's home. His daa had left the jali guild after being disgraced for his affiliation with an Ajabo woman once Danso's existence was revealed post-pogrom. Habba had settled into life as a private healer. The DaaHabba household, with no caretaker, suffered as a result and began to fall, crumble, die. Danso thought his triplet uncles who lived with them made this crumbling happen much quicker by siphoning the few resources his daa had left.

"So, um," he said, "I would like to apologise for today. The day really went away from me. Can I make it up to you at the crossing festival?"

Esheme smiled. For a moment, Danso saw what most others saw: a pretty, young, desirable Bassai woman, dark and pure. Then her smile lasted just that little bit too long, and the illusion was gone.

"Of course you will make it up," she said. "You will kiss me, and then it will be forgotten."

Danso cast furtive glances at the entryway. "Er—"

But she had already pulled him in and put her lips to his. He found them soft and slim and tender, warm. The balmy, metallic fragrance of the ochre of her facepaint ran rings around his nose. He shut his eyes and opened them many times, until she pulled away.

She adjusted his wrapper knot, then ran her palm over his plait again. She kissed his forehead.

"At the crossing festival, then," she said.

She disappeared behind the entryway, and Danso was left alone to dread the return home to face his daa's disappointment and the snivelling whispers of his uncles.

Danso

HE HAD NOT FULLY stepped through the doorway when Pochuwe, the first of Danso's three uncles, materialized in front of him in a flurry of fabric.

"Where have you been?"

A retort rose from the bottom of Danso's belly and travelled up his chest, ready to be unleashed, but, as usual, it stopped at his larynx and lodged there with the other retorts that never became, forming a bulge now too large to go down no matter how hard he swallowed.

"Dehje, uncle," he said in greeting. "I was walking my intended to her maa's."

"Eh." Pochuwe gathered his wrappers, laid them over a thin hand, and studied his unkempt look. "You say you were, but how do we know for sure? Because your lie-lie can be legend." He twisted his angular jaw, an odd feature beneath lazy, rounded, well-fed cheeks.

"I was there," Danso said, which wasn't quite a lie.

Uduuwe and Kachuwe, spitting images of Pochuwe, descended the steps from the upper floor, their wrappers draped across their arms in the exact same manner; it was uncanny. Uduuwe looked at Danso and frowned.

"You weren't at the announcement," he said.

Kachuwe, the youngest of the three, said: "We heard."

Danso almost rolled his eyes. It was pointless asking how they knew. Bassa's network of corridors and courtyards meant everyone knew everything too soon. The colour of one's shit could be common knowledge before one stepped out of the lavatory. But they could just as well have wrung it out of Zaq.

You maybe should've spent that time finding your own houses, Danso thought, but swallowed again. "I said I went."

"When?" Pochuwe asked.

Danso stared at him.

"Toward the end." Kachuwe scoffed. "Zaq told us."

"You think you're a big man now or something." Uduuwe shook his head. "It's like you're forgetting where you're coming from. Are you trying to sabotage this family's name or what?"

"I'm not—"

"What did Nem have to say about you leaving her daughter to attend the gathering alone?" Pochuwe asked.

Danso stared at the cut strap of his sandal again. He should get Zaq to fix that right away.

Pochuwe managed a disapproving click of his tongue and went to settle in a woven chair. The other two followed, regarding Danso in the same pitiful manner with which one looked at a fowl that insisted on taking up issue with the field cattle.

Kachuwe said: "You can't finish us in this family, this boy."

"Every single one of your peers was there," Pochuwe said. "Representing their houses. And you think you're too special to follow the rules of your guild, or what?"

Heat rose up Danso's chest, but he shuffled his feet and shoved it down. "Sorry, uncles."

"Sorry for yourself," Uduuwe said, then poured raffia wine into earthenware cups and passed them around. Pochuwe took a sip, smacked his lips, and said:

"Your daa is waiting for you in his workroom. Better have a good apology ready."

Danso dragged his feet across the welcome room and to the back of the house, cursing every single step that led him closer to his daa's workroom. When he arrived at the door, he couldn't will his feet to enter. He stood there, contemplating.

"If you're going to come in," his daa said from inside, "come in like a man." Danso sighed, said a silent prayer, and pushed aside the woven door.

Habba sat at one end of the wooden healing table that took up half of the workroom. He was hunched over, parsing a herb, separating the stalks from the blades. From the pungent smell, Danso could tell it was the aromatic fever grass, hence the reason the thatch blinds over the large windows were rolled up. Bassa's afternoon humidity settled into the usually cool room. A firepot burned in the corner, adding to the heat.

Danso barely came into his daa's workroom unless he was in trouble or was sneaking in to learn about the medicine his daa worked, something Habba didn't quite agree he should be privy to. His daa thought he was better suited to the intellectual work of the jali, not work that required physical labour at any level. Danso, however, was simply insatiably curious, and managed to sneak in to study the dried fauna and flora—whole or in part—in earthenware jars stacked row upon row, right behind where Habba was sitting. The timber shelves were packed with them, with no form of organisation visible, so that only Habba knew where to find what. Usually, Danso would give up and study the slates hung on the wall, stories of Oon's history etched into them, the only thing from jali guild his daa retained.

It was like being transported into another world, these tales. Tales from not only the mainland, but from across the Pass: the Savanna Belt and its eastern and western grassland plains, the Sahel lying north of that, encapsulating Lake Vezha; and farther north to the Idjama desert, where few people except licensed merchants ever went, as it was rumoured there was not a drop of water to be found there and that was why desertlanders were migrating southward.

Even about the mainland, there were slates from places south of the Tombolo-Gondola confluence, those corners of the mainland very few Bassai ever ventured into. The slates were from both hinterland protectorates, southwest and southeast, as well as the delta settlements—this particular slate told of its humongous alligators and unverified stories of massive water creatures that ate people for fun. If there were stories of some other continent beyond Oon—not that anyone knew if there was one or not, because no one had yet been able to cross the seas to find out—Danso was sure his daa's workroom would have them.

Danso found it annoying that the manuscripts in the university library never told these stories, instead focusing inordinately on Bassa's conquests within the mainland's north, and notable events like the construction of the Soke moats. He thought it was one of the nation's many flaws: simply considering anything non-Bassai to be inferior, and therefore undeserving of attention. These smaller stories, often hidden, were the ones Habba had preferred to tell in his time as jali. For Danso, this room was the one that had sparked his interest in the world outside Bassa, because it held so many worlds in itself, ones Danso vicariously lived in.

Coming in here for a reprimand, however, had a completely different feeling to it. The room suddenly lacked air and the walls stood too close.

Habba didn't look up when he asked, "Why were you absent from today's gathering?"

Lie or truth? Danso thought, biding time for both factions of his mind to battle against one another.

"You know how I hate it when you lie," Habba said.

The lie faction in Danso's chest dissolved.

"I'm sorry," he said. "See, I was deep into writing and got carried away, so I didn't hear the crier. By the time I realised it and could dress up—" He shrugged.

Habba didn't look up, continuing to weed off the stalks with the tip of a small knife. "What were you writing?"

Danso shuffled, uneasy. Another condition of his return to the university was that he would never write down what he had learned in that codex on anything, anywhere, ever. The records, once thought lost in the Second Great War, had been declared too esoteric for public consumption. Two seasons ago, Danso had accidentally rediscovered them written into the margins of another random old manuscript, which was from the restricted section he wasn't supposed to be looking at. After the Elder Jali who caught him passed the discovery over to the Collegiate Council, the scholar community was agog with gossip, exchanging all kinds of tales about what might be in the codex. Danso, who had read just a significant chunk of it (but not all) before being happened upon, snickered at how far off their postulations were.

Unsurprisingly, the scholar community treated the codex just like everything else from the Manic Emperor's time—as the ravings of a madman. The Upper Council, once informed, decided the manuscript be "sanitized"—by which they meant *re-scribed*—for "historical accuracy." The original was to be destroyed and whoever had already seen it was to be sworn to silence, hence the rules about discussing the codex. All of this, of course, had the opposite effect of piquing Danso's interest more. What was so special about those notes? In truth, most of it had been gibberish—discussions about aspects of the two Great Wars that Danso had never heard about in any of the jali songs; descriptions of various peoples Danso had never heard of, so that he didn't know if they were real or fictional; a *lot* of fixation on what the emperor called *stones of sorcery*, or sometimes *stone-bone*. For a while, Danso thought the Collegiate Council might've called that one correctly: The codex was clearly the documentation of an obsessed man constantly under the influence of opiates. But as with most things Danso read, the words remained imprinted in his brain anyway.

"I see you have nothing to say," Habba said. "So perhaps I should show you this…" He reached to the side and pulled out a sheaf of bound papers.

Danso's eyes widened.

"I enjoyed it, actually." Habba placed his knife down to flick through the sheaf. "Such colourful descriptions of nonexistent people and places for someone who has never left Bassa."

Then Habba leaned over the table, manuscript in hand, and tossed it into the firepot.

Danso shot forward, unthinking, as the manuscript's edges started to catch. He was reaching into the pot when Habba rose from his stool, extended a long, thin arm, and grabbed his wrapper at the neck.

"Are you mad?" he boomed, pulling him back. "By moons, are you mad, this boy!"

"Why would you do that?" Danso yelled, eyes on the new fire catching in the pot, his face constricting in agony. "Why?"

His daa regarded him, dumbfounded. Slowly, Habba sat down but did not resume his parsing of the herb. Instead, he watched Danso watch his stories burn, until the fire returned to normal.

"This is self-sabotage, is it not?" Habba asked finally. "You're trying to get yourself in trouble, to get expelled on purpose. You *know* that discussing anything you saw in that codex, in a fictional sense or not, is a sanctionable offence. But you throw that aside, throw aside all our sacrifices, throw aside how hard we *begged* to ensure that you could keep your place and status," Habba breathed. "You think you're persecuted? You think you're the only one who's kept from telling stories? Look at the merchants—to become full guild members, they swear oaths to not speak of what they see beyond the Pass. Look at the desertlanders who come here—isn't Zaq restrained from telling you unsanctioned stories about the desertland too? I know you're a jali and your work is to tell stories, but stories are like knives: weapons or tools, depending on who is wielding them. Especially those that are written down and can be traced back!"

Danso glared at the fire. He refused to blink, refused to let the pain clouding his eyes leak down, refused his daa the satisfaction of seeing his pain. He turned away from the man.

"I'm not done with you," Habba said. "Look at me."

Danso faced his daa. The man looked at him—*looked* at him—and Danso felt his resistance shift, fracture, melt. Habba's eyes always had something swimming in them, like the inside of him was made of burning gold, like he channelled the fire of Menai. Habba rarely laid a hand on Danso, much to the chagrin of his uncles, but his daa could *look*, and the ghosts of Danso's sins would come running to torment him.

"You must understand, Danso," Habba said quietly, rising, "that the world will never be as forgiving as I am."

Habba, taller than most men of Bassa, but constantly slouched like a man who carried the weight of the continent on his broken back, came over to his son. He was thin, just like Danso, with cheekbones that rose high and sharp.

"I can't blame you for spending all your time trying to dig into a past that is better left alone," he said. "It's my fault. I didn't foster you a sibling to spend time with responsibly or become joined to another to share the weight of leading this household. We have no caretaker, so I barely have time to teach you everything you need to know."

Habba walked over to stand by Danso. He was dressed in a house garment wrapped around his midriff to cover his loincloth. Sweat gathered on his back from his task, drips running down the lines of his ribs.

"But you're the future of this household," he said, a hand on Danso's shoulder. "You need to remember that, every waking day, every sleeping night. You must understand what your actions mean for this household."

Danso bowed his head and bit his lip.

Habba sat on the table to face his son. "Look, you're gifted. You've passed memory tests even Elder Jalis struggle with. We're preparing for your joining to Esheme, and you two will be powerful together. You're poised to become one of the best jalis in Bassa and beyond, to even have your stories drawn into the pillars of the Great Dome." He narrowed his eyes. "But you will never become this person if you cannot remember these simple duties." Habba smoothed the plait in the middle of Danso's head. "Is that too much to ask?"

A flurry of responses rose through Danso's chest. What if he didn't want to be great? What if he wanted something completely different, something he didn't yet have a name for but felt deep in the pit of his stomach?

The questions lodged in his larynx and stayed there.

"I don't know who is madder, Emperor Nogowu for writing these things, or you for enabling such nonsense." Habba returned to his table and resumed with the herb. "Now, this won't be complete if I don't punish you. So go and rearrange the yams in the barn. Put the rotting ones at the bottom and the freshest on top. Go."

Danso turned to leave.

"And don't let me hear that Zaq helped you out," Habba called after him. "I want you to spend that time thinking about what we just discussed."

Zaq waited for Danso at the door to the cylindrical hut that served as the barn. He was big enough to almost cover the barn's door, but not as tall as a civic guard, which was why he had ended up a househand in the first place, eventually promoted to Second. Despite the turning light of evening, his complexion was still distinguishably low-brown enough for anyone to peg him for a Yelekuté.

"Zaq, can you imagine?" Danso said. "All my time and energy, he just threw it in the fire like that." He stopped when he realised Zaq was making the customary bow for Seconds. "What're you doing?"

"Nothing," Zaq said, his voice thick and harsh in the throat. "Simply paying required respect to my charge."

Danso looked him up and down. "Why are you talking like that? Did you drink or something?"

"No." Zaq remained bowed. "I just don't want it to seem like I've… forgotten my place."

Danso looked around, then frowned. "Something happened, didn't it? Tell me. Who was it? Pochuwe?"

Zaq said nothing.

"Gettup, boyo," Danso said. "I've told you to stop listening to my uncles. They can't have that kind of authority over me when they don't even pay for the wrappers on their bodies."

"It was not Pochuwe," Zaq said, rising. "It was your daa."

Danso went sullen.

"Well, that's rubbish," he said. "We can do however we like." He looked to Zaq. "And you even listened to him. Since when did we start following anybody's mouth?"

"Since now," Zaq said, his voice taking on an official quality Danso didn't like. "I am required by the nation to remind you of your duty to this land and to this family. I understand our relationship has not been quite… favourable to that. But alas, things must change."

Danso stared at him, aghast.

"You must understand, Danso," Zaq continued. "This is the job I was accepted into the mainland to do. It will not be wise for me to keep risking being sent back because I let you do as you wish. I'm sorry, but now I must be like this with you, please. It's my duty to prepare you for everything, to help you be the best possible Bassai."

"So what happens to all of our good stuff? Our errand hijinks, our mooncrossing gags. Who's going to read my tales and whisper taboo stories of the outlands for me to embellish them with? You're really just going to hang me out to dry like this, Zaq?"

"Sorry." Zaq kept his face as straight as possible.

Danso kissed his teeth with vehemence, unlatching the door. Zaq watched him for a moment, then placed a hand over his. Danso stopped, his hands shaking, fighting back the anger rising to his eyes as tears. Zaq, caught between maintaining a respectful distance and providing comfort, shuffled his feet.

"It was me who told him where your manuscript was," Zaq said, contrite. "He forced me to. I didn't have a choice. I apologise. I really do."

"It's not your fault." Danso wiped his eyes.

Zaq put an arm on his shoulder. "No, it's not. I thought that too, back then, when I used to be stubborn like you and made mistakes I couldn't take back. Your situation is different because you still have this." He tapped Danso on the temple with a finger. "It is your power. It will always be."

Danso unlatched the door and stood at the threshold, staring into the darkness.

"I'll get you a lantern," Zaq said, turning away.

"Zaq," Danso called. "What if I don't want to be the best possible Bassai?" He turned to face his Second. "What if I want to be...anything else?"

Zaq stared at him for a second, then said: "I'll get you a lantern."

Danso stood there and waited for his eyes to adjust to the darkness.

Nem

NIGHT CAME WITH A thunderstorm, and rain poured into the courtyard of the MaaNem household. Bits of hail came with the rain, striking the slate roof with unsettling noise, uncommon in Fourth Ward because Nem's house was one of the very few houses here with a slate roof. The night was not a lit one—Ashu was in a quarter moon, and her sister, fiery Menai, blinked red in reverse gibbous—so that only a series of palm-oil-lit lamps illuminated the courtyard and shone into the street outside.

Nem stood at the threshold of the door to the library's veranda, watching the rain pour from the roof and fill the impluvium in the middle of the courtyard. She sipped raffia wine from a beaded calabash, slowly. Alongside weybo, the highly intoxicating spirit, she preferred the common man's drinks to the fruit wines from the hinterlands that the highbrow of Bassa drank. Nem had grown up in the core of the city herself, had mingled in its streets. Her taste buds weren't simply going to change just because she had clawed her way upward.

She turned back into the library to face the man talking to her. Speaker Abuso was a thin, tall man, as dark as farmland humus. He was the embodiment of the Bassai elite: erudite, diligent, proud. They called him *the one without a curved back*, because he was stiff and upright and held on to the appearance of integrity for dear life. It made sense that he was plucked from the scholar guild very early on and elevated to Speaker for the nation, the voice of the Upper Council, even though, technically, he was not a part of the council itself.

Even now, sitting, he kept his spine straight and prim, his voice so loud and clear that Nem had given up asking him to quiet it down. She settled for not listening to him, then tuned him out as she often did with most men who sat in that chair. Bassa's Idu caste was filled with whiny babies who always came to her, complaining about their problems as if she were a place for respite. Sure, it was her job to help them in exchange for gold or bronze or copper or cowrie or favours owed, but she found herself turning to a habit of not listening, as she already knew how to solve most of their issues anyway.

In this case, however, she wasn't listening because she was mentally parsing the problem that had just landed on her lap, one that she didn't actually have a solution to.

"Are you listening to me, Nem?" Abuso asked. The decorative markings etched into his forehead, smeared with clay and gold dust, twitched.

Nem turned but didn't respond. She admired her collection of stitched manuscripts instead, running her eyes around the shelves set into each wall. Her carved desk sat in the centre, under a handwoven rug. Both items bore her handsigned household seal, the intricate curves a symbol she had designed herself, forcing legitimacy into a household name everyone tried to pretend did not exist. The ceiling was part wood and part glass that bore handpainted versions of the same symbol. A cylinder of candles hung from the middle.

Nem walked back to her desk and sat behind it. She picked up a sheet of paper and a charcoal stylus.

"What're you doing?" he asked.

"Gathering resources," she said. "I will need your household signature."

Abuso eyed her. "I'm not signing anything. I cannot get any more embroiled in this fiasco than I already am."

Nem looked at him across the desk as she wrote. "Whether you like it or not, it was in the line of doing what you asked that we got embroiled in this yellowskin matter. You should have fought harder against the closure if you wanted to remain out of this."

"I am one person," Abuso retorted. "Those against were outvoted."

"Then we suffer the consequences. Dọta knows his caravans will be severely impacted, so he's very keen on getting the yellowskin caught. We should have answers when he comes asking. Even better if we have the yellowskin dangling from a rope in the city square by then. No loose ends, and we still get to make a show of strength. Who knows if there are even more yellowskins out there planning things?" Nem leaned in and wrote some more. "You can help me, or I can find other ways to do this, and whatever you see, you take it."

Abuso's frown deepened as she wrote. "A whole cursed people, unseen for a thousand seasons, suddenly awoken." He shook his head. "Where did they even come from—beneath the sea?"

"You're the educated one here," Nem said. "Shouldn't you know?"

Abuso scoffed. "You think jali training is about knowing what part of history is true or not? My training was memorising a bunch of litanies and knowing how to create more, and perhaps if one is blessed enough, learning how to sing them and entertain too. I didn't learn how to tell if a bunch of island spirit-people are real or not, not to talk of knowing where it came from."

"She."

"Excuse me?"

"The yellowskin is a *she*. Or at least that's what the official who saw her reported."

"You mean the same official who said it changed to high-black?" Abuso snorted. "I might as well believe it is Menai in the flesh." He paused. "What are you writing?"

Nem passed the paper across the desk to him. He frowned at it, reading it from a distance without picking it up.

"That's outrageous. What do you need this many hunthands for?"

Nem stared into his face. "What do you think is our best chance of catching someone we're not even sure exists? We need numbers."

Abuso frowned at her some more, then leaned forward, picked up the stylus, and signed his household name on the paper. He threw the stylus down in frustration.

"None of this would've happened if Oke had just stayed in one place. But no, she had to go gallivanting all over the desert, saying she's looking for some useless bone rock."

Nem said nothing. The bone rock he was calling useless, Oboda had brought back to her after failing to find Abuso's daughter. How he had procured it was a separate matter entirely, a matter that was probably connected to why there was a yellowskin on the mainland. But it was in Nem's best interest not to complicate matters as they stood, so she kept this to herself.

"The next time I hear from you," Abuso said, rising, "it had better be good news. Or it's over in this city, Nem. Remember our agreements. My daughter, or everything you have will be in jeopardy."

Nem snatched her paper back. "I'm aware of the gravity of the situation." She paused. "And I would prefer if you refrain from threats in the future. I do not take kindly to them."

Abuso scoffed, then rose and took his leave, yelling for his Second, who doubled as prime guard. The man opened the door and announced Abuso's leave.

Nem reread the letter, which was addressed to at least five or six ward leaders, consisting of ward chiefs and civic guard captains. A moment passed, and then the door opened, and Oboda walked in.

"He's ready," Oboda said. "In holding."

Nem nodded, rolled up the paper, and handed it to Oboda.

"Give that to Satti and have her send it off immediately. Also—" She tilted her head for him to shut the door. He did. "I have a task for you. It involves retrieving a, um, an artifact. Something you can never be caught doing or caught with, and something I will have to deny knowing about if either of those two things happens."

He nodded, unfazed.

"I will give you the details, but let us deal with this civic guard first."

She rose and walked out of the library, Oboda right behind her, his boots causing thunderclaps with the floor, echoes of the thunder outside.

"Find Esheme," Nem said to the first househand she met outside the door. "Tell her to meet me at the stalls."

· ◇ ⸻ ⸺ ◇ ·

The holding stalls of the Nem household were on the ground floor, but not below ground as with most of the city's holding facilities. Nem thought underground holdings smelled too bad and were difficult to clean. Of course, it was unheard of for a private home to have its own holding at all—detention and jailing were the responsibility of the civic guard and the local government of each ward. But in Nem's line of work, there were times when people needed to be handled outside the usual channels.

The stalls were instead set aside in a separate building from the main household, adjacent to the kwaga stables, carefully locked, guarded, and disguised so that anyone who wasn't looking couldn't find them. Here, Nem stood with Esheme in the semi-stable, semi-prison interior, their water-resistant cloaks dripping from the walk from the main house in the rain. Oboda stood next to them, boots squishing with water as he shuffled, impatient. Outside, rain lashed at the thatch roof.

The man they came to see was speechless upon their arrival. He had been strung up from the rafters by a rope pulley, the strain in his shoulder joints clear from a darkness building there, blood communing at the wrong point. In addition to being starved of food and water, it was obvious he'd been whipped, his back opened with bleeding scars. He was now so faint he looked asleep but was, in fact, slowly dying.

"Do you recognise this man?" she asked her daughter.

Esheme squinted in the light, green with unease as she always was whenever Nem brought her here, but stoic in the face of it. She stood straight-backed and nodded.

"Good," Nem said, an idle hand on her chin. "You should never forget a face that has wronged you. And in this case, not just you; anyone who lays a hand on your intended disrespects this whole household."

"What do you want to do with him?" Esheme asked.

"Oboda will flog him some more," Nem said. "Then, I will make sure he is sent over the border and can never return."

"The border is closed," Esheme said, "so that's impossible. We'll have to do something else."

"Like?"

"Kill him."

Shock didn't quite register on Nem's face, but something moved within her, and it was not a pang of nostalgia. It was something that showed up every now and then when, even after dealing with some of the most despicable people in her line of work, she could not quite come to terms with this side of Esheme. There was something primal about the girl, a vindictive desire to demonstrate always that she was capable of anything. And she *was*, but that wasn't Nem's worry. She was more concerned that whatever path lay ahead of her daughter could be destroyed by this relentlessness before it even had a chance to manifest.

"Are you sure?" Nem asked.

"He is going to die at some point, anyway," Esheme said matter-of-factly. "Better to be buried in the welcoming humus than the harsh and unforgiving sands of the Savanna Belt, where his spirit may never know any rest."

Nem waited.

"Okay, fine," Esheme said. "It shows weakness if we let him go."

Nem turned to look at the civic guard. He had opened his eyes now and was attempting to speak but his lips were parched, unable to stretch properly. Oboda held up a finger to silence the man, then unclipped his runku from his waist and swung it so that it made a deadly whoosh with the air. He set the heavy head on the ground and leaned on the weapon, looking to Nem, but also to Esheme, waiting for a decision.

"You have always said you want me to learn," Esheme said. "You say you want people to think of us with respect. Well, when people think of us, this is what we should want them to remember: that even the slightest errors against us will not be tolerated."

Nem regarded her daughter, perturbed. This, exactly, was why she had insisted that Esheme join the counsel guild. She belonged to that life, to the Idu ways, one that required balance. Not this one of blood and depravity, designless. Nem was doing everything she could to teach Esheme to be streetwise, decisive, ambitious, but also to temper that with shrewd prudence, keep the order of things from going askance. The latter never stuck, though, and each day, Esheme's affinity for the deep end grew in a way that unsettled Nem.

This time, however, maybe she was right. Maybe Nem was growing soft. Perhaps this was why Abuso thought he could bully her. Perhaps she should be doing more to carve her name into the fabric of Bassa.

She nodded at Oboda.

Oboda moved swiftly; in two or three steps, he lifted the runku and swung. There was a crack of thunder outside. Wind swept in, and the fires in the room shifted. Nem placed a firm hand on her daughter's neck in case she tried to turn away, but Esheme did not. Nem was proud of her for it, but concerned she had just let burn a fire she could not extinguish.

Esheme

THE COURT OF THE Fourth Ward, like each within the city, was an exact replica of the noble court of the Great Dome, only one tenth its size. It held seating for less than fifty and had dais space for two judges and a supporting panel, instead of the whole Upper and Lower Councils. Esheme had only been to the noble court once, on a guild excursion, and had never forgotten the thickness of the pillars, the height of the ceiling, the array of benches in every conceivable direction. Since then, she had always thought of the city versions as drab.

Esheme sat at the very rear of the small hall. It was early morning, which meant the court was near empty. Smaller hearings, those between citizens, were held first in the day. The biggest hearings—involving serious crimes like deadly assaults, robberies, and rapes—were dealt with in the evenings, when most people had returned from the day's work and were willing to trundle in and listen to proceedings. As a novitiate of the counsel guild, Esheme was mandated to attend these larger hearings, since they were community-versus-accused. She was also required to attend nation-versus-accused hearings, which were held at the Great Dome's noble court and happened so infrequently that none had yet happened in her lifetime.

The case before her was a silly one, as most were: Two farmers from the same guild, though patrons to rival trading partners, had gone into an altercation over a disputed land border. One had attacked the other with a hoe. Now the attacked man wanted payment for what he had spent treating a head injury.

The counsel speaking on behalf of the accused man was a recent graduate of the university, a woman called Fafa who was only a few seasons
older than Esheme and had just ascended from counsel novitiate to junior
guild member. She waited as the accuser's counsel, an older veteran of the
guild, shattered and dismissed her every accusation. The complainants
themselves sat on opposing benches, looking at each other askance.

Esheme enjoyed attending these hearings. Being so close to the Great
Dome, Fourth Ward held court seriously and often, and Esheme considered these early-morning sparring contests the place where one could
really learn about people, their strongest desires in the minutest circumstances, the things they held on to for dear life. The high-profile hearings
were usually too swept up in furore for individual motives and reactions
to shine through. The early-morning cases provided an up-close-and-
personal view of things, which better suited Esheme's interests. If she
could visit courts outside of Second, Third, and the neighbouring Fifth,
she would, but if rumours were to be believed, anything beyond Seventh
was not a court, anyway. It was a community meeting where nothing
proper happened.

Fafa was making her final argument for the panel, which consisted of
two judges—Second Elders who were Fourth Ward's representatives at
the Lower Council—the ward chief and civic guard captain of Fourth,
and a selected jali who mostly took records. The five listened attentively
as the young woman suddenly dropped the act she'd been maintaining all this time—that of a meek and acquiescent novice—and gave a
powerful speech that revealed updates to encroachment laws that the
attacker had been unaware of, argued for the value lost by the attacked,
and enchanted the panel with a final plea that a few bronze pieces were
nothing compared to a man almost losing his life and a household almost
losing its head.

The panel nodded, and there was a relaxation in her charge's shoulders. The other counsel had his mouth agape, his charge shifting uncom-
fortably in his bench. Having expended all his points during earlier
arguments, the older man gave a closing that was dappled and weak. The
judges didn't deliberate much after. Fafa was smiling long before they
ruled that her charge would be paid over a hundred bronze pieces.

Esheme smiled out of the corner of her mouth as the teams packed up and the panel took a break. The losing side went into an argument immediately after, while Fafa walked out, shoulders high. Esheme's eyes followed her out, admiring the woman's technique. Reel them in when they thought you weak, and strike back when they had expended all their energy, when they couldn't retaliate. It was a trap many weren't supposed to fall into, but Fafa understood the hubris of educated Idu men, especially when they looked at her and saw a small, young woman, fresh into the guild. Winning this case hadn't been a matter of legal prowess. It was a matter of human psychology.

Ikobi came into the hall right then, spotted Esheme, and settled next to her on the bench.

"What is it exactly you gain from these things again?" the elderly woman asked. She said it like she didn't already know the answer, but Esheme knew that what she was really asking was if Esheme herself knew why she came here so often.

"People," Esheme said, same as she'd answered every other time. "Being a good counsel is about knowing what makes people *people*."

"In a way, that's true," her mentor said. "But it's no substitute for classes at the university, at least one of which you will have definitely missed at this point."

"I can always memorise laws," Esheme said. "Besides, all mainland law can be summed up as 'affluence rules and lack follows.'"

Ikobi chuckled. Unlike most Elders at the university, Ikobi considered Esheme amusing rather than finding her grating, a welcome change from how other mentors at the university treated their mentees.

"How so?" the woman asked. "Didn't Fafa just win this case? Her fee will perhaps cost that farmer less than a few crops. His attacker, on the other hand, will be owing his trading partner for a while." She shifted in her seat. "*Influence*, perhaps, is the word you're looking for."

"Affluence, influence, does it matter?" Esheme said. "The word *you* are looking for is *power*. Which is what Fafa just employed anyway, only in a form most don't recognise."

Ikobi wore a look that reminded Esheme of how Nem sometimes looked at her, like pride mixed with an equal measure of worry. However, she did not try to press it as Nem often did. Instead, she rose and knocked on the bench.

"All right, that's enough, get up," she said. "Where's your Second?"

"Outside." Esheme didn't move. "I want to hear a case or two more before I leave." The panel was returning, a few new attendees were showing up, and the next counsels were preparing with their charges. Ikobi's eyes followed them, and then she sighed and sat, deciding it was pointless to argue with Esheme.

They watched the proceedings in silence. The new case was a simple and very tired one: an unpaid loan.

"Who is it this time?" Ikobi asked without turning her head. "Danso or Nem?"

Esheme did not respond. Truthfully, it was both. Both of them were going to be the death of her in this city if she let them. Every single time she thought she had done enough to distance herself from their missteps, they found new ways to drag her back into their muddy waters.

"You can't keep running away from your obligations every time you're upset," Ikobi said. "Those two are your family—or at least Danso will be soon—and you must find a way to deal with them."

Easy to say, Esheme thought. She had always known Danso to be a blockhead, but his antics were getting worse these days.

She didn't hate him, not quite. In fact, she liked Danso a lot. He was intelligent, perhaps the most scholarly man in Bassa if he opened himself up to the possibility. He didn't treat her unkindly for being Nem's daughter, and he took her words seriously. He was also the only person in Bassa who would allow himself to be joined to her. He understood what it meant to straddle the two worlds of being privileged and outcast at the same time, even though the reasons why they were both outcasts differed. And, surprising herself, she wasn't taken aback by his Shashi status and associated complexion—he was a part of the Idu caste regardless, wasn't he?

But what most fascinated her about Danso was that there was a puerile stainlessness about him, like a clean slate to be written upon. The first time they met, a matchmaking Elder Jali from the university had brought Danso before her and Nem, offering a golden opportunity to have Nem's household be *tied to the potential of his greatness*, as the jali had put it. Nem was to act quickly before someone else recognised the opportunity. Nem had taken one look at the impish young man, eyed the written record of his Idu status the jali presented, and whispered to Esheme by her side: "This young man is going to be trouble."

Esheme knew, though, that this *trouble* was simply dough, and if she got joined to it, she could make whatever kind of bread she desired.

Now, she saw a bit of folly in that decision. Sure, it made sense on slate, but in practice, Danso was the chaotic kind of unpredictable, not the more intentional kind she desired. Unlike her maa, who, despite being the antithesis of everything Bassai, liked to stay constrained and predictable by working within the Ideal's systems, Esheme wanted to have not one face but *many*. She wanted to be iridescent, a different colour with every angle. She was already an outlier in Bassa, and Nem wanted her to escape the combined weight of a parent of Emuru status and the stigma of a fixer's child by becoming an *inlier*. But Esheme coveted the opposite: to slip between the circles Bassa had drawn so she could exist unquestioned within or without any of her choosing. Preferably wherever granted her the most freedom or perhaps the most acceptance. All she needed was a place where she did not have to tone herself down.

She couldn't achieve this with Danso exposing her, though. When he wasn't getting into trouble for reading arcane manuscripts, he was failing to wear the proper cloth, to do the proper hairstyles, to show up when required. While Esheme did everything to stay focused on the spaces she aimed to circumnavigate, Danso seemed to be doing everything to leave the one he was a part of. No matter what she did—including sending Oboda to keep an eye out for him in case he'd slipped away from his own Second—he always found new ways to disappoint her.

Esheme sighed aloud. Ikobi snorted.

"You're still young," the woman said. "You have time to make things better. Stop sighing like an old woman with a basket of tomatoes on her back." She rose again. "Okay, time to go. Really, this time."

"The case isn't over."

"Look, we already know he's going to lose the loan." Ikobi pointed. "What do you notice about the complainant's counsel?"

Esheme looked. The counsel, a smallish man with perhaps a few seasons of guild time under his wrapper, kept fidgeting and snatching glances at the debtor, who sat rock-still but every once in a while gave the counsel a hard-edged glare.

"He has threatened him," she said.

"Power, as you said," Ikobi said. "Different form from the last, but same currency."

She walked out. After a while, Esheme followed.

Outside, Oboda untied her kwaga, one ear on the nearby chatter of a group of idling Yelekuté who argued about whether the price inflations caused by the border closure would remain or go down. Esheme got on her animal, lost in thought, and Oboda led her away.

Nem had always told her she needed to get joined to Danso to aid the smoothing of her social creases. But today's cases had fermented the idea that had been brewing in her mind for a long time: that she didn't quite need Danso at all, and honestly, she might not even need Nem. She only really needed one thing, and that thing was power.

6

Danso

The six pillars of the University of Bassa, headquarters of all scholars on the mainland, stood taller at Second Ward this morning than Danso remembered them, more imposing with every step he climbed up to the second-largest building on the continent. The usually welcoming parables cast in bronze on the top façade seemed to snarl at him in High Bassai.

When you pursue two rats at the same time, you catch neither, the pillar of Logic said.

You do not divide forbidden meat with your teeth, the pillar of Religions and Philosophy whispered.

A child does not play outside so much as to forget home, the pillar of History, Geography, and Languages warned.

Danso eyed the pillars, apprehensive. The remaining three pillars of Earth Studies, Numbers and Letters, and Mainland Law had similarly disapproving things to say, to remind Danso of everything he owed, everything he'd done wrong. He tore his eyes away from them and joined the throng of scholars and novitiates filing through the multiple entryways into the main yard.

The grand clock of seasons welcomed them, the four pointers telling of the current rainy season, the current mooncycle, and the exact day and hour. Looking at it, Danso realised two things: The next mooncrossing festival was much closer than he'd thought—only a day away—and he was late for class again.

He hustled through the throng, down the stairs and into the closest passageway, darting past corridors of decorated mudbrick. Bronze busts embedded into the walls and tales written with mica, coral, and cowries swept by as he ran, bound manuscripts under his arm. He didn't need to read the signs for each courtyard with its novitiates seated cross-legged in front of every kind of scholar. He could see the various wrapper colours worn by other university scholars and novitiates, each for its own individual pillar and college, and in tandem, connected guild.

He finally spotted the maroon-dappled-with-yellow tie-and-dye patterns that told him that the final-season jalis, the only scholars who studied all six pillars of all six colleges, were holding senior class in history, geography, and languages. He stopped short of the courtyard entrance, adjusted his wrappers and patted his hair, then peered in. Elder Jali Nogose, a wiry man with a short temperament and plaits dyed blue, had his back to the class: sixteen of them, all in the final mooncycle of jali guild. Well, fifteen, because Danso was missing.

Nogose paced, reciting a litany of the timeline of mainland history, a call-and-response monotone that sounded like a bee buzz. The novitiates responded singsong, reciting the stories of the continent from when Bassa started as a cluster of families building hamlets through the conquest of the mainland protectorates and the building of the Soke Pass.

Danso put his back to the wall, crouched, and crept in. Many in the class turned, then snickered when they saw it was him. Luckily, he didn't have to struggle for space to sit and gain Nogose's attention—he had his own special seat, far away from every other student, the only place he was allowed to sit in every class. Unluckily, being the Shashi-with-a-special-seat in every class made it difficult to be invisible, a quality he badly needed right now.

Danso arrived at his spot and settled in, spreading his manuscripts before him. Nogose turned, paced, then stopped midrecitation. He scanned the class, and his eyes settled on Danso.

"DaaHabba," he said, and the class snickered again. "You shouldn't be here."

"Elder, I swear I have a good excuse," Danso said, putting his finger to the tip of his tongue and sticking it in the air. "I was putting yams in the barn for my daa."

The class laughed aloud this time. Nogose frowned.

"No," he said. "Elder Oduvie has asked that you be withdrawn whenever you arrive. She wants to see you in her workchamber."

Now the class murmured, and Danso knew his day of reckoning might have finally arrived.

—o—···————···—o—

Elder Scholar Oduvie's workchamber was located in the farthermost reach of the university, but on the ground floor, as opposed to those of most scholars, who preferred the upper floors away from the noise of the classes on the ground level. There was a guard at the door—no one fancy, just a man with a sheathed blade for show—and he let Danso in without a word since, as Oduvie's mentee, this wasn't his first time visiting.

The walls of the workchamber rose high. Oduvie, seated behind her desk, was a woman so small the desk had been reduced to suit her. The floor-to-ceiling shelves were empty, and all the manuscripts had been brought down to sitting level, some stacked off-shelf, so that the room bore the look of someone packing up to leave. Oduvie herself was old but showed little sign of it, especially on her face, where she had marked herself delicately, white and yellow beauty spots on her forehead and cheeks quite akin to those used by young Bassai women. Her five arched hair plaits glowed yellow with cheto and her white scholar wrappers were starched and immaculate. She wore jewellery of gold, bronze, and coral beads on her neck, ears, fingers, and wrists.

All of this still wouldn't be out of place if she weren't also a Shashi like him. Oduvie was the only other Shashi that Danso had ever met besides himself, though she was more like the folks at Whudasha—she had one parent from the Savanna Belt, not from the Ajabo islands like he did. Her hair had greyed and shrunk so much that it was less evident how loose her curls used to be, but her complexion stubbornly remained a shade lighter than the typical Emuru, and her nose had a curve that betrayed her desert heritage.

Just as Bassa had done with him and other outliers in every caste, they had weighed the potential value of letting a Shashi into a role reserved for Idu against the stellar acuity they would be missing out on, and concluded that letting in just the token couldn't hurt. Prior to being assigned Danso's mentor, she had unofficially honed herself in all six pillars, from Logic to Mainland Law, and was arguably the most accomplished scholar in the whole nation, and probably the whole continent. Still, she had not been allowed into the jali guild. It was why she had taken his case personally and asked to mentor him.

"Sit, Danso," she said, her head down as she wrote quickly on a sheet of paper. Danso sat, mildly thankful. Oduvie was one of the few people in Bassa who called him by his own name and did not refer to him by his family name, except for when he was in trouble.

She wrote for a while more, then rolled up the paper, tied it with twine, set it aside, and folded her hands.

"You're in trouble," she said flatly. Oduvie never minced words with him. He used to think her harsh, lacking in empathy, but he'd come to see, over time, that that was simply her way of looking out for him.

"Elder, I can explain—"

She held up a hand. "Before you do, I just want you to tell me now. The truth. And nothing but the truth. Will you?"

Danso breathed. "Yes, Elder." He knew that telling her what had actually happened with the meeting would break her heart, but he definitely could not lie to her.

"All right," she said, and leaned back. "So tell me: Did you take it?"

Danso frowned. "Sorry?"

"Nogowu's codex," she said. "Did you take it?"

Danso's heart skipped. "I don't understand. I thought that issue was over? I thought they said—"

"Not if you went back and took it again."

"Went back and—" Danso almost choked on his own spit. "What do you mean?"

"Nogowu's codex is missing," Oduvie said. "And the Collegiate Council believes you took it."

"*Me?*" This was the last thing Danso had expected when coming to this workchamber. "I would *never*. Not after all the uproar last time. Why would I want to jeopardise my life?"

"And that is exactly what I told the Collegiate Council," she said. "But they were adamant, and after a while, I began to consider this as carefully as I want you to now. Denying this so vehemently is you making a statement: that not only did you, who have broken this rule before, not commit this crime, but that one of their Idu scholars or students did. And that is a *huge* accusation we'd be making."

"*Accusation?*" Danso's temper rose. "It's not *me* who is making accusations!"

"Yes, I am aware." Oduvie rolled her chair backward, then rolled herself around the table to set herself next to Danso. Her jewellery jingled as she moved.

"Do you remember your first season here?" she asked, peering into his face. "Just a little boy, youngest ever to grace these walls. No scholar wanted you in their class; they said you couldn't compete with the Idu novitiates, that you would struggle, that you belonged in Whudasha with the others." She always avoided using the word *Shashi*. "But your daa believed, and so did I. They let you in here because we spoke for you. I was speaking for myself when I spoke for you; I was speaking for everyone like us. I saw in you what I believed in myself when they told me that same thing. And I want that door to remain open.

"Your intellectual worth is undeniable. Over a hundred novitiates admitted that first season, and you have topped them every season, including this final sixteen. You are even better than I was, Danso, and they can see that. And that, my boy, is why, for whatever reason that codex is missing, you are a target. And a target makes themself more difficult to hit by making themself smaller, not larger."

Danso was speechless. *Was she asking him to own up?* He bit down the expletive threatening to leave his mouth.

"Listen," Oduvie said. "Denying will give them more firepower, make them more eager for your ruin. Don't be naive, Danso—this is not about whether you took the codex. Don't think for a moment that because you have the undeniable ability to memorise everything you read or sing or see, that that will ever be enough."

There was no simple response to what Danso was hearing, so he kept quiet. Oduvie sighed and leaned back into her chair but did not roll away. They sat that way for a while.

"The collegiate Elders clamoured for your immediate expulsion. As your mentor, I spoke on your behalf and managed to negotiate a deal for you, if you are willing."

Danso sighed. "Do I have a choice?"

Oduvie matched his sigh. "I'm afraid not." She reached over to the table and picked up the letter she had written earlier. "You will be suspended effective immediately. You are not allowed back into this university for classes anymore." She handed him the rolled-up paper. Danso collected it, gingerly. His heart pounded, and he felt ready to break out in sweat.

Oduvie held up a hand, and her wristlets jangled. "However, you will be allowed to take guild finals if the codex is found before then. If you pass, then you will graduate with the others. If you do not, then you go home to your family and find another guild or trade circle to take you." She cocked her head. "Something tells me they will find that codex before then, and of course you will pass, Danso, will you not?"

There was a ghost of a wry smile on her lips, and in it Danso found some solace. He found himself wrapping his arms around the woman in her chair, the smell of her cheto and ochre in his nose.

"Thank you," he said breathily.

"Eish, get away." She pushed him gently. "Don't rub off my facepaint."

Oduvie rolled herself back behind her desk, picked up her charcoal stylus, and gave him a glance that he interpreted as his dismissal. He rose, paper in hand.

"I think it'll be best," she said, without looking at him, "if certain people in your household never know of the contents of that letter, or what we've discussed in this room. Or that I made this very statement I've just made."

Danso nodded and shut the door, a bit too hard. The guard outside gave him an enquiring look. Danso sneered back at him.

·◦·▦▦▦▦▦———▦▦▦·◦·

The library at the University of Bassa was never called by its official mouthful of a name: The University Archive of the Emperor of Enlightenment, the Fifteenth Emperor of Great Bassa, Emperor Tumwenke. Built during her reign—a short one lasting only a few seasons, as she was quickly usurped by her successor, the Leopard Emperor, the Sixteenth Emperor of Great Bassa, Emperor Idiado—the library had remained standing ever since, with the university then built around it. It therefore was the oldest standing structure, and looked like it too, with some portions still sporting straw, wattle, and daub next to the more modern mudbrick and stone. Regardless, this ancient structure held all of Bassa's written histories within its walls, and not a single story written anywhere on the mainland was not first written on manuscript or slate here.

Danso went straight into the library from Oduvie's office, heading for his favourite spot: the space between two adjacent shelves at the tail end of the library. The way he saw it, there was a chance that he could milk the most out of the little time he had left before the news that he was suspended took hold. The aim was simple: There had to be some way out of this predicament, out of this false accusation. Surely there was some mainland law that said he couldn't be suspended without proof? He would ask Esheme for more information later, but for now, the library was the best possible place to find some path out of this. Luckily so, too, since his favourite corner happened to contain some manuscripts on mainland law.

At this time of day, the library was mostly empty in the general areas. The restricted sections, all behind iron gates under keylock, however, teemed with various Elders, jalis, and scholars of other dispensations alike. Most sat and read, memorising sections for later regurgitation in teaching or storytelling at events like the forthcoming mooncrossing festival. Some wrote new stories, some rewrote older ones, while some composed new songs out of the already existent. A sizable number just moved around, browsing manuscripts. Danso wondered how many of those were currently searching for the missing codex.

Danso slipped between floor-to-ceiling shelves set between pillars just as massive, giving the restricted sections a wide berth. Ever since discovering the codex two seasons ago, he had received dagger stares every single time he set foot in the library. If the codex had been his first infraction when it came to restricted texts, then things wouldn't be this dire. Sadly, incessant curiosity ensured he'd racked up a healthy number of broken rules before that incident, from things as simple as challenging

Elder Jalis in class to those as serious as skipping multiple classes because he knew he could memorise ten times faster by reading on his own rather than being slowed down by his peers.

Once at his corner, he browsed, finding manuscripts covering local government court processes, land and loan laws, and trade laws, but nothing about suspension of a novitiate at the university. He did find something about court processes for contesting false accusations, though, which he pulled out and sat on the floor to read.

Intermittent chatter and laughter punctuated his reading every now and then. Sometimes, the passersby looked into his corner and snickered upon spotting him. He had learned, after such a long time, to ignore them. Everyone who looked in this corner expected to find him anyway, since unlike in his classes, he did not have a seat set apart here. He was forbidden from sitting with the other Idu in the general areas of the library, so he had had to make this his own space.

The manuscript held nothing tangible, as most of the approaches were written for Idu or Emuru bringing a case against themselves. There was a small section for Potokin or Yelekuté indentured workers bringing cases against their employers, but it was very short. For Shashi, there was just one line at the very end of the manuscript:

A Shashi shall lose all claim of rights upon crossing the Peace Fence of Whudasha, and shall claim no rights on Bassai land.

Danso shut the manuscript in disgust. *Just wonderful.* He wasn't even Bassai enough to contest his own injustice.

Just then, a group of novitiates walking past spotted him and stopped to chatter, pointing at him. He frowned, replacing the manuscript. One broke away and went off toward one of the restricted sections. Danso gathered himself and proceeded to leave the corner immediately.

"Aren't you banned from this place?" one of the novitiates, a woman, asked. "Crook."

The brazen accusation shocked Danso, but he knew it was useless to try to defend himself to these blockheads.

"That's rather a compliment, don't you think?" he said instead. "I would say *back to sender*, but being a crook requires a gracious amount of intellect, one I can't possibly say you possess."

The group gasped, and Danso gave himself an inner pat on the back.

"Just wait until the Elder Scholars hear you're here," another said. And just as he said it, Danso saw the novitiate who had broken away earlier returning, an Elder Scholar in tow.

Great, Danso thought, then turned about and high-tailed it.

Zaq

THE LOCAL GOVERNMENT OFFICE of Sixth Ward was packed to the brim with people waiting to get in. Like every local government office in Bassa, it opened late, it was understaffed, and the amenities were less than desirable. Hopeful visitors stood in a line and were assigned numbers by civic guards according to how soon they'd arrived. There were several lines of this sort: separate lines for new migrants, migrant assignments and reassignments, migrants reporting performance per mooncycle, and separate lines for nation citizens who were here for matters of business like trade or specialist permits, guild registration, or seeking redress for disputes.

Zaq stood at the front of a line of Seconds. He always woke before dawn, anyway, and was usually among the first to arrive at the office on report day.

The local government officers strode in late, as always, without apology. They moved languidly, like people who weren't in the employ of the city. It took them ages to get into their seats behind their windows and roll up the thatch screens. Even then, they barked at the people who tried to immediately approach them, asking for some space and time to "compose themselves," despite being over an hour late.

As with every time he had to be here, Zaq marvelled at this dedication to mediocrity. It shouldn't have surprised him at all, but each new experience was jarring. Was this the same Bassa, the promised land of gold and humus? The same Bassa whose emperors' names had once evoked fear and trembling in the lips that mentioned them, whether those lips belonged to mainlanders or outlanders? Stories of the nation's well-drilled armies and their demanding leadership had filled his childhood, and he could not believe Bassa had fallen so far from its heyday. In the discussions he overheard among Bassai and immigrants alike, many believed that the lack of a succession of true ideals contributed to this. By getting rid of their emperors and opting for a parliamentarian system of councils, Bassa had, in essence, become a nation without a frowning face or striking hand. The newer Bassai Ideal was supposed to strengthen that, but too many interpreted it as a simple pledge they recited and didn't exactly have to live out in their day-to-day activities.

Prior to crossing the Soke border into the mainland, Zaq had never compromised on three things: punctuality, efficiency, and a zeal for self-improvement. Sadly, being in Bassa had caught up to him too, and he found that he waned on all three counts. He had been subsumed into becoming a part of Bassa's biggest problem, which was really that the Bassai thought they were too big to fail. Past glory had lured them into a sense of excessive optimism.

Finally, the officer at the window in front of his line beckoned that he was ready, and Zaq went and sat in front of the man. Despite it being early in the morning, the man had lit a pipe of tobacco leaves and was gently puffing on it while flipping through a sheaf of papers. He put it down and, without so much as a glance at Zaq, asked for his name and date of entry.

Zaq offered his information, including the name of the household he was assigned to. The man flipped through the sheaf some more, then pulled out a sheet and reached for a charcoal stylus.

"Hmm," he said, chewing on a cleaning stick whenever he put his pipe down. Zaq wondered who wouldn't clean their teeth before coming to work. Back in the small town of Haruna in the Savanna Belt, where he was born before his parents moved to Chugoko in search of work, not only would omitting this simple action be deemed disrespectful, the man would be immediately removed from his position without question.

"Clean record so far, up until this past mooncycle anyway," the man said, spitting chaff from his chewing stick into a nearby waste bowl. "What happened?"

Zaq frowned. "I don't understand."

"Your charge," he said. "Danso DaaHabba, am I correct?"

"Yes."

"I see a report of two misdemeanours for him," the man said. "Which means, twice, you have failed to do your job."

Zaq gulped. "It wasn't—"

The man put up his hand. He wasn't old—a young man, maybe fifty or so seasons, at least five or more younger than Zaq. Back in Chugoko, when he was still a teacher at the seminary, this man could have been Zaq's subordinate. Yet here, he wielded authority like someone who had birthed many Seconds.

"Consider your position before you mention any excuse," he said. "Remember, I'm authorised to make comments in your report about your behaviour. You wouldn't want me to write you up for insolence, would you?"

Zaq gritted his teeth. "No, officer."

"Then keep quiet." He held the point of his stylus into a nearby flame to darken the charcoal. "Your charge has two misdemeanours. It makes no sense that you have none, since he is your responsibility. So I'm going to put you down for one misdemeanour."

The man wrote and wrote, while Zaq seethed. Never in his life had he been accused of being less-than, of not doing his duty to any authority: family, occupation, state. If anything, he would be accused of doing too much. Leaving Chugoko for the mainland was the first time in his entire life that he had gone against the wishes of anyone, and that was why, of course, he could never go back. But when he was promoted from househand to Second and assigned Danso as his first charge, all of his focus and steadfastness had started to veer. He was suddenly losing these virtues, sliding down the hill he'd been climbing up all his life, and he was being punished for it.

After he was done, the officer straightened up, stretched his back so that the bones creaked, and took another puff of tobacco.

"A Shashi, eh?" he said, and chuckled. "What did you do for them to slap you with this one as charge?"

To be honest, Zaq had asked himself this same question a number of times. He had migrated to Bassa to *make it*, and had primed himself to do the work required of him as a Yelekuté. But not a single thing worked out as planned. It was like Bassa had passed him the one thing it couldn't handle: a young man who didn't know who he was, what he was supposed to be doing, and how he was supposed to behave. How was he supposed to succeed with that?

"You know what happens when you come here with another misdemeanour, yes?" The officer blew smoke into Zaq's face as he said this.

Zaq nodded. He wanted to wave the smoke away, but was unsure of what would count as disrespectful, so he let it settle all over his face. He tried hard not to cough and annoy the man further.

"Good," the man said, beckoning to the next Second. He looked Zaq in the eye, to press home the point, to twist harder the knife of his powerlessness. "Because if you come here with one more misdemeanour from your charge, I'll be sending you back over the moats myself."

· ◇ ··· ── ··· ◇ ·

The rest of the afternoon Zaq spent at Mokhiri's quarters. His secret lover was a perky, buxom woman whose cheeks dimpled when she smiled as she opened the door and hurried him in. Even though their clandestine visitations required more precaution during the day, he found that just gazing at Mokhiri's dimples was a great source of stress relief, and on days like this when he had been wound too tightly, he made a great effort to visit. If he was caught by a civic guard—or worse, reported by anyone who discovered that two Yelekuté immigrants were having unsanctioned relations—he would be in the hottest of possible soups. Yet he did it anyway. Zaq was no rule breaker, but if there was one person he would break a rule for—over and over again—it was her.

Mokhiri shuttered the windows as she often did when he visited. They had slow, passionate sex; her on top, him saving the mental image of her face contorted in the throes of pleasure for later use. They lay naked after, sweating profusely in the afternoon heat for lack of ventilation. Mokhiri rose, unclothed, and got them some water. Zaq sipped from his calabash without rising, letting the water pour down the sides of his lips and pool behind his ears.

"We should just get joined now," Mokhiri said. They spoke in Savanna

Common, the only time Zaq ever spoke his old language. A lot of freshly migrated Yelekuté spoke Savanna Common among themselves, or for those who came from the Idjama desert farther north across Lake Vezha, the Idjama tongue or a border pidgin. But if Zaq wanted to be elevated to the upper immigrant caste, he had to be fluent in Mainland Common. In fact, the best Potokin were expected to also be fluent in High Bassai.

He chuckled and playfully sprayed some water at her. "And how will we do that? Voluntarily report ourselves to the civil guard?"

"The ward leaders should understand," she said. "We love each other, and we want to be together. Who are they to tell us if, when, or how to get joined?"

"Yes, I agree they shouldn't dictate," he said. "But you're forgetting one of us must be Potokin, must be able to earn more and be able to take care of children. Imagine if we got joined despite the laws and ended up bearing one of those abandoned street rats? Ashu forbids it." Zaq circled a hand over his head and snapped his fingers.

"I know, but…" Mokhiri sighed. "I'm tired of waiting for our indenture to expire. If they'll just let us go back and then we can do whatever we like…"

"You know I don't want to go back," Zaq said. "And you know they'll never let us leave without milking our indenture to the last drop."

"Exactly my point. They come up with new reasons to extend it every day, telling us we've broken this rule or that rule when we have done nothing different from the average Bassai. Now, we have the border closure, which is just another reason to keep us here." Her dimples appeared and disappeared with a quick purse of her lips. "Unless you're promoted to Potokin tomorrow—and I don't see that happening—then what is the use of waiting? We might as well get joined now. They can't punish us any more than they currently are, can they?"

Zaq sat up to look her in the face. "Mokhiri, please, let's not get ahead of ourselves. The closure is surely temporary. Also, what do you know— maybe it could even fast-track my promotion."

She scoffed. "Have you been listening to what everyone's saying? No one even really knows why they closed it. Doesn't that tell you it's just another excuse to keep us here as long as possible?"

"You know I don't trust gossip from workers who eavesdrop on their employers."

"Or maybe you just enjoy Bassa too much and don't want to leave," she said, looking him in the eye. "Do you even want to be joined to me?"

Zaq's eyes widened. "Mokhiri! How can you say that?"

"Then what is all this defending of Bassa? Look at what they did to you today, writing you down for Danso missing the meeting. How is that *your* fault? Now you get to do extra work to make up for something *he* did. Doesn't that bother you?"

Zaq leaned back into the wall. She was right, it did bother him. Oh, it *definitely* bothered him. But he had mastered the act of separating his feelings from the work that needed to be done. That was the sacrifice he had made when he left.

Mokhiri pressed herself beside him and leaned into the crook of his body. He massaged her shoulder in return.

"Do you ever wonder if it would've been better if we had never left?" she asked in a small voice. "What life would've been like if we had stayed?"

He had indeed wondered. Mokhiri had crossed the border as a child and thought of life in the desertlands with nostalgia. Having left in recent times and under challenging circumstances, Zaq had more mixed feelings.

"Well, for one, there would be no us, yes?" he said. "If this little man from Haruna had showed up at your trading colony, would you have said yes?"

"Yes," she said, then chuckled. "Okay, maybe not, whatever." She pinched him playfully.

He ran his hands across the frizz of her close-cropped hair. "I remember the good parts, though, sometimes. The smell of Haruna's grasslands; being out in the fields with the hot breeze on my face; shepherds shouting at their animals, the smell of goat and cattle dung everywhere. And after I left and moved to Chugoko, I remember eating baobab porridge and rice pancakes for the first time. Glorious. I ate it for so many moons until I couldn't stand the smell of it." He chuckled at the memory. "Time at the seminary was good, too. I loved drinking cane rum in the evening with the other teachers." He paused. "And then I wonder, if I had stayed, maybe I would have become head teacher there by now."

"No, dear," Mokhiri said, lovingly but firmly. "You would not because the seminary thought you a traitor—thinks you a traitor still. They kicked you out because they believed their children weren't supposed to learn the cultures and ways of lands beyond their own. You shouldn't have been punished for trying to do that good work, and it was wrong for your family to side with them and abandon you. We all moved for different reasons, but remember that the real reason is that we didn't have any other choice. We *had* to leave." She patted his hand. "I don't care for Bassa as you do, but it's not lost on me that Bassa offered a chance to build our futures when the desertlands couldn't. So, while I'm no fan of this ridiculous Ideal thing, I get it; it's bittersweet."

Zaq sighed. "Yeah." He clicked the back of his throat. "And I'm with you, honestly. I want it to move fast too. Because if I have to take one more fighting class to qualify for promotion to Potokin, I will die."

Mokhiri burst into hearty laughter.

"Oh, ehn-ehn, you're laughing at me?" Zaq prodded her belly with a finger. "You think it's easy? Getting beaten by men twice my size, smacked all over my body with wooden weapons, all the while being told, *Get up, get up*? I tell them, I can't do this thing you want me to do, I'm not a violent person, I can't hit anyone, just let me learn the motions needed to pass the tests. Instead they hit me some more and say, *Then block, desertlander, block*. My tongue now knows the taste of dust in a way it never did all my seasons growing up in the literal dust. My body aches constantly. I really want it to end."

"I do hope it will end soon," Mokhiri said between chuckles, before settling back into a serious tone. "But that hope is dwindling; not just for us but for every hand this side of the border. Nobody is sure what tomorrow holds for them anymore. And we have the least choices, don't we?"

"We do," he said. "Which is why we keep at it until we can't anymore, I guess."

But he didn't quite believe these words as he always had. The combination of today's events and Mokhiri's words had sprouted a seed in his heart now, one that brought it front-and-centre that the system was rigged against him. All it would take was one mistake—one that didn't even need to be his—to write off his hard work. Who was to say it wouldn't take even less for everything to come crumbling down and leave him in the dust again—abandoned, homeless, useless? Would Mokhiri even love him then? What would he then be without her or his duty to Bassa?

"Once I get to Potokin," he said, "maybe I'll ask to be transferred into some kind of teaching again. I miss it."

"I miss weaving too," Mokhiri said, and they both gazed at the ceiling for a moment, wistful, before she added, "Instead of spending all my days wiping a grown woman's buttocks." They laughed.

"Danso will be done soon," Zaq said. "I should prepare."

"Yes, and Basemma will soon be back too." Mokhiri put a hand between Zaq's legs, at his hardness. "If we can shelve our own desires for so long, though, they can definitely abide us being a tiny bit late, can they not?"

They definitely can, Zaq thought, pulling her to himself. As long as they were together, the world could burn, for all he cared. She was his anchor, and he was hers, and that was all they needed. He only hoped they could hold out long enough before his frustrations led him to do something untoward. His belly was getting full, and all it would take to burst was a prick, like an overripe guava poked by a bird's beak.

Danso

THE TWELFTH WARD RAFFIA market was levels grittier than the central market near the city square. Rather than neat arrays of yams, cocoyams, mangoes, and tangerines, lines upon lines of raffia palm workers wove and twisted and braided and hammered and sewed, making baskets, mats, and other ornamentals. Bunches of drying raffia dangled from shop rafters or scattered on their floors in heaps, contributing to the prevailing smell of burnt vegetation and mould from wet things long stored. The stench of caked sweat, stale alcohol, and fermenting wine mixed to form a sharp olfactory sting that, to Danso, felt like home.

He arrived Twelfth Ward in search of wine, friends, and repose. Going home was out of the question; it would become evident what had happened. He needed to keep up appearances for the time being, and that meant returning home at the same time as he did every day. The rest of the day was available to kill, and the raffia market was just the place.

Some traders had managed to squeeze themselves between the raffia shops. They heaped okra, tamarind, melon, and white star apples on sackcloth. Danso went past two men roasting a goat and choice parts of a cow on a spit. His stomach grumbled but he hurried on, easing past customers haggling in Mainland Pidgin. They wove in and out of words so that the market was always music, an orchestra without a conductor.

Danso was no stranger to the smells, sweat, and disarray of markets, and found them fascinating when he visited for the right reasons. The evident poverty of this market was no deterrent either—if anything, it was unsurprising. It followed Bassa's pattern of everything decreasing in importance and affluence as one moved outward from the Great Dome toward the outskirts. Fifteenth Ward's shanties housed Bassa's poorest, while most of Bassa's noble Idu caste, especially councilhands and senior guild members, lived in the inner wards of Second to Fifth, with First Ward not open to private housing, being the original Emperor's Road. Danso lived in Ninth, which wasn't as upscale as Esheme and MaaNem's Fourth. Fifteen wards in all, squares divided by the mainways, then by streets separating the courtyard groups, which were interlinked by corridors and passageways. Yards housed either private or city-owned units, depending on whether they were zoned for domestic or commercial activities. Every new ward was a repetition of this layout, so that Bassa was an onion, a concentric maze to the foreign eye.

Danso found the people he was looking for seated in a small raffia wine joint situated in a gazebo. Abulele—Abu for short—who knew all the good spots, was the stocky young man who had likely chosen this spot. Tables and cushioned benches were laid out in circles, many empty at this time of day as most drinkers hadn't yet left work. The joints usually didn't allow novitiate-age groups to drink with other customers, so Abu often came with his intended, Uria, who didn't drink at all but whose presence meant the joint owners would refrain from harassing them.

"Aye, boyo," Danso called to them heartily. He never spoke Mainland Pidgin outside of his sojourns to Twelfth. It was unheard of for a jali to speak anything but High Bassai, or Mainland Common if telling stories to less enlightened groups. Even being spotted here could raise eyebrows. It was why he always did the visiting, and not the other way around. Abu up in Ninth would get tongues wagging enough to jeopardise Danso's position at the university. But being secretive was moot today. The worst had already happened, hadn't it?

"Dan-boyo!" Abu rose for a boisterous embrace and back pat. Uria, who was taller than them both and much too good-looking for Abu's hard-edged face, kissed Danso on the forehead.

"Weybo?" Abu asked. He was already reeking from the heavy stench of the spirit.

"Wine oh, I beg you," Danso said. "Make yo man fit reach home well."

Abu clicked his fingers and shouted the order to someone. The raffia wine arrived before they'd even settled, so freshly tapped that the smoke-coloured brew still featured a tiny blade or two of the palm leaf in each cup. Twelfth Ward was known for its good wine as well as its stellar raffia craftwork, which made perfect sense since both things came from the same tree.

"Where Nowssu?" Danso asked, sipping from his calabash. Nowssu was the last of their quartet, which doubled as a savings circle—they each contributed cowries toward one person every mooncycle, until each person had received a collective contribution, and then repeated the cycle. Nowssu was always late, both in arrival and in contribution, because she had to leave the caretaker guild to join her father at his craftworking shop. That wasn't entirely legal. She was still a caretaker novitiate and therefore not permitted to work, but some cowries and bronze pieces had changed hands with the civic guard captains or ward chiefs, and it was common practice for such to continue.

"Beyond the Pass," Uria said, and Danso suddenly realised why she'd looked so crestfallen since he arrived.

The excuse of the savings circle aside, Danso knew their small gathering was stolen time for each in other ways. He, for instance, considered it an escape from everything else that made up his life—it was the only place he could be as close to his true self as possible. It was a getaway opportunity for Abu too. As a talented dancer and stuntsman, one of the best in the performance arts guild, wowing crowds with his acrobatics and performances on stilts during the mooncrossing festivals, he was loved and admired by all. This fame came with the burden of being courted by various families wanting him to be joined to theirs, especially once they knew he was an orphan. Yet he had to keep rejecting them all. He couldn't face the chance of his secret—that he had a condition that meant he could sire no children for them—slip. With the Bassai Ideal's heavy premium on reproduction, he would be vilified. For him, this circle was solace, the closest thing he had to a family, and probably would ever have.

Uria wasn't really his intended; she only posed as one. Her own reasons for joining the circle were probably the most important of all. She and Nowssu were the real lovers here, employing the circle for little else other than so they could see each other in public without much scrutiny. Both belonged to the Coalition for New Bassa, the activist group led by a charismatic man called Basuaye the Cockroach, which called for a return to the halcyon days of emperors as a route to exercising various freedoms. One of these freedoms was to allow people like Uria and Nowssu to become joined to each other, regardless of the fact that Bassa frowned upon such joining because they wouldn't produce children. Different reasons from Abu's, but similar underpinning. Until such a time that the coalition succeeded, though, Uria and Nowssu could only meet openly among friends, and since Nowssu was always so busy, the savings circle was the easiest way to do it.

Now Nowssu was stuck in the Savanna Belt and, with the way things were going, might not be returning for quite a while.

While they let the weight of this settle on them, a group of Twelfth Warders went by the periphery of the market, chanting against the closure of the Pass, yelling rhyming phrases and expletives in Mainland Common. Their castes told the story: mostly Emuru, mixed with a few Potokin. There were no Yelekuté because the consequences of protesting would be too great for them. And there were no Idu because Idu did not really care about anything but themselves.

The chants were haphazard, but Danso was able to snatch enough to understand that the traders needed salt to preserve their food, and the border closure meant less salt imports, which meant higher salt prices, which would spiral into general inflation. Only a day since the closure, and they were already seeing it happen. Meat was being sold off quickly to avoid rotting; fish trade with the Tombolo hamlets and the delta settlements had reduced drastically for fear that the fish wouldn't last the trip down to Bassa. No export meant all craftwork now had to be sold solely in Bassa for low profit. The coalition wanted a reopened border and were not afraid to ask for even more, like for the Upper Council to step away and crown a new emperor if they couldn't do the work.

It was the kind of thing Uria and Nowssu would've joined, being Emuru themselves and having a vested interest. For them, the protests were just as safe as the savings circle—most Emuru didn't concern them-selves with whom one spent time with in private, and were well aware that many didn't quite fit the Ideal's reproduction-only paradigm. There were no laws or punishments against their kind of relationship, but the Idu continued to stand strongly against them, citing a respect for the Ideal that, unsurprisingly, they didn't keep to in other, more detrimental ways. Uria often described the Idu as having *an illicit wedlock with toxic morality.*

Nowssu's notable absence hung in the air as the protest went by, tailed by a few mean-looking civic guards who lingered restlessly, waiting for a reason to gleefully take their runkus, crossbows, and spears to the protest-ers. When the procession neared their gazebo, one of the civic guards spot-ted Danso and slowed, watching Danso with the gaze of a lion stalking an antelope. Another joined him, and they both stood there, just watching.

"You forget something here?" Abu challenged, rising.

"Leave it, Abu," Danso said, but Abu waved him away.

"You better be walking," Abu said. "You can't drag anybody here into holding today, you hear me? Thank moons you cannot lie that we're con-stituting a nuisance—we are not among the protesters, see?" He held up a finger at them. "And don't even try—you don't know who I am, do you? Be moving, unless you want to find out."

The men watched for a little bit longer, whispering to themselves, eyed Danso again, then went back to trailing the protest. Abu sat, curs-ing. Uria put a hand on Danso's and whispered her apologies.

"No, *I'm* sorry," Danso said, laying a hand on hers too. "All this with Nowssu, what you're going through, is much bigger than some thick-headed civic guards."

She smiled wanly and patted his hand. The unspoken understanding that they might not be seeing Nowssu for a while settled between them. Danso wondered how many more people had been affected by such a simple decision.

"These coalition people, even—can they not do the actual thing they claim to stand for?" Abu waved a dismissive hand toward the now-fading crowd. "Then this border can open fast-fast and Nowssu can return. But instead, they want to be protesting, protesting, no change. Just eating everybody's time, collecting money from all over the place. Frauds, is what they are."

"You can't say that," Uria said. "They're trying their best."

"Which best? Please." Abu kissed his teeth. "What do they do apart from getting people's hopes up, only to arrive at personal agreements with the same people that disenfranchise us? What they are best at is turning this revolution into wealth, I can give them that." When Abu was passionate about something—the only time he spoke sense—he could be quite articulate.

"There is value in the cause, regardless," Uria said. "It creates space for people like me—people like Nowssu, people like all of us here—to speak up for the things that affect us most, and to do so without fear."

"I don't know," Danso said. "Abu is kind of right—they aren't all that honest about their motives, are they? But I agree with you that there's value in a voice of the people continuing to exist. Maybe not in its current form, but at least it's there. Maybe, one day, someone can channel that power and use it to make some changes." He cleared his throat and raised his calabash. "Okay, enough about the coalition. Let us drink to Nowssu: Moons willing, she comes back soon."

Abu lifted his calabash. "Moons willing."

They drank. Danso turned to Uria with a grin, trying for a change of mood.

"How is caretaker guild?"

Uria shrugged. "Mad thing, that one. They have us doing household expansion and sustenance plans now. Hiring and managing househands, planning rooming extensions, designing storage for produce in the rainy season." She sighed. "I tell you, we caretakers should rule the continent. We know everything about how to keep a place running."

"Hear, hear," Danso said, lifting his calabash. "I'm testament to that. Look at my own home. If only we had a caretaker. My daa can't even afford to hire one. Instead now he has me working in the barn!"

They chuckled at that. "Why *you*, though?" Abu asked. "Are you not one of them high-and-mighty ones with a Second?"

Danso snorted. "It's my punishment. I missed the announcement meeting." He paused. "And I've been, er, suspended from the university."

He expected shock from the two, the exact way he expected anyone from his household would react. Instead, they stared at him awhile, and then Abu broke the silence with laughter.

"Finally!" Abu said, wiping his eyes. "But that place no fit you anyway. You have more brain than anybody there. Now, do and leave that Esheme woman, and you can be on your way to greatness."

Uria snickered at that. Except Danso, the whole circle disliked Esheme—not just as part of the collective Bassai sneer toward her maa, but because she represented everything the current Bassai system stood for. They referred to her with a dirty Mainland Pidgin slang term that meant *the one who carries shoulders up*, and wouldn't allow Danso discuss their intended joining ever, because they knew for sure they wouldn't be invited. Abu rose and performed a mean impression of Esheme's gait, sticking his neck up and shooting his bum out while walking. Uria chuckled. Danso didn't laugh because it hit a little too close to home, but he was very careful about reprimanding his Emuru friends' disdain toward the Idu. As someone who lived both within and outside Idu circles, he knew they deserved it.

"Boyo," Abu said, sitting back, "but with this closure business, you sha hold that one tight. Because no Esheme, no fucking for you forever."

"Taa, Abu," Uria said. "Your mouth."

"It's true." Abu snorted. "I remember you say you want to go to Whudasha sometime, abi? Better stay and get joined to Esheme. From what I hear, them no dey open nothing anytime soon."

"How so?" Danso asked.

"My daa says he's hearing whispers they're looking for something," Uria said quietly, peeling the edge of the table with a fingernail, "and won't open nothing till they find it."

Danso recalled his discussion with Esheme about an iborworking skinchanger. He couldn't tell his friends that—not just because it was *their* secret, but because they would snicker and ask him if he'd drunk too much weybo.

"I hear it's to slow migration from the outer lands," Abu said. "Say we getting too many hands and not enough work. Say one day, they fit too plenty and overthrow us, like the islanders tried to do in the Great Wars." He pointed to Danso. "No offence to your people."

Danso wanted to say, *None taken*, but it was still hard not to flinch whenever anyone parroted that line about the Ajabo. He couldn't ask for more care in speaking about it—it was all they knew. Also, wasn't he a novitiate of the very guild that had put those words in their mouths? Wasn't he training to continue to do the same?

"How long, then?" he chose to ask instead.

"Until whenever," Uria said quietly. "Maybe until Bassa finishes eating us alive."

They went back to drinking in silence, the gravity of Nowssu's absence pressing in on them once more. Danso held his wine at the back of his tongue, letting the tang soak into his soft palate and thinking about how Nowssu felt to be stuck outside of home. He wondered if he'd rather be in her place, rather be free of home's shackles. He wondered if such a thing was *freedom from*, or *freedom to*, and if both weren't two sides of the same blade.

·—◇ ⋯ ⋯ ◇—·

It took Danso arriving home to immediately remember that, having drunk too much wine, he had forgotten to return to the university, where Zaq would be waiting with a kwaga to pick him up. Too late now. Rather than go upstairs, he went around back and straight to the barn, to work away the wine in his bloodstream. Besides, if his uncles caught even a whiff of intoxication from him, he wouldn't hear the last of it.

The barn door was unlatched, thankfully. The tubers—yams, cocoyams, potatoes—lay in rows on platforms built into the mud-and-thatch walls of the hut. In the dark interior and in Danso's less-than-stellar vision, they appeared crooked. He rubbed his eyes and carefully stepped over the underground storage units, those housing the biggest tubers. Once inside, he stood there, trying to put together a good strategy. He had yet to move a single tuber since he was assigned the job, as the thought of all the work involved paralyzed him. He'd have to do the buried ones last, moving the oldest from the top and the rotting ones to the bottom for immediate usage. He might need Zaq's help after all, and waiting for his return seemed like a good use of his time, given his current state. So he sat down.

A sudden sound in the barn caused him to leap up. He looked around. Nothing.

Another movement. From one of the underground storage chambers. Something lay beneath the thatch cover. *Rats*, he thought. Or worse, a snake. Danso had never killed a snake before.

I should get a light, he thought.

As he turned to leave, something leapt from beneath the ground and out of the dark. He moved just in time to evade its grasp, but not before he caught a flash of something that felt like it didn't fit, in the barn or in any known existence at all. Something bright and yellowlike.

He barely had time to recover, having landed in a pile of thatch and gotten his leg caught. He saw only flashes as it came for him again: bared teeth, bright irises, a blade.

He yelped as he moved.

A force yanked at his wrapper and sent him landing on his buttocks. A hand emerged from the darkness and clamped over his mouth, pressing so hard and high into his nose that he couldn't breathe. Cold, sharp iron landed on his larynx. Something—someone—breathed hard and fast on his neck. The person barked something under their breath, a language Danso did not know.

"Mmhn!" He shook his head vigorously.

The person smacked his mouth, repeated the command, and pressed the blade harder.

He struggled, panic beating drums in his chest. *I don't understand!*

Smack. Again, in the mouth.

I get it, I get it! I won't scream! He stopped moving, his only motion the heaving of his shoulders. After what seemed like eternity, the hand grudgingly withdrew from his mouth.

Danso screamed.

Something hit his head, heavy, and then darkness embraced him.

Esheme

ESHEME DID NOT TAKE Ikobi's advice and return to the university. Instead she went in the other direction, toward the public houses of the neighbouring ward. Fifth Ward was known for being a transition space of sorts, the only ward where there were an equal number of Emuru living side by side with Idu. This meant a huge devotion to keeping up appearances. Unlike in the outer wards, where Emuru felt more comfortable among their counterparts, Fifth was a ward of performance, where every action was designed to increase the appearance of one's importance. It wasn't surprising, then, that it was also the ward with the highest number of public houses that provided hairdressing service.

Since her maa had gotten the local government to reassign her last Second, who had been responsible for plaiting her hair arches, Esheme had to get her arches done somewhere else. Satti had been interviewing householkands, trying to find one who wasn't already a Second to assist with the duty, but none of them were good enough to the level Esheme needed to show her face proudly in public. So she had settled for visiting the public houses for the first time in her life.

Fifth buzzed with energy. It was the peak of the day, with the guilds that closed earliest from work—farming, hunting, building—already making their way back and heading right for the public houses rather than home. This close to the Great Dome, it was mostly senior guild members, dressed in brightly coloured starched wrappers. They filled the saloon sections of the houses, while some began their dalliance with companions earlier than usual, securing upstairs lodging as well as a companion for the night.

Esheme went to the same house she always did—it was one of the few with its own private quarters, which doubled as both private saloon and lodging. It helped that the housekeep was also discreet.

"Send in my usual hairdresser," she said to the housekeep as Oboda secured their kwagas. She handed the man a bronze piece. He frowned at it, dissatisfied. Esheme made a disapproving click with her tongue, then added a copper piece and three cowries. The man beamed, handed her the key, bowed, and went off.

"Greedy bastard," she said, then made her way through the back-yard corridor. On the floor above, on the rear balcony of the house and within view of the door to the quarters, three hairdressers, women, sorted threads, pomades, and accessories. They chattered as they worked, but upon spotting her, they went quiet. Esheme went in and shut the door but put her ear to it.

"That is her, eh?" one of the women said in rapid-fire Mainland Pidgin.

"Yes," another replied. "You will see, she go ask for Igharo. Only for Igharo, nobody else."

"Tueh," said yet another, mimicking spitting. "That household done finish. Maa, crook. Daughter, crook. And to think they let this one enter Idu?"

"No mind them," the first one said again. "If you let pig sleep inside house, them go bring their yama-yama follow come. This one, she go do like moon-sent, parade like turkey outside, raise buttocks for air. But for secret, she and us, no difference."

Esheme shut the curtains and sat before her reflection in the large mirror of polished brass. She closed her eyes and tried to commit their faces to memory. If they thought they would still be working here come sunrise, they were mistaken.

"Think they can spoil my name anyhow," she said to herself. "We shall see."

To kill time before Igharo arrived, she began to loosen her hair, rumi-nating. This was her problem with Bassa. Everyone expected her to just be a piece on a draughtsboard, standing there for them to push around. And Nem believed that if they worked within the rules, and only bent them ever so slightly, then no one would sneer at them both.

But Esheme knew that rules only worked for those who fit neatly within them. She could be the most rule-abiding person, but as long as anyone believed that she was an Emuru by blood and did not belong in the Idu caste, they would treat her as such. She was tired of trying to earn respect. Perhaps it was time to start taking it by force.

·—◦—···———···—◦—·

Evening fell on Bassa, the moons preparing to take to the sky. Esheme, hair now freshly plaited and scented, remained by the window where the dressing had taken place. She watched Ashu and Menai sidle up close, ready to cross paths in a few days. The evening was damp and warm, despite the closeness to the harmattan season.

Igharo, her Potokin hairdresser, slipped out of bed and came to her, clasping his hands around her belly from behind. He kissed the nape of her neck.

"Go back to bed," she told him. "Someone could see you through the window."

"And what if they do?" he asked, nibbling on her ear.

"Don't be silly."

"I mean it," he said. "Why must we hide? I am even an upgrade of your intended."

She smacked his thigh, hard. "Shut up and do as I say."

He obliged but did not get back under the bedclothes. He instead lay posed atop them, provocative, so that she could see him in all his glory. Esheme ignored him, though she had to admit he did have it good. One of the finest in his guild, both physically and in craft, so that he was highly sought after by all, even among higher castes. She had chosen him because he possessed exactly what she needed: soft, caressing hands that worked just as much magic on her hair as they did on her body.

Igharo flopped into the bed, defeated by her dismissal. "What are you so worried about this time?" He propped himself up on an elbow. "Is it your Shashi?"

Esheme shot him a cutting glance. He was getting bold, the young man.

"Who told you that you can talk about my intended like that?" she asked. "Who gave you permission to be so disrespectful to me?"

He held up his hands. "My apologies. I was just concerned about your well-being—"

"Keep your concern," she said. "You're here for one thing, and one thing alone. You can lie there until I'm ready for you, or you can leave."

She went back to staring out the window until he returned under the bedclothes. Sure, he was right. She had indeed chosen Danso because, if she was being honest, she thought him easily manoeuvred. What she had not expected was for him to become a complete disaster to his own self, so much so that he was palm oil on her white wrapper. It *was* only a matter of time before he took her under with him. But that patience was hers to lose, not for others to lose on her behalf.

It wasn't Danso's antics that worried her right now, though. It was Nem's.

After the civic guard's death, local government personnel had visited the Nem household, led by the ward chief and civic guard captain of Fourth. Voices had been raised in the library, as Esheme was used to. Enough time in the household, and she no longer needed a translator to tell her what was going on: They were upset about the manner in which their comrade was dispatched. Esheme had heard Nem use her measured, placating voice in response. *Apologizing but not apologizing*, as Esheme thought of it. The voices died down and the men left in a sulk. Esheme thought Nem should have done a much better job of sticking it to them, but this was just another day with her maa.

Later that night, something else made Esheme even more worried about her maa's choices.

From her upstairs window, she had seen Nem go into the storage chamber of the last floor, a most odd thing because Nem rarely went down there, having a plethora of people in her employ to attend to whatever was required. When Esheme had gone downstairs for a late drink of water, she heard muffled thudlike noises from the floor below. She followed them to the storage chamber, through the throng of newly hired hunthands Nem had hired since Oboda returned from the Savanna Belt, to find the room guarded by her very own Second.

That wasn't the odd thing. The odd thing was that Oboda had actually prevented her from going in.

"MaaNem says she cannot be disturbed," the big man had said, refusing to look at Esheme's face.

"Look at me when you tell me that nonsense," she'd snapped. "She's *my* maa, not yours. Open it."

Oboda didn't have to, because the noises stopped and Nem emerged, barely clothed, looking sickly and sweaty, eyes clouded like she had a high fever. Before Esheme could make sense of anything, Nem came forward and ushered her away roughly.

"Return to bed," Nem said. "You're sleepwalking."

"Maa, what is happening in there, are you okay?"

Nem pressed her lips into a line and pushed her daughter back upstairs. "I'll explain later."

Esheme shrugged her off. "Stop treating me like a child. I'm a grown woman. Tell me what you're doing in there."

"Securing the future," Nem said. "Yours, mine, ours."

Esheme groaned. "Is there a time when you'll never be cryptic? You're quick to bore me with details when it's nonsense matters. You're involved in something clearly significant now, and you choose to shut me out?"

Nem looked at her for a long time, then said, "One day, you will understand these sacrifices." Then she went back to the chamber and locked the door.

Esheme pulled down the window blinds now, throwing the room into darkness, and went back under the bedclothes. Igharo mumbled sleepily but did not reach for her. She wanted to take a nap before the event later tonight, where her maa would be hosting several Idu nobles and Emuru leaders, as she did periodically to curry favours. She needed to be well rested and performing at her best. Yet sleep evaded her.

Being an Emuru and a fixer was mostly why many people took Nem for granted, but a huge part of this was that she was also highly predictable. Esheme believed instead in being the arbiter of one's domain. She didn't quite care what people thought about Nem—her maa could handle herself well enough—but she did care what people thought about *her*. And when her maa was giving off vibes that she could easily be reprimanded by mere ward leaders, that would cascade down to people's impressions of her, wouldn't it? Word would get out, tongues would wag, and the ensuing embarrassment would find its way back to her.

Esheme tossed about. Nem and Danso were working overtime to bring further disrepute to her already struggling status. If she didn't curb these two somehow, one of them was going to succeed sooner or later.

She threw the bedclothes off Igharo, who mumbled words in half-asleep confusion.

"Get up," she said, and Igharo rose slowly and stood off to the side, hesitant, or tired, or unsure.

"Well?" she said, her eyes goading. "Do your work, then."

He got down and put his tongue into her, and she grimaced from how deep he was. Once she found the wetness between her thighs to be sufficient, she reached between his legs and inserted him into herself. She moved him as she willed, guiding his approach, his thrust, his weight upon her pelvis. They sweated, slick between their bodies.

Still, her mind never left Danso, never left Nem, never left her reputation. She didn't even remember to tell him not to come inside her. When he stopped moving, she couldn't remember if the slick between her thighs was his or hers. She pushed him off and welcomed the drowsiness that followed.

Danso

Danso emerged from the darkness with his cheek to the ground, mould and tuber dust gathering at his nostrils. The back of his head hammered, and stars played hide-and-seek in front of his eyes. He rolled over and struggled to sit up, before realising his hands wouldn't separate. They were bound before him at the wrists, and his feet at the ankles. A dirty rag was wrapped about his mouth. The thought of it touching his tongue caused him to retch and almost give in to vomit.

He propped himself up on his elbows and blinked, waiting for his eyes to adjust to the darkness.

The barn came into view slowly. The yams, the shelves. A pair of attentive yellowish irises, attached to a crouching figure, watching for his next move.

He saw her for the first time now, dressed in a single bulbous wrapper that didn't quite seem to make any sense. It looked like someone trying to mimic the Bassai way of dressing, someone who had tied up too much wrapper in the wrong areas, leaving too much body visible. And beneath the wrapper, Danso saw what she truly was.

From face to hands to feet, as much as he could see, her body was the least like humus he had ever seen outside of himself. Bassai manuscripts called it *the creator's colouring*, that which made most mainlanders look as they did—the less of the creator's colouring a person had, the manuscripts said, the less like the humus they were. It was understood that the farther and farther away from the mainland one went, the less of it they had, with desertlanders having only some of it, and islanders having the least. Gazing upon the yellowskin woman now, Danso realised that the people of the Nameless Islands must have not a single drop at all.

She wore something else beneath the wrapper, clothing closer to the wool of animals than the Bassai wrappers of woven cotton, something he had only ever seen recently migrated desertlanders wear. Over her head, she'd draped a cloak, in the way people of lower status on the mainland often did to hide their plainer plaits. She looked young—barely fortyish seasons, just about his age. Ochre ran from her lower lip to the bottom of her chin, in simulation of Bassai makeup.

A yellowskin. From the Nameless Islands. Dressed as a Bassai.

Solid fear gripped Danso at the throat. Even the earliest sojourners north who returned with stories about yellowskin sightings believed they had come upon ferocious spirits. Others who disagreed with the spirit theory said they were ancestorless people with souls that did not travel to the sky upon death, that their yellowed eyes were a manifestation of those corrupted spirits living within them, and that was why they were so feral. While the consensus of the library manuscripts was that said sojourners had spent too much time in travel and returned crazy and deranged from the sun and solitude, Danso suddenly didn't quite believe so anymore.

There had not been a single reported sighting of a yellowskin in over a hundred seasons. Now, one had suddenly materialized in Bassa, inside his own barn. For what other reason than she was here to kill him?

The young woman moved suddenly, slithering toward him, her movements lithe, her eyes keen and sharp. She settled into a squat before him and studied his face intently, her yellow irises searching for something.

Finally, she lifted an index finger and placed it on her lips. *Keep quiet* in the universal tongue of signs. Danso nodded so hard his head could fall off. With the same finger, she dug into the rag at his mouth and pulled it down.

He felt it when they both held their breaths, waiting for him to do something stupid. She smelled hot and oily. Her hand fell to her side and he noticed a belt of leather and polished shells there, a long, sheathed blade with a hilt heavily decorated with gemstones he'd never seen before. Her hand stayed there, waiting.

Danso gulped, confused. So she wasn't trying to kill him, then? Which made sense, now that he thought of it, because she wouldn't have tied him up in the first place, would she?

Something was afoot here, and none of it made any sense.

"Who are you?" he asked, slowly, deliberately.

Visible relief washed over her and she tracked back and settled into a cross-legged sit. Danso pondered for a moment on why a yellowskin would be relieved not to kill him. Every tale of the outer lands he had ever learned as a jali novitiate agreed upon one thing: that all people of the lands beyond the Pass were born ready to put a blade into the heart of the first mainlander they came across. They were uncouth, violent, and uncultured, a far cry from the Bassai way of life, which was the basis for every accepted migrant being put through a rigorous induction program. Whatever barbaric customs and traditions they were used to had to be erased.

Yet this young woman's actions were confusing. Where he expected rash, barbarian behaviour, she was measured and contemplative. She was...human.

He pulled himself up into a sitting position, lifted his bound hands to his body, slowly so as not to alert her, and pounded them on his chest.

"Me, Danso." He pointed at her. "You?"

She cocked her head, then said something to him. Her voice was mellow, rich, as if made for singing. The language she spoke was like water running down a rock, like what he imagined the waves of the great waters would be: high-low. It wasn't any of the languages he had learned as a jali novitiate.

"I don't understand," Danso said.

She stared at him awhile, then rose to her feet. Beneath the poorly tied wrappers, Danso could see her slight frame. She wore no wristlets or anklets, but something jangled as she moved.

She went to the barn door, having already fastened it from inside, and peeked through the tiny space between. Danso watched her, dread mounting as he came to terms with what that meant. She wasn't going to let him go. Not anytime soon, at least.

"They will come looking for me," Danso said, fear keeping his mouth moving, trying to halt her predator-like movements. "My daa and uncles are in the house."

She looked at him again, her eyes saying something that he interpreted to mean that that was the least of her worries. Or that she didn't care. Or that she didn't understand.

She settled on her haunches in the corner by the door, her hand hovering about the blade at her waist. Danso remembered what Esheme had said about a yellowskin being spotted at the border, yet nothing was discovered upon investigation. Before common sense could take hold of his tongue, an intense curiosity about her opened up before him, and he found himself speaking.

"You must be the one that slipped past a battalion of guards." He surprised himself, that he was asking questions rather than screaming for help. "How did you do it? Evade all those civic guards?"

She didn't turn around or show any sign that she understood his questions. Or show any signs of worry. She just...waited. And so, Danso decided he had no choice but to wait with her. Perhaps he could learn something fundamental if he did.

The shadows of late evening had fallen and the gaps in the hut now drew sharp lines across the floor. Night fell quickly in Bassa during the late rainy season, and unless Ashu and Menai took to the sky early, an appreciable period of darkness would occur before nightlight fully arrived. Mainlanders referred to it as the window of darkness. It seemed to be what she was waiting for. Danso was surprised that she knew enough about Bassa or the mainland to know about the workings of the dark window, but he was more concerned about what she intended to do with it. Kill him and bury his body under the cover of night?

He gulped. *Where is Zaq?*

He was tired and hungry and his head still throbbed from his intoxication. He wondered why his daa and uncles had not come to seek him. Zaq, after not finding him at the university, would assume he went home alone as he had done many times, and had most likely moved on to preparing the evening's meal. Habba was likely still busy in the workroom. And his uncles never, ever came to the barn.

He was going to die here.

"Are you going to kill me?" he found himself asking.

Pleading seemed to transcend language, because she looked at him now and, slowly, shook her head. The gesture gave him some relief, until he realised she could actually be saying she didn't understand.

Who was she? How had she gotten here? What did it mean for him, for her, for Bassa, that she was here, right now, alive, and seeking something? All of these questions tugged at him, and the more they took root in his brain, the more his fear was tempered by a more familiar feeling: a deep curiosity so intense that it consumed him to the extent that he no longer felt the pain of his bound limbs.

They stayed at this impasse, Danso growing wearier as time passed. The hut was fully dark now, and he could see little more than her eyes.

Suddenly, the door moved. Someone was trying to open it from outside.

"Danso?" Zaq called.

The girl sprang to her feet and pulled out her blade. The action was swift and silent, one born of habit and reflex.

"No, wait, wait," Danso said, too quickly.

"Wait for what?" Zaq said from the other side of the door. "Danso?"

The girl looked at him. He couldn't quite see her well, but he imagined that her yellowed eyes swam in a way that reminded him of his daa. The manner in which she was frozen sent two messages: a warning and a plea. Danso couldn't decide which to settle on.

"Zaq?" Danso called back, his eyes on her. Her grip on the blade visibly tightened.

"I'm here. Why is the door tied?"

Danso breathed. "I—um—"

He felt her gaze boring holes in his forehead. *Don't*, her stance said. *Don't.*

"Danso? Is everything all right?"

"Zaq, I don't want to be disturbed."

Silence. Zaq didn't seem convinced.

"Remember daa said I needed to think? I'm thinking."

There was a shuffle of feet. Silence again. The woman didn't move.

"Evening food is ready," Zaq said finally. "I came to call you."

"Okay," Danso said. "Give me a while, I'll be there soon."

"Should I get a lantern?"

"No," Danso said, a bit too quickly, because she tensed then. "Just— I'm coming, I can find my way."

"Okay," Zaq said begrudgingly. "I'll be over here, in case you need me."

"Zaq," Danso said, an image of Zaq being sliced apart by her blade suddenly weighing on his voice. "This is a command. Go back and wait for me."

There was silence, then a *hmph*, and finally the sound of fading footsteps. The young woman's body released its tension.

"See what I said?" Danso said, growing in confidence. "They will come and look for me. And if I don't return soon, Zaq will come back and break down this door." He shook his head. "Zaq is a trained warrior from the desert, excellent with the runku. You know what a runku is? That big stick with the thick head? It won't end well for you."

All lies, of course. Danso knew Zaq had been a teacher at the youth seminary in Chugoko, and before that, a lampmaker. Zaq had never used the runku given to him when he became a Second, despite the fact that a Second was supposed to protect their charge at all costs. He'd even once mentioned that, if he could help it, he'd prefer not to use it at all.

The young woman regarded Danso with something akin to pity, then moved in on him with purpose.

"Wait, wait," he said, lifting his hands to protect his face. "I didn't mean it. I just—"

She grabbed his wrists in a grip so strong he could do nothing but succumb. She hooked the blade under the thatch binding and sliced. His wrists snapped free. She moved to his feet and did the same, then stepped back and sheathed the blade, watching him.

Danso sat there for a moment, unsure of how to proceed. From the moment he'd awoken, his only thought had been that of survival, one built of inculcated belief that whenever islanders and mainlanders met, blood was sure to be spilled. Now instead of bolting right for the door, he found himself suddenly wanting to stay, to ask more questions. He wanted to know everything: Where was she from and why was she here? If she came from the islands, then why was she yellow and not sandskinned like his Ajabo ancestors? As someone who had spent his whole life learning, he was unaccustomed to being this ill-informed. Was he just going to let this opportunity go?

Danso rose to his feet, massaging his wrists. The girl watched, tentative. Her lips twitched, as if she was going to tell him something—her name, her purpose, anything. As they each stood there, working up the courage to speak, that was when he noticed it: a couple of lines dribbling down her ankle. The dry, coppery smell hit him at just about the same time.

"You're bleeding," he said, leaning forward to touch it. She stepped back, tugging at her wrappers to cover the area.

"Maybe," Danso said, fearing the words as they came out of his mouth. "Maybe if you show me, I can help you? My daa is a healer and I've picked up some things."

She gave him a small, careful glance, then returned to the door and untied it. He watched her open the door a peek, then swing it just enough to squeeze through. Evening breeze brushed past her and raised dust in the barn.

"Wait."

She turned.

"Will you—" Danso stopped himself. *What're you saying, Danso? Are you mad?*

She stood there, waiting.

"If whatever you're here for is done, or doesn't work out," he said, "will you come back?"

She blinked, and right before Danso's very eyes, her skin, which was once yellow, slowly changed, darkening until it was the high-black of an Idu. Then she put a finger to her lips, slipped out the door, and melded with the night.

11

Nem

THE TRAVELWAGON RODE SLOWLY along mainway four, past the evening throng of street folk. It was gilded with the finest bronze and brass that Fourth Ward residents could have, the kwagas adorned with cowries and draped in coral beads. Hanging on to the travelwagon, dangling like branches, were two private hunthands, so that everyone who looked upon the travelwagon knew, despite it being covered from all angles, that it contained the most influential person in Fourth: MaaNem.

Everyone who encountered them had time to give way. Most stepped aside; a few genuflected to greet them. Nem wasn't quite sure if the slow movement was because people were still anxious over the border closure—the Bassai were always anxious and upset about *something*—or if it was simply because of the usual reason: that they considered her important enough to acknowledge but detested her enough to hold back a public show of respect.

The wagon reached a mainway junction and waited for the hunthands to jog ahead and stop oncoming and crossing traffic so they could pass. Street urchins from the outer, poorer wards, who came into the inner, wealthier wards to beg and scramble for leftovers, ran over from the roadsides, carrying large brushes with crude bristles made from plant fibre, and began to brush the coats of the team of kwagas pulling the travelwagon. The stablehands riding the teams shouted and lashed whips at them. The children danced out of reach with practiced ease and returned just as quickly, petting and brushing the kwagas, who seemed unbothered by their jovial touches.

Nem leaned out of her window at the ruckus.

"Leave them," she said to her driving stablehand. The children took this as their cue to swoop in on her travelwagon, arms out, chorusing a rehearsed plea for a reward for cleaning the kwagas. Nem dipped a hand into a pouch at her waist and put cowries in each of their palms. The children skipped away and the cavalcade moved on.

"You shouldn't encourage them," Esheme, sitting next to Nem, said. Oboda, opposite them both, acted as usual: like he wasn't listening.

Nem lifted her eyebrows at the rebuke. "How so?"

Esheme scowled at the retreating figures of the children. "All they'll do is pick up where their parents left off, producing a never-ending caravan of street spawn. Thank moons we've closed the borders. Any more of these immigrants and they'll completely take over the streets."

Nem smiled wryly. "You don't quite see the difference between influence and affluence, do you, my dear?"

Esheme said nothing, looking out at the workers lighting the streetlamps with long rods, in time for the fall of evening. Nem clicked the back of her throat and wondered what it would take to teach her daughter the more nuanced ways of the world. To show her how things so apparent were always more twisty than evident, and the road to triumph lay in how bendable one could be, as bendable as the roads that led there. But she returned her thoughts to the evening's forthcoming event instead.

The travelwagon drew to a halt outside the Nem household. Standing there was Nem's caretaker, Satti, a slight woman with tight little eyes, small hands, and an iron fist. Most people who came upon her thought they could go over her head, and were quickly corrected. She had run Nem's household for as long as it had existed, and despite her high turnover rates of househands and stablehands, the household's performance remained of superb quality.

Satti looked anxious, though, when she genuflected to greet Nem, which was unusual.

"What is it?" Nem asked, getting out of the wagon.

"We have unexpected visitors," Satti said, and just as she did, the two unexpected visitors emerged from the entrance.

The event was supposed to be a hosting Nem held periodically for guild leaders, civic guard captains, and local government officials in Fourth and beyond. Sometimes an Idu noble attended for some reason, but that was rare. Never had *two* Idu nobles—especially if those two were a First Merchant from the Upper Council and the Speaker of the nation himself—been at her house at the exact same time.

The tension in the air was palpable. Even Esheme looked concerned.

"Nem," Abuso said, staring at her. The other man was First Elder Dota, a burly man swaddled under layers of the finest wrappers and gold that announced to anyone looking he was clearly from Upper Council-hood. He literally ran half the border's merchantry enterprise and owned the caravan Nem had hired to send her hunthands out in search of Abuso's daughter.

"Speaker," she said, and feigned a genuflection that both her caretaker and daughter mirrored. She seethed inside as she rose.

"We have come to enjoy your feast," Dota said. His speech was lazy, like someone who wasn't used to speaking much and got bored just doing so. But under his acute gaze, Nem felt *watched* and tense for the first time. She understood immediately he was not someone to be taken lightly. His family had not been First Merchants of the nation and members of the Upper Council for so many seasons by sheer luck.

"Will you have us?" Dota asked, almost naturally, and any listening ear not keen enough might have even thought Nem had a choice.

"Certainly, Elders," she said, and motioned to Satti. "Let's set additional places for our leaders."

They went inside, and soon after, the invited guests began to arrive, alighting from their travelwagons, househands rushing out to help them. Gold, bronze, brass, copper, and coral winked here and there as the finest wrappers and jewellery worn by the highest of the Emuru filled her house. Being the worker caste, they pulled no stops in attempting to mirror the Idu noble look, stretching the boundaries as much as legalities would allow. The women kept their fewer hair arches high and proud, the men their plaits shiny, and all genders their facepaint bright.

"Welcome to my household," Nem said, greeting everyone as they shuffled in. "It is a great honour to host you tonight. Please, come in. Enjoy all we have prepared."

The main courtyard of the house's ground floor had a lengthy table overflowing with food and wine. Musicians started up in the corner, playing skin drums, beaded calabashes, a flute, and the twenty-one-stringed lute-harp. A jali sang, one of the recent graduates still seeking permanent placement within the guild and thus still open to private hire. She played the role of singer-herald, welcoming the visitors in High Bassai, weaving their names into on-the-spot songs of praise as they came through. One or two danced toward the troupe when their praises were sung and dropped cowries or gold or bronze or copper pieces into their laid-out calabashes. The jali chanted even louder.

Househands swooped in, offering food and fruit and wine. Nem went around, Esheme in tow, greeting each attendee and asking of their welfare. She smiled performatively, eliciting favourable responses.

When everyone had settled in and the feast was under way, Abuso rose and found Nem, pulling her out of the line of sight of Dọta, whose eyes followed them suspiciously.

"Do you have news for me?" Abuso asked hurriedly, once they had hidden away beyond a corner. "Dọta came asking me questions for which I had no answers. I had to bring him here just to pacify him, but I don't think I can hold him off much longer."

"I have no news," Nem said, yanking her arm from his grip. Oboda, who was standing nearby, stepped forward, hand already on his belt, ready to release his runku. Nem gave a sharp shake of her head and he paused midstride, but the dagger looks he shot Abuso did not abate.

"Oh, so you'll set your Second on me now?" Abuso was saying. "You think you're the only one with a Second?"

"No." Nem waved at Oboda to move away. The man did, but never took his eyes off her. She turned back to Abuso. "Look, Speaker, I'm still working on it."

"Well, I gather your Second brought you some artifacts from his sojourn," Abuso said. Before Nem could deny it, he said, "Ah—don't. I already know it's true, so don't bother. All I need to know is if those artifacts are connected to Oke, and if we may be able to use any of them to pacify Dọta."

"Your daughter was involved in some…things," Nem said, "according to the report I received. But no, the artifacts did not have anything to do with her."

"You did not answer the second part of my question."

"We cannot pacify him with anything currently in my possession. Not in any way that I know of." Both statements were lies, of course, and she knew Abuso knew it because he didn't take his eyes off her.

"Listen, I am going to tell you something now." Abuso shifted on his feet, impatient. "You think somehow you're smart, that you can just go outside the border and do whatever you please. Do you know the risk of your actions for this nation? Imagine if Chugoko's leaders got wind of your exploits, or the Idjama chiefs beyond the lake. That's all the treaties we worked so hard for, gone. That's our salt imports, our kwaga imports, our copper and wool you're playing with." He shifted again, getting even more antsy. "If I find out that in addition to erroneously slipping an invader into the mainland, you have also brought something dangerous here, then you are by all means in for it. Expect that I will be letting the Upper Council know what I have found out, immediately." He leaned closer. "I also hear that the Manic Emperor's rediscovered codex is missing? My daughter also broke in and read that codex. I have a feeling these incidents are not unrelated. Nothing with you ever is." He pulled back. "I'm warning you, Nem. Regardless of your line of work, you are not above the law of this nation."

"I told you, Speaker," Nem said, as politely as she could. "Please don't threaten me."

"And you will do what?" he asked. "Please tell me what you're capable of, you low-rent Emuru." He kissed his teeth long and hard and walked away. Nem watched him leave, unfazed but angered.

"Maa?" Esheme emerged from the shadows suddenly. Nem wondered how much of that exchange she had heard.

Almost as tall as she was, her daughter whispered in her ear, "This is perhaps a good time to tell me what is going on." It sounded like half an enquiry, half a reprimand.

Nem smiled and held her daughter by the arm.

"Soon, you will see," she said. "When the right time comes. Information before you need it is just as dangerous as the lack of it. Patience, woman."

She left her daughter standing there and carried on with the feast. Soon it was late, and everything died down. The attendees began to leave, First Elder and Speaker included. Nem bid each farewell at the door, and a few whispered promises of goodwill as they left. Nem took each with grace and smiled, Esheme and Satti on either side of her.

·—◇—⁝⁝⁝————⁝⁝⁝—◇—·

After the feast, when all was quiet and still, and the househands had cleaned up and gone to sleep, Nem went down to the storage room, Oboda in tow.

"Tonight will be much longer than usual," Nem said to him at the door. "Be sure to stay awake."

The man nodded, shut her in, and stood guard outside. Nem took off her wrappers and set them aside. Then she went to the corner of the room and, opening the secret compartment in a bottom corner of the wall, retrieved the wrought-iron strongbox she stored there. She retrieved its key from her wrappers, opened it, and pulled out the objects within.

The first objects were two types of material that were hard and dense like stone, but tough and brittle like bone. One of them was reddish and larger than her two fists put together, the other greyish and in pieces smaller than her fingers. They were both pockmarked and dull, polished by age and elements enough to be recognised as something buried for a long time. The flickering light of the pot's fire bounced off them, giving off an aura of otherworldliness and power.

The other two objects were manuscripts. One of them was hers, a bound leather-wrapped manuscript in which she had been documenting notes about everything she had been learning from the other manuscript.

The other manuscript was the Codex of the Twenty-Third Emperor of Great Bassa, the Manic Emperor Nogowu, which Oboda had helped her steal from the university library's restricted section.

When she had heard the news, two seasons ago, about that Danso boy's inadvertent rediscovery of a manuscript from the Manic Emperor's time, she had wondered, in passing, what knowledge he must have been privy to. Then Abuso had come to her, saying he had discovered that his daughter was funding the Coalition for New Bassa. Apparently, the young woman had been privy to some secret manuscript—she wouldn't say what or where—and said that it had "opened her eyes." Abuso, furious, had lashed out, and Oke reacted by running off and finding a way across the border, after which he had approached Nem for help in finding her.

Then Oboda had returned without the young woman in tow, but with an unbelievable tale featuring a yellowskin man whom Oke had apparently planned to meet, and how the man had started a fire and burned down a popular caravansary on the trade route north. And once he revealed the two shades of stone-bone he had seized after overpowering the man, the last piece of the puzzle clicked for Nem.

She had inadvertently just rediscovered the rarest and most powerful mineral on the continent of Oon: ibor.

But so had Abuso's daughter, somehow, likely through her "secret manuscript," which, upon second thought, Nem decided had to be Nogowu's codex.

Nogowu was known by the populace for exactly two things: being the emperor who crumbled the now-defunct Bassai empire into its current nation-state form, and being addicted to opiates, which had eventually killed him. But there was a third thing, relatively unknown, only accessible to those who could read—and they weren't many: The emperor had an unhealthy fixation with the supernatural. Very few knew this, but it was he who had started the stories of ibor, a mineral that could perform feats akin to the sorcery believed to be wielded by those who did not worship the moon gods. He'd called them Iborworkers, and he postulated that outlanders—islanders, perhaps even desertlanders—and select groups in the hinterlands could wield this power and use it to take over the mainland. While the rest of the nation went to war with the Ajabo islanders simply to get rid of them, Nogowu's belief that they possessed this power was what drove him. But of course, none of this was public knowledge, then and now, because even among his council, few took him seriously. Court scribes had documented some of his ramblings, a few of which Nem had read, but anything by the man's hand had been deemed lost. Until now.

Nem lit a firepot nearby. The joke was on them all now, wasn't it? Because, Nem believed, the emperor had been right.

The daughter of the Speaker of the nation had, out of nowhere, suddenly risked everything to cross the border into the Savanna Belt for a meeting with an islander who wasn't supposed to exist. If that told her anything, it was this: The codex was at the centre of it all. It was the catalyst, the thing to have. It would tell her what she needed to know in order for her to do with the stones what she wanted: to become an Iborworker.

Yet for that to be worth anything, she had to make sure no one else possessed this information ever again.

After painstakingly checking that she had copied all she needed from the codex to her own leather-bound journal, she began to tear out the manuscript's pages, one by one, and toss them into the pot, watching them catch and contort, then succumb into ashes. She did it again and again until the forbidden codex of Emperor Nogowu, the last and Manic Emperor of Bassa, was nothing but black soot at the bottom of the pot. She poured water into the pot to complete the destruction.

Nem rose, picked up a piece of grey ibor, and studied it. All of the pieces, both red and grey, had grooves in them, marked in an indecipherable language, but she would get to those later. Right now, she simply needed to learn the most important thing: how to *use* it properly.

As she had been practicing over the weeks, she inhaled, squeezed the ibor in her palm, then let her mind go, let it find the power of the mineral and connect to it. She floated for a while, seeking, before suddenly, a jarring hold overcame her body as the ibor power surged into her. She Drew it, kept Drawing until she held enough of it in her chest, until the cavities of her insides were filled with its heat. Then she turned to the water in the pot, focused her mind on it, and Possessed it.

The water rose, animated and unwieldy, like a squirming infant. Nem struggled to keep it under control. And to do that, she executed the third step as the codex had described it: She Commanded it.

Stop.

The water froze in midair, suspended and immobile, almost anticipatory. Nem Commanded again, releasing some of the ibor's energy in its direction, and the water formed a globule, neat and iridescent. She offered another Command, and the globule froze into a neat ball of firm ice.

She practiced a few more mental Commands until the energy started to take its toll on her body, and then she let all of it go too quickly at once. The water splashed, hard enough to have wounded someone standing in the wrong place at the wrong time. She ducked, and drops missed her by inches.

She regarded the damage as a tooth in her mouth shook loose. She pulled at it and it came off easily, bloodless. The tooth was almost completely decayed. Nem was very particular about her dental hygiene, so this was simply the ibor taking its toll over time, eating her body from the inside in exchange for its power. The codex detailed specific nourishment regimes for Iborworkers, dietary requirements and supplements to combat the effect of iborworking. Nem hadn't taken it seriously in the beginning, but looking at that rotten tooth now, she decided that was the next thing she had to focus on.

She relit the pot, reading her notes before her next attempt. The codex had offered notes on three shades of ibor and the Iborworkers associated with them: white, amber, and grey.

Of White Iborworkers, he had written: *Fly a distance. Harness the wind. Absorb light from a place. Cloak, like a chameleon.* Nem had interpreted this to mean they could Possess and Command both air and light, force it to do their will.

Of Grey Iborworkers, he had simply written: *Fire. It will do anything.* Nem already knew this from Oboda's tale, where the yellowskin man had Possessed fire against them and inadvertently set the whole caravansary ablaze. The water, however, she had stumbled upon by accident, while practicing.

Of Amber Iborworkers, he had written much more, as theirs seemed a bit trickier.

Initial Possession is the toughest, but creates a bond between mineral, Iborworker, and the Possessed object, the notes said. *May be any object, but must be without life. After first Possession, they may Possess same object continuously with growing ease, like an extra limb.*

Nem had initially thought he'd mistaken red stone-bone for amber, but after she had tried everything with the red stone-bone in her possession and nothing worked, she decided this particular chunk of red had to be something else. Perhaps it wasn't even ibor, even though it had the same form and consistency as the grey pieces. Perhaps it was another type of ibor that operated some other way. Time would tell.

On her next go, Nem tried Possessing both the water and fire at the same time, and when the two came together, they negated each other and brought steam and sweat and high humidity into the room. Nem sat and paused for a rest, waiting for the room to cool down.

In the meantime, she made some more notes in her journal, postulating why ibor might work for certain individuals and not for others. The codex had said that ibor, regardless of the shade, *chose* its worker. His first explanation, which she had already copied into her journal, mentioned that it was arbitrarily distributed, much in the same manner as any other talent. But then, in what seemed like the emperor's later days, his most manic periods, he had jotted a frenzy of notes, not quite legible and not necessarily in one language but in various ones. This part, Nem thought, offered more insight, but she had been unable to copy them. So now she was making her own notes because something told her that there were certain conditions each user had to fulfil, regardless. She believed these conditions simply weren't currently known.

Belief, though, she wrote, *is crucial*. This part, the codex had said. A certain suspension of disbelief in the workings of the world was required: an acceptance of the idea that the body and mind could achieve more than the typical or expected. Nogowu had been writing about himself, explaining that it was the reason he had been unable to work ibor while islanders used it easily, though Nem couldn't be sure if this was true or not. She had learned how to, had she not?

Once the room had cooled, Nem rose again. It was going to be a long night, but that didn't matter. Her enemies weren't sleeping, and neither would she.

12

Danso

DANSO WASHED OFF THE worst evidences of his ordeal before going in for his evening meal. His daa and uncles paid little attention to his looks, anyway, which was proved right when he sat at the lively table and they paid him no heed. Zaq, more perceptive, said nothing, but eyed his stained wrapper and the reddish marks on his wrists, visible when he brought his hand up to take an occasional swallow of his starch meal with palm kernel soup.

Danso ate slowly, trying more than anything to keep his hands from visibly shaking. What that Elder had told Esheme's maa had been right after all.

There was a yellowskin in Bassa, and she was a skinchanger.

But the biggest news of all: Islands still existed.

And the stone-bone mineral of ibor—and its supernatural powers of which the Manic Emperor wrote—it was all real.

Conflict burned within him. Surely he *had* to report this, didn't he? Wounded or not, a yellowskin was a danger to every person in the city. An Iborworker at that! Who knew what she was up to right now, blending in with the populace? Worse yet, she clearly also possessed what he now realised was likely the most important item on this continent.

Yet the part of his mind in favour of not reporting was making a strong argument. Like how, for instance, she had made sure not to harm him, and had left him despite everything he knew about her. This indicated a modicum of trust, didn't it? Was he to betray that trust, then?

Also, this was the first islander to be spotted in so many seasons and if there ever was anyone who could perhaps answer his questions—about the Nameless Islands, about the Ajabo, about what had become of his maa and her people—it was her, wasn't it? If the civic guard caught her, the Upper Council would hang her immediately. All for what—the same illegal border crossing that desert folks did all the time? It was insane. He could never forgive himself for that, especially for missing the opportunity to have his burning questions answered.

Zaq leaned over as Danso simmered with his thoughts.

"Everything okay?"

Danso shrugged. "Yes? No? Maybe?" He put down the starch meal he was in the process of cutting with his fingers. "Tell me, Zaq: How do you know when what you're doing is the right thing? Do you just…decide that the option you've chosen is right? Is it instinct, perhaps?"

Zaq frowned, pensive for a moment. "I…I don't think anyone really knows, perhaps?" He retreated, suddenly in a clouded mood himself. "I guess it is time that tells?"

"Fair." Danso returned to his meal. "I wish I could always know in time. I feel like I never make the right decision, no matter how hard I try."

Zaq thought for a moment, then said: "I see."

Danso watched the table, his uncles telling Habba a story from one of their outings during the day. Danso's mood grew darker and darker as he watched his daa smiling peacefully, eating his meal, laughing with his brothers. How could they so easily brush aside something—someone— that was such a big part of his life, and of theirs before him? He wished his maa were here; perhaps she would give him her ear, ask what troubled him, offer room for him to relay all his tormenting questions. He would ask her if loyalty to Bassa preceded unearthing hidden truths, or if asking the yellowskin to come back had been the right move. He somehow believed she would understand all of this, though a small part of him doubted because he knew too little about her, didn't he?

The turmoil in Danso's chest roiled even more.

"Daa," he said, without looking at Habba, "I want to know what really happened to—" He paused, swallowing. "Maa."

Uduuwe coughed and choked on his soup. Habba passed him water in a calabash to take a swig, washed his own hands, then interlinked his fingers and watched his son. Silence swallowed the table.

"I know you have told me not to focus on that, yes," Danso continued, "but it's important to me. And you"—he looked at his uncles too, here—"are always avoiding this topic. And I believe I'm done waiting for you to be ready to talk about her."

"Danso, you are being disrespectful again," Kachuwe said. "Can you not learn to couch your words well? Can you not—"

"If you don't mind, uncle," Danso interrupted, "I am speaking only to my daa at this moment."

His uncles gasped. "Habba!" Pochuwe said. "Look at this boy—"

Habba put up a hand, watching his son closely. He drank raffia wine from a calabash, slowly, then put it down.

"And what has happened to warrant this enquiry now?" Habba asked.

"Nothing has happened," Danso shot back. "I don't need a reason. I'm a fully grown man, soon to be joined. I have a right to know who I am, where I'm from. I have a right to know about my own maa."

"You are of this household," Habba said, calmly, "and that is all that matters."

"To you!" Danso said, agitated. "To you, to this city, to this nation. Have you ever asked what matters to me?"

"In the grand scheme of things," Uduuwe said, "all that matters is that you shut up and eat your food, and be grateful for what you have."

Danso shot his uncle a hard look. "Uncle Uduuwe, I said I am speaking to my daa. I suggest you focus on eating your food, so you don't choke on all the contributions to this household that you never make."

His three uncles' jaws dropped. They pushed away their plates.

"What did you say?" Uduuwe said.

"I *said*," Danso said, "I want *you*"—he pointed to them each, Habba included—"to either talk about my maa or refrain from speaking to me until further notice."

His defiance rippled across the table and kept things static for a beat. Even Zaq looked anxious. All of them turned to the head of the table, where Habba sat, for a response.

"I understand you're upset by my silence," Habba said finally, dousing the tension. "But you must understand what a bloody time it was. Every image of it is tinged with agony, misery. Our bodies know it, our minds know it—they clench up when we try to recall, wipe our memories so that we're no longer sure if we dreamt it or not. There were children starved, slaughtered, roasted, Danso. *Roasted.*" He looked up. "It is a big ask to revisit such a place, my boy. Even at the expense of... memory."

"So I'll never know?" Danso rose with a loud scrape of his chair. "Is that what you're saying? That your pain is bigger than my lifelong emptiness and doubt? I've been patient, waited and waited for you all to come around. And you're telling me that we're going to continue to pretend a whole part of me does not exist? That *she* didn't exist? You won't even tell me her name!"

"Sit down, Danso," Pochuwe said. "Now."

Danso remained standing, glaring at everyone, and things stood still at the table for a long time.

"I cannot sit and eat with liars," Danso said finally, then shoved his chair violently and went upstairs without a word. He flopped into bed and lay there with the window wide open and the raffia blinds raised. The evening breeze commingled with the scents of his collection of potted plants scattered all about the room and melded them into a sweet-sharp odour that teased. Ordinarily, this would be the time he checked to see if Zaq had watered them during the day, but he remained under the bedding despite the heat, afraid to be alone in the dark again.

Or maybe he was confused, not afraid. They could refuse to tell him about his maa, but what he had witnessed in the barn was proof that stories untold always came to life eventually. He would never unknow what he now knew, unsee what he had seen. Perhaps his maa's story would come to life in this same way.

But right now, he had a duty to his people, to speak up for their safety. As Esheme had said, giving this information to the ruling councils could be worth a hundred gold stones. He could lie in some of the finest feather-beds, ditch this thatch bedding forever. He could bring joy to Esheme and forge the foundation for a long and blissful joining. He could finally gain respect, for himself and his household, across the city.

And the greatest danger overall: If he failed to report this, he was in essence declaring himself an enemy of Bassa. The Bassai pledge of allegiance made no bones about it: *Protect our lands and borders, sand and sea, from outsiders and invaders.* If he kept quiet, he was choosing to become an enemy of the nation. If word ever got out that he had known something and kept it to himself, he would be made an example of. Being Shashi, he didn't need to think twice to know what kind of example it would be.

But. *But.*

He thought about the yellowskin woman for a moment: the sparkle of purpose in her eyes, the feel of someone on a mission. She wasn't just some border skipper—she was here to stay until she finished whatever she came for. That alone increased the chance that she could be here for a while. Maybe she could even return to the barn.

I'll wait, Danso decided, there and then. A drop of wonder had landed on his tongue, and Danso knew that henceforth his thirst would be insatiable. Whether his daa and uncles were willing to acknowledge that thirst or not, it existed, and he was going to quench it somehow.

Danso lay staring out the window, at the two gods of the sky. Menai, whose ring of fire and wrath the Bassai feared and prayed to for strength to strike their enemies, was out in full view tonight. This was not to be a good night, it seemed. Terrible things happened when the red moon shone brightest. Beside Menai, almost close to crossing, her calmer and delicate sister, Ashu, winked, farther away.

It was to Ashu that Danso would pray for strength instead, but strength of a different kind. He had touched something outside Bassa, something that had burst forth from all his dreams and imaginations about everything beyond the Soke border. And she had lived and breathed and bled like him.

Danso closed his eyes and asked Ashu for fortitude and control. Because tonight, he had made up his mind: If he did not get the answers he sought in the short term, then he was going to seek them somewhere else.

He would pack a bag and leave Bassa, go anywhere that promised something even a little more than his household and this city could offer.

Whudasha looked like a good place to start. Across the border, maybe even better. And best-case scenario, to the islands, if they were still there.

Before he fell asleep, Danso again prayed to Ashu for good fortune, for a sign. He asked for a spark, something that told him these were the right decisions. Yet before he drifted off, he kept thinking of what that sign might be, and what stuck to the edges of his mind before sleep claimed him was the image of the young yellowskin woman in his barn.

· ◇ ⋯ ——————— ⋯ ◇ ·

Danso rose very early, long before dawn, and packed a new bag.

Ever since he was a child, Danso had kept a survival clothsack. It started as a childhood fantasy of riding off on a kwaga to Whudasha, to go see how people like him lived. They said the place was only filled with memories of pain, and it was bad for him to be associated with the people there. Later, it morphed into a desire to go find his maa, when no one would talk about her or where she had come from, or why her people left the mainland. He'd kept packing and repacking until, at some point when he was older, he somehow always had a ready-to-go bag lying around for no reason at all. He thought of it as an emergency stash, ready for whenever an opportunity to leave came. He repacked the bag anytime he found he couldn't sleep and needed to process his thoughts.

Today, he packed furiously, emotions warring within him. After all these seasons trying to put thoughts of his maa aside, he was surprised that his thoughts now often drifted to her. This yellowskin woman's appearance had reawakened them in a way that nothing ever had before.

He unpacked all he'd packed so far and put the items back into the bag again, running through a list he'd become familiar with. He stuffed the oldest at the bottom: an old blade Zaq had used for slicing meat; some cowries, copper and bronze pieces put aside from his savings circle; a bunch of wrappers; a tiny clay lantern stuffed with animal fat; a thick blanket. On top of these he packed the more recent stuff: some water he always replaced in a leather canteen; some dried food—shelled palm kernels, roasted groundnuts and cashew nuts, dried coconut, fruits and meat. Over these, he placed the most recent items he'd stolen from house resources: some wrapped herbs, spices, ointments, and elixirs from his daa's workroom. He tied them together in the clothsack and placed it under his bed as usual, then went back to lie down.

Dawn came, and Danso went straight to his desk without a word to anyone. Zaq came with a message from his daa, who had gone out, that he was not allowed to go anywhere that day except classes and the moon-crossing festival in the evening. Danso paid no attention. He opened his journal instead and first began to rewrite, from memory, the manuscript his daa had burned. Then he tossed that aside and began to write only what he had learned about the islands and yellowskins and ibor from the codex, or at least as much as he had read of it. But then he let his mind wander, and wander it did, and what he started to write became a fictional tale, one that he may or may not have dreamt the night before.

His charcoal stylus scratched on sheet after sheet in a loose sheaf. The tale was about a skinchanging woman from the Nameless Islands, who had a child with a Bassai man, a child so Shashi that people didn't know what to do with him, so they threw him into the streets where he waited, and waited, for someone to come and claim him.

He wrote long into the afternoon, a winding tale that went on, searching for answers. It wasn't until Zaq, who had wandered over multiple times to inform him that meals were ready—to which Danso replied, each time, "Leave me alone"—tapped on his shoulder. When he looked up, it was dark, and he knew it was time to meet Esheme at the moon-crossing festival.

Danso

For the second time in a few days, mainway one was packed with people heading for the city square. Attendees had arrived from every corner of the fifteen wards, as well as communities beyond the Tombolo-Gondola confluence that marked the edge of Bassa's capital city-state. The southeast and southwest hinterland protectorates were duly represented, as well as the delta settlements to the south-south and the Tombolo fishing hamlets to the east. Whudans to the west were not invited, as expected. Shashi had no place in such honoured activities. Envoys and delegates from outside the Soke border were absent also, as the border closure had prevented any such travel.

The energy had shifted to one of ecstasy, almost as if the transgressions of the last few days had been forgotten, worry and panic about the Pass closure thrown to the wind with the meeting of Ashu and Menai in the sky. It was a favourite Bassai saying that mooncrossings brought good fortune. It was also a favourite saying that the average Bassai was like a stray dog: Throw them a bone, and they forget their conditions are exacting and their future bleak.

For Danso, the mooncrossing took on a more dismal quality. Now washed, doused in fragrances from the yellow trumpet flower, wearing a fresh plait and proper facepaint, he rode atop Usi, his household's one and only kwaga. He moved through the crowd in a majestic household procession as required of his status as a jali novitiate, his daa and uncles riding behind him in the household's one travelwagon—drawn by a team of domestic asses rather than kwagas, which were imported from the desertland and therefore not easily affordable by the Habba household. Usi's striped coat was polished for the night, her horns shined. Zaq, on foot, led her up the mainway, clicking his tongue and tapping her every now and then, shooing people out of the way of her horn span.

The two moons lined up in full bloom above, so that Menai, with her ring of fire, eclipsed her sister. But Ashu's light, never dulled, shone around, so that their overlap was seen everywhere on the continent as concentric circles of red and white, casting orange light so bright it negated the need for streetlamps.

Their group came to the courtyard, handed Usi off to a stablehand, and went in. The central square was an arena with a performing area in the middle and seating stacked in tiers. The big bonfire was already lit in the middle, signalling the start of the festival, and everyone began to take their seats. Danso bade good-bye to his daa and uncles, who went off to seating apportioned for more common folk. After arriving at the seats reserved for scholars and their novitiates, he bade good-bye to Zaq as well, who made his way to the standing area at the back, reserved for Potokin and Yelekuté who had a reason to be there. Soon, the doors to the arena would be closed, and then all night, the civic guard would perform the unenviable task of keeping the late-coming Emuru, as well as Potokin and Yelekuté— who had only limited entry allowances—away from the gates into the city square, just as they had done with the impromptu announcement.

The square was as bright as late dawn, lit by fire and nightlight, and the night breeze rustled wrappers and caused the air to crackle with the dry onset of harmattan. Dancers and performers prepared in the middle. Danso could see Abulele from all the way up where he was, stretching. He wanted to holler and wave at the boy, but decided he was too close to the scholars to do so without attracting a few stares of disbelief.

He found Esheme seated near a group of scholars, all in white, her hands clasped regally. He came to her, put his fingers to his lips, and bowed in the greeting for intendeds. She looked at him and smiled but did not return the greeting. He sat next to her. She smelled pleasantly of the starflower gardenia, which she had tucked into each of her five arched plaits, newly plaited and oiled. Her wrappers were well starched, and the yellow scented ochre line in the middle of her forehead gleamed. She was ravishing. Danso felt inadequate and a little jealous.

"I came early today, see?" he said, going for a light mood.

"Good for you," she said, and returned to gazing at the arena.

An Elder Jali, one Danso recognised from guild, picked up a bull's horn and said, his voice booming across the arena: "Please, take your seats. The mooncrossing festival will soon begin."

The arena lit up with more lamps and dropped into silence as the leaders of the nation came forth.

The breeze changed, suddenly suffused with sweet smells and the presence of more wealth and affluence than the average Bassai was used to. Pomp and pageantry took centre stage, velvet wrappers and jewellery that could only be described as royal—intricate gold neckpieces; coral and natural flowers woven into hair arches; facepaint of the highest quality of sweet-smelling ochre and gold dust—being paraded in square-shouldered gaits.

Leading the line was First Elder Dọta and the other three First Merchants, who had the guild majority of four out of the ten members of the Upper Council. They traded everything the mainland produced with the Savanna Belt and the Idjama desert beyond it—gold, food, nuts, textiles, craftwork, leather goods. In return, their caravans brought back slabs of salt, kwagas, copper, wool, and other goods that enriched the desertland.

The remaining six were spread across the other guilds. A stocky, seven-arched woman whose plaits looked like wares being hawked in the street came first—she was a First Craftsworker. The next two were the First Miners in charge of the gold and copper Undati mines to the east of the Soke border; the next two First Farmers from the farming and hunting guild; and the last of them was a First Lender.

After they were seated, everyone shuffled back into their seats while the thirty Second Elders of the oft-forgotten Lower Council—two representing each ward—followed in their wake, taking their own seats.

It took a while before anyone noticed that Speaker Abuso was not present. There were a few murmurs of enquiry, before Dọta leaned over his chair and signalled to a side of the dais. Soon enough, an Elder Jali, his high-black skin stretched across his collarbone like filter cloth, stepped forward in his yellow-and-maroon wrappers and shuffled to the middle of the platform, supported by a Potokin Second. Behind him followed another jali, much younger but definitely no longer a novitiate like Danso, lugging a twenty-one-stringed lute-harp, the most cherished instrument of all jalis. Danso had one—passed down from Habba's jali days—but he rarely played it. He was good at every jali requirement except one: singing.

The Elder, Danso knew quite well. He was known within jali circles as the Jali Prime, even though there was no such title. His name was Isago, the oldest living jali on the continent. He was also the stand-in person for when the Speaker of the nation was absent, which was highly unusual, so much so that Danso was witnessing this for the first time.

"People of the Nation of Great Bassa," Isago announced, his voice in a tremor. "Welcome to the new mooncrossing festival. We will now reaffirm our oaths to the nation by reciting the pledge."

The Elder Jali cleared his throat and began to sing the litany that comprised the oath to the Bassai Ideal, his voice high and loud and clear. The jali with him began to play the lute-harp, and the drummers, fluters, and calabashers arranged in the corner of the arena started up as well. The city square resonated with the call-and-response of the pledge.

For common blood, for common tongue, Isago sang.
My sweat, my work, my skin is Bassai, the people responded.
With common hands to Bassa we give;
My sweat, my work, my skin is Bassai.

Danso shifted uneasily as he said this, as he always did. The *common blood* was the most difficult part to get used to, especially when followed closely by *my skin*. His uncles always drummed it into his head that this uneasiness was something he had to get over. So, as with many other times, Danso swallowed the discomfort and chorused the principles of the Ideal with everyone else.

Protect our lands and borders, sand and sea, from outsiders and
    invaders;
My sweat, my work, my skin is Bassai.

To serve this nation with all my heart;
My sweat, my work, my skin is Bassai.
To abide by the rules of its leaders;
My sweat, my work, my skin is Bassai.
To uphold our honour, be worthy of it;
My sweat, my work, my skin is Bassai.
To never turn my back on our land;
My sweat, my work, my skin is Bassai.

He noticed Esheme wasn't singing and nudged her with his elbow.

"I can't see my maa." She pointed to where Nem usually sat, an area allocated to Emuru of high social status. He looked, and Nem was indeed nowhere to be found. Unusual. He could not recall Nem ever missing one of these events.

They rounded off the pledge with a final acclamation:

With your help, oh humble Ashu, oh fiery Menai;
My sweat, my work, my skin is Bassai;
Oh may we, may we succeed
Oh may we, may we be Bassai enough.

The arena reverberated with cheers. Then dancers trooped out in their masquerade outfits of bright colours and fearful masks. A roar went up. The music started. Bone flutes and curved horns sounded, and skin drums pounded. This was the one aspect of his duty as a jali and Idu that Danso truly enjoyed. Soon, he was caught up in the excitement of it all, hailing for Abu, who was on stilts, performing a series of acrobatics and somersaults alongside the rest of his troupe. The crowd cheered, and some fanatic supporters rushed into the middle but were pursued and restrained by civic guards.

The performers then morphed into more frenzied dances as if possessed by Menai, performing daring acts of bravery like eating fire. They moved on, later, to group acrobatics, forming human pyramids. Each time, they drew the crowd's admiration.

Danso found himself completely lost in the spectacle, the weight on his shoulders gone, the heat of the bonfires rising and rising. Esheme remained seated, uninterested.

"Maybe she'll be here soon," she said once, but Danso was paying no attention. The one-handed boxing match between wards was about to begin. Danso cheered hard when the contestant from Ninth was called up. The boy himself pumped his chest with his punching hand wrapped in a large swath of padded fabric, his grappling hand kept bare.

The boxing match started, and Danso found himself yelling at the fighters. As usual, the arena increased in rowdiness, some people tearing down the strung decorations in frustration, and getting pulled out by civic guards and sent back into the streets. Danso didn't even notice when Oboda suddenly pushed through the crowd and whispered something to Esheme.

"What, what?" Danso said when Esheme tapped him, craning his neck to get a good look at the wrestling circle below. Something was wrong: The fight had been stopped, and the judge was being spoken to.

"Danso!" Esheme gripped his arm tightly.

He turned to her. Her eyes watered and she seemed distraught. Behind her, Oboda looked grim.

"What's the problem?" Danso asked, confused. At the same time, the arena was falling into silence, as Isago rose again, but this time, so did the Upper Council. An aide walked by Isago, whispering rapidly into his ear.

"I'm not sure," Esheme said. "Word is going around that something has happened to Speaker Abuso."

"Dear people of Bassa Nation," Isago said in his trembling voice, "I am afraid an unfortunate incident has struck us tonight. The mooncrossing festival is now cancelled. Please return to your homes as safely as possible immediately."

Murmurs of confusion and consternation rippled across the crowd. Danso turned to Esheme, Oboda standing behind her protectively.

"What happened?" He looked at Oboda. "Do you know?"

Oboda shook his head. Esheme paid no attention, looking around instead.

"Oboda," she said, slowly, "when last did you see my maa?"

14

Nem

NEM STOOD AT THE window of her bedchamber in the dark, watching the faraway glow of the massive bonfire in the city square. She was alone, not quite the way she would've wanted it, but it was only a few hours until Oboda returned with Esheme. If the choice had been hers, she would've preferred for Oboda to be stuck to her side constantly, but since his return from the long trip to the Savanna Belt, even before the discovery of the yellowskin intruder and her learning to use ibor, Nem had always known she wasn't the one in need of the most protection.

She went into the washroom, undressed, took a chunk of coconut oil soap and rubbed it all over her body, then scrubbed at the dried blood on her hands and feet with a bath stone. The parts of her body that had experienced some scorching hurt a bit, but she was thankful they did not burn. What hurt most was her fingernails, a few of which had fallen off in exchange for her iborworking tonight, leaving blood-red flesh behind.

The night was deathly silent because most people were at the moon-crossing festival. The house registered no movement or voices, as most of her hunthands were outside, guarding the house's perimeter. She wished for it to be this way on most days, but in the wake of news about the intruder and the ensuing border closure, this was unsettling.

The sights and sounds of her night activities came back to her: waiting until the Speaker and his household were all in the house, preparing for the festival; locking the doors; Drawing on grey ibor and Commanding the fires; watching the house light up, the occupants' silhouettes dancing in the flames, their screams carrying in a rending chorus. *This is what I do for the safety of this household*, Nem thought, to herself, but mostly toward her daughter, hoping the girl could hear all that distance away. *This is what I do for you, so you may have a life better than mine.*

She dried off and put her wrappers back on. Her pouch of ibor fell with a soft thud. She retrieved it and, in the nightlight coming through the window, examined its contents for completeness. The chunk of red ibor and the smaller grey pieces were both there. She tucked the pouch back into her clothes.

When she emerged from the washroom, a figure was standing by the door. A young woman, dressed in Bassai wrappers with a cloak over her head, as dark-complexioned as the next mainlander. But a trained eye like Nem, who used to sojourn beyond the Soke border at the behest of various merchants, spotted her yellow-brown irises and immediately knew that this person had never lived one day on the mainland.

"You can drop the act," Nem said, suddenly stiff. She fought to keep down the anxiety that began to grow in her. "I know who you are."

The girl whipped the cloak backward over her head. Her hair was tied in short knots, so Nem knew she was right. Definitely not Bassai. Then slowly, like water pouring down a rock, the girl's complexion changed from black to yellow.

"Glad to finally meet you." Nem feigned casualness, circling slowly, so that she placed the girl firmly within her sights, her own back to the window. "You've come for this, I presume?" She lifted her hand with the pouch in it.

The young woman did not respond, but her eyes twitched in response. Nem waited and moved slowly, breathing, squeezing the pouch in her hand, listening to the yellowskin girl's breathing. The girl took one step, two steps, light on her feet, keeping up. Nem waited until the girl was right in view of the window before she swivelled sharply, reached for a nearby lantern, and threw it outside.

It was a gamble, hoping that the most basic panic signal—lantern-out-of-window—would be recognised by men who were upset not to be in closer proximity to the festival on a mooncrossing day. Somehow, the archers had stayed sober enough to be alert. Shouts of recognition came from the raised stations around the house as the lantern crashed into the ground below.

Nem ducked in time, right before a number of arrows whizzed into the room.

The yellowskin girl lifted an arm and waved it in a gentle sweep. A soft thump engulfed the room, like someone had hit the air with a sledgehammer. In the darkness, the girl's eyes flashed bright, an amber-orange the colour of tree sap. From her belt, a long blade unsheathed of its own accord, as if wielded by an invisible hand. It went straight for the arrows, faster than the eye could see, and knocked each one aside, so that their trajectories were altered. They veered to either side of the girl and thunked into the mudbrick walls.

The blade, its hilt of gemstones dancing in the nightlight, hung in the air, as if awaiting further instruction.

Amber, Nem realised. She was using amber ibor to control the blade.

"I do not wish to hurt your men," the girl said, her eyes returning to normal. Her High Bassai was crisp and clean. "They have done nothing to me. Give me what you stole, and I will not harm anyone."

Another rain of arrows came in. The girl didn't look at them, just registered a twitch in her composure. Her eyes flashed again, and the blade responded. Arrows scattered all over the room.

Nem snorted and sidled past the window, buying time. "Don't be silly. I work with hoodlums like you every day. There is no way you're leaving me alive if you can help it. And if you do, you're even stupider than I thought."

"You are a murderer," the girl said matter-of-factly. "I harm no one who doesn't force my hand."

"Oh, but you are," Nem said, inching away enough to keep the girl within sight of the window. "You have murdered the Speaker of the nation and his whole family tonight."

The girl frowned. "I did no such thing."

"Yes, I suppose that's probably true," Nem said. "But once the bodies of the Speaker and his family are discovered—or who knows, maybe they are being found as we speak—you will have."

The girl's eyes narrowed. "What have you done?"

"Only killed a lot of birds with one stone," Nem said. "This stone, to be exact. So go on, kill me. Then everyone will *really* believe you did it."

Hate hung heavy in the girl's gaze. Her blade moved, slowly and surely, toward Nem's neck.

"You are right," the girl said. "You don't deserve life."

There was thundering in the hallway at that very instant, and the door burst open. Three of Oboda's hunthands filtered into the room, large and unspeaking. Nem sighed with relief when she noticed that these were the best of Oboda's best, armoured hunthands trained in the hinterlands. They were dressed in skirts, chest plates, and iron headwear, and carried shields, spears, and short axes as opposed to runkus. They filled the room, their headwear almost touching the decking above. The girl turned her back to Nem and faced them.

They lunged at one another with grunts, metal clinking, bodies thumping. They knocked out the other two lanterns in the room and plunged it into darkness, nightlight the only thing aiding visibility. Nem couldn't see who was winning, save for the occasional *oomph*, but she could see the girl, half the size of each hunthand, moving with alarming speed and skill, her blade swishing this way and that like a second invisible fighter. Nem crept below the window, her hands searching and searching, until her fingers found the pouch, discarded when she fell.

She poured out the grey ibor pieces into her hand and tucked the red chunk away. She breathed, then Drew from the mineral.

The ibor responded, a fierce rush of heat up her chest. It surged through her, power balling up in her stomach, filling up every nook within her. *Too much, too much*, she found herself screaming inside, realising she had panicked and drawn from all the pieces at once. Her teeth chattered. She inhaled, making space, accumulating.

She searched for a release, somewhere, anywhere, but all of the fire in the room was gone. She turned her attention toward the bathroom, searching with her mind's fingers until she found the bathwater still there. She let the power move from her and Possess the bathwater. Her vision dimmed as she did, losing consciousness.

Go, she Commanded it.

Water flew out of the bathroom with the force of a hundred men, splintering the door and knocking it off its hinges as it came. The girl was fast, faster than the men, and she saw it in time. She ducked and rolled. The men were not lucky. The water came for them, freezing into ice as it rushed toward them with a vengeance. By the time it splashed all over the wall, the men too were splashed all over, limbs and torsos and intestines and blood frozen into place so that the wall was like a museum of gore preserved. The only things that remained whole and untouched were their weapons.

The girl, still on the floor, whirled around in surprise.

"Oh, you thought you were the only one?" Nem found herself chuckling at the naivety. "You thought if you kept it from the mainland long enough, no one would figure it out?"

"I am going to kill you," the girl said coldly, then jumped toward Nem, almost catlike, so that she seemed to float for a moment.

Nem panicked, Possessed the water again, drawing all of it from every corner of the room. She twisted all the power in her gut, suddenly unaware of how much she had taken in, of what her limits were. Her teeth chattered in a ghastly manner, her body shuddering from the weight of the power expended, but she Possessed every bit of liquid existent there, converting it into tiny pieces, icy arrows with sharp, pointed edges.

She Commanded it all toward the girl.

There was enough time for her to see the girl's expression of confusion switch to horror, and her eyes flashed amber for a moment before a number of ice arrows pummelled into her.

The girl crashed straight into Nem at the bottom of the window, which had a low rise. But something Nem hadn't anticipated happened next: The girl reached out for her as she collided with the rise, and both women toppled through the window.

Nem felt herself become weightless, carried by the wind. For a moment, she thought she could use iborworking to get out of it. She reached inside herself for the power but found none. She squeezed her palm to Draw more power but found it filled with ashes and grain. It took her a moment to realise she had emptied all of the power within the ibor pieces, and they had disintegrated as a result.

Nem turned to look at her companion as they fell through the darkness. The girl was ensconced between two of the men's shields as she fell, ice dripping from the dents where the shields had repelled the attack. Yet right before the mud-and-cobblestone ground of the backyard corridor rushed up to meet her, Nem could see, where the billowing wrappers allowed, the girl's skin start to dapple with blood.

15

Danso

ALARM RIPPLED THROUGH THE crowd in the city square. People snapped their fingers, hissed curses, and dispersed in haste. Danso stood in front of Esheme as she panicked, his breathing quickened, his ears pricked, catching the whispers floating from people's lips. Her face contorted in worry and anger, but also fear.

Someone went by and he heard the words "... *intruder from beyond the border...*" and everything clicked into place for him.

The excitement of the night was sucked out of Danso, and his mind returned to the barn, the taste of tuber dust on his tongue. He remembered that light in the yellowskin girl's eyes, that calm, focused desire. Her mission, whatever it was, had caused this ruckus. But more importantly, it meant her reason for being here was done, over, fulfilled.

Esheme was still speaking to him, saying that they needed to find Nem immediately, but Danso wasn't listening. She reached out and grabbed him in a tight hold, but Danso was no longer there with her; he was in the dark interior of his daa's barn.

"I have to go." The words were out of his mouth before he could take them back.

Oboda and Esheme frowned at the same time.

"What?" Esheme said.

"I have to—" He pointed in a random direction. "Home—I—sorry."

Her frown twisted deeper, as did Oboda's; he was watching Danso carefully.

"Danso?" Esheme's face moved from astonishment to disgust. "What is wrong with you?"

Everything. His heart thumped. The sudden desire to get back to the barn rose to his throat and spilled over.

"My daa," he lied. "I must get home."

"Isn't he here—" Esheme started to say, but Danso yanked his wrist from her grip. Esheme's jaw slackened.

"Danso?"

But he was already moving, his legs reacting quicker than his brain. He brushed past Zaq, who was racing up to meet him, and was away before the enquiry could leave Zaq's lips.

He didn't remember how he got to Usi, how he snatched her reins from the stablehand who helped him loosen her tie. He wasn't sure if the sound of his name being called by multiple people was real or imagined, but he didn't look back to confirm. He leapt onto the saddle and charged away.

People scampered out of the way as he cut through the exiting crowd, running the kwaga harder than he ever had. Usi's horns were almost horizontal, and anyone with half a brain knew to give her the required berth to avoid being decapitated by their sharp points. He ran her harder than he'd ever done in his life, not caring who saw, not caring who screamed questions. He breezed past the Moon Temple of Menai and Ashu, past the now-abandoned marketplace, past all manner of sense and thinking. He let his thirst carry him all the way to his daa's house.

Bringing Usi to a halt at the stable, he jumped off without tying her and went around back, to the barn hut.

The door was open. It was never open.

He approached, slowly, breathing deeper and quicker than his lungs could withstand.

"Hello?" he called out, and waited. No response.

"It's me."

Silence.

"I'm not here to hurt you." He swallowed. "I promise."

Silence.

He stared into the barn, half-lit with nightlight, sanity returning and washing over him like the dew of morning.

How stupid could you be? he thought. *By Menai, what were you expecting?*

This was a person who had attacked his very nation. What did he think he was doing, rushing over here? He flopped to the ground, exhausted. Perhaps it was the thought that, for a moment, he might have had a window to the outside world that had consumed him. The hope that he could somehow be part of somewhere else, something other than his basic Bassai existence. Now he had disrespected his intended and embarrassed his family by running off in this way, and he was going to pay for it. Moons help him if the yellowskin was eventually caught and it came out that he knew her whereabouts and said nothing.

It was over for him, one way or another. He would have to resign himself to whatever came his way now, whether he liked it or not. He rose, dusted off his buttocks, and turned away, shoulders stooped, arms hanging loose.

He had barely taken three steps toward the house when a weak voice called out behind him.

"Wait," it said.

Danso turned, slowly, frozen. It took him a moment to realise that what had been spoken was Mainland Common, and another moment for him to recognise it for the plea that it was.

A figure, bowed at the waist, moved into the nightlight. There was no wrapper draped over her head this time, and it revealed her hair to be short and yellow, gathered and tied in a pattern of knots with unfamiliar forms of jewellery woven into them. The Bassai wrappers were gone, and Danso saw her skin now: yellow and bright, pockmarked in a few places by scarifications. She straightened, her hand supporting her ribs. Red ran between her fingers. The night breeze brought a metallic odour toward him.

"Help," she said.

It hit Danso right then, the reality of what lay before him. This was a chance, an opportunity of many proportions. He could fix his first mistake—in fact, fix all of his mistakes—right now. His decision to keep silent could be overlooked if he spoke now. He could redeem himself in the eyes of Bassa, in the eyes of Esheme, of his family. The young woman before him was wounded and weak. It wouldn't take too much to offer her up on a platter of gold to a nearby civic guard. He could claim that reward, and he and Esheme could live that life she'd always dreamt of.

Yet as she stood there, hunched, breathing heavily, he knew that, as with most things about him, this life with Esheme in Bassa was simply a nice dream to have, because it was just that: a dream. The thought of it brought no satisfaction to him, no flutter in his belly. Instead, what quickened his pulse, what took a firmer hold in his chest the more he thought about it, was that he was not going to turn this yellowskin woman in at all.

He was going to help her.

Like her, he knew what it meant to be misrepresented. He knew how it felt to visibly carry around the weight of a heritage one did not ask for, to be always wrong and never given the chance to be right. And he believed that she had come back here, not just because he'd *asked* her to, but because she understood that too.

"They're saying you attacked our Speaker," he found himself saying, trying to force his thoughts to circle around, to succumb to common sense.

She shook her head and winced in pain. "No."

She wobbled, and he reached and caught her just in time. He knelt and laid her across his thigh. Her deep yellow eyes caught the mooncrossing, pools of nightlight floating in tears. Her breathing was rapid and shallow. Her woolly clothing was sticky-wet with blood, and there were scratches all over her limbs.

All sense of reason flapped away like a bat and Danso found himself gravitating toward her, drawn. He grabbed her about the midriff and pulled her across the backyard to the side of the house and upstairs to his daa's workroom. She yelled and whimpered all the way up, but he managed to prop her onto the treatment table.

"I'm sorry," he kept saying. "I'm sorry."

She bit her lips and wept quietly as he rummaged through the workroom with only nightlight for guidance, looking for where his daa had stored the healing salve, an anti-infection and anti-inflammatory paste made from aloe sap and neem leaves. He found a dry version of it in a clay pot at the bottom of a shelf. He retrieved it and added ground cloves for the pain, a few drops of spirit, and mixed it into a paste.

When he peeled her garment aside, he found wounds so alive they could've been given their own names. Skin torn apart by blunt material that looked like it went clean through. The openings were too small to be arrowheads and were shaped oddly. They were ripe for infection, so the sooner he saw to them, the better her chances.

He dipped a washcloth into distilled spirit and wiped at a wound. She howled.

"Sorry. I'm sorry."

Heavy sobs racked her body as he cleaned and cleaned, her tears running freely. He scooped from the paste and smeared it, starting with the edges and reserving some for the cuts and bruises on her limbs and face. Her skin was hot and fuzzy, strands of hair so yellow they were invisible.

Accessories of metal and other unrecognisable material clinked on her body as he turned her here and there, especially an array of what looked like small teeth that she wore on her upper arm, embedded into her body. She gripped a sealed pouch tied to her waist fiercely and held it close to her body, despite the pain she was in.

He worked faster, the thought of anyone returning to find him there giving haste to his hands. He needed to get her somewhere hidden and safe immediately. The first place that came to mind was back into the underground storage in the barn where she had assaulted him.

He tossed the clay pot aside, wiped down the workroom, and pulled her off the table, slinging her arm over his neck.

"Hurry." He hustled her out of the workroom, back down the stairs and across the yard to the barn.

Two silhouettes emerged from the rear of the house, calling his name. Danso froze.

"Danso?" Esheme said, and then a click, as Oboda unbuckled his runku.

Danso

FOR A MOMENT, ESHEME'S eyes showed excitement and pride when she saw him with the yellowskin girl. Then slowly, her expression changed when she noticed the way he supported the girl's weight.

"Wait," Danso said. "Wait."

Oboda spoke, slowly, deadly. "Put down the invader."

"Wait," Danso said. "She said she didn't attack anyone."

"Are you helping her?" Esheme said, dumbfounded. "Is that what you're doing?"

"She said—"

"Put down the invader," Oboda said again.

Esheme grew pale. "*She said?* SHE SAID?" Even in the dark, he could feel her anger building as she pointed at the yellowskin woman. "*She* attacked my maa and killed *three* hunthands. They say they found my maa lying in a pool of her own blood in the corridors, and here you are saying SHE SAID?"

Danso gulped, then looked to the girl, who was grunting something to him in protest, but he couldn't make it out. *Surely, she couldn't have?* It made no sense. Both in one night? Not with those injuries. Why would she even attack Nem *and* the nation's Speaker? Abuso was nothing but a scholar. But then, he remembered the codex going missing from the library. Were the two trying to learn about ibor, perhaps? Now *that* definitely sounded like a thing Nem would do.

"Are you even considering this, Danso?" Esheme was saying. "Have you become *mad*?"

Yes. Yes, I have.

"Put down the invader," Oboda repeated, and moved the runku into a firmer grip in his other hand.

"Can you all just wait?" Danso said, laying the yellowskin girl onto the ground slowly. "Maybe she can . . . explain?"

"Maybe *you* can explain to the Speaker's grieving family," Esheme said, suddenly advancing toward him. "Maybe you can explain to my maa, to me. Maybe you can explain to the city, to the councils, to the nation. You can tell them that you chose to forsake your nation and ally with those who attack us." She was a few feet away now. "You can do that, or you can hand over the yellowskin."

"Esheme—"

"Oboda," Esheme said. "Grab them."

It happened too fast. First, there was a feeling, like the air had become solid. Danso felt a distant rush of heat come together, the weight of coalescing air on his skin.

He called out a warning, but it was too late.

The blade swung from the yellowskin girl with a whoosh, swift and clean in the night air, aimed directly at Esheme's heart. But Oboda saw it at the same time Danso did. The Second stepped forward, shoving Esheme hard, out of the way. She flew like dried raffia, slammed into the barn wall, and fell to the ground softly, unconscious. The knife went forward, missing its target, then boomeranged back to the yellowskin woman and into her sheath.

Danso whipped about. Her eyes shone amber, dancing in the nightlight. It held for a moment, and then the shine went out, and she crumpled from her haunches onto the ground.

Oboda moved in two, three strides and was upon them both, his runku lifted. Danso froze and shut his eyes, waiting for the impact, for the sound of death.

There was a crack, from somewhere far away from his head. A thud. Danso held back a moment more before peeking.

"Oh, no," Zaq said, "what have I done?"

Oboda lay on the ground, his runku discarded. Zaq held his own runku loose, like something strange that he was only just realising he owned.

"Oh, Menai," Zaq said, the runku falling from his hands and to the ground. He dropped to his knees and bowed. "Oh, what have you made me do..."

Danso stood there, rooted, unable to hold his jaw together. What had he just witnessed? *Did she...*

He shivered. This was not a dream.

Everything Esheme had told him about the Elder's conversation was true. The yellowskin girl was an Iborworker.

He looked at her now, lying motionless on the ground. She was real. Ibor was real. Iborworking was real. Islanders were real and alive.

The weight of truth fell on him. Thoughts and possibilities swirled in his head, so that he swayed on his feet. He had a choice to make, right here, right now: unsee everything he had seen, unknow everything he now knew; or allow the tug of this knowledge to take him where it would. And he saw, with mounting dread, that no matter the choice he made, both available options potentially led to the exact same demise.

"Zaq," Danso said.

Zaq, his head still bowed deep into the ground, muttering things— invocations, prayers—did not respond. Danso could hear, in the distance, the voices of people returning to their homes. Very soon, his own daa and uncles would be here too.

He went over to Zaq and shook him by the shoulders. "Get up, Zaq. We need to go."

Zaq looked at him, incredulous. "Go? Go where?"

The decision came to him, stark and clear, just like when he'd left the city square. He knew it then: This was it; the sign he'd asked for.

"We have to leave," he said, firmly. "We have to leave Bassa."

Zaq frowned. "What are you talking about? We can't *leave* Bassa, Danso. No one *leaves* Bassa."

"We will," he said. "Get up. We'll go to Whudasha. We'll go through the Breathing Forest."

"Are you *insane?*" Zaq's eyes were large as grapefruits. "Nobody goes into the Breathing Forest!"

"Yes, exactly," Danso said. It was as if his whole life had prepared him for this very moment, and he suddenly felt ready, agile, alive. "No one will follow in pursuit of us once they learn we have gone in there. If they, like us, enter the Breathing Forest, they will be unable to return to Bassai society as well. We stay in there long enough, and who knows, they may forget about us and believe we have perished."

"And they'll be right!" Zaq said. "We won't even last the night!"

A lot of things had been said about forbidden forests like the Breathing Forest, especially in some of the songs Danso had learned as a jali novitiate. Some spoke of creatures like the green-moss-covered dwarves that lived deep in the earth, that ate a human whole. Some spoke of dragon-pythons in the swamps down south. Others of bush dogs and ghost apes and carnivorous trees and lightning bats. But none had provided any single evidence to back up such claims.

Claims, yes, thought Danso, because he knew it for sure now: Those beasts lived in minds and songs and myths alone. If there was anything he had learned in the past two days, it was that Bassa was very good at telling stories that painted only a part of the picture, the only part they wanted people to see. He could bet his life—and he would—that the Breathing Forest was nothing more than just a regular forest, in the same way that he had found a woman whom he was once taught didn't exist hiding in the yam storage behind his own house.

"We'll be smart about it," Danso said, cresting this new wave of assurance. "Once we enter, we can take our time, avoid the bushroads. If we follow a trail parallel to the Gondola, we can get to the Bight of Whudasha in a few days, unharmed and without attack."

Zaq was exasperated. "Are you suggesting what I think you are?"

"Yes," Danso said. "Self-exile."

"Moons, Danso!" Zaq said. "We can't go to Whudasha. We're not Shashi!"

Danso went silent.

"I mean, *I'm not*. I can't leave Bassa." Zaq rose, breathing heavily. "We must plead our innocence. You weren't the one who attacked Esheme, it was the invader. I was protecting you when I attacked Oboda. I was performing my duty to my charge."

Danso looked at his Second for a long time. The man's devotion had truly blinded him to the gravity of what he'd just done, hadn't it? If he left Zaq here, it wouldn't be a case of whose version of events to believe—even though they would *definitely* take Esheme's word over his. It was a case of making an example, a bloody one. Danso couldn't allow that blood on his hands.

"You're going to die if you stay," Danso said flatly. "If you think I'm going to leave you here after you saved my life because you want to blindly believe you'll be pardoned for attacking a Second who was protecting *his* own charge from the current greatest threat to Bassa, you're more insane than I am."

"I can't," Zaq was saying. "I have too much to lose, I—I can't."

"You can," Danso said. "No matter what you think, there is nothing left for either of us but pain. Not after this. At least in Whudasha, we'll be covered by the Peace Treaty."

Zaq shook his head. "No, no, no."

"Then stay, but only if you want to die," he said with a finality and conviction that surprised even himself. But he didn't have time to debate.

He ran into the house and up the stairs to his room. He grabbed his packed bag from beneath the bed, slung it over his shoulder, stopped by his daa's workroom to pilfer some more medicine, and was soon back to the ground. He found Usi grazing, and after a thought, he grabbed her reins and led her around to the barn. The voices of arrival were much louder now, as the people of Ninth Ward returned to their homes. He was out of time.

Zaq was still there, uneasy, but seemed to have conceded defeat. Danso ignored him and pulled at the girl, who was still passed out on the ground. She looked frail and powerless just lying there, and Danso couldn't help but think it was ironic that *this* was who the greatest nation on the continent was afraid of.

"You want to help me or what?" he said to Zaq.

Zaq gasped. "You mean—"

"I'm taking her with me? Yes."

"No, Danso, no," Zaq said. "That will be the final runku to your head. That will be admitting guilt of collusion with an invader!"

"If I'm guilty of anything, it's being a human being," Danso snapped. "Am I supposed to leave her here to die?"

"Yes," Zaq said. "That is expected of you as a Bassai—"

"Don't you dare bring the Ideal into this," Danso said. "Don't help me if you don't want to, but don't do it on account of Bassa."

He pulled the young woman along the ground. Zaq waited a moment more, then came over to help, exuding disapproval all the way.

They draped her over the kwaga, just in front of the saddle. Usi was one of the bigger kwagas, so her saddle was large enough to squeeze in a two-seater. When she was purchased, Danso remembered the trader joking that she'd been trained with elephants in the desert to carry much more load than the average kwaga. Thinking of that now, Danso felt like the moons were smiling on him. It was as if everything had colluded to make this day possible.

Danso got on and looked down at Zaq, who had picked up his runku but was still hesitant.

"One last chance, Zaq," Danso said, reaching out for his Second, sombre. "I—" He paused. "I don't want anything to happen to you because of me."

Zaq looked back at the two bodies on the ground, unmoving. The sounds of citizens returning to their homes were now prevalent. There was a long moment of hesitation from Zaq, a heavy sigh of regret.

"Fine," Zaq said, slowly. "Fine."

He got on, and the three turned and cantered off westward.

the breathing forest

Esheme

ESHEME AWOKE IN A strange bed. Her head and right shoulder hurt. The walls of the room she was in looked familiar but the space felt different, as if she had been here in spirit, but not physically. Her memory was foggy, like she had stayed too long in a deep sleep. It took her a while to gather that she was in her own house, but in a place that she hadn't visited too often and that looked completely different from the last time she was here almost a season ago: her maa's room.

Maa. She shot out of bed. Pain whizzed into her head and she suddenly felt faint.

"Easy," someone said, and pushed her back, gently. "Easy, Maa-Esheme."

Esheme lay back, confused by the use of the term of address reserved for household heads. The speaker was Satti, the caretaker. The small woman had been keeping vigil at the bedside, and was now staring at her, cautious. Esheme searched her crow's-feet eyes, saw distanced respect in them and worry lines on her forehead.

"What happened?" she asked groggily. "What day is it?"

"Still mooncrossing day, maa," Satti answered. "We're well past the midnight hour."

"Why are you calling me maa?" Esheme looked around. "Where is she?"

The small woman's face went through a set of conflicting emotions, an irregular trait of hers. Nem had hired Satti in a very unconventional

manner, as with many things Nem did. Satti's late husband had died in
a hunting accident, and Nem not only brought her into the household's
employ, she procured official records for the woman's joining—to Nem
herself. No ceremony, but the local government office had Satti listed
as Nem's wife. Satti was eternally grateful to Nem and acted it in every
waking moment. If she was now referring to Esheme as maa, then that
meant—

"Where is she?" Esheme asked.

The woman glanced between Esheme and the far end of the room,
where a curtain had been hung to cordon off something.

"Let me see," Esheme said, rising to a sitting position.

"Maa, I don't think—"

"Stop calling me that," Esheme snapped. "I said I want to see."

Satti went to the curtain and slowly pulled it back.

The first thing Esheme noticed was the prevalent colours: red and
white. White for the bedding and clothing, red for the blood spilled on
them. Her maa lay completely naked, with half her face open in a lesion
that dragged from temple to chin, so that her jawbone stood out starkly in
the midst of open flesh. Her face was wrapped to protect it, but the blood
had seeped through the cloth. Her plaited arches had been loosened and
her hair now lay wild over the bed, some of it sticking to the sweat on
the good side of her face. From the way she lay, her body propped up by
blankets, ropes connecting from her limbs to the ceiling to keep them in
specific positions, Esheme could see how broken her body was. There was
a visible sag in the space that her lower left ribs should've occupied, and
clear fractures in at least one arm and one leg, both in unnaturally askew
positions in a way limbs never should be. She lay like a corpse, her skin
ashy, and but for the slight rise and fall of her chest, she could very well
have been dead.

Esheme couldn't tear her gaze away from the woman in the bed. She
found herself staring, frozen, waiting for something warm and wet to
dribble down her cheek, for the mixed emotions roiling within her to
condense into tears and emerge from her eyes. Nothing.

Once, when she was twelve seasons old, a man from the hunter's guild
had shot a brown antelope in the one of the forests along the Tombolo

River and brought it to Nem as offering for some favour past. The animal had still been breathing, soft and labourious, despite the many days' journeying to Bassa. Esheme had stood there and stared at its clotting wound, the arrowhead still stuck in its side. The hunter had broken its knees at some point to prevent it from getting up and running away. She had stood there, watching the animal suffer, and felt absolutely... nothing. Even as young as that, she knew she was supposed to feel some sort of sadness or pity, but she didn't have a name for what she felt, or better yet, didn't feel.

She looked upon her maa now and felt the same way: a multitude of conflicting responses—Fear? Anger? Surprise? Pity? Vindication? Sadness? They negated one another in a way that culminated in the near absence of a response at all. She looked upon her maa and felt... nothing.

"She was truly found sprawled in the corridor behind the window of her room, as the rumors said," Satti was saying, her voice trembling, fighting to remain stoic. "The bone doctors said her spine is fractured and her skull is dented from the fall. She may or may not wake up, but judging from the carnage in the room—they say the men had to be picked up in pieces and carried out in sackcloth—she is lucky to have survived. She is the one person to have survived any attack by the invader so far."

Esheme grappled with the feelings tussling in her belly. She was sad her maa was injured, right? She was glad she was alive? *Of course, of course.* Her mind said yes, but her body offered no response.

Satti yelled for a househand. Two young desertlander men rushed in, one of them with a bowl of water and rag, who dipped it and wiped Nem's body. Esheme winced as the boy ran his hand over her maa, touching her indiscriminately. Satti noticed her displeasure and gave the boy rapid-fire instructions, so he was more careful. The other boy replaced the cloves burning in a small clay pot by the bedside and set a new bunch aflame, probably as instructed by whatever healers had attended to Nem.

"Help me up," Esheme said. Satti shooed the boys out, locked the door, then did as she was told, walking Esheme to the bedside. She felt woozy but could walk okay, so she waved the woman aside. The heavy stench of boiled and burnt herbs hung by the bedside. Her maa looked peaceful, as if she hadn't been expecting the attack. There were no visible cuts on her body, but various portions were clouded in large bruises darker than her low-black complexion.

Esheme stood there and waited again to feel something, but her quest for empathy soon devolved into blaming. If asked, she could not say what her maa had been fighting for that had put her in this situation. What exactly had she been doing?

For all their time as maa-daughter, Nem had only been forthcoming about things that were already common knowledge—like how she conceived Esheme with a man she wasn't joined to (and had him disappeared to prevent any funny ideas in the future). The few things Esheme knew about her maa, she discovered piecemeal: Nem liked to eat okra in boiled rice, liked to pick up street strays and aid them, hated small talk about mundane things like the season's harvest or the councils' antics. Nem liked to work late in her library undisturbed, liked to speak little if she didn't think her listener was worthy of attention, liked to speak to Esheme in riddles, particularly those appended to lessons about streetwise acumen. To not know what she had been doing to draw the ire of an outlander—a suspected Iborworker, for that matter—was not strange.

What was strange, Esheme realised, standing there, was that if she were asked what her maa *wanted*, she couldn't quite say. Did Nem love her? Definitely. Nem would do literally anything to ensure that Esheme got what she needed to move up in the world. Esheme didn't always agree with those choices, but Nem was a slave to the same system she wielded for her own purposes, as much as she was also derided by it. *Why* she chose to remain in that role, though, Esheme could never deduce. For all the lessons she taught Esheme about ambition, Esheme considered Nem quite unambitious herself.

The woman who lay broken before Esheme was, in essence, half a stranger. Esheme decided it had to be for this very reason that she was unable to mourn Nem's gradual slip into eternal darkness. But it would also look bad if she just stood there staring at her maa like a statue, so she constricted her chest until she had squeezed forth a tear or two.

"Ah, MaaEsheme," Satti said, patting her back. "You have to be strong and have hope. For all of us."

Esheme sniffled. This, at least, was true. She was now MaaEsheme until her maa woke up. She nodded, stood straighter.

She noticed that Nem was severely emaciated in a way she hadn't been just a day ago, like she had suddenly been struck with a terminal illness. Her hair seemed to have lost all of its vitality, and she had a wound or two that did not look like an attack injury, but cracked and patchy skin lesions, the kind Esheme had seen in severely malnourished street children.

"Why does she look like that?" Esheme asked. "Did the bone experts say anything about why she seems malnourished?"

"They did," Satti said. "They said she is showing symptoms of kwashiorkor."

Esheme squeezed her face. "How is that even possible? Doesn't kwashiorkor require multiple fortnights to develop?"

"They were just as alarmed. They said it is what makes her injuries much worse, because she needs to be nourished back to health before her body can even start to heal. This was all they could do, until further notice."

"This?" Esheme shook her head. "She'll be dead before morning. We need someone who understands bodies beyond just bones. Is there no one else you could call?"

Satti blinked again, hesitated.

"What?"

"Scholar Aifu is the best here, but is away on a trip to the hinterlands," Satti said. "It'll take days of hard riding to pursue him and a sweet tongue to make him turn back. The next closest by distance is to bring in someone from Chugoko over the border, where they have good natural healers. But the Pass is closed to immigration, so we'll first have to find someone who can puncture that system for us. Something MaaNem maybe could've done if she were awake, but..." She trailed off, leaving unsaid the fact that Esheme did not have the same influence as her maa. "Anyway, that leaves only one qualified healing practitioner in Bassa who can maybe handle this case: Habba."

The name fell on Esheme like a shower of water, and all at once, she remembered. The nightlight of the mooncrossing, the sting of betrayal when Danso chose the yellowskin over her, the pain in her shoulder as she slammed into the barn. She flinched at the memory, and it must've come out as a dangerous expression on her face because Satti gasped and took a step backward.

"Then let us get Habba," Esheme said.

"Habba and his brothers have been detained," Satti said. "The Upper Council thinks Habba knows where Dan—" She cleared her throat, unsure if she could say the name yet. "Where his son and the invader went."

Esheme balled her fist and released it. She took a few breaths, steadying herself.

"Well then, we have to find someone *tonight*," she said. "My maa's life is more important than keeping the only healer who can help her locked up where he's useless to everyone. So either we get him out, or we get someone else fast."

"Ah, that's just as well." Satti's voice lowered. "There is a First Elder from the Upper Council here to see you, and maybe you can speak with him on that matter."

"See me?" Esheme frowned. "Who is it?"

"It's Councilhand Dọta."

"*Dọta?* Why would he want to see *me?*"

Satti regarded her like one would a child one had to repeat everything to. "Because you are the head of household."

Esheme paused again to consider what this meant. Something sinister was truly afoot. All her worst fears had come to pass: Danso had finally disgraced her in the worst way possible—almost killing her in the process, even—and Nem had not only gone and nearly killed herself, the burden of her dubious dealings was suddenly on Esheme's own lap. A burst of hot anger flooded Esheme's chest. She fought it down.

"All right." She cleared her throat, stood in front of a mirror and adjusted her wrappers, and wiped at her eyelashes. "I guess I'll go see him at once, and maybe he can help. Where's Oboda?"

"Resting. He took a big knocking, trying to protect you. He recovered quickly enough, though. It was he who brought you home."

"Okay. Get me one or two men to come with me." She waved for the caretaker to aid with putting her together. Satti grabbed a nearby comb and began working her hair, replaiting the arches where they were loosened.

"Is it just Dọta here, or all of the Upper Council? Did Abuso make it?"

Satti frowned, then her eyes opened wide. "Oh. You don't know yet."

"Know what?"

"Speaker Abuso's house was burned to the ground during the moon-crossing festival, with his whole household inside," Satti said. "Not even the kwagas made it out alive."

Danso

THE FIRST THING THAT struck Danso about the Breathing Forest was that it wasn't dark. He had always envisioned it so, along with tightly clumped inhaling and exhaling vegetation that hindered any manner of good sight. However, the nightlight of the mooncrossing made it easy to see at least a few feet ahead of themselves without the aid of a lantern or fire, so when they arrived at the threshold of towering bamboos that guarded the length of the rainforest entrance, they recognised it at once. Along the line were all kinds of signs, written and otherwise, imploring them to turn back and avoid entering the forest, even by mistake. It wasn't surprising that the entrance wasn't guarded: The Bassai held the Breathing Forest in high regard, as one of the oldest places on the mainland dating back to a time before human feet stepped here; back to a time when the continent was almost believed to move and breathe as it wished. It was widely believed that this forest, along with others to the east and south of the mainland, still retained vestiges of that time, malevolent entities included. Danso had learned a few jali songs about brave but stupid adventurers who entered these forbidden forests and went missing and disappeared forever. No one in recent times ever attempted to enter and find out if it was true, because every word out of an ages-old jali's song was the undeniable truth and that was that.

Danso, who had sung those words himself, had always been sceptical of the veracity of stories that postulated that one would get gobbled up by the forest floor, or that beasts living within the earth were what made it rumble, and they came up and pulled any intruders into the ground. Compared to facing the aftermath of his actions, he was more than willing to take a chance on Bassa's word. There was a higher likelihood of staying alive that way. Besides, wasn't this what he had always wanted? To go missing from Bassa forever?

"Protect us, oh Ashu," Zaq said, circling his hand over his head and snapping his fingers to ward off evil spirits.

They dismounted the kwaga and attempted to cross the threshold on foot, Usi in tow. Here, they came across the first sign that the journey was not going to be a smooth one. Usi suddenly froze, refusing to go forward. She barked at the forest, at nothing. Zaq urged her forward by rein and foot and push, but she stood firm at the threshold, and even turned around despite his efforts, barking all the way. Zaq whispered to her, petting her striped coat and holding her horns to keep her steady. She took a step or two in agreement, but promptly balked again and resumed barking.

"Even *she* knows it is dangerous," Zaq said.

"She's a kwaga, she doesn't know anything," Danso said, getting down. "We'll just have to leave her and go on foot."

Zaq opened his mouth to say something, then changed his mind and helped Danso strap his bag. Then he put the girl on his shoulder—Danso thought she didn't look too heavy, thankfully. They tried to get Usi to go back, but the kwaga stood there, stubbornly, snorting and stomping her hoof.

"Let's just go," Danso said finally. "She won't follow us in anyway."

They were right. Usi kept barking as they left her, whining in a way that clearly said she didn't want to follow but didn't want them to leave either. Zaq kept looking back and making calming tongue-click sounds at her. Her barks followed them until they crossed the threshold and the full glory of the Breathing Forest came down on them.

The temperature dropped instantly: The once warm and humid night breeze dipped to a cold draught that beat against Danso's skin and caused the fine hairs on his arm to stand erect. Behind the line of bamboos, the vegetation thickened to a dense cluster of rogue dwarf palms and pawpaws, flirting with the slim, tall hardwoods many feet overhead.

Between them, a thick understory of shrubs and creeping plants fought to stay relevant, and weeds and wildflowers covered the ground. It was impossible to see far or walk in a straight line beyond three paces. Sound wasn't good either: Cricket, frog, and nocturnal bird noises drowned out everything. The light too changed. It took Danso a while to realise why it was not the bright, white nightlight of both moons but an angry, reddish glow.

"Ashu's light does not penetrate the canopy," Danso said, a smidgen of doubt suddenly creeping into his voice.

Zaq performed the hand-over-head finger snap again, a Bassai gesture to ward off evil. "Even you have to agree that to travel by Menai's light is a bad omen."

Danso eyed him. He had always found it odd that Zaq, an immigrant, was a more ardent believer in the moon gods than Danso had been his entire life. This was probably due to the strict indoctrination process desertlanders went through. It was obvious in how worship gatherings at the moon temple were packed with twice as many Potokin and Yelekuté than Idu or Emuru. Even the rites that mainlanders performed were more out of habit than deeply held belief.

"We should go back while we still have a chance," Zaq said.

Danso did not respond, but instead pulled out a lantern from his pack and lit it by setting a charcoal cloth aflame with a firestriker. Of everything he feared about the stories of the Breathing Forest, Menai's light didn't quite figure into it. He thought there was a perfectly sensible explanation for why the forest breathed—whatever that meant. After seeing what the girl had done tonight, he had begun to incline toward appreciating every option.

The forest pressed in on them as they skirted around things, moving so slowly that Danso was sure if they had pursuers, they would've been caught by now. There was no pathway in the understory, but there was enough distance between most trees, in a fairly straight direction, for them to pass, especially with Zaq lugging the girl on his shoulder. So far, they hadn't met any corpses or skeletons, a good sign. Danso was very close to gloating that his instincts had been right.

They moved as quietly as they could, a near impossibility. Every now and then, they heard something that caused them to stop rock-still: a cry, a sharp movement, anything piercing the chorus of crickets and frogs and nightbirds. Grass slapped at them, nature violently shooing them out of her territory. Everything was green shaded by red, slimy and wet, stems and low-hanging branches covered in moss. Danso had learned about rainforest plants and animals in earth studies class, and had thought that that information would be sufficient. The farther on they went, though, the more he realised that was only a slice of what existed, and that he was not as prepared for this as he'd thought.

Suddenly, there was a roar from somewhere, and a strong breeze came. The ground on which they stood moved. Danso staggered and Zaq came bumping into him. The girl on his shoulder groaned.

"What's that?" Zaq asked.

"Is it...a quake?"

Another strong gust came, prolonged this time, blowing out the lantern and plunging them into darkness. The trees swayed, leaning hard, and the ground lifted and settled. There was a long, throaty roar, like a hungry animal.

Danso held on to the nearest tree and Zaq held on to Danso, one hand keeping the girl on his shoulder. But even this tree leaned, too low. Then there was a cracking sound as the roots pulled out of the ground and the tree tilted.

"Move!" Danso yelled, and the two leapt forward in the darkness as the tree leaned even lower. They didn't look back to see if it fell.

Another gust came, and the forest responded in a long wail. Brushes swept side-to-side with violence, and trees flapped their branches like wings, raining down twigs and leaves.

Danso lurched forward, his arms out, grazing one obstacle after another and shouting directions to Zaq over the wind. Even without the lamp, he knew they had entered the forest from the east end, and if they kept going in something akin to a straight line, they would remain parallel to the Gondola tributary and therefore still be heading westward. All they needed was to stay pointed in that particular direction.

How long they went on like this, Danso could never be sure. What he would remember would be the wetness of the understory as he stepped into the dew of grass, the overpowering stench of rotten green, the sighing and wailing of the forest about him, the ground inhaling and exhaling as roots dislodged the loose forest floor. The pain, as his body scratched and bumped into various impediments, him trying not to figure out if he had just bumped into tree or animal. The increasing lack of assurance about direction, about whether Zaq and the girl remained in tow behind him, as he darted and veered away from obstacle after obstacle.

Then he tripped, a quick reality check, and Danso put his hands forward to brace his fall. Except his hand touched air, and he pitched forward, falling faster, faster, the forest chorusing above him.

19

Lilong

LILONG'S DAA STOOD BEFORE her, a memory of a pale man in a scraggly beard as yellow as his skin. He was dressed in woolen garments, rare shells and stones stuck into his headpiece, gleaming onto his face. His earrings dangled, a tiny stick of stone-bone attached to their ends, so that anyone who looked at him at once knew he was both a Grey Iborworker and a member of the Abenai League of Warriors, an important keeper of the secrets of the seven islands of the archipelago. He had bright yellow eyes on a face that was always crestfallen, so that to Lilong, he was a bundle of contradictions: an exciting man who was always disappointed with the world.

Lilong remembered it so clearly that she could feel the heat of his breath when he sighed, the smell of the akara balls frying in the kitchen of their house, a little way away from the cliff where they stood; the *flap flap* of dhow sails in the distance, off the coast of their island of Namge and its tiny docks. The balmy afternoon breeze caressed her cheek, warm and tender.

"Again," he said, and shoved her off the edge of the cliff.

The memory was yanked away violently, like an owner retrieving their property, and the air around her whooshed, the earth's merciless force pulling her toward the ground. She didn't need to open her eyes to see, to know she was falling. The pieces of ibor indented into her upper arm tugged at her consciousness, recalling the memory of her daa training her on how to use ibor to break her fall.

She didn't need the ibor to remind her, though. She had survived the fall outside Nem's window. She would survive this one just as easily.

She went into action, muscle memory taking hold. First, she Drew, pulling the power into her chest and thinking about the kind of obstacle it would take to break her fall in a way that wouldn't hurt her but would also make her landing less impactful. She tumbled and brushed against every possible thing, humus and wetness pouring over her, and then she felt something that had the warmth of life, something that wasn't trees or animals—*people*, her mind said. People, falling like she was.

Lilong shut her eyes in concentration and did what she had to do.

In all her training, she had barely taken on anything heavier than tiny objects, mostly things that could be used as weapons. But occasionally, her daa had made her try Possessing heavier objects, even though this was frowned upon by their league of warriors back home because too many had died trying to perfect this exact act. *Stretches your ability*, her daa had said, and not only had he been right, he was now justified. It was the exact thing that had saved her at Nem's window, and would save her now.

She Possessed her blade easily, Commanding it to slash at the next few trees it could—branches especially. The blade slashed in a flurry of quick motions. Several of them began to fall with her, but slower, getting stuck in other trees. She reached out with her consciousness again, pushing the ibor's power into the darkness, trusting it to latch on to the lifeless branches which, now severed from their life-giving roots, were eligible for Possession.

Her body protested painfully in response to so much power being spent at once, the way it always did when Possessing something for the first time. The pain from her wounds came alive, as if ignited. Lilong yelled into the wind, but she persisted, her Possession grabbing hold of the branches.

She Commanded them to fly.

They came as called, first to her, the biggest of them rushing, wedging under her armpits and pulling upward to slow her descent. Her legs smacked into something solid—*pain*. She pushed herself upward off it, breaking her fall, and eased down gently, onto what she decided must be the branch of another tree.

Then she reached out with her mind again, the vegetation reverberating with a pulse in response to the power. She was suddenly hyperaware of the direction in which the branches moved, could sense as they barged past every obstacle, rushing toward the falling bodies as she had Commanded. They found them just in time, a few feet from the ground, and just as Lilong had thought up the haphazard command, they positioned themselves over each body like a pivot and spun the bodies in the adjacent direction of their fall.

Each body hit the ground with an unnaturally muffled thud and roll. There was an *oof.* Lilong felt about with her mind again, sensing the warm breath of life in each body the same way she sensed the cold absence of it in objects she Possessed.

Then Lilong realised she couldn't stand, that her legs were in fact useless, no longer containing any strength. She put out an arm to lean on something, but her hands found air, and she fell through vegetation and hit the ground.

Esheme

INSIDE THE LIBRARY WAS cold with the absence of Nem. It filled the room in every way—from the overpowering shelves of manuscripts and her personal knickknacks in brass, copper, bronze, wood, and literally every sculpting material on the continent, to her household symbol signed into every possible thing. It told the story of the woman who owned this room: that she was a well-travelled, well-learned woman, and Esheme, sitting behind the large desk, realised she didn't quite know this version of her maa either.

Esheme had always been uninterested in the details of Nem's work as a fixer. She knew it involved Nem spending a lot of time meeting everyone: from the nation's high-and-mighty to its low-and-lowly. However, it also meant too little time at home, which Nem tried to make up for by dragging Esheme along to one meeting or the other. Esheme, who was never comfortable with these gatherings, usually sat in the periphery and pretended to be interested.

But as time wore on, she had begun to use these meetings to learn more about how the mainland worked, how to bend around its curves, how to poke holes in its weaker points, how power was wielded in Bassa, who was untouchable and who wasn't. She considered it useful upon graduation into a full counsel of mainland law. So, despite distancing herself from the meat of her maa's work, she appreciated the meetings just as she did the court proceedings. But somehow, the life she had eschewed for so long had found its way back to her anyway.

Esheme turned her attention back to the man before her. Prior to her entrance, Dọta's Second, a scowling, towering Potokin with a shiny shaved head, had poured him one of her maa's premium fruit wines without asking permission. She came in to find Dọta seated behind the desk, in Nem's chair, his Second behind him. Esheme had to make do with the visitor's chair, which was a perfect metaphor for who she truly was in this situation.

Dọta leaned back, swirling the wine in a brass gourd, listing his body to the side and regarding her as if he wasn't sure if he was going to talk to her or spit at her. Esheme had never been up close with this man, reputed to be the most opportunist and ruthless merchant in all of the guild. Couple that with him being a First Elder of the Upper Council and having close to a monopoly on import-export proceedings at the Soke border, and she did not necessarily expect him to be a nice and welcoming person either. She wasn't surprised to find him cold and calculating, even more so than her maa, his eyes documenting her every movement with unnerving vigilance.

Esheme sat still and waited. Dọta cleared his throat and said: "You know why I'm here."

"Yes," Esheme said. "On behalf of my maa—the moons pardon her—I am sorry for the loss of your friend and colleague, the Speaker of the nation, at the hands of—"

He held up a hand. "I'm not here about Abuso, his soul travel well. I'm here about matters more pressing to me, and to the nation."

Esheme realised he expected her to say something.

"May I know what these pressing matters are, so I may help you with them if I can?"

Dọta frowned. "Are you playing with me?"

"No, Elder," she said. "I don't know what you refer to."

"Surely your maa must've told you," he said, grouchy. "I've been told you tally along to many of her dealings."

It was no use trying to be naive: Dọta owned this room the same way he owned the border. Nothing went by there that he didn't know of. Whatever he was involved in with Nem and Abuso must've been big, and if he wanted to meet with her despite Nem fighting for her life, then it was also extremely urgent. No use playing games.

"My apologies, Elder, but I am not party to all of my maa's dealings," Esheme said, and it was true. Nem did take her places, but barely any of the significant ones. Mostly, she sat through discussions over matters of crisis management and gag-order payoffs, with a case of retaliation sprinkled in here and there. One of the reasons she remained dissatisfied with Nem's work was that in the end, she was never in the room for the things that mattered.

Dota looked at his Second, and his Second wrinkled his nose.

"Fair enough," Dota said. "Regardless, I am owed something important, something that is at the core of all of this tragedy befalling the nation, including the tragedy that has befallen her today—may she recover well. I am here, at this moonforsaken hour, to collect."

"And what might that be, if I may ask, Elder?"

Dota sat forward and crossed his hands on the desk. "Your maa, via Abuso, rented a caravan of mine for a trip north. Now, I'm sure as a counsel novitiate, you are familiar with the terms of such a lease? If they return from the outer lands with anything that poses a danger to civil life on the mainland, then a portion of their assets are forfeit to the government, with a share allocated to me for the disruption in my business. Unless, of course, they can neutralise said danger before it materializes or impacts business proceedings and civil life significantly."

He cleared his throat. "Now, Abuso and Nem not only managed to stow an invader across the border inside *my* caravan, I'm privy to the knowledge that the hunthands Nem sent also returned with the most powerful mineral this continent has ever seen, one that has been missing from this side of the continent for hundreds of seasons: ibor."

Esheme was not shocked by this information. After the encounter with Nem in the storage room, her suspicions that her maa was involved in some way with the panic that swept over Bassa due to the border closure rose a notch. Suddenly changing up her Second once Oboda returned from the Pass—*for security reasons*, she'd said—meeting with Abuso in the dead of night, hiring a bunch more hunthands, being uncharacteristically twitchy and a hundred times more cryptic than usual. The argument with Abuso at the feast solidified things for Esheme, and the attack at the barn by the yellowskin was the final piece to the puzzle: Nem was playing a deadly, dirty game that involved a mineral that was not supposed to exist and possible supernatural powers.

If there was anyone who was likeliest to have unearthed an ancient, mythical mineral that supposedly possessed the continent's greatest power, Esheme knew Nem was just the person. The real problem here was that Bassa's prime merchant was now sitting in front of her and asking for it.

"Forgive me, Elder, I don't mean to be disrespectful," Esheme said, picking her words carefully. "But surely you know that ibor is nothing but a myth? The jali songs say—"

"The jalis say what they need to," Dota said, placing his empty gourd on the desk. The Second took it and went to refill it, a golden-hilted knife on his waist clinking against the metal of his belt, obviously a gift from his employer. Esheme's eyes followed the Second, her countenance wavering. She regained control of herself.

"Now, since both things entered the mainland," Dota was saying, "the border has been closed and Bassai citizens have been murdered. I would say that constitutes significant danger to civil life and my business, wouldn't you?"

"I would."

"Good." He drank from his gourd. "Now I, in my utmost benevolence, have decided to forgo reporting this piece of information to the requisite authorities." He chuckled at the joke, seeing as the requisite authority was indeed himself, being perhaps the most successful member of the Upper Council. "I intend to keep this information, and other knowledge that I have, in exchange for something much smaller in your possession: the retrieved pieces of ibor, and the Codex of the Manic Emperor Nogowu."

Esheme frowned. "Nogowu's codex? The university library has that."

"Not after your maa stole it."

Esheme was speechless for a moment. What was *happening*? First Danso had been caught with it two seasons ago, and now her maa had stolen it? What was so special about that dirty old thing?

"Is there anything else I need to know?" she asked. When Dota frowned, she added: "Forgive me, Elder, I am just trying to get my bearings, so I can aid your quest in the best way possible."

Dota pursed his lips and smacked the gourd on the desk. "Very well, if you must know." He leaned forward. "Your maa also murdered Speaker Abuso and his household because he was going to report her dealings to the Upper Council."

Esheme started a fierce rebuttal, but Dọta put up a hand.

"I'm not here to argue it with you. I have solid information on these things. You may even say firsthand knowledge. And besides that, we both know what your maa is capable of—the whole nation knows it. No one is going to doubt she did all of these things. I don't care about the invader, and I honestly think Abuso was weak—good riddance. I simply need my ibor and that codex. Failure to provide either, well." He leaned back. "I'm sure your household could survive the forfeiture of a significant portion of your assets, but once it is known that your head of household stole the codex and killed the nation's Speaker, I will come here with civic guards and remove you and your whole household physically, and confiscate everything until there is nothing left of this house." He looked to the ceiling to drive home his point. "Not even your name will be remembered after I'm done."

Esheme watched the man closely. Her maa *had* been absent from the mooncrossing festival when Abuso was murdered. And she wouldn't put it past Nem to steal from the university library. But the real problem was not these secrets being divulged—the real problem was that Dọta had this household in the palm of his hand, and if Esheme was not quick and smart about shoring herself up, she would be going down swiftly. If there was anything that was not the Esheme way, it was going down without a fight.

What had her maa been doing with this ibor, for moon's sake? Was she trying to...become an Iborworker?

"I know what you're thinking," Dọta said. "That people will speak up for you, perhaps allies of your maa. Well, they can try. But you forget about your intended."

Esheme frowned. "I'm not sure what his actions have to do with me."

"Oh, everything," Dọta said. "Aiding an enemy of the nation casts a big stain, doesn't it? A stain so big, perhaps, that everyone around such a traitor then becomes a pariah. Look at what happened with his family, for instance. You were only saved that because you were attacked as well. But if you think that stain will not touch you, you are mistaken." He sipped some wine. "And if I do not get what I want, I will ensure that it does."

Esheme massaged her aching shoulder. *What a mess of a night.* Her maa was dying, her intended was a fugitive, the most powerful person in Bassa was blackmailing her into paying a debt she did not owe, and she did not have what she needed to pay.

But, she thought, remembering one of Nem's aphorisms, *within every disappointment lies an opportunity.*

"If I find this...ibor and the codex for you," Esheme said, "what do I get?"

Dota raised an eyebrow. "*You* get to not lose everything, is what. If I were you, I would be thinking about how to get Nem awake quickly, before she dies with all the knowledge."

His bluntness stabbed her, but she suppressed any response. "Perhaps I can get your support in trying to solve this, then? Help us both get what we want sooner?"

Dota kept his eyebrow raised, then let it down. "What do you need?"

"I'm sure you can pull a few strings to get Habba released? He is the only healer currently skilled enough to nurse my maa into reawakening as soon as we want. Otherwise, we wait, and we both lose."

Dota eyed her with what she thought might be reluctant admiration. Without looking at his Second, he said: "Ariase, we will make sure this young woman gets what she wants, won't we?" His Second grunted in response. To her, he said: "He will be kept on a short leash, guarded around the clock, and contained to the room. He'll still be *arrested*, just not in local government holding." Esheme nodded.

Dota rose. "I'm giving you only three days, starting now, to find me that ibor and codex." He smoothed his wrappers, the imported northern silk woven into the front of them uncrinkling in one wave.

This is a powerful person, Esheme reminded herself. *Best to play along.*

"Three days," she repeated.

He considered her for a moment, then said: "You don't want to know what happens if I don't have them after three days."

He left the room, his Second scowling and clinking behind him. Esheme released her breath.

So this was it, then? Her maa's wish was fulfilled. Like it or not, she was now completely immersed in Nem's world of skulduggery.

Esheme

OBODA WAITED FOR ESHEME outside the library door, amid a throng of househands and a few hunthands. All stood at attention when she emerged from the room. She looked around for the arrival of someone important, then realised they were standing at attention for *her*. She was looking at the whole household, sans her maa. And this household, it seemed, was looking at its new leader.

Oboda had a large bump on the side of his head, illuminated by the lamp hanging by the door, yet he stood there as if nothing had happened.

"You are awake," he said.

Esheme nodded at him. "And you? You're fine?" She understood that had been his way of asking about her well-being.

The man affirmed without speaking. He was better suited to Nem, being a man of very few words. Esheme realised it was for this very reason that her maa had assigned him first as her own Second, then later as her daughter's Second. He was the one person Nem trusted Esheme with in her absence.

She put a hand on the man's big arm in conciliation, then said:

"I intend to have a very long and serious chat with you, but I will wait until morning, when I am stronger."

She made to leave for bed, but Oboda reached out to halt her progress without touching her, then nodded at Satti. Satti barked at the househands and everyone scrambled. Oboda waited for them to leave before gathering his wits about to speak. He bent and whispered into her ear.

"Esheme-maa, before you continue with further matters," he said, "there is something I must show you."

.⋅◇⋅⋯⋯━━━━━━━━━⋯⋯⋅◇⋅.

Going to the holding stalls, over time, had become associated with death for Esheme. She had watched Nem question various people, or Oboda and his men work a person over. Nem's holding stalls were known across the city, but only in whispers, and not even the ward chiefs or civic guard captains ever came by to find out if they truly existed. Her maa was funny like that: She'd barely be seen doing any heavy lifting, but somehow she always got things moved.

This time, though, there was no one there when Oboda took her inside and started to rummage about a heap somewhere. Esheme stood in a corner, cold in the early-morning air. She remembered the execution of the civic guard in this very place, and burned in anger once more, thinking about how the person whose honour they had been protecting offered no such honour in return.

She would face Danso and his betrayal in a bit. Especially when he was caught, which wouldn't be too long now. The nation definitely would not let the death of its Speaker go unpunished. Despite what Bassa liked to believe, its leadership was afraid of the force of the people: of their wagging tongues and propensity for easy assemblage once in high tempers. Dọta's haste was because he knew if the news about the yellowskin and the ibor ever got out, the people's response would be unpredictable. There would be a swift desire for a scapegoat, and whoever was within easy reach—be it Danso, be it someone in Bassai leadership—was going to be chewing that tough hide for a while.

Frogs croaked outside, and the night air grew cooler. Esheme tightened her wrapper about herself, wondering how Oboda kept warm without upper-body clothing. Immigrants to the mainland were only allowed lower-body clothing—their torsos were to be kept open, to prevent hiding anything of any form, the law said, especially when they were in gatherings or in the presence of their employers. Strips of cloth were allowed to cover breasts, and blankets were allowed only for cooler weather.

Oboda didn't seem to mind. He found what he was looking for, brought it over, and held his lamp over her head so she could see.

It was a small strongbox, made of wrought iron and decorated with bronze. It was well worked too, edges polished to smoothness by an expert craftworker. It was locked, not with a latch but with a keylock, which was unusual since keylocks in ironwork were reserved for things that needed to be kept really, really secret.

Oboda produced the key, a small but weighty piece of iron. Nem's name was cut into the bow.

"She say to give this to you," he said. "In case."

Esheme regarded Oboda with newfound appreciation. Nem, who had a soft spot for broken things, had adopted him when he'd first come over the border as a boy. He'd come without a family, fleeing hunger and starvation after a devastating attack on his nomadic clan, an attack he'd survived by slaying every single attacker with the femur of a fallen dromedary. He had stowed away in a caravan—much like this yellowskin—and slipped past the Soke border illegally. After being finally discovered on the mainland, he was due to be repatriated. But Nem had thought that such fearlessness and penchant for survival were useful skills, and asked to take him under her wing instead, promising the civic guard captains that she would keep him close and out of trouble, which she had managed to do thus far.

Esheme had known all of this and kept him at arm's length for that very reason. But with this singular action, he had redeemed himself in her eyes. She could see, now, the sense in her maa's trust in him, and how devoted he was—and would be—to her and this household.

Oboda held the box as she put in the key and opened it. The lock groaned from a lack of oiling, a clear sign the box itself hadn't been opened much. She lifted the top, and by the yellow light of the lamp she saw that it contained a small bound manuscript, wrapped in leather covering, as well as a piece of something red that looked like it could be stone or bone or both.

Stone-bone, she thought, and knew, immediately, exactly what it was.

Esheme took it out and examined it. Polished in a way that it could be really old bone, but pockmarked in a way that it could be stone. It was chipped on one diagonal side and smooth on the others, which told her it had been broken off from another larger piece. The symbols carved into it were of a language not taught at the university, so it definitely wasn't from the mainland.

She examined the manuscript next, which seemed ordinary except that the leather was soft from being stored in the cold, with mould on its edges from wetness at some point. She unbound the twine, flipped the latch, licked a finger, and leafed through the manuscript. Her eyes scanned the first page. She flipped. Scanned the next, then the next, and the next. Then she closed the manuscript.

She had only skimmed the first few pages, but they offered sufficient answers to all the questions she had awoken with. The stone-bone's capability. What her maa had been doing in that storage room. Why the yellowskin was possibly in Bassa. Why Dọta wanted it. Why she had to ensure that under no circumstances could he lay his finger on any such thing.

She decided, standing there in the cold, that this was her first duty to this household: She was going to learn everything this manuscript contained. And then she was going to *use* it.

22

Lilong

LILONG WOKE TO THE sounds of the two men coughing. Her eyes adjusted to the weak light, and she saw their outlines: panting, rising gingerly, checking their bodies for injuries. They were oblivious of her lying in a darker spot, too weak to move, her head pounding. They muttered to each other, as if afraid to disturb the night sounds engulfing them.

"We're okay," the Shashi boy, Danso, was saying, looking up. "Thank moons, it doesn't seem we fell too far." Then he paused. "Zaq, where is she?" He tapped the other man. "Light, we need light. Quick, search, let's find the pack."

There was a flurry of activity that Lilong found difficult to keep up with. Her headache beat harder. She rose to a sitting position but did not try to stand yet, gathering the strength required to do so.

Soon, there was a strike, then a flame. Light engulfed the area about them.

It was the other man, Zaq—a desertlander, she could now see by the light—who saw her first. He startled, then wordlessly tapped his charge, who turned and saw her as well. She must've seemed akin to a forest animal kneeling in the vegetation like that, because the two ventured no closer, instead blinking back at her and keeping the kind of distance one kept from a predator.

"Zaq," Danso finally said. "Put your runku away. We don't want to scare her."

"Put—" Zaq tapped his waist, looked about him, then threw a hand up. "I lost it."

Immediately after the word *runku* was mentioned, Lilong's mind responded as it was conditioned to: *attack*. But her body only coughed in response. She couldn't move her limbs in any meaningful way. Her heart began to race at the thought of being so slow. *Slow is dead*, her daa always said. She had expended *way* too much ibor in one night, fallen *twice* from significant heights, and had lost blood, but it was no excuse.

Remember, Lilong, she thought. *Slow was what got you into this situation in the first place.*

She rose cautiously, wincing as various parts of her body pinched and flared in response. The men watched her with concern. She wobbled, unable to differentiate between the growing hurt from expending ibor and that from falling. There was pain in her shoulder, neck, and finger joints—something was broken or dislocated somewhere, for sure. She was more worried about the injuries she wasn't yet feeling—those eating into her from within, ibor taking and taking its price and leaving a crevice that might grow too large before she would discover the damage done, the holes left.

She leaned against a tree and tried not to vomit.

Danso finally handed the light—a burning piece of cloth tied to a broken branch—to Zaq and came forward, his hand raised. Lilong's mind instinctively thought of her blade, of wherever in the understory it was discarded now, waiting for her next Command. But as before, her body was not ready.

"Dehje." Danso was standing in front of her now, and he let the bridge of his hand rest on his forehead and nose, bowing slightly. It took a moment for Lilong to remember that it was the formal Bassai greeting. Or maybe it wasn't just her? It did feel out of place, standing here in the middle of a forest, and yet a Bassai man covered in red mud, with leaves and twigs in his hair and wrapper, stood so erect and proper—so *Bassai*—in greeting her. Another oddity struck her: It was the first time she was observing someone do this who did not look quite like the typical mainlander or immigrant. It felt... *off.*

"Remember me?" he said. "Danso. From the barn."

She stared at him. He took a step forward, then another. His Second put an arm on his shoulder.

"You saved us, didn't you?" He looked eager, almost excited. "I saw the branches, cut clean—your blade, right?" He bowed slightly again. "Thank you. We might have been dead right now."

Lilong gauged their surroundings, gritting her teeth to stave off the warring in her stomach. Something wasn't adding up, but she couldn't quite put a finger on it, and her head wouldn't let her think properly. *Why had they fallen in the first place?* She wanted to ask, but suddenly her mind went to the pouch tied to her waist. She hastily felt for it and was rewarded with the feel of the heavy mineral inside.

She sighed with relief, and it came out like a gurgle, which gave way to a cough that gave way to emptying the contents of her stomach. She leaned on the tree and turned away from Danso, vomiting over her shoulder. It tasted of blood. *Cost of the quest, Lilong,* she told herself as she wiped her mouth. *You got what you came for.*

Danso had concern written all over his face.

"You should sit down," he said. "I can help with some herbs from my pack. Some rest, and you'll be in better shape to journey on." He paused. "Then maybe later you can tell us all about yourself, call it even."

It was that word, *even*, that did it. The Bassai term for it translated to something closer to *equal* or *the same* in the Island Common she spoke back home. If there was one thing she was sure they were not, it was alike.

She locked eyes with him. This young man clearly harboured the idea that they could be some sort of *friends*—Lilong almost gagged at the thought. Despite the fact that he was clearly devoted to the Bassai Ideal—look at his clothes and hair and everything—did he truly not understand that the only reason they were even standing here, talking to one another, was that she didn't have any other choice?

But his eyes remained eager, like a baby seeing a toy for the first time. This one clearly was looking for comradeship and did not understand what was at stake here.

Lilong studied her surroundings again, now better aware of the dense vegetation, the red moon's angry glow. Every direction looked the exact same. There was no way she would figure out how to get out of here alone.

You can't cut him loose, can you? she thought.

She turned her attention back to him, uncomfortable with how close to her he stood, the closest any Bassai she wasn't trying to kill had ever come. Even in the nightlight, she could see his eye glint, inquisitive, enquiring.

"Where is this?" she asked.

Zaq, the Second, made a squealy sound in surprise. "High Bassai!" He cocked his head. "How are you speaking High Bassai?"

She frowned at him. Now, *this one* made no attempt to hide his suspicion, continuing to regard her out of the side of his eye. Maybe this one she should kill.

"We're in the Breathing Forest," Danso said.

"The Breathing Forest," she repeated, pieces of information coming together in her head. "Is that westward?"

"Indeed," Danso said. "We were aiming for the coast, see if we could follow the route of the Gondola. See if we could get to—"

"The Bight of Whudasha," she said, shaking her head, swearing in Island Common. *Stupid stupid stupid!*

Danso frowned. "Excuse me?"

But she wasn't paying attention to him, instead suddenly alert. She gritted her teeth, Drew on a smidgen of ibor, located her blade, and Commanded it toward her. It flew through the vegetation, startling the two men. Danso took a step back from her.

"What—"

"You brought us into a hunting ground, you fool," she snapped.

Zaq's eyes widened, but Danso furrowed his brow. "That's not—no one followed us—"

"Not by your people, by something else," she said, turning in circles, listening hard for anything beyond the pounding in her head and in her chest. *Where is it, where is it?*

"Hunting ground for what?"

"Beasts," she said. "Beasts that will tear us from limb to limb in one move."

Danso went solid. He knew what she was talking about, then?

"You mean—they're real?"

"Of course they're real," she snapped. "How do you think we fell down here?"

"No, it was not—the forest, it was breathing—"

"Yes. And each time it breathes, they hunt beneath the cover of noise and wind." She spun around again, balancing her weight with the tree. "Tell me, which of them was it? A tepe? Ghost ape? Skopi? Biloko? Belly snake?" She swivelled again. "Speak!"

"I don't know!" Danso said, turning about as she did now. "We didn't see anything."

Lilong spent another lengthy moment listening but heard nothing of note. Calm had returned to the forest. She sheathed her blade with reluctance.

"We are safe for now," she said. "But only until the next breathing, which could happen any time. And even before then, we must be alert for other dangers. To leave this forest alive, we must move intentionally. Westward, you said?"

"Yes," Danso muttered sheepishly. "But it'll take...days..."

"I said *intentionally*, not quickly." She winced from the vehemence in her rebuke. "Listen, trying to move too quickly puts us in even more danger. We must be both careful and alert, which means no reckless actions. Let's not forget your people will not give up either—they will definitely be waiting for us at whatever points of egress exist here."

The two men looked at each other. Not so sure of themselves anymore, were they?

"Maybe we should go back to Bassa," Zaq said. "Shorter distance."

"Oh great waters, you two are stupid," Lilong said, settling her weight into the roots of the tree. "If all you have are stupid ideas, then we might as well part ways now."

Doubt and uncertainty hung between the three, an executioner's axe waiting to drop.

"But you came back," Danso said, finally.

"What?"

"You believe I'm stupid, but you came back."

Lilong bit her lip. He was right: She *had* returned to his barn of her own will, hadn't she?

Because a part of you wanted to be wrong, Lilong, she thought. Truly, had she not hoped, upon escaping the border, that there might be just that one person, Bassai or otherwise, who would look at her differently? Someone who would understand her plight and aid her in some way? And now fate had granted her such a person, yet she still combated this newfound alliance. Was this her resistance to her daa's *there-is-good-in-everyone-in-the-world* adages rearing its head?

She surveyed Danso anew. Her whole life as a warrior of the seven islands had revolved around two things. One: that every person beyond the seven islands of the archipelago was a liar, murderer, and greedy bastard who wanted to suck them to the marrow of everything good, ibor included. Two: that it was best to know as much about these liars, murderers, and greedy bastards as they knew about themselves, because to know your enemy inside out was the key to defeating them. But the way Danso looked at her was completely lacking in the hate and malicious intent she kept expecting. All he did was stand there, eyes laden with curiosity and interest and surprise. The same look she had remembered in her moment of pain, that had convinced her to return to the barn. Maybe it was the look itself, then—how alien and unexpected it was—that scared her. Hate, she understood quite well. But this—whatever *this* was—she was wary of.

"I may not quite have the resources it takes to defend us against the dangers of this journey," Danso said, sitting on the ground before her, "but I am a jali novitiate, and I know this land like the back of my hand. We have fallen and lost our path now, yes, but I can get us back on track soon. I just need to find where we are adjacent to the Gondola's route. You somehow know so much about these forests—maybe you can tell us more later—but with your knowledge and mine and Zaq's, we can all get where we want to be: out of Bassa for good. Just trust me."

She waited for him to see the absurdity of his ask. Surely he wasn't *that* naive? He was asking her, an islander, mortal enemies of the mainland—so mortal that the mainland had committed to their erasure from the minds of its people, assured that if they did not exist in minds, they did not exist in body—to trust him, the embodiment of everything the mainland stood for. But there he sat, earnestness in his forward-leaning posture, and it occurred to her what was really happening. For the first time, someone was asking Lilong to look beyond their makeup, those things that identified them as islander or mainlander or desertlander, and was asking for a trust that belied those markers—human to human.

"I don't trust you," Lilong said. "But we must get out of here, so I will rely on your judgement."

Danso nodded his thanks. "You will not regret it."

"And when we get to Whudasha?" she pressed. "It's just another Bassai protectorate, so what stops them from turning us in once we arrive?"

"Well, I've thought about this," Danso said, motioning to Zaq to join them. The desertlander came and stood over them with the light.

"You're trying to go over the Pass, right?" Danso asked, pointing to her. "Well, you can do the…complexion thing you did at the barn the other night, yes? Blend in. No one would even know who you are in Whudasha. And no one will bother us"—he pointed to himself and Zaq—"up there."

"What complexion thing is that?" Zaq asked.

"Long story," Danso said with a wave. "But the Peace Treaty—made post-wars, yes?—says that that no one on the mainland can attack a Shashi in Whudasha."

"I know what your Peace Treaty is," Lilong said. "What I'm wondering is why you think no one will break it to arrest you—us. You do know there will definitely be a bounty on our heads at some point?"

"Well, I'm Shashi, so—"

Lilong snorted. Sure, Whudasha was the land where the mainland sent everything undesirable, including all those like him with so-called *confused* heritage. Perhaps Danso sought a place that felt closer to home, that offered more answers about himself. That, she could understand. But if he thought he would fit in seamlessly enough to guarantee safety there, then his naivety really knew no bounds.

The stridulating of crickets stood between them for a while as they contemplated their fate. Lilong leaned into a semi-lying position, her breath just as raggedy as when she awoke.

"I'll admit this is not a foolproof plan," Danso said. "But it's either this, return to Bassa, or live in this forest forever. I don't see how the other two are better options." He pointed to Lilong. "And you need to see a proper healer. I have some salve and some herbs, but that won't take you far. Whudasha is the closest safe place."

Lilong refused to give him the satisfaction of seeing her wince and give credence to her increasing pain. But he was right: She would really need proper help soon if she was to eventually make it back over the border.

Whudasha it was.

"We must leave this position," she said. "We're easy pickings if the next breathing comes along. And even without that, making camp here opens us up to snakes, skunks, raccoons."

"Cover and some flatter ground," Zaq muttered, speaking up for the first time.

"Yes, that's exactly right," Lilong said. "We need tree cover and flatter ground." She looked to Zaq with some surprise, and maybe a tinge of newfound admiration.

"Seconds are trained in wildlife survival," Zaq offered, by way of explanation. "To protect their charges."

"I see," Lilong said, but she sensed a niggling question embedded in the statement, one that asked who was supposed to protect the Seconds.

"I'll get the pack, then," Danso said, wandering off.

Once alone, Zaq regarded her with a look she interpreted as disdain—surprising, as she thought they had just shared a moment of connection. Besides, desertlanders were closer kin to islanders: siblings in oppression, adjacent in complexion, united in disaffection with the mainland. But then she remembered: This man was no desertlander. He was just as Bassai as Danso. Perhaps even more so.

Lilong leaned further into the roots and sighed. This was going to be one nightmare of a long journey.

23

Esheme

THE NEXT MORNING, ESHEME needed another drink of fig nut and lemongrass brew in order for the pain in her shoulder to subside to a slow throbbing. She would've asked for a second helping, but she had more important things to take care of and needed to keep a clear head.

She dressed and went straight to the library without morning food. On the way over, househands greeted her, genuflecting: *MaaEsheme, Eshememaa*, and the titles were like iron grinding against her teeth. Her maa wasn't dead yet, yes? But the mantle was there, and someone needed to take it up in the time being, and that person was her. The Bassai thing to do would be to embrace it with both arms, but Esheme did not want to be Nem's replacement. She did not want to be Nem, period.

She locked herself in the library. Early sunshine had begun to peek through the raffia blinds and birds chirped and kwagas barked and harrumphed in the distance. She settled behind the desk, retrieved the bound manuscript that she had kept on her person since last night, opened it again, and began to read.

She read until early afternoon, until the sunlight slanted into the library through the blinds. Then she ordered a late breakfast of yams and stew with smoked fish from the Tombolo hamlets to the east. Afterward, she brought Oboda into the library. He came in and sat before her, patient. Esheme paid very little attention to household staff—she couldn't even remember the names of her last two Seconds before him. But something about Oboda's aggressive simplicity and relentless focus was unnerving. In a way that was actually fine by her, Esheme realised, but very, *very* bad for others. Which, of course, made him a much better Second than any she'd ever had.

"I am going to tell you everything I have learned from this manuscript so far," she said. "And because I know how capable my maa is at withholding the truth, I want you to stop and alert me when I get to anything that is a half-truth or a lie."

Oboda did not offer any form of affirmation, but she knew him well enough by now to understand that that, in itself, was affirmation. She cleared her throat.

"On your last trip over the border, you went to find the daughter of Speaker Abuso, by the name of Oke," Esheme began. "She left the mainland without her daa's permission, and has not been seen for a long time. She ran away when Abuso discovered she was using his resources to fund that movement with the Cockroach—the Coalition for New Bassa, yes? He wanted to bring her back as punishment and clear his name in case it was ever revealed that a member of his household was supporting near-treasonous activities. So he hired my maa, who borrowed one of Dọta's caravans and sent you in search of Oke." She paused. "How am I doing so far?"

Oboda nodded.

"Good." She cleared her throat. "I don't know what happened in the Savanna Belt—my maa documents that you returned a man or two short, and without Oke. But you did not come empty-handed, yes? You brought pieces of ibor, as well as that yellowskin in stowaway." She flipped the pages of the manuscript absent-mindedly. "Now, the documentation here doesn't offer much more than that, but I want you to fill it in for me. I have two questions. First, how did you lay your hands on that ibor? Second, how did my maa use it to burn the Speaker and his household?"

His lack of shock at her revelations was unsurprising. Too much time spent with Nem, it seemed, had dulled both of them so much that her likely assassination of the Speaker of the whole nation surprised neither of them.

"She practice in the storage room," he said. "Thas' how she done it."

"I see," Esheme said, pursing her lips. "You did not answer my first question."

Oboda sighed. Esheme didn't think she had seen that expression from him before.

"Oke was meeting a man," he said. He paused, perhaps trying to remember exactly how things happened, perhaps trying to translate a concept in his head from the Mainland Common he knew to the High Bassai he barely spoke.

"What man?"

"A yellowskin man."

"Ah. That's who you killed." Things slowly clicked into place for Esheme. "You didn't find Oke, so you killed him, and as part of your conquest, you brought back his ibor." She made a click at the back of her throat, seeing it clearly now. "That is why the yellowskin girl followed you here. She is here to take it back."

Oboda nodded slowly. Was that shame in his eyes? Did he feel guilty about his actions contributing in a way to Nem's situation?

"It's not your fault," she found herself saying. "*She* sent you on the mission. My maa brings these things on herself, not the other way around."

He frowned slightly, perhaps annoyed at her criticism of Nem. Then his expression softened, as if he'd agreed she was right, which of course she was.

"Do you know why they were meeting?" she asked. "Do you think, perhaps, Oke wanted to use ibor for herself?" She paused. "Or…for the coalition?"

Oboda just shrugged. Esheme sighed. His usefulness had peaked.

"You may go."

He rose and went out. Esheme retrieved the strongbox from where she'd stored it beneath the desk, pulled out the red piece of ibor again, and examined it. It was much smaller than the description and drawing Nem had put into her manuscript. Going by that chipped edge, Esheme decided the larger remaining part was with someone else, and if Dọta was asking for it, it wasn't him. It had to be the yellowskin—that must've been what she had returned for, and must have retrieved after attacking her maa.

If a yellowskin was willing to brave the risk of capture and death to retrieve a simple red stone-bone, then it had to be even more important than the grey ibor her maa had described learning to master.

Esheme gripped it to see if she would feel anything. Nothing came to her, not in the way Nem had described her own reaction in the manuscript. Perhaps this one was employed in some other way?

She returned to reading the manuscript, until the slant of the sunlight from the blinds began to droop. There was nothing new in the manuscript about red ibor. Most of the recent stuff was Nem detailing her daily practice with ibor, as well as information she had gleaned from reading choice parts of the codex before documenting that she'd burned it afterward.

Great, thought Esheme. *There goes the second part of my debt.*

She flipped to the back. Nem had been journaling from both sides of the manuscript at once: the front section contained the most recent entries, while the rear section was more of a business journal, detailing everything about her dealings with people and travel and merchandise. It also contained lists upon lists of everyone who owed her in gold or favours or other kind of barter. Contracts upon contracts, contacts upon contacts. First and Second Elders and councilhands of all kinds, senior government personnel, civic guard captains, senior craftworkers, scholars, healers, earthworkers, farmers. One segment named a few rival fixers in the city—not that they mattered, as no one would go to them if they could go to Nem first. The tail end contained common mainland folk with only a given name and no household name, simple men and women (and sometimes, even children) forming a network of whisperers, gatherers, muscles.

The real question for Esheme, though, was this: How was all this information supposed to help her solve her Dota problem?

There was a soft knock on the door, and Satti peered in.

"Maa, some news, if I may." Esheme waved her in.

"Habba has been brought in, and he has begun to see to MaaNem," Satti said. "He promises she will be stable soon."

"Hmm."

"He also says you can see her."

Esheme shook her head. *Not now.* She couldn't distract herself with that.

"I'll wait until she's awake," Esheme said, then paused. "You were shaken yesterday. Are you fine now?"

Satti, a quite private woman, found the attention disconcerting. She shifted on her feet. "I . . . have no choice but to be fine, maa."

"Yes, I understand your devotion and I commend it, but you've been on your feet ever since this started. Perhaps you should go home, spend some time with family or something."

Satti cocked her head. "My family lives in the hinterlands, maa."

"Oh." This was the first serious thought she had ever given to the lives of the house folk. "I never knew that. You left them just to come here?"

"I owe it to MaaNem," Satti said matter-of-factly. "They can afford to eat because MaaNem saved me."

Esheme saw that she had unsettled the woman quite a bit, so she waved it all aside. "Well, then. Anything else?"

"Yes, maa," she said. "Word has reached us that the kwaga on which Dan—your intended, and his group, escaped, has been found somewhere around the edge of the Breathing Forest. It's assumed they're escaping the city through there, and headed for Whudasha. It is also assumed they will not survive the forest."

Esheme made a back-throated click with her tongue. Sounded like Danso all right, pigheadedly charging into a forbidden forest. Why did he have to make *everything* difficult for everyone? Finding and recapturing him and the yellowskin had just taken on a whole new dimension.

"The Upper Council has also increased the bounty," Satti continued. "A hundred gold pieces *per head* for him, the yellowskin, and his Second, dead or alive."

Esheme ruminated on this after Satti left. That piece of news was the only good thing she had learned so far. *Three hundred gold pieces.* If she managed to capture Danso and the yellowskin herself, this problem was halfway solved. She would regain respect and honour in the sight of the nation, and soiling her name was going to be that much harder for Dọta, for a start. And even if he pressed his luck, with that kind of gold, she could hire the right number of guards and hunthands for protection, and pay the right people to dispute any badmouthing of her household in the streets, sow discord, and flip whatever narrative Dota might have spun about them.

Danso would get punished for his wrongs, she would get revenge for the yellowskin's audacity to attack her household, and she would then fully possess all the ibor available, including the other piece of the red stone-bone. And if worse came to worst, she could even pacify Dota with the smaller of the two pieces.

It was the perfect solution. It was also the most impossible solution. But it was what Nem would do.

She gathered the manuscript, tucked it under her wrappers, and made her way down the hallways of the house, clutching the piece of red ibor tight in her palm. She made sure to skirt the area around her maa's room. There were many questions that needed answering, but only after her maa awoke.

She found Oboda and pulled him into a corner.

"Gather your hunthands and leopards," she said, her voice taking on an edge. "You're going to find Danso and his supporting cast. And if you do it in record time, I will hand you a chunk of that bounty."

24

Lilong

THE FIRST THING LILONG noted at dawn—and was immediately incensed by—was that Danso and Zaq were nowhere in sight. *So much for no reckless actions.* For a moment, she considered leaving them, but the thought was soon dispelled when she heard sounds of movement and someone—Danso, clearly—speaking aloud without a care, all worry of being tracked or traced forgotten. Soon after, the two men emerged from a nearby thicket surrounding the spot they had chosen for camp, carrying a number of fruits in the crooks of their arms, including cocoa pods, green oranges, and wild mangoes.

They stopped when they saw her. Then she looked in the direction they were staring and saw a patch of her tunic wet, red. She felt a trickle down her belly, down her legs. More blood.

Danso handed his fruits over to Zaq and came over, making a move to touch her. She gripped his wrist reflexively. He sucked in a breath, more out of surprise than fear. For a moment, they studied their hands next to each other, how different they looked: his Shashi complexion that resided somewhere between the humus-dark mainlander complexion and something much lighter but not islander-yellow; against hers, exactly islander-yellow, completely lacking any humus-adjacent colouring in both skin and forearm hair. His eyes were a deep, dark brown, striated, and she wondered what her own brown-yellow irises looked like to him.

"Let me see," he said slowly, real concern written on his face. "I've supported my daa enough to tell a few things for myself. Trust me."

She studied him some more for a moment, ruminating on the word *trust*, then succumbed.

Danso peeled aside the bottom of her garment and hissed sharply. "Ooh, that looks…bad. Why didn't you show me this?" He looked genuinely upset. "The fall must've exacerbated the injuries." He gave her a direct gaze. "Tell me again how you got these?"

She stared at him. How could she explain *water arrows as strong as iron* to him? Could his mind process that?

"Of course," he said, as if finally accepting the fact that she was not going to tell him anything she didn't need to. He returned to his task of revealing each wound. There were four of them, the four that had hit her where the shields couldn't cover.

He shepherded her back to the tree and made her lie down, investigating other parts of her body for injuries. Only when hands that weren't hers started to gently prod at her did she feel pain in places she hadn't felt before. There were at least five or more sores in her mouth, and after inspection of her teeth, he announced she had gum bleeding. Her joints were swollen and hurt upon touch. Even in areas he didn't touch, she felt dull throbbing pain: neck, nipples, eye sockets.

"This is odd," he said at last. "I'm familiar with your wounds, but I'm also seeing fresh symptoms of severe malnourishment that weren't there yesterday." He felt the side of her neck with the back of his palm. "Yet you don't have a fever."

How, again, could she explain that that was what ibor did: It took all the things that gave one's body vigour and converted it into the power that it wielded, and with the amount of ibor she had spent over these past few days, she was lucky to be walking upright?

"I will be fine," she said instead. "Let me rest a bit, and then we'll move before the next breathing."

"Oh, you can't go anywhere like this," he said, rising. "I don't know how you were standing yesterday night, but I can tell you that if you stand today, you will not be standing long. Your wounds are not clotting quickly enough, so they'll keep opening up and bleeding, which means unconsciousness won't be far off, which makes all the haste pointless anyway." He looked around. "Maybe we can find a place nearby to hide for the next breathing?"

"And what if your people have decided to make an exception and follow us in here?"

"Never," Danso said. "No Bassai will willingly enter this forest. Not even on the threat of death."

"Even your military?"

Danso frowned. "What military?"

"Your Bassai army."

He snorted. "Bassa does not have an army. Where did you hear such a thing?" He cocked his head. "I thought you knew everything about us."

"Your civic guards do not together constitute an army?" she asked.

"The civic guards?" He chuckled. "No, no, not in that sense. I understand they can be mobilized in a war, yes, but we've not had such a thing in forever, so Bassa no longer keeps an active military. Can't afford the upkeep if you're not fighting anyone. We do still siphon resources from protectorates all over the mainland, though, but now we sign fealty treaties and install warrant chiefs for that." He rose. "If we should be worried about anyone, it'll be hired hunthands trying to earn a bounty placed on our heads, if there's one. Can't be sure how far Bassa will go for that, though, if they'll decide we're worth it." He paused, observing her, his hands akimbo. "Listen, I don't have anything to hasten your clotting, but I can try some more salve and dress the wounds properly this time."

He returned to Zaq—who busied himself with sorting the fruits, pretending all of this was not happening—and pulled supplies from his pack.

Lilong's fingers felt for her pouch again and felt the weight of ibor in it. This alliance was great and everything, but she had to remain focused on the sole purpose of this mission: Get the red stone-bone back home. It was not just her sacred duty to protect the item and its secrets—including that of its very existence—it was also her responsibility to ensure that the existence of the islands themselves remained obscured. She had already partly failed, between being spotted in her natural yellowskin and dallying with these mainlanders. But every other secret yet uncovered, the very last bastions of power the islands possessed, she was going to protect with her life.

Hopefully, they will understand my choices, she thought, adjusting her body into a more comfortable position. They had to. She had broken the rules by leaving unsanctioned, sure, but it was all for a good cause, yes? She *had* to fix her daa's mistake, and not just for the good of her family. The course of the whole continent depended on it.

Danso returned and gave her a few pinches of crushed cloves. After she'd licked enough of the almost tasteless powder, he set to work. She winced at first, when he began to clean the wounds, and then he began to sew, and she responded in a low wail that seemed to go on forever, with him whispering *shh, shh, it's okay* intermittently.

Once the agony was over, Lilong blinked tears, breathing hard.

"Eish, that was rough," Danso said. "But at least now you can rest."

Lilong observed him for a bit. "Where did you . . . learn all this?"

"What, the medicine? Oh, my daa is a private healer and physician. For the herbs, I've collected plants since I was a child." He wiped his hands on a rag that looked like a piece of his own clothing. "Mostly started because I loved the way they smelled, you know? Then it became fun to know their names. But you spend enough time between a healer daa and the university library, and you begin to recognise the properties of most plants just by identifying them."

Lilong wondered how such a puerile concern had morphed into a valuable skill. Where she was from, people devoted their lives to the learning of such things. She watched him, perhaps a bit fascinated, but also confused. How could someone so sharp also be so stupid? How could both things coexist in one body?

Danso, in turn, watched Zaq, who had now spread a piece of clothing on the ground and was praying on his knees, forehead touching the earth, facing the direction of what she understood through her studies back home to be one of the two moons they worshipped.

"Zaq, we won't be leaving here for a while," Danso said to him. "Perhaps we can work up some proper food?"

Zaq gave an audible sigh and grumbled something. Danso frowned, then went over to have a word with the Second. They argued out of earshot for a short moment. Then Zaq got up, gathered his things in exaggerated movements, and went to rummage through the pack.

Danso returned to Lilong.

"Sorry about that," he said. "My Second and I are not really in a good place right now."

So full of contradictions, aren't you, this man? she thought. One moment, he was defying every possible Bassai instinct, wilfully becoming a fugitive to aid an intruder to his nation. Then in the very same moment, he was disrespecting his Second's need for prayer to badger him into doing what he wanted. Someone who was only a Second in the first place because Bassa decided everyone beyond their self-imposed border was less-than. She snorted. You could take the man out of Bassa, but taking Bassa out of the man was another thing entirely.

"What's so funny?" Danso asked, dressing her wounds in cloth bandages.

"Nothing—*ow.*"

"Sorry, sorry."

Lilong watched him work, his touch delicate, his hands those of someone who had never done any manual labour in their life. Hands that cared. All the care Lilong had received in her adult life had always come from people she knew: family, friends, colleagues from her league of warriors. But from a stranger? It was a new and unnerving feeling. She appreciated it—relished it, even—but all the while she was fighting the reflex to stick her blade in his neck just for existing.

Give people a chance, her daa said all the time. *Trust the world a little bit.*

I'm trying, daa, I'm trying. But it was going to be a long and tough road, seeing as the last mainlander her daa had given such a chance had led to him burning up the Weary Sojourner Caravansary and getting fatally wounded. Nothing in the world was going to make her trust anyone that much. But maybe this man, with his wild and nonchalant curiosity that made him both stupid and dangerous and the worst kind of person to trust, ever—maybe she could offer a morsel. He did possess a capability for kindly consideration that had been in her favour so far. He'd offered to attend to her wounds, what, three times now? Even after she'd attacked him, that first time. He'd had his doubts, but he had looked beyond them, past her complexion. He was clearly a better person than she was, because she didn't think anything could convince her to betray her own nation like this.

"I realise I don't even know your name," Danso said, cutting into her reverie.

Lilong regarded him for a second. Could she, really?

She looked toward Zaq, who had begun work gathering enough dry kindling to start a fire. She needed at least *one* of these two on her side, and it wasn't going to be that Second.

A name was a harmless thing to give. For now.

"It's Lilong," she said. "Now let's find some cover for the next breathing."

25

Esheme

Esheme spent the rest of the day in the storage room, which had long since ceased to be used for anything resembling storage. Now, all that lay here were remnants of her maa's activities. There were more ashes in the firepot than usual, and scorch marks on pretty much every wall. The floor was damp and mould grew in the corners. Putting together the journal's words and what lay before her, Esheme could almost re-create everything her maa had done in this room.

And so, Esheme put down the manuscript, retrieved the red ibor, and, recalling every painstaking detail, spent the rest of the day attempting to follow each step and do the exact same thing.

She found that her mood darkened by the late hour, when nothing she had done yielded any results. She had tried everything, including the intense concentration her maa had mentioned, trying to *connect* the energy of her own body with that of the stone-bone. The notes said, *Be one with the stone-bone*, but no matter how hard Esheme tried, she and the red stone-bone steadfastly remained disparate entities, pretty much like with every other stone in the yard.

She was further upset by an admonition that followed the noted instructions: *Be intentionally patient.* Her maa, even from a coma, was still giving her vague and annoyingly cryptic advice. She stuffed everything back into the strongbox, hid it in the secret storage compartment she'd found, and returned to the library, staring out the floor-to-ceiling window overlooking the courtyard with the impluvium.

Her maa often stood here and drank, thinking. Esheme had never asked her what she thought of, and realised now that this must have been her scheming, planning, strategizing. As much as all she wanted was for Nem to wake up and come deal with the problems she'd created, Esheme realised something: She might be more cut out for this role than she'd care to admit.

She frowned but did not leave. Instead, a memory engulfed her, one that took her back to when she had just reached lower guild age and had begun at counsel guild, preparing to go into the university. A fellow classmate, a notorious bully of a boy called Nosawe, had referred to Nem with a colloquial term in Mainland Pidgin reserved for people found too undesirable to be joined to someone else. But in calling her that, Esheme knew the reference wasn't really about her maa's inability to get joined but her own position as a child without a daa: a bastard.

Esheme wasn't known for getting into physical fights. She considered herself more strategic, choosing to hurt people in other ways, by jabbing them in already existing sore spots when they least expected it, and in a manner so severe they never got the chance to return for a retaliation. But that day, something had shifted in her, and she had *moved*. She remembered thinking not about her maa, or even her absent daa, but about the fact that this young man had thought he was going to disrespect her and get away with it, and that was simply not going to happen. Her aim had been to teach Nosawe a lesson, knock sense into that flat head of his, and she had gone for him with fists. He had been too stunned to retaliate in any other way than to keep pushing her away, and ended up with a bloody nose for it.

Esheme was suspended for a fortnight, and had thought her maa would be furious. Instead, when called in for a chat with the guild leaders, Nem took the whole story in stride. She thanked them gracefully and took her daughter home, even stopping their travelwagon midway to buy roasted maize from a street vendor, something she rarely did. They had eaten it together on the trip back, munching in silence, Nem present, but also somewhere else. Esheme had been confused, and when they'd reached home, Nem had left her without a word, to return to her work.

It wasn't until she returned to counsel guild that she realised that Nosawe was no longer in her class. She asked around, and heard under whispers that the boy and his family had gone over the Pass on some sort of adventure-retreat trip and hadn't been seen since. It was rumoured they'd been attacked by vagabond desertlander cannibals and eaten alive.

She caught on quick. Of course Nosawe couldn't have gone on such a trip without help; his parents had limited proximity to the merchants who could facilitate that sort of thing. Esheme had gone straight to Nem and accosted her, in this very library even. Nem paused from writing something to look her up and down, then said:

"Why did you fight, then?"

Esheme, expecting resistance, or even denial, was taken aback. "What?"

"Why did you fight back, if what he did wasn't wrong?"

"He *was* wrong."

"Yet you don't want him to face the consequences of his actions?"

"I do," Esheme said. "But you should have let me do it."

Nem put down her stylus. "Really?"

"I started it. I was going to finish it."

Nem nodded, returning to her writing. "And the consequences? Would you take care of that too, or would I have to step in and take over when it gets too much?"

"I don't need you to be my fixer." The words were already out of her mouth before she could take them back.

Nem flinched. Esheme remembered it now as one of the first few times her maa ever showed stark emotion.

"I'm not trying to be your fixer," Nem said at last. "I am trying to be your maa." She paused. "I am trying to make space for you to be more than I could ever be."

Esheme turned from the window now, opened the door, and signalled to the househand outside.

"Get Satti."

She shut the door and returned to her maa's chair. She wasn't sure how to feel just yet, but she definitely knew one thing: Her maa trusted her, relied on her, believed in her. Regardless of how she felt about this woman, about all of this scheming and the sudden bestowal of duty upon her, she had to do what was good for the household. She had to do what was good for herself.

She picked up a charcoal stylus, retrieved a sheet of paper, and at the top, wrote her own name, *MaaEsheme*, and copied the household symbol next to it. Then she began a letter to Igharo.

The message was simple. They were to cease and desist any interactions indefinitely. She did offer reasons—she wasn't a monster—even if they were lies: She needed to focus on her maa, she needed to return to her studies at the university, she needed to take up the role of leading the household. Her reputation was even more important now. He was to remain away and, if he ever saw her in public, never acknowledge her. And he was never even to entertain the idea of whispering anything that had happened between them to another soul. She thought about adding a threat in there to demonstrate how seriously she would take any flagrant disregard of these instructions, but decided against it. It was empty barrels that made the loudest noise. There was more weight in things left unsaid.

Satti came into the library and announced her presence with a throat clearing. Without looking up, Esheme said:

"Satti, I am going to ask something of you."

Satti's silence was enough of a question.

"I want you to appoint a person or two to handle your caretaker duties," Esheme said. "From today onward, I will need someone to trust. With Oboda off in search of the fugitives, that person is you, and I will need you to start playing a different kind of role."

Satti nodded. "I'm at your service, MaaEsheme."

"Good." She rolled up the letter, wound twine around it, and handed it across the table to Satti. The woman came forward and took it.

Esheme did not immediately let go, holding the woman's eyes. Satti looked distraught and a tad confused, as anyone would be in the face of such uncertainty. But behind that, Esheme could see the strong resolve that had caused Nem to bring her into the household in the first place. She decided she was making the right choice.

"You will deliver that letter in person to a name and location I will only give to you verbally," she said, letting go of the paper. "This task is a test. Do not fail it."

Satti nodded and tucked the letter into her wrappers.

26

Danso

It was well past midday before Lilong's health started to improve. Birds circled high above their heads and announced the sun's peak. In the western horizon, Menai had ducked behind the clouds like a ghost, and only Ashu stayed up, her grey, dappled face hanging morosely in the sky.

Now lit by daylight, the rest of the Breathing Forest opened itself up to them. The scavenging trip earlier in the morning revealed to Danso that the forest was just as thick and tightly congested as earth studies education had led him to understand most mainland rainforests would be. The canopy above them stood high, the understory composed of thickets filled with thorny shrubs, and the ground cover was slippery with weeds, nearly marshes in some places. Then there were the noises. Strange kinds, all of them. Sometimes it was birds flying in unison; other times, small frogs with vocal cords twice their size. Mostly, there was an incessant squeaky-creak that could be anything from a branch swaying in the wind to a bush dog lying in wait. And of course, mosquitoes, houseflies, and tsetse flies, all buzzing by the thousands. None of the three had happened upon a snake yet, but with the number of other crawling reptiles they'd already encountered, Danso was sure it was a matter of *when* rather than *if.*

Then, there was the breathing.

It had happened only once more since, during which Lilong advised, dangerous as it seemed, that they stay anchored to a nearby tree and remain as still as the swaying allowed. Preferably one of the less massive trees whose roots didn't get pulled up by the heavy winds. *We move as the forest moves, so we are indistinguishable from it,* she said. *That is how we survive.* Her advice did little to quell Danso's trepidation. To him, every sound the winds made was a growl, the shrill call of a predator. But the breathing had lasted for less than half an hour before dying without event. He had calculated all of it—the time between the two events, how long it lasted—with the aim that they could predict the next one and plan accordingly.

Now, he studied Lilong as she lay resting, asleep. Under the late midday heat, she was still dressed in what he decided would be clothing from the Nameless Islands: a bloody woollen cloak with a hood. She sweated profusely in it as she slept, but he didn't want to bother her by taking it off. Besides, he had only his clothes to offer her, and with the way she looked at him, she would simply refuse out of spite.

He, however, held no such feelings. Instead, he found every single aspect of her being fascinating, so un-Bassai. She had no holes punctured in her ears, for instance, and no rings circled through them at all. Save for the fake Bassai facepaint, which she still hadn't cleaned off, she did not have any other body adornment. On the mainland, that kind of bareness was reserved for cattle, pigs, and goats, perhaps with a sole ring or mark as a sign of ownership—an unmarked animal was a free-for-all. He found it a struggle to stop thinking of her bareness as distasteful.

There were other things too: some indentations in both her upper arms, holes where various pieces of a tiny amberlike, stonelike, bonelike material were stuck in. He had run his hands over them, feeling their smooth yet pockmarked texture, and he immediately decided what they were—ibor. The Manic Emperor had described them so well, with all their smooth and opaque faces dappled with scars, that Danso felt like he had seen them before. Some of the holes were empty in a way that told him those particular pieces might have been lost or given away or used up somehow.

He also realised he had never met someone with short hair before. The Idu always wore their hair in plaits, and though some lower-status Emuru who could not afford to maintain plaited arches kept shorter hair, that only happened in the poorest parts and farthest reaches of the mainland. Potokin and Yelekuté kept their heads bald as a requirement for all immigrants, so that was different. Lilong's short, yellow hair was the antithesis of everything that was Bassai, the complete opposite of people like Esheme.

Esheme.

The thought of her made him feel cold. He had finally become her worst nightmare, as she was always saying he would. Yes, they shared a dissatisfaction with the Bassai system, but Esheme was in favour of staying on the mainland and rising above it. She'd always found his interest in Whudasha irritating. Now that he had actually gone and left, managing to get her injured in the process and aid an enemy of the nation while at it, there was well and truly no going back with her. Even if Bassa forgave him for some reason, Esheme would ensure that her wrath haunted him forever.

During their little trip for fruits earlier, Zaq had muttered about keeping an open window for a possible return, and Danso had seriously considered it. Being Shashi would weigh significantly in how he would be treated, but perhaps his Idu side could offer a buffer. If somehow the moon temple decided to look favourably upon him, he still wouldn't be let near the university for sure. What good was he in that city without the one thing for which he was useful? He was not half as good at singing as most jalis were—Habba's handed-down lute-harp almost never left its hanging place in his room—so he could never become a herald like some new graduates or disgraced, low-rent jalis did. And though he was good at memorising and telling stories, he wouldn't be allowed to do that either. He would be just another Shashi in the city. Soon enough, they would send him off to Whudasha anyway.

But only once he remembered that he would have to deal with Esheme did the fantasy finally crumble into dust.

He could face his daa, his uncles, his friends, Oduvie, even Nem. But Esheme, he knew he could never face. He would never be able to sit next to her again or look her in the eye. He would have to avoid her for the rest of his life, because even if she didn't one day show up and murder him in his sleep—he wouldn't put such a thing past her—she would haunt him with her silence and dagger glares for the rest of his miserable

Bassai existence. That was, if he could ever be Bassai again after aiding an invader.

He shrugged himself out of the thought. What was most important now was deciding where they were going next, how they were going to navigate their way back to plotting the Gondola's route and following it out to where the forest ended and the coast began.

"Lilong," he called, finally deciding she had suffered the heat enough. Her name still sounded foreign on his tongue, the end syllable rising like a mountain. She started from half sleep, reaching for her blade, then paused midway, recognition dawning upon her. She rose slowly, wiping her face with her clothes and dusting ants off her body. Her skin seemed to glitter with the sweat, the midday sun caressing it like kin. Danso, surprisingly, felt inferior.

"How are you feeling?" he asked.

She stared at him funny. She *always* stared at him funny as if unsure about what she was doing with him, what manner of madness drove her into this alliance in the first place. He could understand that. He'd been wondering the same thing about himself.

"I've seen worse things," she said, and stood, swaying for a moment, but working herself so that she didn't show it.

"Try to reserve movement for when we need it," Danso said. "When we get to Whudasha, someone might have better food and more potent herbs to quicken your recovery."

She stiffened at the word *we* but said nothing. They stayed in that awkward silence for a while. Zaq had wandered off to find the next camp and some wood for it, taking the knife Danso had packed to mark the trees and find his way back.

Remembering the fruits, Danso reached into his pack and brought out a couple of mangoes and a wild soursop, offering Lilong one of each. She took the mango but eyed the soursop.

"What's that?" she asked.

His eyes widened. "You don't know what a soursop is?" She shook her head. "It's like this sweet-sour thing, very refreshing. Look." He pulled the spiky fruit's skin apart from the head. The green skin opened up to juicy white insides with black seeds. He pinched a fingerful and dropped

it into his mouth, savouring the tang. Colourless juice ran down his arm.
He pinched another and handed it to her.

She frowned, placed it in her palm, then licked it tentatively. Danso
giggled. She shot him a look before taking a bite in her mouth, swishing
it from side to side. Danso laughed at her quizzical expression.

"This tastes...good," she said at last, surprising Danso with a little,
wry smile.

"Ahn-ahn, so you can even smile," he said, and her face changed the
instant he said it. She withdrew into her silence and went back under her
tree, peeling at the mango skin with her teeth. The only sounds between
them were the respective slurps of sucking fleshy fruit insides.

"Why did you come back?" Danso asked.

Lilong paused her eating for a moment, then returned to it as if he
hadn't asked anything. Her response didn't surprise Danso, and he
waited a moment before asking again.

"Please stop asking me that," she said. It was not a plea or request.

He put down the soursop. "Someone else who wasn't me might've
talked. Especially after being attacked the first time. But you still came
back."

Lilong ate the last of her mango thoughtfully, threw the seed away,
then rose and said: "I have to go see to something. I will need a rag and
some water from your pack, if you don't mind."

"You haven't answered my question."

She glared at him until he raised his hands in submission and pulled
out the items, asking what they were for.

She raised an eyebrow. "Woman's business. Unless you want me to
explain it to you in detail."

"No, no," he said, quickly, handing her the items. "Forget I asked. Just
make sure you're...safe."

She snorted. "I don't need your protection."

Danso went away from the spot, admonishing himself for almost
embarrassing her. He found a spot of clear ground with enough sunshine
seeping through to determine the sun's position with stones and an erect
stick: almost due south, it told him. Then, from memory, he began to
draw the map of the mainland he knew, based on this direction. He drew

and recited the geography as he had learned, with everything described by its orientation from Bassa:

Soke, the north, the ragged mountains;
Bassa, the seat, the heart of the nation;
The Gondola and Tombolo, they cut the land in two;
Whudasha to the west, fishing hamlets to the east,
The southern hinterlands, each side of the confluence;
The delta settlements, the land meets the waters.

The recital was much more elaborate than that, but he had crafted his own abridged version. The longer version went into much more detail, naming the tiny towns in each hinterland protectorate, as well as the little that was known of the delta swamp settlements.

As he drew and elaborated on just the portion between Bassa and Whudasha, Danso thought about how Lilong, a stranger, knew just as much about Bassa as he did, perhaps even more. Despite being university educated and having read one of the rarest manuscripts on the mainland, he was still unprepared for what the world had in store. The hands-on knowledge required to navigate real life he still had to learn through a warrior from an invisible island.

This was going to be one hell of a journey.

He surveyed his work. Feasible. They would need to get to higher ground first, but he might be able to pinpoint their exact location soon enough. And since the Gondola flowed westward, toward the coast, from there he could point to the Bight of Whudasha by crow's eye.

By moons, he was going—dare he say it—*home*, one way or another.

27

Esheme

THE MOON TEMPLE OF Menai and Ashu was a multistoreyed building with a central hall that spanned all storeys in height. Stairs ringed the temple, steep, narrow, and dank, so that whoever got to the top was usually left breathless, leading to a popular Bassai adage that prayer was absent without work, and those stairs were how one got their work done. The idea of renovating the temple was the longest-standing debate at council meetings and had even once been opened up to the people for opinion, but the final decision was always the same: The temple had served the mainland for hundreds of seasons, through the First and Second Great Wars, and the mainland remained prosperous because its prayers to Menai and Ashu had always been answered here. It helped that the older the building got, the more the city raked in from pilgrimages made by those in the farthest reaches of the mainland. This income stream was made more potent by the fact that every mainland protectorate—except Whudasha—was required to demonstrate fealty to Bassa by sending an agreed number of delegates on such pilgrimages every season. Of course, said pilgrimages would now be greatly reduced in the wake of the border closure. As it stood, temple offerings were already dwindling, and templehands had begun to seek transfers to other guilds and positions.

Esheme, as she climbed the steps to the topmost floor, did not think that tourism was a good reason to place such a burden on the inhabitants of the city. For the first time in a long time, she found herself sweating, doing labourious work. The three househands trailing her weren't puffing as much, and she didn't like looking so weak in front of them. She held her breath until the top floor before releasing it in bursts. She was MaaEsheme now. She had to act like it.

She was ushered into her maa's praying chamber on one of the upper floors by one of the many priests. Ordinarily, Esheme would have been stationed on one of the lower floors, despite being an Idu, while her maa, who was Emuru, surprisingly got one of these upper floors. Esheme thought the Bassai caste system was confused—she sat in a special reserved seat much better than her maa's during mooncrossings, only to come to temple and be demoted to a lower floor. The offered explanation for this—that allocation of places here was based on cumulative time spent with the gods over one's lifetime, and not on social status or exuberance of devotion—made absolutely no sense, since Esheme had attended temple much more than Nem had ever gone. It also did not explain special places being reserved for the highest payers, especially pilgrims who were willing to spend more than the average citizen. She knew Nem paid to hold this space simply because she needed it to broker connections with other high-and-mighties of Bassa.

Most eyes in the room stopped to regard her as she came in. The floor was sectioned off between Idu and Emuru, and some people even had their own special partitions, especially those who she could tell were members of the Lower Council or other high-ranking guild officials and top tradespeople. First Elders had their own floor entirely.

She stared back at the questioning looks, aware of what they were thinking. How could a young woman, barely what, thirty-six, thirty-seven seasons, not even past guild finals, be up here? She replied with her own hard stare. There was no law that prevented a young successor from taking up this space, and they had to deal with it. She settled into Nem's spot—a raffia mat with a household symbol woven into it—sat with her legs folded, and bowed her head.

It had been Satti's idea to make a public appearance. As much as deference would allow her, the caretaker had frowned on Esheme's refusal to go visit her maa, who, while responding to Habba's care, refused to wake up. Satti thought that if Esheme found it too difficult, too painful to see her maa like that, then maybe she could *at least* make a public appearance to show that she cared and was praying for the recovery of her maa. It was the Bassai thing to do.

Esheme shut her eyes and turned her face eastward, in the direction where Ashu currently lay, and in the same direction in which the white moon god's altar had been set up, high in the far corner where everyone could see. The white moon god's representation was so familiar by now that she didn't need to see it to internalise the image: the head of a hen dressed in Bassai wrappers and wearing cowrie and coral jewellery. Ashu, the humble giver, the one to whom they prayed for succour. This representation was cast in bronze and placed above the lamps of the altar. There was a jar filled with humus on the altar, and sweet-smelling herbal spices burned in a clay pot, to symbolise the connection between sky and earth, the two pillars of everything the Bassai held dear.

As Esheme sat there, she realised she didn't have anything to pray for. Well, at least not to Ashu, whom she was supposed to ask to put some *good* in her, to help her turn from her lackadaisical ways and away from nonchalance and anger. But the longer she sat there, clenching her lids shut, the more she knew she was praying to the wrong god, for the wrong things.

She turned around on her mat and faced the western wall of the red moon, Menai. Menai's representation was also cast in bronze but was dressed in armour and had a leopard's head wearing a golden headdress. There was the same humus and spices, but these spices were less gentle, harsher and sharper in smell and colour of smoke, so that the whole altar seemed to snarl.

Esheme was the only one turned to face Menai's altar, and it attracted attention. Bassai always pretended to not pray to Menai. It was a brazen act to face Menai's altar squarely and pray to her for all the things she was associated with: rancour, wrath, vengeance.

What Esheme really needed was strength, and it was only Menai she could pray to for the kind of strength she needed. Strength to fearlessly survive this period as the head of her household, to decide what needed to be done without apology. Strength to look Dọta in the eye and deal with whatever he brought her way. Strength to survive this nation and its people. Strength to take on the world.

As Esheme shut her eyes and whispered, her prayers soon tapered into silence. Again, she realised she was praying for the wrong thing. So she rose, gathered her wrappers, and went down the stairs.

It was time to face her truth. It was time to face her maa.

◦——⋯————⋯◦·

Esheme's travelwagon had only just pulled out of the temple and back into the road when a group of ten men on kwagas rushed in and blocked their way. Her stablehand pulled the team to a stop, and her escorting househands jumped down to do their best to cover the door to the wagon in anticipation of an attack.

Instead, Esheme pulled aside the blinds of the wagon and poked her head outside. She cursed herself for stupidly believing she was not under threat and sending her only real protection away on a search with all his men.

A man jumped down from the lead kwaga, a desertlander. He was lean and had a high-brown complexion, and a permanent scowl made him mean-faced. He was dressed in a way that told her he was Potokin: His whole body was covered in wrappers in a way one barely saw with desertlanders. Esheme struggled at first to remember where she had seen him before, until she heard the clinking as he approached and spotted the golden-hilted knife clinging to his belt.

"Ariase, right?" she said, and waved her househands away from the door. "What is the meaning of this disrespect? Couldn't you have come to my home—"

"Young maa," Ariase said, and the expression bit Esheme in her chest. "You should not be here."

Esheme took a moment to contain her anger, then said: "Is that so?"

"Yes," he said, without batting a lid. "You should be seeking the artifacts the First Elder has asked for. Any time not spent doing this is time wasted, and the First Elder is not pleased with that. You have spent a day already, with no dividends. The First Elder has asked that I remind you what he is capable of. He asks that I remind you of the assets in his controls and what he could achieve with them."

Esheme stared at him. Who did this dirty desertlander think he was talking to? Had it come to this in this nation, then? That some random outlander could dare stop her in the middle of *her* city and question her? Was this what people thought of her maa's name now? Was this how people thought of her household?

She wondered how much of the issue lay with him being Potokin, a good number of whom were Seconds to high-ranking Idu. Because the nation never quite spelled out the limits of their elevation from average desertlander to the closest thing to bona fide citizen an immigrant could be, they let their access to the Idu get into their heads and thought themselves at par with real Bassai. And sometimes, people got drunk on this power and overextended themselves.

Esheme gathered her wrappers and stepped out of the travelwagon into the afternoon heat. She stood in front of the man, almost matching him for height. At least she got that from Nem.

"Have you been following me, Ariase?" she asked, incensed. "Are you telling me where I can go or not? Are you *threatening* me?"

The desertlander was unmoved. "I'm doing as instructed by the First Eld—"

"Fuck you and your First Elder," she said, poking a hand in his chest. The men around him shifted in response, but he made a small, sharp motion with his head, and their hands left their waists and sides, where their runkus and blades were.

"Young maa—"

"Call me that one more time," Esheme said, shoving him. He didn't move much; he was a solid man. She shoved him again. "Try it. Call me."

The afternoon pressed heat and tension down on the group. They waited.

"I meant no disrespect," Ariase said, finally. "I have only come at the wish of the First Elder to remind you of your duty to him, as instructed."

"And to show me a glimpse of what the consequences could be like if I don't deliver, is it?" she asked. He said nothing. "I have the message, thank you. Now, here's one for you and your employer." She stepped forward and closed the space between them. "This is my city. Nobody, I repeat, *nobody*, can run me out of this place I have given my life to. Not you, not your First Elder. I am MaaEsheme, of the household of Nem and all of those who have come before her. We were here when you crossed into the mainland, and we will be here when you leave. Remember that."

She turned to go, then said, without looking at him: "Tell First Elder Dọta that I will give him what he wants. I may not give it to him in the two days left, and that is just as well. But let him know that if he makes a move against me or my household before I have had a chance to make my case, I had better not live to retaliate. Because if I do . . ." She let the statement hang. "Remember, Abuso thought he was invincible too."

She got in the travelwagon and shut the door, then instructed her househands with a wave of her arm. They got back in their places.

"Now move, before I run you all down," she said, and shut the blinds.

DaaHabba looked much skinnier than the last time she had seen him, and he was already a thin man. Esheme found the man seated in the antechamber to her maa's room. The conditions of his release—that he could never leave the room or Nem's bedside—meant that the antechamber had become his living quarters, with a small sleeping and eating area. He was allowed to use the lavatory upon escort. The only two hunthands Oboda had left behind stood guard outside the room, with rotating shifts to ensure that it was always guarded, another release condition.

Habba welcomed Esheme into the antechamber, wearing his usual plain clothes and calm demeanour. He didn't look like someone who was going to run away anytime soon, and had the air of someone dedicated to the cause of keeping his patient alive. This was very much the kind of person she had always known him to be: straightforward, focused, dedicated. The complete opposite of his son.

Esheme smiled at him when she entered the room. He rose.

"Esheme-maa," he said, and genuflected slightly.

"Dehje, Jali Habba," she said, the bridge of her hand on her forehead and nose in greeting. Most people still used the title from his jali days, even though he had not done anything as a jali for a long time.

"Please, you don't have to do that," he said, almost begging. "I should be the one indebted to you right now. I should be on my knees, apologising for my son's behaviour."

"Oh, no, please, stop it. It's not your fault. We both know how strong-headed Danso is."

"You must understand, he is just a broken boy." Habba was at his most conciliatory. "He has a lot of love and care in his heart, but he's just misguided about where he's putting it. It is perhaps my fault—I broke him by ignoring him for too long. I should've done more to show him the way."

"Perhaps." She shrugged. "But there's nothing we could've told him that would've changed his mind."

"I know." Habba sighed heavily. "I just hope he is at least found safe and sound."

"Yes," Esheme said, but she did not, in fact, hope he was found safe and sound. She hoped he and his new yellowskin friend were in bad enough shape to be found easily, captured, and returned to Bassa. Then she could have all she wanted sooner.

"I hope they're feeding you well?" she asked Habba.

"Yes," he said. "More than I could ever have hoped for in the local government cells. I am in deep gratitude to you, Esheme-maa. I hear you persuaded them into this."

"And I thank you, too," she said. "For helping her."

He shook his head, resignedly. "It's the little I can do." Esheme caught, in his weighty tone, apology again for his child, and it struck her yet again, how different Danso was from his daa.

"If I may ask one favour?" His eyes drooped, hopeful.

"Go on."

"Perhaps, you could talk to … whoever you talked to about me, to see that my brothers are released too? They had nothing to do with all of this, I swear to you. Nothing."

"Oh, I know they didn't," Esheme said. "I'll see what I can do."

"And perhaps, when he returns," Habba continued—Esheme noticed he didn't say *if*—"you could speak on his behalf? You would put in a good word about his behaviour and lessen his punishment?"

Now this she could not promise, so instead she said, "I can see my maa now?"

It wasn't really a question, and Habba caught on and stepped aside solemnly.

Inside, the room smelled different than the last time she had been here. A new stench of spirits and burning herbs commingled with the older stench of blood and stale urine. Nem lay covered in fresh white sheets, looking peacefully asleep. Esheme signalled for the door to be shut, and only when it latched behind her did she release her breath.

"What have you done?" She moved toward the motionless body on the bed. "Why are you doing this to me?"

She settled into the chair next to the bed and stared at the barely perceptible rise and fall of her maa's heart.

What do you want?

She wasn't just asking Nem this question, not really. She was asking everything: her household, the city, the moons, herself. Especially herself.

What do you want?

She looked at the woman lying in the bed. Even in her coma and paralysis, Nem was still asking things of her. But this time, Nem had left behind problems that couldn't be solved by adhering to the Bassai Ideal. Any solution required her to become some iteration of a fixer, the one thing they agreed was against Esheme's best interests. To survive this period of turmoil, she had to first *become* Nem, to see and understand the situation as Nem would have. She would have to see through Nem's eyes, think Nem's thoughts, attack the problem the way Nem would. And, after all was done, she would have to *unbecome*, so that the only thing left would be the core of herself. Esheme, pure and unadulterated.

She stared at Nem upon coming to this conclusion, her plans of action falling into place. The more she laid the pieces one in front of the other, the more they made sense.

There was a letter she had to write.

28

Oboda

OBODA SAT AT A waystation on the Emperor's Road to Whudasha, eating a white star apple and spitting the seeds into the nearby bush. The waystation existed at the intersection between the bushroads—the well-trodden paths that people took to the Gondola River—the Emperor's Road to Whudasha, and the main egress points of the Breathing Forest. The three crisscrossed each other in a manner so uncanny that the waystation ended up in the perfect centre of these three and was named the Three-Prong Waystation for it.

The Three-Prong Waystation was also the biggest on this route and therefore could take all of his men, while also allowing him the opportunity to utilise the emergency pigeon outpost to send and receive messages if he needed to. But since waystations were public property, it also meant he couldn't stop any other hunthand on the bounty trail from using it, which left him in the peculiar situation where he had to share the same space with various men that weren't his own.

He smacked his tongue and hard palate together, savouring the tang of the star apple. A group of men—not his—played a crude mancala game in the camp nearest to his, digging two rows of six holes into the dirt and dropping stones into them in sequence. The men bantered as they played, in full bounty-hunting dress and armour, weapons sheathed and ready for the draw. Oboda had taken all of his own hunthands save for one or two, alongside a hired hand or two who were particularly skilled in tracking, archery, and spearfighting. Alongside them were three leopards from his private leap. His favourite, Viasi, a rainforest leopard with a golden coat rosetted in black, stood by him now, sniffing at the star apple seeds he spat out and disappointed that they weren't meat.

He patted her on the head and sucked on the hard skin of the fruit, draining the pulp of juice. They had been waiting, what, three days now? Still no sign of the fugitives. Ever since the bounty had been upped, the number of people looking for them had doubled alongside it, and the number of camps at the waystation steadily increased over the last few days. Every hunthand seemed to be taking the same approach: simply waiting to see if the three would make it through the Breathing Forest.

There was a strong belief that fewer than the initial three would emerge from the forest, and even if they did, they would be starved, tired, and unprepared for attacks, which made for easy capture. It was a big bounty for small work, and every hunthand in Bassa wanted an easy slice of this mango. Add to that the fact that most Bassai had suddenly become insecure about what their economic futures would look like following the Pass closure, and it made sense that this particular bounty had become overpopulated quickly.

He often heard hunthands discuss how they were likely to share the bounty if they nabbed the fugitives. The promise of this had gotten so far into some heads that one hunthand had decided Oboda was the biggest rival and had attempted to murder him at night. But he did not bank on the fact that Oboda almost never slept. He'd cracked the man's skull in one runku swing, then fed his body to Viasi. When the other hunthands woke by morning, they were unsure which affront to the guild's rules was worse: the errant hunthand or Oboda's violent response. Oboda's silence dared anyone to act, and no one thought themselves adequate to take up the challenge. Power, Oboda had learned, was taken by force, not offered up on a platter. Asking for permission was anathema to him; it demonstrated weakness. The weak got eaten alive, and ever since he lost everything in the desert attack that brought him over the border, Oboda knew he did not have the luxury of ever showing weakness again.

The first set of hunthands had begun to leave after a day or two of waiting, though, convinced that the group had either died or been taken by the spirits within the Breathing Forest, as with everyone who had ever gone in there. *Even the most inept Bassai would cross that forest in three days*, they mused. *They are dead, for sure.* Of course no one went in to confirm this. Oboda's own men were just as disillusioned about entering the forest, so eventually, everyone just sat and waited.

Oboda did not believe in the evil spirits, beasts, and various nefarious entities that were said to exist there. He did not believe that nonsense about the forest being cursed or sacred or belonging to the moons or whatever. Left to him, he would march in there himself and make sure those three bodies were lying cold in the understory. But the problem was that anyone who as much as stepped foot into the Breathing Forest couldn't return to Bassa—even if they made it back. The Bassai considered every being returning from the Breathing Forest as soulless, their soul having been stolen by the forest spirits during their time there. Not only were returnees to be stripped of whatever position they'd earlier occupied, they'd be forced to become devoted to the moon temple, serving its priests and living as outcasts of society forever as a way to earn their final journey to the skies through devotion to the moon gods. Even the odd animal that strayed from the forest into the bushroads was slaughtered immediately and offered up at the temple's altar. No, his life, his purpose in this world, was for something much greater than scrubbing temple floors.

He adjusted his chest armour about his neck, uncomfortable in the heat of waning day. He and his men remained dressed and kept the kwagas saddled, in the event anything happened quickly. He had seen the work of the yellowskin on MaaNem, and on his men once the ice had melted, and knew that this was not someone to be taken for granted.

He was still embarrassed about having failed his duty. He hadn't yet told anyone of what had truly happened when he faced the yellowskin—too disgraceful to share, and he was glad for the lack of witnesses. He'd had a chance right there, with the yellowskin weak and injured, and he had failed his charge, failed his household. He itched to right this mistake, and was more than prepared, more proactive, so as not to be caught unawares when he came across the yellowskin again.

He had heard the rumours about all that the yellowskins could do—change their complexion to look like anyone else's, manipulate various elements, turn into animals, become invisible. He had always thought of the mainlanders as more prone to belief in petty sorcery than desert-landers like himself—every unexplained phenomenon, they attributed to wielding evil power sourced from the corrupted spirits of ancestors who were never burned and sent to the moon gods. But what the yellowskin had done with her blade—that was no sorcery. He had witnessed a similar thing, with fire, back at the Weary Sojourner Caravansary. He had to be prepared for anything, since he was unsure what else she could do.

In keeping with that aim, he had brought his whole troop and their arms. He needed to not only outnumber her but also outsmart her. He could send Viasi too, excellent climber and good swimmer that she was, to locate and deal with the three. But she too wouldn't be allowed back into Bassa. She'd be captured and killed on the spot, as the Bassai believed, to prevent the scent of bad luck that would follow her from the forest from polluting the populace.

He reached into his bag, tossed the leopard a dried rodent, and watched as she ate. Rules, rules, rules: That was all they cared for on the mainland, wasn't it? He loved working for MaaNem, remained committed to her, but she was all about keeping things relatively civil, wasn't she? He sighed. But she understood and respected him, something he had fought for all his life but never had to fight for with her. She treated him as an equal, as someone who she believed understood her actions. This was why he swore himself to her.

Esheme-maa was different. A bit more like her maa than she cared to admit, but the complete opposite of MaaNem in that she was fiercely protective of the things that mattered to her, whether they went against the tenets of the Bassai Ideal or not. There was something in her that MaaNem lacked: a deep-seated darkness, dangerous yet delicious. When MaaNem assigned him to her after hearing about the yellowskin, he'd only needed to watch Esheme for a few days to see why she needed to be protected. While MaaNem was quite disaffected, separated from the things she did and showing little response toward events and deeds many considered vile and despicable, Esheme possessed the capability to do those same things, but with a highly emotional response, making her all the more dangerous.

And yet, that was exactly the kind of person the household needed to keep its name in this time of adversity.

Oboda rose and dusted the sand off his buttocks. He was never going to find the fugitives this way. If he went back to MaaEsheme with nothing but conjecture that the three must've died in the forest, unlike with MaaNem, he wasn't sure what would become of him after delivering such news.

He went to his own camp, Viasi strutting alongside him, and then running off to join the rest of the leap. He had barely sat down when he heard the flapping of a homing pigeon arriving. He looked up at the pigeon outpost and recognised the bird as one from Nem's household coop. He sent one of his hunthands to return with the message, which the man did.

The little piece of paper had the Nem household symbol behind it, and the letter itself was one simple, frantic expression that he could at least read by way of the few phrases of High Bassai Nem had taught him:

Don't return without them.

Oboda folded the letter and ate it afterward, as was his custom with Nem. He returned to his tent, satisfied that he had been right about MaaEsheme. She was not going to accept a paltry answer from him. He had to do something more. If the fugitives were any kind of smart—and he knew that boy, Danso, was quite the brainy individual—they wouldn't emerge from the Breathing Forest here, or through the bushroads, or the Emperor's Road. They would likely attempt to escape somewhere else, and he knew just what that somewhere else might be.

See, he, Oboda, was smart too. He had watched Esheme, but he had also watched that boy, her intended. There were Shashi in Whudasha. Danso was Shashi. It wasn't difficult to put those two things together and realise where they were headed. And there was only one place to go through if one wanted to land in Whudasha without taking the usual routes and without emerging here for all to see.

"Boyo-oh," he called in Mainland Pidgin. His men, lazing about, stood to attention. "Scatter camp and prepare for saddle. We go make camp for another place."

"Where?" one of them asked.

He reached down and patted Viasi, who had returned, solemn, and now purred under his touch.

"I no know yet," he said, contemplative. "Somewhere with..." He fought for the word for a moment and, when he found it, stabbed the air with his finger, as if pinning it there.

"Somewhere," he said, "with surprise."

29

Zaq

ZAQ KNEW HE WASN'T supposed to be angry. There were many things to be thankful for. They weren't being chased down, for one. At least, not yet. The consequences of entering the Breathing Forest were weighty enough to foster hesitation, but it was only a matter of time before one person made an exception, after which following that person's actions would become easier for others. Especially for civic guards, who could claim backing from the leadership—and would likely get it. For hunt-hands, if the bounty prize was big enough, they might be happy to take it and never return to Bassa again.

But apparently, he was the only one thinking this, as his companions were more fixated on whether they were being hunted by some mythical beast. Danso spent ample time doing two things alone: trying to pinpoint their location each time a breathing event occurred and deducing the timing between them. So far, his efforts weren't necessarily completely useless, but neither had they been yielding significant fruits. They still hadn't pinpointed their relative distance from the Gondola, and his estimation of the pattern of breathing events seemed to be neither right nor wrong, only sufficiently close to be lucky the once or twice it occurred each day. Lilong mostly slept and tried to gain strength. This left Zaq to do most of the work of breaking and making camp for the past four nights, which they had to do in a different place each day, upon Lilong's insistence. *To avoid being easy prey for anything tracking us*, she'd said. Sounded like a perfectly good reason to Zaq, if only he weren't the one doing all the work.

Each of these days was different. On the second day, a downpour had drenched them. Zaq used a broad plantain leaf to catch and funnel enough water to refill their stock. He'd also picked up some more fruit. For meat, Lilong had killed a rodent, her knife moving with swift and menacing alacrity that made Zaq uneasy. Turned out it was being chased by a snake, which she then also had to kill after it almost bit Danso. On the third day, finding a spot had proven treacherous, as the terrain had suddenly become steep and inclined for reasons unknown to them. Finding a new camp spot had taken much longer, and they'd had to deal with one breathing event during this time. By the time they found camp, they had been so exhausted that no one ate anything. They'd simply made a fire and crashed into sleep.

But for Zaq, the days passed as if the same. He awoke with Mokhiri's name on his lips, his heart aching badly for her. At night, he would look up at the stars and wonder if Mokhiri was looking up at them too. He wondered what she thought about his absence, how she felt. Angry? Sad? Worried? She had to have heard by now that he was a fugitive alongside an intruder and her helper. Did she still believe in him—believe in them? If he returned unharmed tomorrow, would she still want to be with him? These questions plagued him whenever he slept, and he navigated each day in a sullen trancelike state of repetitive motions, wondering what devil had possessed him to listen to Danso and come along on this journey. If he found a chance, should he take it? Would Bassa take him back now? Did he pose a greater threat to himself—and to Mokhiri—if he returned than if he pressed on? The questions rattled around in his brain like peanuts swirled in a fist.

Now, at sunset on the fourth day, he was nearly at his wits' end. Lilong's strength had returned to a considerable level, and Danso had announced they were finally able to move on to higher ground, where he said pinpointing their location would be much easier. But Zaq's concern was this: *How come the girl got to dictate their every move?* How was she yet to let on so much about herself, but Danso was constantly letting on everything about them? Even that tiny little pouch of hers, tied to her waist for dear life, she had yet to divulge what was in it.

Tonight, she and Danso sat by the fire, chatting away, while Zaq prepared the pack for the next day's journey. *How has she won him over so?* he asked himself as he listened to them banter. Wasn't this the same Danso who had found it difficult to bond with his own intended in this way? Yet here he was in fraternity with this invader, this murderer.

Zaq rummaged through the bag, furiously stuffing in everything they weren't using for the night. Little shit had not even apologised for ruining his life. If they were caught now, Danso was a Bassai Idu man and would at least be accorded that honour, even in arrest and possible execution. He, however, no matter how hard he had worked to be close to the Bassai Ideal, was a Yelekuté, the closest to a nonperson there was. He might not even get to open his mouth in plea. He didn't leave his old life behind to cross the border and die like this.

The two of them, completely oblivious to his predicament, continued to trade childhood myths.

"They used to tell us if a yellowskin points at a pregnant woman and laughs, evil spirits would steal her baby and replace it with a yellowskin," Danso was saying. "And that if we stay in the sun too long, we'd turn to yellowskins."

"Well, our Elders used to tell us you lot were cursed, too," Lilong replied. "They said your people didn't have souls, and that was why you couldn't use ibor."

"They told us *you people* were cursed. They said Menai punished you by removing your top layer of skin, that's why you're yellow."

"What—" Lilong shook her head and made a click in the back of her throat. "Okay, I don't like this game anymore. Let's look at your map."

Danso did as she said, spreading out the makeshift map he'd been drawing with charcoal on a piece of clothing over the last few days.

"Okay, so once we make high ground tomorrow, we will definitely be able to locate the Gondola before the day ends. With that much rainfall from the other day, we can even locate it by sound."

"But we're not *following* it, though, right?" Lilong said. "Just tracing it?"

"Of course," Danso said. "You never know who could be on the bushroads. We just need to locate where we are relative to it, then follow its flow direction coastward. Combine that with the sun's location, and we can trace our way pretty easily to the bight."

"How long do you figure from here to Whudasha?"

"Two to three days on foot, barring mishaps. Once we clear the forest, things should be much easier and move much faster."

"Well, you would think a savanna is less dangerous than your forest, breathing or not, but you would be wrong."

"A what now?" Danso said, and even Zaq turned to look at her then.

Lilong pulled a stick from the fire, blew at it so that only the black charcoal end was left, and then drew on the map. Menai hovered, so it was bright enough to see by her red light. Zaq finished his task and drew closer to them.

He was familiar with the divisions of the mainland and roughly knew where everything was—the local government councils ensured every immigrant did. However, he saw that she was circling a particular area, not far from the edge of where the Breathing Forest was supposed to continue down to the coast.

"Here," she said.

"No, that's just more forest," Zaq said.

Lilong frowned at him. "You don't know?" She looked to Danso, who shook his head too.

"Forests are dying, changing to grasslands," she said. "Everywhere on the continent."

Zaq and Danso looked at each other.

"Wait, wait," Danso said. "For a start, savannas only occur *outside* the mainland."

This was true. Chugoko, which Zaq had left before crossing into the mainland, was the largest city in the Savanna Belt, nestling between the Soke border to its south and the Sahel to its north in a way that ensured that all trade toward the mainland went through it. Zaq knew what Lilong was talking about when she said *savanna*: the dwindling water, the lack of dense vegetation, the wide-open land that offered little protection. But Zaq also knew that Chugoko was the closest thing to a savanna the mainland could claim proximity to. There was no way there was one on the mainland itself.

This young woman was up to something.

"There is a wetland savanna forming here," she said, pointing again. "One of the things I learned about the mainland was that if one arrived by coast, one could take either the Emperor's Road or the savannas and bushroads to get to the city." She pointed to where he had drawn the Tombolo, the river that went in the opposite direction of the Gondola, sporting similar forests and ending where the fishing hamlets would be. "There are also savannas forming in these forests. In fact, I would make an educated guess and say all your forests are being encroached on by grassland."

"And you learned this from where?" Danso asked. "I'm a jali novitiate and I've never heard any such thing."

She squeezed her nose at him. "Then it is your jalis who need to update their knowledge. Our league of warriors sends skinchangers into the desertland every now and then to bring back news about the world beyond the seven islands. I was training to do that before I came here. We may have never come to the mainland before, but your deported immigrants—the actual people who know your land better than you do because they engage more often with it—bring us all the stories we need. We islanders believe it is our duty to glean this information, to know more about our enemies than they do about us."

Danso looked down, sheepish. Zaq, unconvinced, said: "Well, those stories cannot be right."

She looked at him. "You believe your fellow desertlanders are lying?"

Zaq pursed his lips. "I'm not saying that. I'm saying, yes, the vegetation could be thinner upon approaching the coast. But it's the Breathing Forest all the same."

"No, it is not," Lilong said. "All over the continent, forests are dying. And I know you lot think you're special, but your forests aren't. Why do you think there have been increased migrations toward your border? Food and water shortages have been increasing steadily for seasons. You take all these things from the land and do not replenish, and the land remembers." She pointed at the encircled portion again. "Portions like these are most at risk. The animals and plants there are changing habits and adapting in accordance."

Danso and Zaq looked at one another.

"Still cannot get over how you know more about the mainland than I do," Danso muttered.

Lilong's lips thinned. "Focus. Listen to what I'm telling you. We must prepare for the savanna. It can be quite as dangerous as in here. Perhaps even more so, since there is no hiding place." She paused. "I in particular must prepare even more."

"Because?" Danso asked.

"I don't do very well in the sun." She put up a hand before Danso could open his mouth. "No, no further questions, please."

Zaq frowned. Something was afoot with this young woman, wasn't it? First she was manufacturing savannas on the mainland out of thin air, and now she was giving instructions on how they were to proceed. How could it be that a random person he would never have engaged with in his everyday Bassai life was suddenly dictating his very future? Had he really fallen this far?

"So you won't offer us more information about yourself or your people—or even whatever it is you're carrying in that pouch—but you suddenly want to tell us how we must get to the coast?" Zaq was surprised at the harshness of his own voice. "You want us to follow the word of you, a stranger from nowhere, over that of the manuscripts in the University of Bassa, the only university on this continent?"

Lilong regarded him with the expression of an exasperated parent. "First of all, yours is not the only university on this continent—"

"Do I look like I care what you believe?" Zaq said. "From the moment you stepped into our lives, your actions have been trying to get us killed. And I'm supposed to just suddenly trust your word now?"

"Zaq?" Danso frowned. "Where is all this coming from?"

Lilong's gaze toward Zaq darkened.

"Prior to a few days ago, people like me did not exist to you all in this land," she said, her formerly benign tone now developing edges. "In many ways, we still don't. So don't speak like I'm the one causing your problems. You had problems long before me." She pointed to the stone-bones embedded into her upper arm. "I've done nothing but expend myself and my resources to protect us all since. Remember how you almost died falling? Or by snakebite? If you want, I'm happy to spend this energy protecting my interests alone."

"Wait, you two—" Danso was saying.

"Isn't that what you've been doing all along anyway?" Zaq pressed. "Isn't that why you murdered our nation's own Speaker?"

Lilong rose in one move, suddenly standing over Zaq. Danso stepped into the space between them, his back to Lilong. He held a hand between each, his eyes on Zaq.

"Okay, Zaq," he said. "We have established that she did not kill Abuso."

"And you believe her?" Zaq said, rising to match them. "You believe something unprovable from the mouth of a stranger over the word of your own land?"

Danso regarded him quizzically. "What is wrong with you? You're acting crazy."

"Me, crazy? *I'm* the crazy one?" Zaq pointed to the map. "Fine, let's say there truly is a savanna. I grew up in one, so I can tell you there's no way we will not become easy pickings for just about anyone or anything once we get into that open space. This forest may be just the thing saving us now. Set aside the reality that there will definitely be civic guards and hunthands prowling the edges, waiting for us to emerge. If we manage to evade them, do you not know what lives in savannas? That is where leopards are caught before taming, Danso. Wild, ferocious things, not those you see that Oboda and his hunthands have, no. We're talking hyenas, cheetahs, lions." He pointed to Lilong. "*This woman* knows that, and she's using it to scare us, steer us in a direction for moons know what. Following her word has been dangerous from the start—every step we have taken with her has put us in more danger. And it's *me* who's the crazy person for saying we should question her motives?"

"I trust her judgement," Danso said, after looking thoughtful for a moment. "So far, she has not demonstrated any bad faith, and she has every right to be suspicious of us. Yes, you, too, have every right to be suspicious. But I'm asking you to trust me, as your charge. Trust my trust in her."

Lilong scoffed. "You know what? I cannot." She threw her charcoal stick into the fire, sending up embers. She dusted her buttocks, turned away, then turned back to them for a moment.

"You know what?" she said. "He's right. You shouldn't trust me. But what we need to survive this journey is not trust, it is fortitude, something you two clearly seem to lack. But if you don't already know that all three of us need a bit of each other to survive, then you two haven't really come to terms with this journey. Maybe you need to talk to each other, sort out your personal problems." She regarded the two men. "I'll be over here."

With that, she wandered away. Danso faced Zaq.

"You're not angry at her," he said. "You're angry at me."

The accusation caught Zaq off-guard. He bit his lip and forced himself to stay silent. If he opened his mouth, he was not sure of the words that would be spoken.

"Say it," Danso said. "Say it with your chest."

So I have to spell it out? Can't he see? All Zaq wanted was for the nation to know he was a dedicated immigrant, that he wasn't really one of those desertlanders who came here because they had no choice. He *chose* to come here, to leave his whole life behind. That had cost him, and he didn't plan to return, not ever. There was nowhere to return to.

But here was Danso, nonchalantly taking that away from him. What would he say to Mokhiri, if he ever saw her again? What arguments would he make now for his advancement to Potokin? Danso's thoughtlessness had started for him a path of regression, a backward journey whose continuance would inevitably lead to the same border he had given everything up to cross, abandoned all on the other side to commit to. And rather than take responsibility for that, here Danso was, trading childhood stories and playing house with the very reason this journey had begun at all. He had chosen to lie with the enemy at Zaq's own expense.

"Zaq?" Danso said.

"You didn't even ask me," Zaq said. "You made me come, a decision that will change my whole life, and you didn't even consider the weight of that sacrifice for me. You didn't wonder, *How can I protect Zaq, who doesn't have the same privileges as me?* You made me come, because you think me dispensable."

The fire crackled into the night, ensconced by cricket and frog sounds.

"Zaq, I thought..." Danso said.

"I should never have followed you here," Zaq said. "I will regret it until the day I die."

He turned away, back to the pack, making the decision there and then: He was *done*.

By Menai, once they arrived in Whudasha, this journey was over for him. He would find a way to return to Bassa, beg for forgiveness. He would even lie if he had to, say he was kidnapped and bewitched by the yellowskin and her sorcery. It wouldn't be hard to believe, would it? He could persuade the moon temple to waive the punishment for entering the Breathing Forest. He'd done it under duress, had he not? That should count for something. And even if they disagreed and insisted on punishing him, at least he would go down with more honour than getting caught and dragged back like a runaway goat.

Danso

THE REST OF THE night was spent in tension, Danso taking first watch with Zaq and second watch with Lilong. Zaq refused to speak to him throughout, still angry. Danso gave up after a while and they both sat in silence. This wasn't the first time they had quarrelled, but this felt different, like something had cracked between them. Danso was unsure whether to feel guilty about dragging Zaq along. He thought he had been doing him a favour, but in retrospect, he realised maybe he had simply been projecting his own desires onto his Second. But that remorse was now countered by Zaq's staunch position about returning to Bassa being the better choice, even when that place was at odds with Danso's very existence. He found himself incensed that an outlander, one who had been bullied at every turn by the mainland itself, turned out to be the anti-islander in this group. How could both those things exist in one mind? Just the idea that Zaq held ill feelings toward Lilong because she was from a different place so angered Danso that the air between them was stiff with unresolve.

Lilong sat close at second watch, closer than she'd ever been since they met. He could feel the heat of her body next to him, elevated, though she didn't look feverish. He couldn't tell if the yellow in her eyes was the usual or a result of jaundice.

"Are you okay?" Danso asked, reaching to touch her slightly. She flinched and he withdrew. "Your temperature is so high I can feel it all the way over here."

"I'm fine," she said, wiping sweat from her brow.

"Look," he said, "I don't know if it's your way to mask how much you're suffering, but—" She shot him a look, but he pressed on. "*But*, those aren't small wounds. You have to take it easy before you collapse."

"Then you leave me and continue on your journey to your people." She looked at him. "That is most important, right?"

"What? No." Danso sighed. "I mean, yes, it's important, but not at your expense."

She scoffed. "And you care because what?"

He wanted to tell her the truth. She was a window to a world he had only dreamt of, and the fact that she was sitting here now, talking to him, was a manifestation of his dreams and a vindication of his blind belief. Did people just let dreams come true walk away? Did people just let windows into their past, their future, the possible key to discovering the essence of their very being, die from stupid wounds?

He gulped and said nothing. She retrieved a small whetstone she had made out of a rock she'd found, pulled out her gemstone-hilted blade— longer now, up close, than Danso had initially thought it to be—and began to polish it, slowly, piercing the night with its ringing.

"We were told all the islands had sunk, did you know?" He scratched his head. "I grew up thinking of my maa below the sea, wondering if she was cold. Now, I don't know what parts of what I know are real or true anymore. And I want to. I want to know and be free." He looked up. "You asked why I care? About you, about all of this? That's why. Because you—and all of this—are my chance to learn that truth."

She stared at him for a bit. "Tell me: What else were you told?"

Danso shrugged. "What *wasn't* I told? That my maa's people came here to escape their sinking islands. That they waged war on Bassa using sorcery, so Bassa drove them back to their sinking islands. That their men raped our women, and their women bewitched our men into childbearing, so that Shashi like me could be born. Apparently, the Ajabo wanted to take over the continent by bearing an army of Shashi children." He scoffed. Now that he thought about it, how could he believe such a story? It sounded so thin, in retrospect. "As the jalis say, when all the antelopes in the forest are dead, the hunter's tales are all we have left."

"And you believe them, these hunter's tales?"

Danso shrugged. "Honestly, I don't know what to believe anymore. But that is why I want to know, so I can believe."

Lilong nodded. Cricket noises and owl cries bit into the quiet, punctured intermittently by the ringing of her rock against her blade's iron.

"They were right, though, about the islands sinking," Lilong said, and Danso raised his eyebrows. "Yes. I told you Oon has been dying for a long time. Deserts drying up, but also the great waters eating away at our islands. It should be just as apparent on your coasts, if you looked close enough, but you Bassai never go there, so you never see. For us, it is our everyday reality. My people have never travelled to the opposite side of Oon, so I'm sorry I can't tell you if the Ajabo islands have sunk. But old tales of their demise still circulate, if you listen hard to stories told in the fringes of the desertland. Our forebears sure believed them, and they must have inspired the decision to stay hidden, protect ourselves from the mainland's greed." She paused her sharpening to punctuate the moment. "My people believe it was lies, by the way, all those stories about the Ajabo. If they left their islands, it was out of fear of them sinking, not that they came seeking to conquer the mainland. If my people have to leave tomorrow, it would be for that reason too. I believe the Ajabo only wanted to keep their people safe, alive."

Danso thought it sounded like something he believed his maa would do.

"Bassa is the culprit here, the ones who wanted the ibor they arrived with but not the people themselves," Lilong continued. "And when your emperors targeted them, they did not surrender it, and must have had to defend themselves with it. Your last emperor used that excuse to crush them by the strength of numbers, so much so that they chose an honourable return over dishonourable death on a foreign land. They built new dhows, powered them with the last of their ibor, sailed over the great waters, and went back to die on their sinking islands."

"A moment," Danso said, a finger up. "What do you mean *dhows*? Bassa stopped trying to sail because the seas proved too erratic, low tides extending like the Emperor's Road, waves as high as many iroko trees stacked together. But you're saying the Ajabo crossed these same seas in some sort of ibor-powered—dhows, you called them?"

"Without ibor, whatever water vessel one builds is crushed to death before it even leaves the beach. But if you know how to build a sturdy dhow and gather the right combination of Grey Iborworkers to steady the waters, you can. We do it all the time."

"Interesting. I believe our scholars once tried to figure out how the Ajabo crossed but couldn't. It was why the mainland gave up any form of seafaring." He filed that away mentally. "Anyway, we'll come back to that. Now that we're on the topic, tell me: In your stories, did any mainlanders—say, our last emperor—wield ibor? Or is it just you island-ers who can?"

Lilong was thoughtful for a bit. "I believe anyone can use ibor, not just us."

Danso's eyes widened. "Really?"

"No—well..." Lilong shifted in her seat. "My people believe other-wise, but I think anyone, not just islanders, can learn to wield at least one type of ibor. It's just a mineral, right? The power is inside it. One's ability to connect is like any other talent, like being able to play a lute, for instance. Everyone has hands, see, but playing a lute either comes naturally or must be learned over a long time. In the same way, anyone may stumble upon their connection to ibor, but may also find it with the right training. Back home, the Abenai League—the league of warriors dedicated to protecting our secrets, of which I'm a part—they train those of us with the most natural connections. Not necessarily to learn how to *use* this power, but to understand the responsibility of possessing it, and how to avoid hurting ourselves and others.

"Our only luck is that, as far as we know, ibor has only ever depos-ited on islands, and that's possibly why today's mainlanders would never encounter it enough in the first place to figure out that they could use it. More difficult if they don't even believe the islands exist."

The Manic Emperor's words were starting to make sense to Danso. Nogowu had written that the first landers—what Danso deduced to be referring to the Ajabo—had never been keen on migrating inland. That was how Whudasha as a protectorate was first founded, and the first iteration of the Peace Fence built to keep them there. But somehow, Nogowu must have been the only emperor to discover their use of ibor.

I led a delegation to engage with the first landers, he had written in the codex, *to ask of them what price for their full integration into the mainland. This, my antecedents had only tentatively attempted, but I was determined to bring the first landers under my prerogative, and do so by force if I had to.*

Now, Danso realised Nogowu had pretty much asked the Ajabo to exchange their ibor for induction into the mainland. Their refusal had sparked the Second Great War, under the guise of them being a threat to the mainland. This had to be why Lilong's people hid, wasn't it? They knew if they mingled with the mainland and desertland, someone would finally figure out that anyone could use ibor if they tried hard enough. And after witnessing what Lilong could do with it, Danso could clearly see the danger that information posed. Perhaps it was better for the continent that the islanders and their secrets stayed away. Perhaps it was better that the histories of mainland-island interactions told at jali guild held more fabrication than truth. Perhaps a good lie was sometimes better for all.

"This...connection to ibor," he said. "How does one come about it?"

"We get tested as children," said Lilong. "Again, like playing a lute. Put it in your hands, see what you do with it. The Abenai League decides what strain of stone-bone your connection is strongest with and if you're worth training further. Mostly, they teach us basic iborworking—Draw, Possess, Command. After that, just like a musician, you play whatever tune comes most naturally. Some learn quicker and get better very fast; some never progress beyond basic. Everyone uses ibor differently—no two people employ ibor in the exact same way."

"And then a mainlander figured out how to connect and use it." Danso could see it now. "That's why you came here, isn't it? It was Nem, wasn't it?"

Lilong muttered a quiet "Yes," and held a breath before saying, "But I did not cross the border for the ibor alone. I followed because she tried to kill my daa."

Danso frowned. "That's not—possible. Nem has not left the mainland in a long time."

"Not by her own hand," Lilong said. "She sent her hunthands to find someone, someone it turns out my daa was meeting and sharing ibor's secrets with. He ended up being attacked, and all his ibor was stolen from him." She looked to the sky. "He was trying to help us, you know? Perhaps trying to garner more allies—he always believed we should do that. It is impossible for us to continue hiding, he said, that with so much migration happening all over the continent, we would be discovered soon enough." She shook her head, as if trying to clear the memory. "The Abenai League—they want him tried, if he ever heals from his injuries. He had yet to awaken when I left." She looked up again. "I wonder if he has now."

Danso nodded slowly. Frogs croaked in the silence between them.

"I left by slipping away at night," Lilong said. "Travelled a long way, tracked his path to the Weary Sojourner Caravansary. It was in ashes. Found the housekeep, who told me the story of my daa's altercation with the hunthands, then pointed me toward the border, toward the men who had started it all. I tracked the caravan. I had to get that ibor back, or my family was doomed. My plan was simple: slip in, steal it, return without incident. But things went sideways, and I ended up stowing away with them over the border. And now, here I am, stuck in a forest, heading nowhere near home." She swore in an alien language, which Danso knew was a swear because they sounded the same in every language. "A nightmare, this. Everything that could go wrong has."

"Well, at least you got what you came for?" Danso eyed the pouch. Lilong eyed him back but said nothing.

"So they found you because of the stowaway. But how did you discover it was Nem?"

"I trailed the big one, what's his name?"

"Oboda."

"That one. I saw him with your woman friend. Followed her, she led me to you. Then I followed you and ended up in your barn."

Danso's eyes widened. "You used me to get to Nem?"

"No, I needed a place to rest and heal. The complication I spoke of earlier? Bandits, before I found the caravan. I had to fight them off, and I got injured. That's why I ended up stowing away so long in the caravan—because I needed to heal. Wielding ibor is harder when I'm weak or injured, and I ended up spending too long in the caravan. By the time I could use ibor again, we were over the border, and I was spotted before I could change skin. After so much hiding and running, I needed a safe place to continue my recharge. Your barn just had some good hiding places."

"And you were there for how long?"

"A day? Two? It was dark, I don't know. Your Second came in once or twice, briefly. But when you came in, opening up the underground hatches, I knew I'd be found if I didn't act." She looked at him. "I didn't plan to attack you or anything. I also did not plan to eat your yams."

"Oh, so you were the one eating our yams? We thought it was rats!"

"They tasted like shit." She wrinkled her nose in disgust. Danso thought it was almost cute. He pantomimed vomiting and they laughed.

"And then you found Nem," Danso said.

"And then I found Nem." Lilong turned her neck so it creaked. "The big one worked for her, and therefore I knew she likely had what I sought. I had to wait until the festival night to find an opening. I expected the house to be mostly empty and with a decent sweep, I'd find wherever she might have buried it. Turned out she didn't attend the festival." Lilong shrugged. "I didn't plan to attack her either. My one focus was my duty to the Abenai League, and to my daa. Still, though, she got what she deserved."

Danso found the feeling of not being too moved over Nem's demise discomfiting.

"I couldn't take the chance that it wouldn't respond to her, mainlander or not," Lilong said. "Ibor can be very selective about who it responds to, and no one knows what the criteria are, just like we don't know how talent is distributed. The Abenai League has been protecting this secret for hundreds of seasons. I couldn't let it slip."

Danso could get with that. He remembered Habba's stories of the Shashi pogroms, of how he had connived with dissenting groups at the time to hide Danso away, passing him from family to family while Bassai citizens hunted every Shashi in the capital city. He had done this for seasons, until the Peace Treaty was signed and he could finally reveal Danso without fear. Of course Danso had been much too young—a baby, practically—to remember anything. But he saw the fire of pride in his daa's eyes whenever he spoke of this. It was the same kind of fire in Lilong's eyes now, the kind that said, *I would die before letting this secret go.*

"So you were trained to...?" He waved over her. "To do the skin thing?" Now that he had got her talking, he wanted to ask as much as he could.

"Mmm-hmm." During his reverie, she had begun eating some nuts they had picked up earlier. She spat out the chaff. "Top layer of your skin is dead, did you know? Inanimate, so it's susceptible to Commands by the kind of ibor I can wield. I'm able to Possess it just like my knife, but in a different way. First time is always the hardest—you can die if you do it wrong—but it gets easier after that."

"Hmm." *Look at me,* Danso thought. *Brightest jali on the continent, yet everything I know is either useless or a lie.* Apparently, when it came to the things that mattered in the world, he knew absolutely nothing.

"Your people," he said. "You never told me what you're called."

Lilong paused for so long that Danso asked: "Is that a bad question?"

"Not really." She threw away the rest of the nuts, then began digging absent-mindedly at something on the ground. "It's just...if the Abenai League knew I was telling you all of this, I would be instantly executed." She laughed, almost as if she relished the idea. "Maybe not getting out of here won't be such a bad thing after all."

Danso was unsure if she was joking or not.

"Ihinyon," she said.

"Sorry?"

"That's what we're called. Ihinyon. In Island Common, it means *seven,* for the number of islands in the archipelago."

"Wow. And here we were just going about calling you Nameless."

"We *want* you to think of us as nameless. But we're anything but. In fact, each island has its own name. I'm from Namge, the largest and closest to the continent, but there's also Hoor, which is next to us and second largest. After Hoor, there's Ololo, island of our toughest warriors. Then there's Edana and Ufua, the twins. After that, Sibu-Sibu, our food basket. The tiniest and last island, Ofen, is our baby. Much is still undiscovered there, with only a few hamlets scattered about." She straightened, a semi-wistful smile on her face. "I'm proud to be Ihinyon. I'm proud to be yellow, and if given the chance, I wouldn't rather be anything else."

Lilong resumed her whetstone polishing. For a while, there was nothing but the rock on iron and crickets and frogs breaking the silence.

"You can see your leaders are trying their best to keep us enemies, right?" Lilong said out of nowhere. "Stoking the fires of hatred? They know the Bassai need something to hate, and they have made it us, if only to obscure their own misdeeds. They have turned us into demons and murderers that we're not."

"Well," Danso said, "the attacks on Nem and the Speaker don't help that cause much."

She shot him a silencing look. "I did not kill your Speaker, I've said this. That woman Nem killed him and blamed it on me because she knew no one would doubt that the yellowskin did it."

"No, I didn't say—"

"I don't care what you said, you implied it." She threw both whetstone and blade down on the ground in frustration. "You mainlanders are all the same, murdering and exploiting people all your lives, then pointing fingers when you get the same in response. I've just told you of the atrocities first committed against me, but somehow it is me under scrutiny?"

Danso opened his mouth to say something, but Lilong put up a finger. "Nem deserved to die. I would gladly kill her again if it means she, or anyone who comes in her name, does not hurt anyone else. My days of hiding and silence are over. One thing you will learn, Danso, is that many times, killing people may be the only path to freedom, because the only other option is losing your own life."

Zaq awoke, grumbling groggily. "What's going on?"

"Nothing," Lilong said, and stood. "Go to sleep." To Danso, she said: "I'll go take my watch over here."

The rest of the night was spent in silence.

Esheme

CLOAKED BY MIDNIGHT, ESHEME tucked herself further into the corner of the Fifteenth Ward corridor in which she stood.

She had never gone past Tenth before. She was so used to clean passageways richly decorated with art that when she arrived here, she almost felt like she was no longer in Bassa. All her temperate ideas about what the poorer wards could possibly look like immediately dissipated when she spotted the first coterie of giant rats, deposited faeces, and homeless people. She suddenly thanked the moons for her choice of clothing—an old, threaded bunch of wrappers—and Satti's suggestion that her plaits be loosened and replaited into just one arch. That was the only reason no one really looked at her twice now. She was as close to the average woman of this ward as she could possibly hope for. Luckily, it was also night, which helped mask how polished her skin was, how confidently facepaint sat on her face, so that only someone who looked closely enough could tell she was a fish out of water here, an Idu in Potokin and Yelekuté land.

Everything here was sparsely lit, the corridors even less so than the mainways. Handheld palm oil lamps carried by passersby cast smoky lights on the red earth of the corridors. A civic guard or two showed up every now and then, but they paid her little attention, choosing instead to harass those who looked much poorer and more vulnerable than she did, shaking them down for bribes and paying no attention to actual dangerous-looking types.

All of this was familiar, but only distantly, and much stranger now that she was standing in front of it, like a new injury that only hurt upon sight. It felt odd because Esheme remembered meeting a lot more Poto-kin and Yelekuté that weren't househands and aides when she was a child. Now, the gap between castes had stretched so far that the inner wards felt like a separate nation from the outer wards. The Pass closure perhaps made it worse, and being so far out of sight of Bassai leadership meant that no matter how dire the effects were on these people, they would be completely ignored. There was truth in the popular Bassai adage: *Everything deteriorates with distance from the beating heart of the Great Dome.* A heart could only do so much for the organs too far to feel its influence.

Squalor wasn't the only defining trait she noticed about Fifteenth, though. There was also a difference in the way the people moved. A distinct energy existed alongside the palpable despair in a way that would never exist back in Fourth or any of the innermost wards. There was a reason they called Fifteenth the *laughing capital*, because despite all of the most depressing news in Bassa coming out of here, the response of the people wasn't anger—it was humour. She had heard more laughter here than she heard daily back in Fourth. She knew it was only a mask, though, a coping mechanism. The outer wards also had the highest incidences of looting, unhinged violence, and petty unorganised crimes that led to fatalities. In counsel guild, they had a saying: *A dying people do not laugh unless they are willing to die as one.*

Esheme scooted further into the shadows, hugged herself and wrapped her wrapper tighter. She was suddenly worried about standing there alone. She wasn't really alone—Satti stood a few feet away, alongside one of the two hunthands Oboda had left behind. She didn't want to spook the person she was meeting, so she'd asked them to keep a distance. But in this moment, she realised she needed something she hadn't needed in a long time: comfort. Warmth.

She squinted into the dark, trying to make sense of the faces that went by her, to see if any of them was the person looking for her. She couldn't even quite catch the conversations that happened between people as they went by. They spoke a form of Mainland Common so heavily slanged it sounded like border pidgin—probably influenced by the high Yelekuté population here.

Suddenly, a man approached her, harried and stone-faced. Her first instinct was to give the danger sign she and Satti had agreed upon, thinking the man an attacker. But he wordlessly produced a piece of paper. She didn't need to look at it to know what it was. She had written this letter.

She nodded, and the man said: "Follow me."

Esheme whistled low, the *I'm okay, don't follow, wait for me* sign to Satti and the hunthand, and followed the man.

He took her down a winding corridor or two, then promptly disappeared, leaving her standing in the dank courtyard of a shantylike building that, at first glance, looked like it had no doors and was closed up with bamboo. Then a section of the bamboo opened in invitation, and Esheme stepped into a room of smoke and oil lamps and came face-to-face with the man she sought.

Even before Dọta's Second accosted her at the Moon Temple, Esheme had already been thinking about getting reinforcements to protect herself and her house. She did not command the same authority as Nem did, the same ability to colonize minds. Having her maa laid low like this, coupled with the blatant and public disrespect by Ariase, everyone now likely thought of her and her household as ripe for the taking. She couldn't abide that. She had to find protection in the interim, especially now that Oboda was away.

So she'd opened up her maa's journal and found the contact she was befuddled yet unsurprised that her maa had. She hadn't necessarily been looking for this man in particular—she simply sought someone who met two requirements: One, they were not above accepting gold and copper from a fixer's daughter, and two, they were out of reach of intimidation and control by any of the highest powers in the land. Of the few in Bassa who met these two conditions, this man was the most likely to be uninfluenced by Dọta, and of course her maa had the secret information about how to contact him. Esheme wrote him a letter and had Satti deliver it as the journal instructed.

"That's a good trick," she said.

The leader of the Coalition for New Bassa might have dressed down to fit into the ward like she did, but his sharp-edged cheekbones also told a story of the perils of advocacy. Basuaye came from lowly beginnings but was one of those people whom the sky gods created with a special gift.

He had the ability to speak in a way that people would listen and, most importantly, agree. There was even a Bassai term named after him—to be *basuayed* was to be convinced, to the point of advocacy, about something one didn't necessarily understand. It had been touted that he employed powers of sorcery to achieve this, so effective was his tongue. But no evidence had been brought forward to prove it, even though many had tried, especially those who didn't want him speaking about the decline of the Bassai nation, about the continuous poverty-induced expansion of the outer wards toward the hinterlands, about its leaders and how they did nothing for the people but siphoned the land's resources for their own welfare.

Most Idu and at least half of the Emuru population were especially critical of him. He not only criticized Bassa's caste enforcement, exposing its hypocrisy and design to keep out people deemed worthy, but also spoke to mismanagement of resources, decisions that impacted the people and the land poorly, the injustice and impunity of the civic guard. In the beginning, he was punished in every way possible short of death—threats, arrests, torture. Every member of his family had been either captured or killed. But Basuaye kept coming back, which gained him a huge popularity and earned him the nickname *the Cockroach*. Now, his name was known across the nation by enemies and supporters alike, which made any blatant attempt by the government to neutralise him impossible. His advocacy had grown beyond the man and become a movement, crystallized into the present coalition, now an institution with its own leadership and support that outnumbered both Bassai leadership and security forces alike. Hundreds of people all over the nation carried out demonstrations in his name, calling for a return to the heyday of emperors, when the nation's power and resources were at an all-time high and Bassa's might waxed strong across the continent.

Yet the man who stood in front of Esheme, both hands tucked into his wrappers, looked nothing like the tough, weathered, cockroachlike man she had always envisioned him to be. He was elderly and thin, appearing more like a scholar than anything else, but with steady eyes and a firm stance. He appraised Esheme slowly, as if this were an interview and not a hurried, secret meeting in a Fifteenth Ward safe house.

"Your maa," he said by way of greeting. "How is she?"

"Recovering," Esheme said. "Slowly."

"Hmm." He sat, and waved for Esheme to do the same. The room was partially decorated—good furniture, a piece of art or craft work or two—despite it being a hideout. Esheme imagined that he had one or so of these in every ward.

"I would've come to visit," he said, "but, you know."

"I understand."

"I hear she tried to fight off an invader who—if I'm hearing correctly— was using ibor?" Esheme nodded slightly, and Basuaye shook his head. "This woman. How do the oddest things happen to follow her?"

They both made disapproving sounds from their throats, together, like an old, married couple, then chortled at their shared protectiveness.

"Will she live?" he asked, when finally solemn. It was a question no one had dared ask, that everyone was afraid to. Esheme could now see why he graced the pages of her maa's journal. He was important enough to fear little, and fearless enough to risk things others couldn't. Just the kind of person she wanted in her corner.

"Does it matter?" Esheme said, finally, admitting to herself, for the first time, that it didn't. "She will never be the same, even if she wakes up. My household caretaker said that she overheard the healer commenting that she might never walk again."

He nodded, slowly. "I see your visits have been limited." He looked over her, devoid of accusation. "I would have the same reaction, if I had Nem for a maa."

"I need your help," she said, straight to the point.

"I know." He retrieved a pipe, pinched some tobacco into its chamber, and lit it, blowing smoke to a side. "Who is it?"

"A First Elder. Trying to blackmail me and my household."

He nodded, pensive. "How long do you have?" No question about what was owed.

"Not long. He will be at Abuso's funeral, most likely, as will I. I don't suppose I will walk out of there without giving him what he wants, even if it's just assurance that I will provide it. And even that assurance, I don't have."

"And this thing, is it in any way related to the invader who attacked your maa?"

Esheme paused, watching his face. He seemed genuinely curious and nothing more.

"It is." When he lifted an eyebrow, she said: "I have sent my own men to capture the invader. Until that happens, I cannot give the First Elder what he wants. I need protection."

"So you want this First Elder delayed."

"If it'll keep me and my household alive, yes," she said. "He hasn't explicitly said he'll do anything—but he's a powerful man. I must be cautious."

"Indeed." Basuaye put the pipe down.

"You will be well compensated."

He put up a palm. "Please, don't insult me. If you found a way to contact me at all, then you already know I owe your maa. And if I've agreed to listen to you, then you'd better believe I already want to help you. But your money is not the decider here—"

"I know you need it." Esheme offered a triumphant, wry smile. "I know you lost your largest source of funding and I know it was the Speaker's eldest daughter, who has now gone over the Soke Pass. This means you are suddenly short of support, and very soon, your campaigns will dwindle as a result."

He paused for a while, perhaps considering how she had come upon that information, and weighing how much to tell her and how much to hold back. Then he made a face that showed he had decided none of it mattered at this point.

"I never said we don't need your money. The coalition has fallen on hard times with having to run on fewer resources and all of that exacerbated by the Pass closure. So, yes, I *will* need your money, and am very much interested in it. But I'm actually not in the position to make the final decision on assigning you protection."

"Who is?"

"My generals," Basuaye said.

Esheme frowned. "I didn't know you had generals."

"Oh, I don't." Basuaye smiled. "I do not have generals at all."

Esheme caught the drift. Now it made sense how he managed to survive attacks. You couldn't ambush someone who had secret ambushes of his own.

"If you need help to delay the councilhand, then we can work toward that. One of my generals will have to *choose* to work for you, though. They are not my employees and I cannot make them do anything."

"All right, then," Esheme said. "Let me talk to them."

"Not here," he said. "Not today. We will schedule another meeting for that. Remember, I have no generals, so I can't be seen meeting with generals I do not have." He winked.

Esheme had never given much thought to having a daa, a male presence in the house. The concept was alien, like a tree branch sprouting from a dog. But sitting here with this man, a certain camaraderie had arisen between them that nudged her mind in that direction for a moment. She shook it off.

"Before then, though," Basuaye continued, "let me do one better with your proposition. If this goes through, how about, instead of *delay*, we go for bigger? Rather than go for the limbs, how about we go for the throat?"

She angled her head at him. She did not quite like the turn in this conversation.

"I'm listening," she said, simply.

"I mean, look at you," he said, leaning back to appraise her. "Despite all the things in your household that could've steered you differently, you ended up accomplished. That's the definition of commitment, right there. You are the epitome of the Bassai nation in its peak glory. And if there is anything the Coalition for New Bassa needs to further its cause, it is someone like you: a living, breathing representation of the Bassai Ideal."

"I won't join your activism group," she said. "I'm not made for that."

"Indeed, you're not," Basuaye said. "The University of Bassa has fostered in you the wiles of aristocracy, and your maa has fostered in you the wiles of the street. You have the best of both worlds. You may be young, but no matter—our most revered, historically, were in the prime of their youth. Nogowu the Manic Emperor was still but a boy when he took over this nation."

"So you want me to become the face of your campaigns? And ruin the little good graces I have left?"

"Not exactly." He shifted in his seat. "Our people say, *An arrow insists it is flying when, in truth, it is expiring*. Take a look at Bassa right now.

We're weak, ripe for the taking if anyone were bold enough to overlook our past glory and conquests. Our Speaker was murdered by *one* invader, for moon's sake. The Coalition for New Bassa wants nothing but to make the mainland great again. But the truth is we cannot do it alone—we need the people to rally behind us, because that, my dear, is where true power lies. And that, as well, is why you have come to me—because you need the power of the people too, just in a different way. I'm saying, why not kill multiple birds with one stone?"

Esheme was impressed—and perhaps a little bit envious—of Basuaye's capability to be convincing. She saw, now, its dangerous potential. She shook her head before the seeds of whatever he was planting took root.

"I need you to stop," she said, irate, "and tell me what you want in plain terms."

"You want me to help you use a power amassed by the people to delay the First Elder." He jabbed a finger into his palm. "I simply want to use this opportunity to push my own message a little bit further. We could consider it a service exchange, one that could perhaps crystallize in a discount on compensation."

"I see." Esheme twisted her lips in thought. "What are you thinking of?"

"The people need a conduit for their scattershot rage," Basuaye said. "Bassa's leadership is faceless, with nowhere for the average citizen to direct their grievances against the land. I have so few seasons left in me that I can no longer play that role. I may not be able to give the people something to hate, but I can give them another conduit, another face and voice through which they can channel their anger."

"I am not going to speak at your rallies."

"No, you won't," he said. "You only need to speak once, at Abuso's funeral. A name only needs to exist on lips to become alive. It doesn't always need a constant face."

She frowned. "I *am* already scheduled to speak at the funeral, on behalf of my maa as a fellow victim of the intruder's attack."

He nodded. "Exactly."

Esheme considered it thoughtfully. "Look, I'm not planning to say anything that—"

"Would invite more wrath than is already directed toward your house?"

He smiled. "Your maa has allies and associates, yes, but also countless enemies. Once they see you up there, a young woman, untethered to anything solid, they will swoop down on you like a pack of hyenas. *This* could be your solidity. If you speak in solidarity with the coalition, and are seen with protection that looks like coalition, people will surely brand you a coalition sponsor, but it will only be those who already hate you. What you're not seeing is all the people who will suddenly be on *your* side, who will suddenly be interested in what you are saying. And once you're in the public eye, it becomes more difficult for anyone to brazenly attack you or your household. Easy mango, we both get what we want."

Esheme pondered this. It really *was* killing many birds with one stone. Besides getting Dọta off her back, whatever came of this could be a means to achieving other suddenly important goals. If she ever got hold of that ibor, she would need something more than Basuaye to keep Dọta away permanently. Gaining the support of a force as big as Bassa's own populace sounded just about right.

"I'm not agreeing to anything," Esheme said, after some thought. "But let's assume I agree. What would you have me do?"

"Oh, nothing major," Basuaye said. "Go home, prepare to meet my generals. If they agree, I will give you specific words to speak and then a few directions on how to proceed."

"That sounds too easy. I'm wary of things that sound that easy."

Basuaye smiled. "Nothing about this is easy, MaaEsheme. Our people say, *If you want to catch a fowl, you pursue the whole brood, because you don't know which one has the bad leg.* The coalition has tried everything possible to put the power of the common citizens back into their hands, and we will continue to try. This speech is only one fowl. We will continue to chase the whole brood, and that, my dear, is not easy work."

Esheme decided she might like this man after all. Not because he had chosen not to refer to her by the diminutive *Esheme-maa*, but because his tongue was sweet in a way that made her feel wary, yet comfortable in its purpose. He harboured the same kind of clear focus and purpose that she associated with herself, and that, she could live with.

Danso

AFTER A TENSE NIGHT, Danso, Zaq, and Lilong packed up camp and began their sixth day in the forest without a word to each other. Danso offered Lilong some more cloves for the pain and she received them in silence. Then he stepped into the lead, clothsack wrapped about his back, blade and waterskin in hand, and led the group forward in his best approximation of the nearest point of high ground.

They went forward until evening before arriving at a point where Danso could begin to plot his projections of a westward, coastward direction. They camped near a tiny brook, likely an offshoot of the not-too-distant Gondola, to refill all waterskins. The sun had hidden behind a cloud all day, which meant the journey had been less energy-consuming than expected. Yet the forest remained so humid that they still sweated until their clothes were damp.

They started up again the next day. Overnight, Danso had worked with information he'd gleaned about the sun's positions over the course of the day, and determined that their current path was actually headed toward the Gondola rather than parallel to it. So, with careful plotting, he set a course that was truer westward, approximating that they could hit the coast in a day or more of intentional walking.

Next morning, they hadn't gone far when Lilong suddenly stopped short. Zaq, who moseyed absent-mindedly behind her, did not see in time, and bumped into her.

"Ow," both of them said, and looked daggers at each other.

"Watch yourself," Zaq said, stepping around her to continue his journey.

"Something is wrong," Lilong said, slowly, a deadly seriousness Danso had not seen in a while taking over her face. "Something might be following us."

Danso paused. The forest had grown slightly thicker as they made for higher ground, pressing in further on them as they navigated a narrow way perhaps made by animals. He had been attempting to name most things he saw—elephant grass, ferns, wild tobacco, touch-me-nots, dwarf plantains—until the plants became too many, slapping them with dew as they progressed. It grew quieter the higher they went in elevation, with nothing around them but vegetation and the odd reptile breathing underwater in a nearby swampy area.

"I don't hear or see anything," Danso said.

"It's not..." Lilong struggled to explain. "It's more like *tracking*."

Danso froze. "Is it—a *beast*?"

"I can't tell," Lilong said, her eyes darting. "But..." She trailed off.

"Moons!" Danso exclaimed. "I thought you said they hunted during the breathing!"

"It's not—" Lilong sighed, then turned to face them. "Okay, listen. I will have to explain something to you two. But you must promise to stay calm." Without giving them time to respond, she reached for her waist and loosened the pouch tied to it, slowly. Danso heard Zaq gasp just a little, echoing his own feelings. Never in their seven days had Lilong ever let that pouch out of sight or away from her body, even that one time she took a bath when it rained. But now, she untied it completely and brought something out.

"I need to tell you about this," she said, holding up an object. Danso immediately recognised it as ibor. It had the same consistency of the others he'd seen embedded into her upper arm, though this one was of red shade and significantly larger.

"Is that..."

"Ibor, yes," she said. "But this one is special. It is what I came to the mainland for. This, right here, is the last and only known occurrence of red ibor on the whole continent. In the seven islands, we call it the

Diwi—our word for *hope*. This Diwi has been in my family for generations, and we have protected it all this time. That is, until your Nem stole
it from my daa."

Danso moved toward her slowly, hand outstretched. "Can I...?"

Lilong's head tilted slightly, but she let him approach. He came forward, ran his fingers over it. It felt just like those in her upper arm—
smooth, pockmarked.

"How come it's not responding to you like the other pieces?" he asked.

"Because," she said, "red ibor is an instrument no one has yet figured
out how to play."

"It...doesn't work?"

"Or we don't yet know how to use it. We don't know which."

"Then how do you know it's ibor?"

"Oh, it's ibor."

He touched it again, fascinated. "Okay. So what about this Diwi then?"

Lilong pulled up the sleeve of her tunic with her other hand, wincing
slightly from her still-healing wounds. The action exposed the tiny pieces
of amber ibor embedded into her arm.

"This," she said, motioning to them, "is how ibor is carried. Tooth-
sized, each lasting about fifty regular Possessions." She motioned toward
the red stone-bone in her hand. "But this? This is ibor in its rawest form,
as found, lasting hundreds, a thousand Possessions. So we break it down,
make it easy and accessible because no one person should lay claim to
such raw power. But another reason why we do it is, well, the stories say,
when any kind of ibor is this large, it tends to attract... things."

"What do you mean by *things*?" Zaq asked.

"Beasts," said Lilong.

Danso's jaw dropped. *"What?"*

Zaq let out a small cry. "I knew it! I knew that beast thing had something to do with you—everything bad always had something to do with
you."

"Keep calm!" Lilong admonished, looking around them. *"You* brought
me into this forest, remember? Besides, I've kept us safe, have I not? I'm
not obligated to tell you why we're being hunted, only that we are. And
your behaviour now shows me I was right."

They stared at one another. Danso wondered how this new information now affected their plans. It was one thing getting by without knowing, but another thing making plans now that they knew.

"What attracts them about it?" he asked.

Lilong bit her lip. "Do you know where ibor comes from?"

Danso shook his head. The codex did not offer anything about the mineral's history.

"We Ihinyon believe ibor is a piece of the sky," she said. "Pieces that fell to earth a long time ago and caused a cataclysm. These pieces of sky melded with the bones of the beings who perished in the resulting fire, and that gave us ibor." She rolled the red chunk into her other hand, put it back into her pouch. "Some of those beings did not perish, though. They have existed among us for thousands of seasons, seen only in rare sightings."

"So, like the Ninki Nanka and all those fabled beasts?"

"I can't say which are real or made up, but we study them all in our league, just in case," she said. "Our understanding is that each beast varies in how friendly it is to us people, but since we believe most eat meat, we assume they will be willing to tear us to pieces upon sight. One thing we are sure about, though, is this." She patted her pouch. "When ibor is this large, with this much power concentrated in one place, they can all sense it. And they will follow it once they do."

Zaq made a sound at the back of his throat. "I can't believe it. A target—a *target!* On our backs!"

"A target that your stupid people stole and brought here, not me," Lilong retorted.

"That's what you sensed just now, isn't it?" Danso was thinking, putting pieces together. "You feel something. You can tell when they're nearby because you're an Iborworker."

"Well, it's..." Lilong shrugged. "Maybe? I've never seen one, so I don't know. All I know is ibor sometimes makes you feel...things. It's like a system of thought-senses, see. I feel things, but sometimes they're just feelings. Other times, they're not. But I try to keep vigilant regardless." She motioned to them and began to move carefully. "We can keep going, but I suggest we keep our eyes and ears wide open. And perhaps, let's not stop for camp until we're sure the area is safe."

Zaq muttered a profanity in a border tongue as they went on. Danso was lost in thought, thinking about everything he had learned about ibor and the islands and the stories from his time.

They went on for at least another hour, before Lilong stopped again, frowning.

"What now?" Zaq said.

"Shush," said Danso. "What's that?"

Beyond the usual sounds of the forest that engulfed them so much they had become used to it, there was a howling, like a heavy wind coming from afar.

"Breathing!" Lilong gasped, and darted.

Breathing? That can't be right, Danso thought. He had calculated them all. They weren't to expect another for at least a few hours.

"Move!" A hand—Lilong's—pulled him. "Take this tree, now!"

Sure enough, the wind arrived at once, without build-up. The ground responded, undulating, up-down, up-down. Danso grabbed the slender tree next to Zaq and Lilong and wrapped his hands and legs around it, swaying as it did.

Then he heard it: a hollow sound beneath the wind, like air blowing through a pipe.

A large shadow passed over them.

"Moons!" Zaq said. "What—?"

There was a screech, a loud and piercing call. A large flapping, the beating of wings, something sweeping over the canopy. A large animal passed low overhead, so swift it had swished out of sight before Danso could tilt his head to look up. Leaves and twigs from the canopy, disturbed by its passing, rained down in its wake. Then it was behind the trees, out of sight, the forest's swaying making it even more difficult to determine its position.

In the clear sky of bright day, a pang of lightning snapped at the clouds, and thunder rumbled low with it.

"Oh no," Lilong said, growing ashen.

"What is *that*?" Zaq screamed over the howling wind.

The animal came into view again with a screech, sinewy wings tucking in fast, directed descent.

"That," Lilong said, her eyes turning amber, "is a Skopi."

33

Lilong

THE SKOPI MOVED TOO fast for anyone to do anything about it, least of all Lilong.

She barely had time to Command her blade to attack before the lightning bat was in front of them, swooping low, its curved, ironlike talons out and shiny. Large with beady eyes, it cast a shadow over all three of them. Lilong did the first thing that came to her mind: She Commanded her blade to cut off the pouch.

The blade had barely finished its work, and the pouch had barely left her body, when the bat dug into her shoulders and picked her up. It dragged her across the forest floor, its skinny wings whacking at her face as it lifted her into the trees. Danso and Zaq and her blade and her pouch receded, growing smaller.

Lightning peppered the sky, crackling with ferocity. She might've heard Danso call her name, or maybe it was just the wind whooshing in her ears. Her lungs caught too much air at once and pinched the inside of her chest.

The Diwi was her only thought. *Save the Diwi.*

Lilong Commanded her blade again, quickly, before it was too far out of reach. She sensed it like a faraway light, growing brighter, then it burst through all of the vegetation, ecstatic, obedient, and went right for the bat, sinking into flesh and drawing blood.

The Skopi screeched and let go. Only then did Lilong realise the folly of her action.

Thankfully, they hadn't cleared the trees yet. Lilong grabbed for a branch of the nearest tree, lost it, and fell a little distance before gaining enough faculty to Command her blade again. The blade flew and dug itself into the tree trunk, flat face upward, and Lilong slid down and put a foot on the blade, grinding to a halt.

The Skopi circled around and plunged, heading straight toward Danso. Lilong gave her blade a quick series of Commands. It slid out, dropped down a few feet, and embedded itself in the tree again, so that Lilong dropped with it and balanced on the blade once more. She did it another time, and another, then jumped to the ground and landed on her feet. The force of the landing jarred her body, and she winced as her injuries protested.

Down her line of sight, she saw the bat bearing down on Danso, who had picked up the Diwi after it had tumbled into the understory. He turned to see the bat headed for him, for the thing in his hand. His eyes widened, and he made to throw the stone-bone away, divert the bat's attention from him.

"No, don't!" she yelled, Commanding her blade at the same time. It ejected from the tree and shot forward at high velocity, cutting through the mass of green and stem.

The Skopi was only a foot from Danso when the blade struck it, going through the back of its head and coming out through the front of its neck.

There was a quick splatter of red, most of it splashing over Danso. The bat screeched and collapsed on him, the chorus of both his and the bat's screams producing an eerie harmony. They fell together, their bodies tumbling into the understory.

Lilong ran forward. *Please be okay, please be okay.* Zaq, who had fled into hiding once the bat revealed itself, came forward gingerly, calling Danso's name. Only then did Lilong realise that, all this time, her concerns had been fixated on the Diwi and not the hand holding it.

She and Zaq arrived on the scene at the same time. The Skopi was dead, no doubt. But something else was wrong—it would not stop twitching. It was as if even in the afterthroes of death, there was still life within it, as if something else that was not its body was powering it.

Zaq stood there, panic plastered all over his face. Lilong bent forward and pushed at the bat, putting her shoulder into it until it rolled over. And there, lying beneath it in the mass of understory vegetation, was Danso.

In his hand: the Diwi clutched tight. His eyes: alight with the blaze of red ibor, of a Red Iborworker. The eyes of the Skopi: red, bright, docile, faithful in accompaniment.

Then Danso gasped for air and rose, and the Skopi rose with him.

———————————

For a long time, everything stood still and no one spoke. The lightning had ceased and the trees and vegetation had stopped shedding everything that was broken in them. Dread and confusion clung to the air like smoke.

Danso unclenched his bloodied hand and let the Diwi fall to the ground. His eyes changed slowly, from red to brown and white, and so did those of the Skopi, which stood off to a side on all fours, wings tucked in, blood still dripping from its neck. The bat did not move further, but did not return to death either, instead posed there in some form of stasis, as if waiting for a command.

Danso looked at his palm.

"I feel…funny," he said, then promptly blacked out and fell to the ground.

Lilong rushed over to him, still trying to recover from the shock of what she had just witnessed, still processing the gravity of what had just been revealed.

After hundreds of seasons, the power within the Diwi had finally found its bond.

With a mainlander. To Possess and Command a Skopi.

The concept tore a hole in her brain. She felt the urge to question everything, to give it all up, throw her hands in the air. Red ibor had been inert for hundreds of seasons, but had suddenly awakened *now*? To *this* man?

This man, however, wasn't doing so good. A pallor had gathered beneath his eyes, and a scaly rash had broken out about his body. Lilong opened his lids and found his eyes dull, sickly. She took his waterskin and poured water over his face, then forced some into his lips. Zaq, on the other hand, just stood there, speechless with shock, perhaps asking the very same questions that were rattling about in her brain.

How did this happen? How was a random mainlander suddenly able to use red ibor, something not a single Ihinyon person had been able to do in forever? Was it the Skopi that had caused it to awaken? Or was there something special about Danso? If neither, why hadn't someone else discovered this a long time ago? Why *now*? She understood now that the bat could be possessed likely because it was dead and inanimate—the rule was the same for amber. So this was what red ibor did, then? Possess things that once contained life?

"Help me get his legs up," she said to Zaq, who didn't move until she turned to face him. "Forget the bat, it's not going to do anything until he wakes up."

"How do you know?"

"Do you see my blade moving unless I Command it?"

Zaq glanced at the bat again before he shuffled forward, muttering prayers under his breath. He held Danso's legs up while Lilong loosened his wrappers to increase circulation. All of this took her back home, to the number of times she had had to revive novice warriors of the Abenai League, especially those who had just been allowed to touch and channel ibor for the first time. Save for a lucky or very talented few, almost everyone fainted. Some never woke up.

She checked Danso's breathing. Weak, but evident. She sat back and nodded at Zaq to let him know he could let his charge's legs go. The Second did as asked but stood there afterward, his legs shaking.

"You should probably sit down," Lilong said. "He'll soon awaken."

He sat, docile, staring at nothing but making sure to reserve a glance or two for the inert bat.

"He will be fine," Lilong said. She didn't really know what else to say to someone who hated her guts.

Zaq said nothing in response. They sat there together, waiting. It felt like waiting for someone to return from a dangerous hunt. There was an equal probability that they would walk out of the bushes triumphant, or one would have to go in and find their body.

"What just...happened?" Zaq asked finally, but he didn't turn to face her when he asked it, instead keeping his forward gaze as though if he looked her in the face, he might die.

Lilong shrugged. "He has bonded with the rarest ibor on the continent," she said. "He has become—" She almost choked, just trying to say it out loud. "He might just have become the most powerful person on this continent."

"But...*him?*" His face betrayed the lack of understanding of that choice. "Why *him?*"

"Honestly?" Lilong shrugged. "I have no idea. But I'm sure we'll find out at some point."

Lilong parsed her mixed emotions. On one hand, she was glad someone had finally cracked open the mystery of red ibor, and this was good news to bring back to the Abenai League. On the other hand, a Shashi mainlander had done it with her own family's heirloom—not so much good news. Plus, she didn't like the idea of Danso knowing he suddenly possessed all this power. She had seen what that realisation did to people. They became reckless, foolhardy. Danso was already those two things. Imagine what he would become with access to red ibor.

She lunged and picked up the discarded Diwi. For a moment, she expected something to happen—for the bat to react, perhaps, or for the Diwi to respond to *her*, for her own eyes to turn red, and for her to Draw and Possess and Command. But instead nothing happened, and she just knelt there, with the Diwi and dirt in her hand, the Skopi in stasis.

She put the stone-bone back into her pouch and tied it to her waist, deciding there and then that she was never going to let Danso touch it ever again.

After a while, Zaq took Danso's pack, pulled out a couple of the wild eggplants they had picked up, and handed them to her.

"Thank you," she said, surprised at the gesture, then decided this was probably the only time she would ever get the opportunity to ask him the question she had always wanted to ask.

"Why do you hate me?"

He froze. Obviously, being a Second perhaps meant he didn't often have to answer direct questions about his personality. He ruminated on it for a moment, tossing his own eggplant from hand to hand.

"I don't hate you," he said, finally. "I hate what my situation has become. I hate that I cannot get what I want, and I hate that everything that is happening is colluding to ensure I never do." He looked at her. "I hate that your coming started it, but I don't hate you."

Lilong nodded. She completely understood—that was exactly her life right now, too.

"Everything that is happening." He waved his hand in an encompassing gesture. "Danso messing about in Bassa, you arriving, me attacking Oboda, us running away, and now *this*—supernatural powers, conscious weapons, undead beasts." He shook his head. "My life can never go back to normal after this, can it?"

Your life has never been normal, you just didn't know it, Lilong thought. The concept of indentured servitude had always seemed wrong to her, even when she first heard about it as a child. That the desert populations thought it was an okay price to pay to live on the mainland was baffling. Yes, the mainland was where the continent's best resources were domiciled, but that was pure luck, wasn't it? There was nothing normal about someone selling their lives just for that. But who was she to tell him that when her life wasn't any better? Besides, he probably already knew all of this, and her repeating it back to him might make him retreat even further.

"I always thought my life was best when living for truth," he was saying. "But I lost everything from my former life trying to chase something I thought was true. At least with Bassa, I'm not seeking that—I know what to expect, what to do to get what. But here I am again, faced with new truths. I'm afraid..." He stopped and bit his lip.

"You're afraid that if you look it in the eye, you will believe it again," she said. "And you don't want to."

"People do not want truth," he said. "They want a stable, secure lie. I have lived enough to see that truth is not worth the sacrifice. That is not a mistake I am willing to make again."

Lilong ate her eggplant with a new feeling about Zaq. She was still wary of him, sure. But she no longer detested him. He was just a person struggling with all the things every person struggled with, and she could not fault him for that.

A short time after that, Danso coughed and opened his eyes. He sat up and looked at himself, frowning.

"I don't..." He regarded his blood-soaked chest, his skin, his feet, as if discovering himself anew. "What...?"

"How do you feel?" Lilong asked.

He looked at her like he was seeing her for the first time. "What has happened to me?" Danso looked at the pouch, now secured firmly to her waist. "What is that thing you have brought to us?"

"Eat something." She passed him her last remaining eggplant. He took it, looked at it, then tossed it aside.

"I want you to tell me what has happened." Then he saw the Skopi standing there in stasis and froze.

"*That* has happened," Lilong said.

Danso stared at it for a long time. When he turned back to her, Lilong did not like the look on his face.

"I'd like to try again," he said, arm outstretched for the Diwi.

Something cold and bitter gripped Lilong. Every original piece of rage she had felt against the mainland returned with a fury, compounded by this new situation. How was it that the most oblivious mainlander possible, someone who did not care about the Ihinyon, someone who had not spent their whole life protecting the secrets of the archipelago, someone whose daa did not get fatally attacked in the course of protecting the stone-bone; how was it that *he* got to command the Diwi, the most sacred of all ibor on the continent?

Lilong rose and dusted herself off.

"We should get moving," she said, her expression firm and stolid. "We must exit the forest as soon as possible."

Zaq looked at her, perplexed, and then, reading her rage, quietly picked up Danso's pack. Danso remained in place, baffled.

"What did I do?" he asked, but no one answered him. Zaq strapped his pack and looked to Lilong to lead the way. The two looked at Danso and waited for him to rise.

When Danso did finally rise after some difficulty, the Skopi became alert. When he began to walk, the bat turned and moved with him. It stopped when he stopped. Danso frowned, then moved again. The bat moved, then stopped again when he did.

"Moons," Zaq said, exasperated. "This thing is going to follow us, is it not?"

Something curled in Lilong when she saw the look on Danso's face— the look of someone who had just realised how much power he possessed. He turned that gaze toward her, and her disposition toward Danso shifted in that moment. She no longer felt cocky, no longer felt he was inept and needed watching like a child. Instead, she now felt like *she* needed protection. From him.

Danso turned and continued down the path, the large bat following in his wake. After a moment's hesitation, Lilong followed, and so did Zaq.

A few steps later, Lilong stopped to tie the pouch tighter to her body. More than ever before, she was going to have to guard the Diwi with her life.

34

Esheme

THE NEXT TIME ESHEME heard from Basuaye, it was with word that the meeting with the generals was scheduled to be held at the coalition's headquarters. Apparently, while the safe houses in which they congregated changed every now and then, the headquarters didn't. It was, therefore, the one thing they guarded with their lives.

When the appointed time came, Esheme rode with Basuaye in a rundown, rickety travelwagon shielded with raffia shades that looked like it belonged to some really poor farmhand. She peered between the blinds, wondering if he was testing her, expecting her to complain and long for the comforts of her Fourth Ward life. Perhaps he had paid little attention to the risk she had taken to meet with him in the first place, how she had altered her clothing and appearance. If he was testing her, he was testing for the wrong things.

They arrived at their destination soon enough: a little house in a nondescript area of Fifth Ward. Basuaye swept aside the ratty curtain and ushered her in. It was dusty and sparsely furnished, but looked obviously lived in.

They went through the main house and emerged in the courtyard, which was bare and with just enough odds and ends to, again, give off the impression that someone lived there. In the middle was a ratty, threadbare rug. Basuaye went to a nearby portion of the mudbrick wall and pushed it. The rug jerked. He moved it aside completely, and in the vacated space lay an opening. Within that opening lay stairs.

"Watch your head," he told her.

They descended slowly and came into a large, lit room that was much warmer than the cool harmattan air of late morning outside. There were three people in the room, who did not respond at first upon spotting the Cockroach. But once the three-arched Idu counsel novitiate appeared behind him, the three people drew weapons in one choreographic motion and pointed them toward her.

Basuaye held up his hands. "Easy. She's the one we're meeting."

The generals—one woman, one man, and one who was neither—kept their weapons up.

"What in the mountains of Soke do I see before me?" the woman spoke. "Is that the progeny of Nem the Fixer?"

"Yes," Basuaye said. "Why don't we all sit?"

Ulobana—a tall, lean Emuru woman—dropped her hand but did not sheathe her blade. Esheme eyed her warily. The woman wore no arches but let her hair hang loose and tattered, something Esheme noticed was fast becoming a silent protest choice among subscribers to the movement. Civic guards had a field day with such people, but something told Esheme that any civic guard who dared get embroiled with this woman did so at their own peril.

"Well, well, well," Ulobana said. "Never thought I would see the day when someone above Sixth would dare to join our ranks." She eyed Esheme over. "And a prime student of the Ideal at that! Priceless."

"I'm not joining your ranks," Esheme said.

"Well, not immediately." She smiled wryly. "Maybe we could lure you in with our wily and welcoming ways." She turned to Basuaye. "Imagine that, eh? Turning a prized treasure of the nation, a devoted Idealist, into a symbol for the coalition's resistance *against* the Ideal."

"I'm in the room, you know?" Esheme said.

"Oh, we *know*," the bald-headed general said, and twirled their weapon, a hatchet.

"Now, now, Igan," Basuaye said, "don't let that temper of yours take hold just yet. Why don't you all sheathe those things and we can talk about why MaaEsheme is here?"

Igan did not put down their axe. It was almost as if Basuaye had never spoken. Instead, they pulled out a piece of oily cloth and began to clean the blade of it.

The room, though below ground, was better furnished than the safe house. Furniture aside, there was more colour here, even some attempts at decoration, like the circular woven ornaments gracing the walls. It seemed to double as some sort of living quarters. Of the three generals, Igan looked the most likely to be the current occupant or some sort of caretaker, as they were dressed in less formal clothes and wore no sandals.

"It is an honour to sit in the same room with the movers and shakers of the coalition," Esheme said, smiling at Basuaye.

"Oh, no, dear one," Ulobana said. She pointed to herself and Igan. "*We* are the movers and shakers." She pointed to Basuaye. "*This* is the face." She pointed to the last general, who opened his mouth and showed the dark space where a tongue was supposed to be. "And Tamino just does what he is told."

Esheme frowned at the man. "What happened to your tongue?"

"He doesn't like to talk about it." Ulobana shouldered Igan and cackled at her own joke. Igan did not even break a smile.

"That's not funny," Basuaye said. "He still has ears, you know." He addressed Tamino: "Ignore her, you know she can be a child."

Tamino shrugged noncommittally, as if to acknowledge that Ulobana made jokes in poor taste all the time.

"We all know why we are here, so I won't waste words," Basuaye said. "We lost our main source of funding, and someone has offered us a lifeline: money in exchange for protective services for a period."

"Oh, well, it's not quite as simple as that," Esheme said, her hand clasped over the other, mirroring the way one leg was crossed over the other. She realised she looked like a spitting image of Nem, uncrossed it for a moment, then thought, *who cares*, and crossed them back again.

"And what is it *quite*?" Igan asked.

Esheme glared at them. "Excuse me, do you have a problem with me? Do I know you?"

"You don't know me," Igan said. "But I know your kind. I see you. And as far as I'm concerned, whatever hunts you might as well burn you down and scrub your ashes off the face of the continent. One less of you equals a victory for all."

"That's okay, Igan," Basuaye said in the placating tone of a parent.

Esheme narrowed her eyes at Igan. "You will want to take that back."

"Or what?" Igan said, holding Esheme's eyes while wiping the already shining axe blade even more furiously. The two held a long, heated gaze.

"You have to forgive Igan, our newest general," Basuaye said. "A prized hotshot, just like you, so a little cocksure. You've heard of Bassa's Left Hand of Darkness?"

Esheme's anger slowly morphed into amazement. "*You* are the Left Hand of Darkness?"

In recent seasons, it had been rumoured the coalition had a secret weapon no one had ever seen. A sort of shadow warrior who struck indomitable fear into the hearts of civic guards and private hunthands hired to disrupt coalition activities and assault its members, with Basuaye as a prime target. No matter who the higher-ups hired to carry out these dirty tasks, they always ended up, if the stories were to be believed, murdered in various creative ways that definitely sent a message each time. Every possible method had been employed: from bloodless murders like cassava root sap poisoning to the gruesome ones like flaying a civic guard or axing them alive from crown to genitals, their faces divided midscream. The bodies were always found at dawn, which meant the murders happened overnight, and at one point, the embalming guild had concluded that the wounds were consistent with someone who was left-handed. The legend of Bassa's Left Hand of Darkness was born right then.

The profile and influence of the coalition rose a notch once no civic guard or private hunthand wanted to touch any coalition follower without cause for fear of covert retaliation. Basuaye himself had publicly denied this, of course, saying that the actions were those of a lone hyena who had no association with the movement.

Esheme looked Igan over properly now, with newfound appreciation that must have been evident in her expression. Igan paused and changed countenance, becoming shyly self-aware, and made a great fuss of putting their axe away in exaggerated movements. It helped that they were mostly a nondescript person—no defining markers anyone could truly remember, though Esheme would remember those very pink lips and tight, tiny eyes for a long time to come. With their complexion and bald head, they could pass for a desertlander househand if they decided to, which explained how they could surprise people who didn't consider them a threat and get easy access to otherwise fortified places.

"Don't think I came to you because I am helpless," Esheme said finally, retraining her gaze to address the group. "I am perfectly capable of handling myself, thank you very much, and whether you agree or not, you could use the money. I am not in opposition to your cause, but don't take that to mean I am in support of it—I simply do not care. My goal here is to secure some independent protection, and that is that. Take it or leave it."

Silence engulfed the room. The generals regarded one another. Igan looked to the floor and said nothing.

Tamino, for the first time, looked at Esheme. He held her gaze, then signed something with his hands. Ulobana translated.

"He says we are not some private hunthands for hire," she said. "And I agree."

"I never said you were."

"He says, don't think you can sway us with money," Ulobana continued translating. "And again, I agree." She signed something back and forth with Tamino, then said: "It goes against the values of our cause. We won't do it."

Esheme sighed. *They haven't been listening.* Again, like everyone else, they took her at face value, thinking, *This one is Nem's child,* and were therefore unwilling to consider her own pain points, her struggles as they existed beyond that designation.

She rose. "When I came in here, you recognised me in connection to someone else, not as myself. About me and my struggles, you know nothing. You do not know what it means to be me, to be caught in the warring between powers, to be the grass that suffers when elephants rumble. You do not know what it means to fight for space every single day of your life, to emerge from the shadow of the elephants, only to find out that you need to protect yourself all over again." She gazed at each, pointedly.

"But then again, you *do* know. And that is why you have signed up to the coalition. We may come from different castes, and our struggles may be different, but our reasons are rooted in the same soil."

Her words held up the room. Basuaye nodded like a proud parent, but said nothing.

"I'll do it," Igan said quietly.

The shock in the room was evident. Even Esheme herself was surprised.

"You've been swayed by that speech straight out of a counsel guild manuscript?" Ulobana said. "You know it's not genuine, right?"

"I've not been swayed by anything," Igan replied quietly. "I'm not doing it for her." They looked up at Esheme, squarely. "I'm doing it because the coalition has a purpose, and if this action ensures that purpose is fulfilled, then so be it." At least, that is what their mouth said, but Esheme thought their eyes said something else she couldn't read.

If Igan was her only choice, she would take it. What better person to have at one's side at such a time than Bassa's Left Hand of Darkness? That aside, Esheme thought Igan possessed something else: a sort of readiness to believe, an unspoken faith. She recognised it because she often saw it in Danso.

"Well," Basuaye said, in the tone of a chairperson adjourning a meeting, "Ulo, Tamino, unless you have anything else to say, I think we're fine here."

Ulobana shook her head in disappointment. Tamino shrugged noncommittally.

Basuaye clapped his hands and turned to Esheme.

"Our people say that *it is the clothes that we respect*. They also say, *Behind soft lips, sharp teeth bite*. Well, you will be both our respectable clothes and teeth behind soft lips at that funeral, MaaEsheme. So we welcome you, and we embrace your hand in our future."

35

Esheme

THE BASSAI FUNERAL CUSTOMS required the eldest child to lead proceedings in the event of the death of the head of a household. Said child received the tributes, organised the hostings, and performed the required rituals on everyone else's behalf. But in Abuso's case, his household was gone, children included. Of course, his only daughter, Oke, was still alive over the Pass, but Esheme believed she was one of very few who possessed that information. All of this meant that Abuso's siblings commandeered the ceremony.

The ceremony took place in the city square, since Abuso was a pillar of society and therefore deserved a befitting farewell. Drapery, strung coral, and flowers decorated the square, all red, the colour for death. Every attendee was dressed in wrappers and accessories of the same colour. Abuso's body was placed on an ancestral altar in the centre of the square. Later, it would be set on fire, the burnt body ground to ash. His siblings would take his ashes to the highest point of the Soke mountains and scatter them, so that the winds there might convey his soul safely to the moons, to be with his ancestors in the sky.

The Bassai thought of themselves as souls interconnected with those who had come before, placed on the only continent in the world, on the most fertile and blessed of lands, to exploit for the purpose of fulfilling the desires of the moon gods. Individual well-being was intricately tethered to the wellness of the social units to which they belonged, in life, and even more so in death. They considered journeying to the moons alone too perilous for a bodily experience, so they ground their dead to ash and had them travel safely moonward by wind.

Seated at what would've been Nem's place—solitary and guildless, as Nem had no such associations—Esheme watched the proceedings with interest. The ceremony began with a ritual dance of send-off. The Chief Priests of the Moon Temple, a woman called Ebose—the only person dressed in white as homage to Ashu—and a man called Ilobi, representing Menai in red, came forward. They brought goats to be slaughtered, one each for Abuso and his deceased forebears, invoking their spirits into each animal. Then, in order of seniority, Abuso's siblings—two men, one woman—danced around each slain goat to the beat of drums, windpipes, and shekeres, tailed by hired dancers. Ordinarily, the family would be large enough to carry out this ritual, but it would be a shame if the Speaker of the nation had only three dancers at his funeral.

The dancers sweated, waved their arms, and twisted their bodies in exaggerated moves. The medleys came fast and jovial, since Bassai funerals were, in truth, a celebration, despite the long faces of the attendees.

Afterward, a hired jali came forward and announced the rest of the funeral activities that would take place over the next few days. He explained the planned processions, led by the siblings, again, with the eldest carrying on their head a box of fine wrappers, gold and bronze jewellery, and other fine accoutrements symbolic of the deceased's property and status. The jali ran off the remaining activities on the list, which mostly meant various levels of wake-keeping and partying, but Esheme had tuned out once she saw Dọta preparing to speak.

It was time.

Dọta's speech was short and succinct, primarily denouncing, in his words, the use of dirty and unspeakable powers to cause havoc in the communities, and to the leadership of Great Bassa.

"The nation will do all it can to fish out the culprits of these despicable activities," he crooned in High Bassai. "Believe that we have set upon this task, and will see to it with the utmost promptness."

Esheme snorted quietly, looking around, wondering if anyone noticed the selective wordage that avoided any talk of ibor or the yellowskin. Everyone seemed to be nodding, unsurprisingly. So much proximity to adversity had made them weak, complacent, abiding. She found it painful to watch.

After Dọta came each of the Upper Councilhands, paying tribute to their fallen colleagues. What Esheme could see, as they stood there and puffed out their chests and forced everyone to think of them as all-powerful, was the scared faces of ten weak people who knew they were under attack, who hoped they could speak reverence back into everyone.

It struck her, right then. There was no strength here. Not in the people standing up there, not in the people listening, not in those outside these walls. All manner of strength, and the power associated with it, was gone from Bassa. Basuaye was right: Bassa did need something to shake it up. If anything was to change—via coalition or other form—then a show of some kind of strength was required. And if what she was going to do next would put more wood into that fire, then even better.

When it was her turn to speak on behalf of Nem, Esheme rose and started down the steps, toward the podium. Igan, who had been standing in the back with the rest of the Seconds, came forward, dressed in separate waist and torso wrappers like a desertland immigrant.

Hushed voices. Esheme held her head up and kept moving, knowing that if she looked, what she would find would be surprise plastered on the faces of the attendees: that this young Bassai woman, strutting confidently toward the rulers of the nation, was currently the most influential person in the inner wards who was not a merchant or councilhand or part of the ruling group in any way. They disliked that for the same reason most people disliked Nem: because power in hands that couldn't be fully controlled was always unsettling. Of course they did not know of her own uncertainties, that her Second here wasn't a Second at all, that she too was under attack and needed protection. But she marched forward, remembering what Nem used to say about power: *What matters is not where it actually is, but where people* think *it is.*

"I am Esheme MaaNem," she said, once she had ascended the podium, "and just like you here today"—she motioned toward the siblings of the deceased, who sat in special reserved levels—"I've been thrust into the forefront of my household. To stand for my household and its name, to lead it. Not because you and I want to, but because it has been demanded of us, required by sudden demise. And though my maa is still alive, I stand before you today, and you before me, as MaaEsheme."

She looked to the ancestral altar where Speaker Abuso's body lay, remembering the words Basuaye had carefully crafted for her.

"This was a leader of Great Bassa, someone who gave every fibre of his being to serve this great nation. And in the course of his work, in the solace of his home, evil has come across our borders and found him and taken him to the skies."

There was hushed conversation, murmuring. Esheme pressed on.

"Oh, do you not know?" She whipped around to look at the Upper Council behind her, their expressions growing more aghast. "The Speaker of our great nation was murdered in cold blood by an assassin risen from the depths of the Nameless Islands."

A hush, hisses. A tremor passed through the crowd. Civic guards nearby stepped forward in reaction to the Upper Council rising, to everyone looking around, unsure of what was happening, what to do, whether to stop it or not. Esheme capitalized on their moment of hesitation.

"Yellowskins!" she shouted. "Yellowskins on the mainland, but our leaders have hidden this from us, have lied to us. Instead, they have shut us in with a border closure to hide their failings, making us even easier pickings, just like your Speaker, just like my maa."

"Now, that's enough," Dota said. "Thank you, Esheme-maa. We may now move on to other things."

"No, let her speak," a voice came from the lowest levels of the crowd, where common folk sat. "Let her say what she knows."

Everyone turned. The man standing had a long, weathered face and was dressed in wrappers that didn't belong in the arena alongside Bassa's highest, but stood like he owned the place anyway, and the people who looked up at him responded accordingly.

"It's the Cockroach!" people whispered, and rose, some—mostly coalition plants in the crowd—reaching out to touch him like a venerable god. He ignored them, keeping his eyes on the Upper Council and the platform of address.

"Quiet!" Another First Elder had stepped forward, shooting eye daggers at Basuaye. "You do not have the authority to speak here."

"I am a rightful citizen of this nation," Basuaye said. "I speak for the betterment of myself and my people."

"Yes," a number of voices—again, coalition plants—affirmed from various places in the arena.

"Who spoke there?" another First Elder asked. "Guards, find them!"

"And get this man out of here," Dọta said. "How dare you disrupt this day of respect and reverence?" He turned to Esheme. "And you—"

"And me what?" Esheme said. She turned back to the crowd. "Will you be silenced while your people are killed, Bassai nation? Will you?"

"No!" voices chorused again.

"Shut up!" Dọta said. "Shut up, all of you."

"We will not be silenced," Basuaye said, his honeyed voice thick and booming. Esheme saw, now, how he did it, how he pulled people to himself with words. "We will speak and tell the truth: We are under attack. We have been under attack for a long time, and our leaders have been shielding the truth from us. No more!"

The response was louder this time. The civic guards pushed past the crowd, closing in on Basuaye. The First Elders looked grim. Even the Second Elders of the Lower Council, who seldom did anything but vote at council and milk its proceeds, looked on, aghast and disapproving.

Something about the commotion ignited a fire in Esheme, buoyed by the whole performance and the part she was playing in it.

She had run out of Basuaye's words, but did she have to be done? Not quite. *Attention,* she decided, *is power, too.* There was value in outfoxing everyone who judged her not by her strengths but by their own wants and impressions—Dọta, who needed her to remain meek and silent; Basuaye, who needed her to speak the coalition's words alone; citizens, who thought her just the opportunist daughter of an opportunist fixer. Forcing attention to turn to her was as risky as it was rewarding; her name on everyone's lips was much safer than she would ever be from Dọta if she stayed holed up in her maa's household. And she knew just what to say to create a second edge for this sword, to forge something she had been unable to for so long: respect.

Her lips curled, words gaining new energy in her mind. She drew from within and proclaimed them with everything she could muster.

"Death to yellowskins and invaders!" she said, fist pumped. "If our leaders won't do it, give us an emperor!"

Every last civic guard in the city square moved.

An emboldened cheer came from the group nearest to Basuaye, soon picked up by every possible corner where common folk sat. Dota stomped forward to the dais, face twisted in anger, forehead shining with sweat.

"Seize her!" he screamed. "Seize them all!"

Two civic guards appeared beside Esheme, but before they could do anything, Igan drew their axe, and everything went berserk.

Esheme could never quite understand what happened after that moment. She remembered a tumult, people crying out various things—warnings, commands, enquiries—mixed with general incoherence. She remembered the clanging of metal on metal, the huffs and yips that accompanied weapons being swung and thrusted. Someone must have hit or bumped into her, because she remembered falling, and seeing a multitude of feet running and shuffling. She remembered one of these feet kicking her in the head, and then she lost all sense of time and understanding from there on.

One thing she would never forget, though, was someone lifting her, carrying her away from the scene. She remembered looking up and the person's face was her maa's. Then the person looked down into her eyes, and she realised it was Igan, before the blackness took her.

36

Danso

IT TOOK ANOTHER DAY of skirting the Gondola and its bushroads before Danso, his Skopi, Zaq, and Lilong broke the threshold of the Breathing Forest and arrived in the savanna.

First they saw the Breathing Forest start to die. The last brook they passed by had dried down to sand and stone. The undergrowth thinned to simple gamba grass, and the vegetation became sparser and sparser. The air moved from rich and humid to sharper and drier.

The savanna was merciless at midday. Aside from the sudden increase in thorny plants that scraped their bodies and held on to their wrappers, the heat climbed up several notches. With no forest cover to shield their skins from the sun, the rays beat down on them with a vengeance, so much that Danso's rashes became unbearably itchy. Humidity compounded things by making it difficult to breathe. Danso's braid, which could never really stay in the Bassai plait anyway, loosened and fell onto the shaved sides of his head, damp against his face. It felt alien, this new way of wearing his hair. Alongside a whole resurrected animal now following him, it felt like the person he once knew had been completely erased, like a stranger inhabited his body. Was he still Danso, the same one who had left Bassa? Or was he some new amalgam of everything he now knew since leaving?

Earlier, he had tried to ask Lilong about red ibor, about why the Skopi insisted on following him. She'd only offered a half-hearted explanation: The first Draw from an ibor piece formed a connection that could only be broken by the Iborworker's passing or the stone-bone being used up. For White and Grey Iborworkers, this did not hold, since the inanimate matter they possessed was ubiquitous and formless. For Amber—and from the look of things, Red—Iborworkers, that connection was passed down to the first thing they Possessed, which was why the Skopi remained, waiting for another Command. The heavy lifting in Iborworking, she explained, lay in Drawing. Commanding was only a matter of the right focus and concentration. Possession, however, was the most passive state, and could remain for anything from a short moment to seasons. A Possessed entity might even respond to a sleepwalking Iborworker.

Danso soon realised this to be true: The bat responded to his own unspoken desires, even without him being in contact with the stone-bone. It not only followed him but stopped when he thought it should—like when he went off to relieve himself. After a whole day of doing this, Danso and the bat had fallen into a rhythm where he simply thought of where he wanted it to go, and it went there, even without a Command.

He had asked, again, for her to give him the Diwi so he could learn better how to handle the bat's presence and actions. The hard look Lilong gave him could have stopped an antelope cold. He tried his luck again a few hours later, and she snapped at him for picking up the Diwi with his bare hands in the first place. He avoided mentioning it from that point onward.

Once they crossed into the savanna, things became more dire.

Prior to leaving the forest cover, Lilong had fashioned a wide-brimmed hat from rogue plantain leaves, which she now wore to ward off the sun. But it seemed to be doing only so much good, as she reacted harshly, turning redder than he'd ever seen her, the yellow of her eyes and hair even paler. Earlier, she hadn't been able to read the map he had drawn, and he'd wrongly assumed she couldn't read in general. Now, he realised it was the sun partially blinding her. She couldn't even see the things he pointed out.

"Lilong," he called, and even though she showed no sign of having heard him, he pressed, "if the sun bothers you this much, perhaps we should stop?"

"I can manage," she shot back.

"Okay," he said. "But maybe, I don't know, change your complexion to one more favourable? Perhaps to combat the effects better."

"Don't be silly," Lilong said. "I'm an Iborworker, not a sorcerer. I alter shades, not properties." She made a disapproving sound with her lips and teeth. "Plus, I like being yellowskin, thank you. Can't be wearing your generations of oppression on my body longer than I need to."

Despite her insistence on powering through, they eventually stopped. Lilong went off to change her collection rag for her moonblood, their backs to her as she squatted behind a tree, the sun peppering them relentlessly. When she returned, she looked even redder. Even Danso himself had started to feel the harshness of the sun by this time, sporting burns on his exposed shoulder and neck. Coupled with a mouth full of cold sores and a bad case of diarrhoea, both bestowed upon him by his use of ibor, he felt a fever coming. The only person who seemed unaffected by the heat was Zaq. The presence of the Skopi, however, was of more importance to him, as he ensured to maintain a wide berth from it.

Soon, Lilong began to struggle to breathe, stopping to dry heave a few times. She allowed Danso to check her wounds, turning her face away so they wouldn't speak. He failed to find any particular reason for her new ailment, though eight days of foot travel through unforgiving terrain was just as good a reason as any. Her skin was tender but none of her wounds had reopened, which was good news. Bad news: She did have something akin to a high fever.

"Does your amber ibor take more out of a person than any other kind?" he asked. "Because, I mean, you're far worse off than I am."

"That's because I've been steadily working ibor for days, and you've touched it once." Her words had jaws, snapping with each syllable. "Plus, you don't have multiple unhealed injuries, are not susceptible to the sun, and have not been bleeding out of your genitals for the last few days."

He nodded. "Sorry. It was a stupid question." He straightened. "We should hit the coast by tomorrow morning. Manage with me until then, okay? We just need to touch the fence, that's all. Once we touch the fence, the Peace Treaty covers us. We'll be safe and sound."

Despite the heat, the savanna fascinated Danso. It was unlike anything he had ever seen in Bassa. The soil was different—reddish-brown, less of humus than that of the forest. It was grassland all right, but as Lilong had explained, it clearly used to be something else. There were trees, especially the thorny gum trees with seed pods used to make dyes—which, according to his earth studies class, were supposed to grow near the border, closer to the desert. The mainland's vegetation was simple: thick rainforests in the centre, thinner clumps on the coasts, swamps in the south region of the delta, and drier climate close to the Soke mountains. A savanna in the west, just a few days out of Bassa, was eyebrow-raising. It felt like the Breathing Forest had reached this place and then withered, leaving behind remnants of itself.

They pressed forward in near silence. Lilong stopped to spit a few more times, complaining about a taste in the back of her throat. Danso fetched gum from one of the gum trees they came upon leaking a good amount of it, and he fed it to Lilong mixed with water before drinking some of it himself. He'd seen his daa use this mixture in treating colds, coughs, catarrh, diarrhoea, dysentery, and sore throats. Her condition improved only a bit. A triple threat of natural body reactions to climate, injuries, and the price of supernatural power was way beyond Danso's ability. The only choice was moving as fast as they could into shelter, and hoping she didn't die before they made it to Whudasha.

They came upon evidence of past excavations, some of them small and now partially filled in, some of them large enough that they were cavelike. Danso couldn't tell by looking alone what they had been digging for. Lilong quipped that they had probably been looking for ibor, which Danso simply took to mean that ibor was foremost on her mind at the moment.

The topography here was slightly harder and rockier than the red mud of Bassa, so Danso knew they were much closer to the coast than they'd anticipated. He even thought that, if he listened closely enough, he could hear the sounds of the sea—if he knew what that sounded like.

Lilong became much weaker and complained of a headache as the hours went by, so that they were forced to stop and rest much earlier than they'd anticipated. Zaq suggested they make camp in one of the excavations, and they chose one still large enough to fit them all, avoiding the sharp edges as they entered. Danso had to think about keeping the Skopi outside, but once he'd thought that, the Skopi simply went off, found a nearby tree, and hung upside-down from it. For the first time since the connection, Danso was quite scared of the bat.

It was dark inside the excavation, and when Zaq lit a fire, they found bones of dead animals there. The place was also filled with twice as many mosquitoes as they'd had to battle in the Breathing Forest.

"The fence," Lilong asked, speaking for the first time in a while. "How does that work?"

"The Peace Treaty covers anyone on Whudasha soil," Danso said, "and since the fence around the coast touches the soil, then anyone who touches the fence with any part of their body is covered."

"And if someone breaks the Peace Treaty?" she asked. "Attacks us regardless?"

Danso shook his head. "They would be risking public execution."

"Even if we're fugitives?"

"Even if."

She nodded. "Let's keep that hope, then."

"I'm not too worried about that. I'm more concerned about what you'll tell them when we get there." He paused. "Have you decided?"

"No," she said.

"Do you think it'll be really bad to tell them...everything?"

Lilong frowned. "Why would I want to do that?"

"I don't know—I guess maybe they, like us, deserve to know the truth."

Lilong scoffed. "Truth, truth, truth. Everybody thinks they want the truth until the truth is staring them in the face. Just look at how your own people reacted to the sudden truth of my existence." She kissed her teeth so vehemently she almost went into a coughing fit. "You think it is just lies that break lives? The revelation of truth, especially one that people would prefer not to accept, does the same. This heirloom has been protected by the Abenai League for seasons for a reason. I'm not just going to trust random strangers with that information." She pointed toward the mouth of the cave, toward where the Skopi hung. "And I suggest you better keep that hidden away as well."

"I'll do as you say," Danso said, "but I disagree. I think everyone deserves the truth, whether they like it or not. It's the only path to true freedom."

Lilong shook her head. "Such an idealist, just like my daa. And where it led him, it will lead you too. Somehow you think escaping your little city makes you a liberator of all peoples. But you're still tethered to all of the privileges of its Ideal, even if you can't see it." She pointed to Zaq. "You call this man your Second, even after we've left Bassa. Why is he still under your command? You may have left Bassa, but you're not really free until Bassa has left you."

Danso sat with that for a while. He hadn't thought of it that way. He watched Zaq for a moment, making plans for dinner.

"Maybe you're right," he said, finally. "I've been selfish. I've made mistakes. And that's on me to fix. But I still think everyone deserves truth, deserves their liberty. I left Bassa to seek truth, to resist lies. I don't know of anyone who wouldn't want to be liberated from lies."

"Then you really are naive." She said it like she pitied him. "Why do you think your Whudasha is behind a fence? A Peace Fence, they call it, but who is this *peace* for? Bassa does not want to look its own failures in the face, so it has shoved them out. Want to know what true liberty is? Looking at the uncomfortable manifestations of your wrongdoing, every day. But Bassa has power, and power gets Bassa anything it fucking wants. Power is what creates truth, and liberty with it. Not the other way around." She adjusted the position in which she half lay, half sat. "This is why, sometimes, it is better to keep the truth a secret until people are ready for it, or limit access otherwise. This is better than revealing an unstable truth."

"And so you lie to people, what, for their own good?" It rushed out of his mouth before he could hold it in. "Or what, you kill people for the good of the continent? If that's the creed of your league, what makes you any different from Bassa, then, holding your own people captive with half-truths? Shouldn't everyone get to decide for themselves?"

"The *difference,*" Lilong spat, "is *consequences.* We may possess a decent power, but it remains incomparable to Bassa's size and influence. One tiny mistake, and we're done. Look how my daa's actions have put our whole existence in jeopardy. Telling these secrets would go against what I'm doing here, which is trying to fix that mistake." She sat up, suddenly stronger for someone he earlier thought was going to die. "But I don't expect you to understand that when you're always running head-long toward every shiny thing without considering how it affects oth-ers. Let me tell you right now: If you do anything to put my goal at risk, I swear to the great waters of Ihinyon, I will cut you down without remorse."

Danso's jaw hung in shock from the vehemence in her announce-ment. Even Zaq paused his work to register the scenario. He opened his mouth, then changed his mind midway and returned to his work, leav-ing them to deal with their troubles. Danso felt a quick sense of déjà vu then, remembering when it was Lilong leaving him and Zaq to deal with their issues. How the tables had turned.

Is it true, perhaps? he thought. *Am I . . . selfish?*

"If you believe this," he said aloud, "then why didn't you just kill me in the barn?"

"I ask myself that question each day since," she spat. "At least then you were still more curious than anything else, more interested in the stories you lacked and so greatly desired. And perhaps because that was in my favour then, I did not see how dangerous such selfishness—which leads you to turn on your own city—can be." She lay back down, adjusting the Diwi pouch still tied to her waist. "You say you want liberty, but you can never be free alone. None of us are free until all of us are. To be free of Bassa requires power—power in service of all. Not for you to derive joy from controlling a beast."

With that, she turned away and closed her eyes in rest.

· ◇ ⋯ ━━━━━━━ ⋯ ◇ ·

The three made plans for the night. Danso spent most of the time think-ing about everything she had said. The part about the Bassa Ideal still living in him stung. He sat there and mused, fighting his warring emo-tions alongside a growing headache, the cold sores in his mouth, and the irritating rash from his ibor use that had begun to itch again.

Zaq continued preparing dinner in silence. Danso, restless, paced, and when the silence got too heavy, he began to sing one of his jali songs to keep lucid. This one told of the first landers, of how they came to the Bight of Whudasha, how they brought misfortune and destruction to the land with their unwholesome practices, and how the Bassai had to fight them off, to force them back to the sinking islands whence they came. Now that he knew what he knew, the words of the song became like chaff in his mouth. He switched to whistling just the tune for a while, then gave it up for another, a litany he had memorised for guild finals: a timeline of Bassa's history, from the digging of the Soke moats and the setup of the border till date.

He had barely gone far when Lilong asked him to stop.

"What now?"

"Half of what you're singing are lies," she said, "and I've heard enough lies for a lifetime."

Danso was quiet for a while. "Sorry, just habit. These are songs every jali must learn."

"Then write new ones. Or do you want to be party to lies told to generations?" She rose again from her formerly supine position. "That first song said the first landers attacked Bassa upon arrival and tried to take over the mainland. It said that's what caused the Second Great War." Her voice hardened. "There was no Second Great War. Your power-drunk emperors wanted to seize ibor from the Ajabo. They resisted, and they slaughtered them in droves. They sent *your people* into hiding, declaring open season on anyone who found them on the mainland. Do you call that a war? They should call it what it was: the Second Great Genocide. The Ajabo opted to perish in the seas, opted to die with honour rather than be slain, and their secrets—the secrets of ibor, which we now try to protect—were used to deceive the continent."

She was breathing hard. Danso opened his mouth—perhaps in surprise, perhaps to respond—but found that nothing came out. Yes, they had discussed this back in the forest, but laid out like this, from the mouth of someone who was not Bassai, it hit him like a blow to the gut. Blind surrender to the everyday motions of the jali guild had caused him to compartmentalise, to make excuses for the lies he peddled in song, for the falsehoods he propagated in order to fulfil his duty. And even now, after he had learned of the secrets of ibor, he struggled to let go.

She was right, after all. He might have left Bassa, but it would take a long time, and a lot of intentional personal effort, for Bassa to leave him. Perhaps it was time, as she said, to write new litanies? In fact, buoyed by that, he pulled out the rag on which they had drawn the map, flipped it, took a charcoal-tipped twig from Zaq's fire, and decided that this night and every one after it, he would write down at least a little of everything he now knew to be true about the world: from Nogowu's codex to Lilong's tales to the things he had seen with his own two eyes.

Zaq, who had been listening all this time without a word, finished the meal in dead silence. The final course was smoked dry meat, most of it being what Danso had packed, and some okra they'd picked up in the forest. They ate it with bread, sitting in separate corners, not speaking. Danso decided to repair things with Zaq, and went up to him. His Second scooted away and kept him at arm's length.

"How wild are the animals out here?" Danso asked, trying for regular conversation.

"Wild," Zaq said, after deciding he had no choice but to answer. "I pray we don't come upon any."

Danso commented on the excavation they were in, how it resembled the kind people talked about when they described illegitimate mines, compared to those in the mining protectorate of Undati and the now-abandoned Dead Mines at the foot of the Soke mountains. Zaq was minimally responsive.

Defeated, Danso gave his attempts a rest for the night. *Perhaps the light of sunrise might alter this sourness,* he thought. So even when Lilong threw up all her meat and broke into a sweat despite the coolness of night, Danso tended to her with a wet cloth and boiled some of the gum tree extract in water for her to drink without speaking to her at all. Zaq went to bed without asking whose watch it was, and Lilong fell asleep much earlier than expected. Danso was left alone with the dying fire, staring into the darkness and the moons above reflecting in the eyes of his Skopi outside.

He had never been more uncertain about his future in his entire life.

37

Zaq

ZAQ ONLY PRETENDED TO be asleep for less than an hour before the snores from his fellow travellers filled the hollow excavation. He rose and picked at his bedding, trying not to make any noise. The bulk of the snoring came from Danso, whom Zaq knew to be a heavy sleeper. He banked on Lilong, the lightest sleeper of all three, being too fatigued from illness and the day's exertion to awaken, and he wasn't wrong. Neither of them moved when he rose and crept out to the opening in the ground.

Nightlight was in full character. The savanna looked different bathed in this silvery glow. Ordinarily, it would've been beautiful, but the Skopi hanging there made it too uneasy for Zaq. The grasses were too tall, and the trees too far apart and isolated, and it seemed like there was definitely something lurking within, biding its time for him to emerge enough to be within reach. Wherever there was prey, there was always predator.

But he had to go, didn't he? He had dreamt about Mokhiri again, the night before. This time, she had been calling his name, asking him to come back home. He had told her he couldn't survive alone—what did he know about defending himself? He couldn't even graduate to Potokin! But her cry had been persistent, had convinced him it might be a sacrifice worth making.

He gulped and took another step, listened. Was that a rustle? He couldn't say. He had spent enough time in the fields in Haruna to see what happened when a lion or cheetah or the odd wolf decided to wander from their habitual terrain to try for food in the settlements. Sometimes, even ten men couldn't defeat them, especially when they came in packs. Sure, all the adages were there—*Do not turn your back on a lion; You must look a predator in the eye*—but had any of these people ever done these things? Had they ever tried to escape into the night, when the predator might not even notice you were looking it in the eye?

He took two other steps. Wind, now cooling but still bearing a modicum of the day's heat within it, like dregs at the bottom of a raffia wine gourd, tousled the grass. Tree branches swayed in the distance. There might have been the call of an animal, or he might have heard that in his head. Either way, he couldn't tell: Was it far or near?

He turned his eyes to the Skopi again. The bat, black as night, remained unmoved.

Nothing was ever going to be the same again—that was a fact. There was no way the Zaq who had crossed that threshold of the Breathing Forest would ever return to Bassa the same Zaq who dutifully went about his reports at the local government and to the combat training sessions for promotion to Potokin. This Zaq could never cook evening meals at the Habba house again. He had seen things that could not be unseen—one of them was hanging upside-down on that tree right now.

What was the point of fearing the savanna, then? He might get mauled, or not, it made little difference—his old life was gone and over. Even if he returned, he would be demoted, becoming a slave to the temple. If that was the life that awaited him in lieu of death, wasn't death better?

But . . . there was still Mokhiri. There was *always* Mokhiri.

He took one step back, another, then another. He retreated into the darkness of the excavation, back to his spot, and smoothed out his bedding. He lay, curving himself into a ball.

He would survive, first. Then he would make it back to Bassa. Whatever might happen to him, he didn't quite care at this point. But he remained hopeful, because, if anything, at least he would get to see Mokhiri's face again. And that, in itself, was sufficient.

Danso

THE FIRST GROWLS CAME beneath the wind, lurking around the edges of the breeze. Danso didn't quite hear them, flitting between dreams and wakefulness, until upon a swift moment of clarity, he was suddenly able to distinguish the intermittent chuffs—a sucking back of breath between growls—from the flurry of air.

He jumped, startled. Had he fallen asleep on watch?

He listened again. The growls were there, from someplace outside, maybe far, maybe near, like something had found them and knew it, but was not yet ready to attack.

"Lilong," he said, quietly, shaking the girl. She didn't move.

"Lilong," he said again, and instead Zaq awoke.

"What, what?" Zaq said.

"There's something outside," he said.

They listened. The growl came again, this time stronger, menacing.

Zaq stiffened. "Oh, Ashu," he said, suddenly weak. "They've found us."

"They who?" Danso said. "It's a wild animal."

"That's a leopard," Zaq said. "Very likely a hunthand's leopard."

They stayed quiet, hoping it would go away. The growling seemed to be coming from various directions, as if the animal was pacing.

"I think it might be hunting the bat," Zaq said. "If it hasn't attacked us already, then there's no hunthand nearby. It must've strayed. Its hunt-hand will likely be tracking it and be here any moment."

Danso's hands trembled. *Focus*, he told himself. *You're supposed to be the smart one here. Think!*

"We must leave immediately," he said. "We have to get to the Bight of Whudasha right away and touch that fence. That's the only way we're staying alive."

They didn't bother packing up. Zaq only grabbed the pack as it was and left the bedding and everything else. If they were lucky, they might not even need these things anymore. And if they were unlucky, they definitely wouldn't.

It turned out Lilong had finally succumbed to whatever ailed her and was not only difficult to wake but unable to stand and stay conscious as well. Danso had to support her with one arm over his shoulder and the other over a grudging Zaq's. Her skin burned against his and created sweat where they touched.

They had to create a diversion, or the leopard would catch up without even trying. There was only one way to do it.

Are you sure about this? he asked himself. Lilong would definitely object if she were awake, but what other choice did he have? He did not come all this way only to be eaten by an errant leopard at the last, and he knew she definitely didn't either.

He dug his hand into her pouch and grabbed the Diwi.

The power of the mineral coursed through his body, filling his chest as it had done the first time, until every part of him felt like it was filled with heat. He turned his focus toward the Skopi, as he had seen Lilong do with her blade. The ibor power reached forward of its own accord, opening him up to the bat, Possessing it.

Two eyes lit up red in the darkness. Lightning streaked across the sky above.

Danso felt yanked out of his own body, and then he was upside-down, yet at the same time not. He had trouble deciding where he started and where the Skopi began, and if he was either or neither or both. His senses had tripled, quadrupled: the night suddenly too bright, everything too loud, breathing too hard. A pulse was going out from his face, and with it, he could sense the direction and placement of everything about him, including the pacing leopard. He felt large, connected to everything, and something even bigger and fiercer spreading across the sky above: lightning.

The ibor nudged him for a command, pushed his mind to make a choice.

Go, he Commanded the bat, the position of the leopard and the image of what he wanted the bat to do with it very clear.

The bat rose and surged into the darkness. A moment later, it struck something, or something struck it, and Danso heard it screech again. A tumble ensued somewhere in the dark that they couldn't see. He let go of the Diwi and pulled out of the connection. Sharp pains of an aftereffect hit his bones, chest, teeth. He gritted his teeth and steadied himself.

"Now," he said to Zaq, and they crept out of the excavation into the hot and humid night of insect noises and bites, swishing through the grass as they dragged Lilong with them, huffing and puffing. With low visibility and the sun no longer present to provide direction, Danso didn't know where they were going. He tried to find the bat by gripping the stone-bone again, but felt nothing. Maybe the leopard had killed it for good? Every now and then, he paused to listen to see if they were being followed by either, but heard nothing significant.

"We have to keep going," Zaq kept saying. "Even if the leopard is gone, its hunthand could still find us."

"How did they even find us?" Danso said, pondering. "We skirted the bushroads."

"They put a bounty on our heads!" Zaq was terribly upset. "You thought we were just going to harbour a fugitive and get a free pass to escape to the one place on the mainland with a Peace Treaty?"

Of course Zaq was right. Leopards meant either very serious independent hunthands or employees of influential families, and Danso could think of one particular family with a vested interest in having them recaptured.

"Think they're from Nem?" he asked. "Or..." He gulped. "Esheme?"

"Does it matter?" Zaq said, irritated. "We get found, we won't even have time to say our last prayers."

They kept going, for what seemed like an hour, then two, then three, and soon their legs and shoulders began to weaken. When they could take it no more, they collapsed in the grass in the middle of the savanna, breathless.

"Can't—go—any farther," Danso said.

"Shush," Zaq said, and took a swig of water from the skin before offering it to Danso. He peered into the darkness, set his ear to listen beneath the sounds of crickets, flies, mosquitoes.

Danso took a swig and forced some through Lilong's lips. It ran down the sides of her mouth. She hadn't changed much, flitting in and out of consciousness.

"We need to get her to a healer, fast," Danso said.

"I'd say we leave her and run for our lives, if you ask me," Zaq said, his back to Danso, head jerking as he scanned. "It's her or death, at this point."

Danso shook his head. "We've come too far. Can't give up now."

"We very well can," Zaq said. "And maybe you can't, but I very well can." Zaq rose. "I can't do this with you anymore, Danso. I can't. You have to choose."

"Zaq, stop."

"No." Zaq threw down what was left of the pack and dusted his palms together ceremoniously. "I'm done making sacrifices for you. If you want to die with her, so be it. I'm going to Whudasha. You can come with me, or you can lose your life trying to protect a stranger."

Before Danso had time to respond, Zaq turned and disappeared into the darkness. Danso wanted to call after him, but worried about alerting whatever might be around. He rose quickly, adjusted Lilong's pouch to himself, threw her arm over his shoulder, and hobbled his way forward.

"You don't even know the way," he whispered harshly into the darkness, hoping Zaq could hear him. "Where are you going?"

No response. Danso continued to hobble forward, stopping at intervals to catch his breath and move Lilong over to his other shoulder.

The Skopi dropped out of the sky and landed next to him, almost completely soundless. Danso fell to the ground in fright. The strong metallic smell of blood hung around the bat, but it did not move, just stood there on all fours, waiting, until he began to move again, and it followed him.

He was unsure of how far he'd gone. An hour more? Two? Everything became timeless, directionless. Nothingness blended together until there was no discerning, no lines to separate the awareness of things. Danso felt, for the first time since leaving Bassa, like nothing mattered anymore, like if he died here and now, tonight, he would be proud of what he had achieved.

And then, a sound. Or, more like a *feeling*: It came first as a breeze, like the atmosphere here had suddenly changed from static to breezy. A distant snoozy lapping, splashing, roaring.

The coast. That had to be the coast.

He readjusted Lilong on his side and hurried forward. They had to be close to the fence at this point.

With no sight in the darkness, Danso ran into a man. And just as he did, he heard the low growl of a leopard again, coming over the distant sound of night and sea.

The man was Zaq, standing rock still. They held down their screams together at the same time.

Ahead of them was a row of lights. One row, low, like from burning torches. The other row, high, farther behind, like from sentry posts. Likely from the fence, Danso thought. But the low lights were from men, hunthands, and another leopard with eyes piercing the darkness. From what he could see, at least one of the men had nocked an arrow in a bowstring and had that pointed in their direction.

"They found us." Zaq put up his hands, slowly, in surrender.

Danso laid Lilong down in the grass, gently, slowly. Her pouch turned askew, and the Diwi fell out and into the grass. Danso cursed and bent, feeling in the grass in search of it.

His hands grasped it, and then many things happened at once, fast.

He rose, Diwi in hand, to shouts from the men with the torches, yelling something indecipherable because they were too far. He saw the leopard, no longer at the side of those who held it in check. It bounded gracefully, parting the grass straight like an arrow, headed for him.

Danso squeezed his eyes shut and Drew.

An unimaginable rush and heat and energy flowed through his body, too quickly, too *much*, so that it took him over and he suddenly was unable to breathe. And the force took hold of his mind and asked him to *reach reach reach*.

So he reached.

He felt a million quick throbbings of air, the tiny particles of its form coming alive, beating, breathing, gathering in anticipation for something. And somewhere within all of this, Danso imagined shouts and commands, growls, the *thwack* of wood leaving a bowstring, the *whoosh* of an arrow sailing through air.

A pain struck him in the left shoulder.

He Commanded as the ibor asked.

A burst of energy descended from the sky and struck the ground. Heavy thunder-not-thunder rippled across the savanna, the beat large and round and weighty. He felt the reverberation in his chest, felt grasses stick up, erect, felt everything nearby shudder, squeal, fall.

And Danso too, as with everything around him, hit the ground.

39

Biemwensé

WHENEVER THE LITTLE SCOUTS brought news to Biemwensé, they stood at the door to her hut and clapped until she told them to come in. Housing in Whudasha was rebuilt too often and too quickly for swing doors, so that meant mats were hung over the doorways instead. It was people without good training and discipline who walked uninvited past these mats and into homes, without alerting the owner and allowing them time to settle into some decency. Worse yet when this happened much too early in the morning before first light had descended; when the house-owner's sight was so severely depleted—like hers—that, a long time ago, she had stopped bothering to peer in an attempt to see.

So of course Biemwensé was severely irritated when two of the scouts she had hired to scan the edge of her property periodically—young boys only wee seasons old—rushed into her home while she was in the middle of her early cassava and okra soup meal.

"Yaya," the voice she recognised as the older one—the fledgling archer, skinny from when she'd last felt him—said breathlessly. "Yaya, we found people."

"And that is why you cannot clap?" she said, flinging the small rolled-up mound of cassava meal in her hand in their direction. She heard-felt them duck. "So because you see something in the savanna, you come and be entering my house anyhow you like? Especially at this early-early hour?"

"Sorry, Yaya," they chorused. But they did not giggle afterward, as they were so used to doing, so that she knew it was something serious.

"What did you see?" she asked, washing her hand in the nearby bowl of water.

Silence.

"Talk, boy," she said. "Don't be wasting my time."

"Bodies," the littler scout said, almost a whisper. "Many bodies."

whudasha

Esheme

THE DAY AFTER THE funeral, Esheme had Igan hang around the house to provide extra protection while she recovered from the ordeal, with the promise of more payment to the coalition. To Esheme's surprise, Igan put up much less resistance to the idea than expected. They spent most of the period together in the library, Esheme splitting her time between rereading Nem's journal and being inquisitive about what was happening in the streets.

Out in the city, protests doubled, tripled. Like most spearheaded by the coalition, unrest sprang up in many of the outer wards and grew inward as dissatisfaction about the border closure clashed with the new information that it had been shut down for more insidious purposes. Reasons for being incensed varied: Immigrants wanted increased efforts to have the yellowskin caught and dealt with before her actions affected their own chances; the Emuru wanted all traitors tried for treason and the yellowskin hanged in the capital square; the Idu wanted a show of strength from Bassa, a gathering of an army to march to the desert's coasts and seek out the yellowskin's origins. At the core of every group's request was one thing: *Remind everyone that we still possess venom in our sting.*

The Upper Council, rather than address any of the concerns, sent civic guards into the outer wards as usual, with the aim of quashing any rising dissent. The only pacifying bargains they offered were to high-ranking influencers in the inner wards.

"So this is how you lot work at the coalition," Esheme said to Igan as she rested her eyes between reading. "You wield tales. Except, instead of jalis telling them, you just make a city crier of every Bassai possible."

Igan gave a wry smile. As someone who had rejected the readily imposed label of *woman*, eschewed the description of *man* as employed derogatorily against people who looked like them, and chosen instead to self-identify outside of either, Igan had a knack for quiet moves of grand resistance. They took every opportunity to demonstrate this proficiency, especially in how they delayed responses, offering a portion of an answer only when they deemed fit. They wielded silence like their axe, employing it like its own manner of speech. The coalition seemed like a natural fit for someone like this—unfathomable. Except, for some reason, Igan didn't seem particularly ecstatic that the alliance had yielded fruit for both parties.

"Tell me," Esheme said, fascinated, and perhaps more drawn to them than she cared to admit, "what did you do before the coalition?"

"Private hunthand," Igan said. They stood watching the courtyard, almost like Nem would have, except less leisurely, with a stance that said they were poised to pounce into battle at any moment.

"Why did you leave? The coalition pays better?"

Igan angled their head. "No."

Esheme decided to hold and match their silence, waiting for the second half of the answer. She enjoyed this push-pull with Igan, almost a cat-and-rat game, except Igan was no rat so it felt more like cat-and-cat, which made Esheme relish it even more.

"I joined because I was looking for someone to really do something for the nation," Igan said, giving in. "Enact the kind of change everyone is afraid to."

"And you think Basuaye will?" Esheme asked.

Igan angled their head again. "No."

"Oh?" Esheme lifted her eyebrows. "Because he is too old?"

"Among other things."

"Like what?"

Igan let the silence fall into another lull before saying, "The coalition has existed long enough for things to have changed. Things have not changed. Therefore, the coalition is ineffective in its purpose." And that was the last thing they said for the rest of the period.

Despite that, Esheme decided she enjoyed Igan's presence in the house for more reasons than one, and believed everyone was better for it as well. Except Satti, of course, who spoke openly about what a vagabond like Igan being associated with the household on a near-permanent basis would do to its reputation. Esheme wanted to tell her that their reputation was already in tatters and had nothing left with which it could save them on its own. But how could one explain a toothache to someone without teeth?

Esheme flitted between her room and the library, resting her head after each meal and some medicine sourced from Habba. A few visitors came by, most attempting to pay respects to Nem, but Esheme refused for anyone to be let through. Even when Ikobi, her mentor at the university, showed up to enquire if Esheme was ready to return, she did not have the woman shown in. Instead, she continued to study the remainder of her maa's journal.

Yet as every hour passed, her heart rate increased because she knew exactly what was coming, the one visitor she was really waiting for, and it was only a matter of time before it all arrived at her doorstep.

The confrontation she expected did indeed arrive toward the end of the day, when the sun had started to cast slanting shadows. She heard the clatter of kwaga hooves and urgent calls to halt, in a way that told her a group of free-riding kwagas had arrived. She went down to meet them, and as she had suspected, it was First Elder Ọta's Second, Ariase.

He came dressed differently from the five civil guards with him, marking himself separate from the others. All were battle-ready and armed to the teeth: spears, axes, runkus, daggers, bows. They looked like they were going to war, which they might as well have been.

Esheme stepped outside, Igan and Satti on either side of her, and the one available hunthand behind them. Igan had their hand placed squarely behind their waist, where the reach of the double-headed axe strapped to their back extended. The axe had a long handle with two sharp edges, a design Esheme had not seen on this side of the mainland before. She had asked them about it, and Igan, in what Esheme was coming to realise was typical behaviour, did not feel obliged to offer any explanation. Instead, they had looked one another in the eye until both had became uncomfortable with the silence.

"Esheme-maa," Ariase said by way of greeting.

Esheme did not respond to his greeting, but stared at him in silence. After a while, he gave in and said:

"May we speak inside?"

"No," Esheme said calmly. "You are not granted permission to enter my house. Whatever you want to say, you can say here."

Ariase's jaw tightened. As the Second to one of the most powerful men in the city, he likely often responded to any challenges swiftly and violently. But today was different. Today, Igan was standing there, and if word had already gone out correctly—even though it was word that couldn't really be verified—then he knew exactly who Igan was.

Esheme put her faith in this and was rewarded. His gaze flitted constantly to Igan and back to Esheme, and every word that he uttered, he thought of very carefully.

"It is a private matter," he said.

"Everything stopped being private the moment you accosted me in the street and your First Elder tried to arrest me at the funeral for nothing. Henceforth, every dealing between yours and mine becomes public."

"Very well," he said. "I was instructed to keep this as quiet as possible, but have it your way." He cleared his throat. "I have been sent by the First Elder. You are to come with us."

Esheme scoffed. "What for?"

"For your treasonous offences against the nation, a list of which I am willing to read to you." He signalled to a civic guard, who began to read a list. "Accusing Bassai leadership of falsities; making false declarations with the intent to incite unrest among the Bassai people; joining forces with a treasonous group—"

"Will you shut up," Esheme said. "I am a counsel novitiate, for moon's sake. If you're going to bring stupid charges against me, at least make them real." She stepped forward. "If your First Elder seeks to accuse me, he can do it in the noble court of the Great Dome, in the full hearing of the people. If he wishes to speak with me on a private matter, he can say it to my face, in person. Otherwise, I would like you to step off my property. Unless, of course, you would prefer to be removed."

Things stood for a moment, and then Ariase's hand went to his weapon at the same time as Igan pulled their axe from their back.

As if on cue—and completely on cue, for Esheme had planned for it to happen just so—an organised coalition protest swarmed onto the scene. Esheme had requested a group so mixed that no one would suspect preparedness. They chanted about the exact same things the coalition had been chanting every single day since the Pass closed. They moved into the scene innocently, asking what was going on, whispering to each other, but keeping it loud enough to reach the hearing of Ariase and the guards.

"Who would attack our voice?" they said. "Who would put a hand over our mouths and bind our lips? Who would take away the one who gave voice to the secrets kept from us? Who, who, who?"

Esheme had gotten the idea from Igan's reports through Basuaye—who had also escaped the scene unscathed, as usual—that the coalition had been sure to spread the events at the funeral like a bushfire, especially to the outer wards. The truth of proceedings had been embellished slightly, and her words polished for memorable effect, so that every citizen came away with two understandings: that Esheme had unearthed the long-hidden truth behind the border closure and clamoured for the glory days of an emperor, and that the coalition agreed with her that enough was indeed enough. They hired singers and heralds with lower morals than a jali to sing litanies and parrot her words until they became gospel. Even the outer wards began to warm up to Esheme in a way that no inner-warder had garnered support for many seasons. The coalition capitalized on this to boost their ranks and rake in even more followers.

Getting a few of those earnest folk to play a part was easy, and Basuaye was willing to draw this out as long as possible. It was a win-win.

Ariase watched the protesters increase in number, watching the guards get agitated by the number of people who had suddenly invaded their space. He returned his gaze to Esheme and her group, very aware of what was happening.

Esheme held his eyes. *Your choice,* her gaze said. *If you think this is going to be easy, try it.*

They held that way for a very long moment, before Ariase resheathed his golden-hilted blade and nodded slowly. The civic guards did the same, and tensions ceased for a beat.

"Well played," he said. "Just know that once I leave here, that is the last of all niceties from us."

"And from us," Esheme said. "Expect anything."

Ariase got back on his kwaga and turned off without another glance at her. The dust of their kwagas was chased by chants from the coalition members, who had, in the midst of everything, surprisingly been joined by a few real passersby. In their chanting, Esheme discovered the new name they were calling her: Esheme the Brave.

Esheme the Brave. She tossed the name in her mouth, savoured its taste. *Sufficient for now, perhaps,* she thought. But *brave* was only a small part of what she really wanted people to think when they spoke her name. She didn't yet have the exact word for it, but she knew it had to be one that invoked a feeling Bassa had not felt in a long, long time.

41

Biemwensé

THE SUN ROSE ON Whudasha like an orange blanket spread over the coast. Its rising hues bathed land both claimed and unclaimed, the debris and barrenness left behind in the wake of the sea's low tide. It was a strange land, Whudasha, not because it was on the coast, which—together with the great waters of the seas—was an enigma in itself, but because much like the people who lived there, it was not one thing or the other.

Biemwensé walked, for instance, over sand that was somewhere between desert brown and coastal polished. Tiny patches of gamba grass and clumps of shrub dotted the coast as far as the eye could see, interrupted here and there by palm trees and rock formations of varying shapes and sizes. Whudasha was that one place on the continent that wasn't sure what it wanted to be—desert or beach or mountain or forest—so it simply chose to be everything. Walking from her house on the edge of the protectorate, just within distance of where the eastern edge of the Peace Fence marked the end of the mainland and the start of the coast, Biemwensé went past all four manners of being in which the land had chosen to exist.

In the horizon behind her, the great waters of the sea winked back at the sun, both holy bodies setting out for the day.

The eastern portion of the Peace Fence was quiet and empty, very much unlike the other portions of the lengthy structure. If there was one thing Bassa loved to build—or dig, in the case of the Soke moats—it was lengthy structures of demarcation. And since they didn't care to build anything worthy for anyone with a drop of outlander blood in them, the fence was made of bamboo. Disintegration had taken hold of it, due to little maintenance since the Peace Treaty's signing. But the fence was never really built to fortify or protect anyway; it was simply a reminder to everyone on one side that they were worthy, and everyone on the other that they were not.

At the western and northern corners of the fence, Bassai civic guards were planted on the mainland side and Whudasha Youth on the coastal side. But the eastern portion had no such thing. Anyone approaching it had to come through both the Breathing Forest *and* the recently formed savanna, and it was highly unlikely anyone would survive those two places, so it was moot to waste hands on guard here. Wild cheetahs and hyenas did all the work that was required.

But Biemwensé was one of the few people who lived there, shunted over to the edge of the protectorate for reasons that made her boil every time she thought about them. She had to take matters of protection into her own hands. The parentless, abandoned children who routinely crossed the fence to scavenge the savanna, risking death by both wild animal and Bassai civic guard, all to set traps for hare and antelope, could do with some help. She had hired a few of them to keep lookout on the eastern perimeter in exchange for food. They crossed the fence anyway, but they stayed true to their word and kept watch. Every now and then, they returned with news about hyena and cheetah and the odd elephant sighting. They never came back with news about people. Especially not *dead* people.

The sun had taken shape when Biemwensé arrived at the sentry station from which the boys said they had seen the bodies. All of the other lookout children were gathered there when she arrived with her two boys. Climbing up to the lookout was physically impossible for her, so if she was going to assess the situation, she had to go beyond the fence.

"Show me the place where you cross," she said.

The children hesitated. She sighed.

"I know you still cross to trap hares," she said. "I will not report you. I just need to see."

The skinny archer boy who brought the report—Afanfan—said: "Maybe you will close your eyes, Yaya, and we will lead you."

"Don't be stupid," she said. "I don't even see well with them open."

But she closed her eyes all the same, and they led her through places that she navigated, as she did a lot of the time anyway, through sound and smell and touch. The open portion of the Peace Fence, when she went past it, smelled of rotting bamboo and was slippery to the touch. The grass was wet with mildew. When the grass beneath her feet began to grow taller, rising to tickle her ankles, she knew they had crossed the threshold where the coast ended and the savanna began.

"There," Afanfan said, and Biemwensé opened her eyes.

When the children had said *bodies*, she'd thought, *human*. But the first body she saw was actually a leopard. From the ring about its neck, it must have been tame. Which was why, a little distance from the leopard, the body of a person dressed clearly like a hunthand—body armour, strapped weapons, warrior bodypaint—did not strike her as odd.

What struck her as odd were the two other hunthands lying in the grass, also dead. All three men had parts of them charred and smelled like roasted meat, their armour melted into their skin and faces permanently contorted like what had attacked them had done so midscream.

The last time bounty hunthands came to Whudasha, Biemwensé had been much younger, still had good eyesight, still had family who were alive. They had tracked a group of runaway desertlanders, househands who had thought they could escape their indenture to the nation by getting on the coastal side of the Peace Fence. There was no guarding of the fence at the time, because there had been no need—mainlanders with as much as a drop of outlander blood were still getting killed so often that any such person who wanted to stay alive was wise to move to Whudasha.

These immigrants had sadly interpreted the treaty to mean it included them. The hunthands arrived a few days after the desertlanders had crossed. The treaty meant they couldn't cross the fence either, but every Whudan knew what harbouring them meant for the coastal protectorate. So the Whudasha Youth rounded up the desertlanders and handed them over to the hunthands.

The hunthands were supposed to return the escaped househands alive. But the death of one could be easily forgiven, so they made an example of one of the three. A grisly eye-gouging, throat-slitting, bowel-emptying example. The smell of blood and guts had carried in the sea's wind for days after. No Whudan dared clean up the remains. Vultures picked off what they wanted, and the wind and hyenas took the rest.

"Go back to the fence and make sure nobody crosses," Biemwensé said to the rest of the children, who turned away reluctantly. "You two, stay," she said to Afanfan and his little partner who had brought the news—his name was Owude.

Biemwensé walked through the grass slowly, squinting, asking her eyes to do more than they could and her brain to solve this puzzle. First, three hunthands didn't stray this far away from Bassa with their leopard for no reason. Hunthands chased specific bounty, and three of them, this heavily armed and with a leopard, meant they were chasing something big. Second, hunthands didn't die easily. These were people who tracked, chased, and captured things for a living—animals, artifacts, people. They weren't easily conquered.

Third, there was no blood. These three had been fried to death.

Ahead, she spotted something in the grass. Someone. Well, *someones*. She went up to them.

She saw the desertlander first, lying a little distance from the other two. The sight brought back memories of the Whudasha Youth dragging the desertlander toward the hunthands, who pulled out their curved knives and grinned. She turned away, and next to each other, almost side-by-side, were a young Shashi man with an arrow in his shoulder, congealed blood around it, and a young yellowskin woman.

All three were untouched and had none of the burn signs of the others, leopard included.

She was about to ask herself all the questions about what three such disparate individuals had done to place themselves within sights of such hunthands in the first place, when she noticed the last body, nearly hidden from sight by the tree from which it hung upside down, eyes wide open yet lifeless.

The Skopi was as tall as she was, and probably much bigger once it had those folded wings spread out. It was black all through—fur, talons, leathery wings—so that, standing so still, it could have been mistaken for a part of the tree. It did not respond to her presence.

Biemwensé stood there for a long time, regarding the scene before her, piecing things together.

The last time she had even heard anything concerning yellowskins from the islands of the eastern archipelago, she had been much younger, and what she had even heard was that they had gone down just like the Ajabo out on this side of the continent. But then, look here—not only was there one on the mainland, over a hundred seasons later, but there was also a Skopi standing there with her, a bat that only existed in reported speech and had not been seen by the naked eyes of anyone currently alive.

What were they all doing here, being chased and attacked by private hunthands? If stories were to be believed, then the Skopi had obviously struck the hunthands with its lightning. Which made no sense because that bat was clearly very dead.

She stood there, befuddled, until an unnamable feeling in her showed itself to be curiosity, then morphed into something akin to pity, and then, surprisingly, something more primal, like kinship. She squatted and put a quick finger to the sides of each of the three young necks. Alive, all of them, but weak rates.

Healer instinct kicked in. She was going to help them.

"Yaya," a voice said, and she almost jumped. Afanfan and Owude stood behind her.

"What is that?" Owude asked, pointing at the Skopi.

Good question, Biemwensé thought.

"Go and tell the others," Biemwensé ordered them, rising. "Prepare to dig holes. Big holes for bodies."

The children nodded, indifferent. Being Whudan meant living daily within an atmosphere so grim that death and everything that came with it—digging graves, for instance—became just another thing that people got to experience. Biemwensé mused that children so young didn't have to go through life in this way, but reality was a persistent force that would disagree.

"How many, six?" Afanfan asked.

Biemwensé looked at the bodies before her. "Three," she said. "You people can eat the leopard."

The boys turned to go, excited.

"But before that," Biemwensé said, "what about you help me move these ones, and I give you some okra to cook that leopard with?"

When they stooped to move the boy, something fell out of his hand. It was a red stone that looked like it could also be bone. Biemwensé stared at it for a while, trying to convince herself it definitely could not be what her instincts were telling her it could be. She had heard many stories about a powerful mineral that looked somewhat like this, and might have once existed on the mainland. Of course she was overreaching—this *definitely* couldn't be *that*—but she had already seen both a yellowskin and a Skopi in one day, had she not? Why was the idea of ibor so far-fetched?

When they moved the boy, the Skopi jerked into motion and jumped down from the tree. They ran. After a distance, they realised it was only waiting. They returned and tried to move the boy again. The Skopi followed. It followed them every single step they moved the boy, so Biemwensé decided that everything she knew and understood about the world right then, she must throw to the wind.

42

Biemwensé

THE SHASHI BOY AWOKE first.

He came to screaming, clutching at his chest and calling for someone named Habba who, after three screams, Biemwensé surmised from his mumbled High Bassai, had to be a parent or guardian. The boy's eyes were tightly shut, as if he was too scared to open them, so she had to throw her weight over the edge of the bed, put an elbow into his midriff, and pin down his arms. He calmed down but did not open his eyes, and instead drifted back into troubled unconsciousness.

The desertlander awoke next. He woke up like a devil, eyes open, noiseless. He might have even been awake for much longer, unmoving, if Biemwensé hadn't turned and found him lying there, his bald desertlander head shining, his gaze fixed pointedly on the Shashi in the bed across him. He did not even turn or flinch when Biemwensé got up and went to his side of the bed.

"Feeling okay?" she asked, first in Whudan and, when he did not respond, then in Mainland Common.

He looked at her like someone who had been awoken from a sleep he did not want to wake from. He was upset, the kind of upset one took to bed at night and awoke with at daybreak. Biemwensé wondered if he was even happy to be alive.

"Where am I?" he asked, in Mainland Common.

"Whudasha, Coastal Protectorate of the First Landers," she said. "But if you want to be specific, you are in my house, on the eastern edge, where

I found you and your friends lying at the threshold where the savanna meets the bight."

He seemed uneased by the word *friends*, but didn't respond, that mini scowl still plastered over his face. Biemwensé wanted to slap it off him.

He sat up slowly, testing his body. She waited for him to ask about the others. Hospice training taught her that within the first few moments, people who had been hurt in a group usually asked about the others. This one seemed uninterested in the welfare of his fellow travellers.

"Guess what I also found?" Biemwensé said. "Three hunthands and their leopard. They're not here because they're dead, scorched to death. So if you have the story of that unfortunate situation ready, I'm going to continue helping your friends while you tell it to me."

She went back to the beds where the other two lay and resumed working on the herb concoction she was mashing and brewing for the yellow-skin girl, who was in the most precarious situation. The other two were in better shape compared to the girl, who had a myriad of ailments: internal and external wounds, heatstroke and exhaustion, all in the middle of her moonblood.

The desertlander did not speak for a while, like he was stunned. When he did speak, it was the last thing Biemwensé expected to hear.

"I must leave," he said.

Biemwensé stopped and turned to look at him. "Excuse me?"

"I need to get out of here," he said flatly.

"Out of Whudasha, or out of my house?" Biemwensé asked. "To be honest, I'm happy to have you out of my house. Out of Whudasha, however, that is not going to happen anytime soon."

The desertlander frowned. "Because?"

"Because, you idiot, the Whudasha Youth will want to know, first of all, why you killed three registered Bassai hunthands right outside our Peace Fence. Then you'd have to explain why they were hunting you. And if that's not enough, you'll have to explain *this* to them."

She pointed to the corner, where the Skopi was hanging from one of her rafters. It had not moved or done anything else but hang like an upturned statue in that corner since following them home.

"You want to tell everyone about *this*, too?" she asked, pointing to the reddish stone-bone, which she had laid next to the Shashi boy.

The desertlander looked at both things with one side of his eye. It was a gaze laden with disdain.

"I don't know," he said after a drawn-out moment, too drawn out, so that Biemwensé decided he knew exactly everything, and confirmed her own suspicions.

She went back to her work, the silence providing agreement for what must've happened.

"The hunthands," she said. "They died of burns, yet not a single other thing around them was even blackened. No fire anywhere, not even around you three." She laid down the facts, maybe for herself, maybe for him. "None of you three were hurt in the same way, so it was precisely targeted, and you were only affected by the blowback of the force of the thing that killed them. Your Shashi is the only one who was hurt by an actual recognisable weapon."

"Then why don't you ask *him*?" the desertlander shot back, a little too vehemently. He retreated into himself right after, in a way that Biemwensé knew that he wasn't used to pushing back, was someone who had practiced reining himself in for too long, and now he was letting it all out too much, too often.

"What is your name, boy?" she asked.

He gave her a long look before answering: "Zaq."

"Zaq," Biemwensé said. "That has a Savanna Belt ring to it. Haruna? Chugoko? Reangi, perhaps?"

Zaq frowned. "And how would you know of such things?"

Biemwensé smiled a little smile. "I have lived many lives that have taken me places."

"But you're—" He motioned to her body. "You know."

"Shashi?" She smiled some more. "Of course. But Whudasha has not always been a protectorate, remember? There was a time, when people like me, people like your Shashi friend here, used to be treated like actual people on this land. A time when we could roam without being targeted for death simply for having a drop of blood that did not adhere to the humus of the Bassai Ideal. Some of my ancestors knew their way around this land long before the Peace Treaty. They knew the tales it held, the tongues it spoke." She returned to her work. "And even after your Bassai overlords decided that desertlanders mixing with mainlanders was taboo, even after the post-war pogroms forced all of us here, our ancestors still had mouths and many of them knew well to pass down the right stories. I am not just me, you see. I am all of my ancestors in one body."

The boiling of her herbs filled the gaps the silence left in the room. Outside, it was late afternoon, but it was quiet. Only the sounds of her employed children, doing whatever they always did when she wasn't looking, far, far away, could be heard.

"So did your Shashi kill those men?"

"He is *not* Shashi," the desertlander said vehemently, a bit harder than he'd probably expected. Biemwensé put one and one together and realised he must be one of those Seconds—as they called these protector-cum-hand types up in Bassa—and the young man was his charge.

"Well, he *is* Shashi," Biemwensé said. "That is what he is and that is what he will always be recognised as, so long as he lives on this land. But at least he will be glad to be here in Whudasha, where that word bears no shame." She gave him a pointed look. "True freedom is not refusing to show pain when being whipped, but reclaiming the whip with which one has been flagellated."

She pulled the concoction off the stove. The steam and balmy scent of it filled the room.

"Good for him," Zaq said, rising to his feet gingerly. "I, however, cannot stay. I need to leave immediately and return to a place where my presence actually means something."

"Then by all means, go," Biemwensé said. "But the only way you are leaving this coast without first meeting with the Whudasha Youth is to return the same way you came, or to go into the bed left by the seas and wait for the waters to return and swallow you."

The desertlander stood pondering for a moment, swaying. Biemwensé did not offer him help or reprimand.

"I will meet with them," he said with a finality. "I will go to them first, so they will know I have nothing to hide."

"Do as you will." Biemwensé pointed to a bunch of wrappers in a corner. "I selected some old wrappers. You all stink. At least wear something that won't kill the whole town with its smell."

Zaq undressed with his back to her. He wound the new wrappers from the waist down, despite having no requirement to do so now that he was out of Bassa and was no longer beholden to the code. Biemwensé chuckled. Take the man out of Bassa, but you cannot take the Bassa out of the man.

"How do I find them?" he asked when he was done.

"Looking like that?" She motioned to his clothes, but also his skin. "I would say they'd find you, the moment you step into the other parts of this protectorate."

He nodded and made to go.

"And what do you suppose I do with these two?" Biemwensé asked, cooling the concoction in a calabash so she could force-feed the young woman.

Zaq looked at the two as they lay, again. This time, his gaze was near expressionless, without thought or feeling or life behind it.

"I no longer have any responsibility to anyone," he said finally. "Do as you will."

Biemwensé

THE SUN WAS READY to begin its descent for the day when the Shashi boy was finally able to speak. He squinted at Biemwensé, disoriented and clearly uncomfortable.

"Elder Oduvie?"

Biemwensé squinted back. "Who?"

He frowned some more and said something in High Bassai. She picked up the cadence of a question.

"I am Biemwensé," she said in Mainland Common, "but you can call me Yaya like everyone else."

"Yaya." He nodded, slowly, and looked to his shoulder, now treated and wrapped. "Thank you."

"Hmm." She rose and towered over him. Biemwensé had always been a big woman, bigger than the average mainlander or islander—even desertlander.

"How are you feeling?"

The young man frowned, searching for the words to describe his situation. But rather than answer the question, he asked: "Zaq and Lilong, where are they?"

"Well, the desertlander left," she said. "The yellowskin, I have put in my own bedchamber. Risky if somebody walks in here uninvited and the first thing they see is...you know, *her*. That will not be...ideal."

"He...left?" he repeated, as if he did not hear the rest of her statement. Then he went on to stare at the wall in front of him for quite a while before turning his gaze around, putting his surroundings together.

Biemwensé's house, like most in Whudasha, was built round, so it had no edges. It was a massive hut, in essence, built by more hands than tools: mud and clay carted from as far inland as was allowed, wood and raffia palm thatch from the coast. It made sense to build this way: quick, inexpensive. The waters of the sea were not a friend, not a trustworthy thing. They had taken and taken from the coast for so long a time that it made no sense to build anything permanent anymore, lest one day it be washed away. Temporariness was a necessary way of life here.

Biemwensé's house was divided into five chambers: the room where they lay currently, which she used as a kind of apothecary, constituting three beds and an array of mud shelves built into the walls; her own bedchamber; a receiving area up front; the kitchen out back, which extended like a yawn into the yard behind; and the storeroom next to the kitchen, which she had now converted into a bathroom and toilet so that she didn't have to walk far to an outhouse to relieve herself.

The shelves sported what she herself thought was an unhealthy amount of fired and decorated pottery, in all shapes and sizes possible. She barely used calabash like everyone else, and instead opted to make and paint her own pottery as a hobby. When she wasn't diagnosing and attempting to treat people from Whudasha East and Central, she was making pottery, which she sometimes sold at the main market in Central. She painted, too, sometimes, on her own walls mostly, but her eyesight had gotten too poor to keep that up.

It was the shelves of pottery that the Shashi boy's eyes stayed upon. He smiled a little, even.

"They're beautiful," he said.

"Thank you," Biemwensé said. *No one has ever said that before,* she wanted to say, but remembered that those who visited here were always either too sick or too hungry to care.

He looked in the other direction, and only then, in the far corner of the room, did he see and recognise the Skopi there. Panic came into his eyes then, and he looked at her, waiting for her to respond in some way.

But she remained calm, making sure to communicate as much as possible that she had no ill intent.

"What happened?" she asked, instead. "To you people?"

The boy frowned in concentration, as if he were only physically here but mentally absent.

"I can't..." He looked up. "I can't remember." His eyes pleaded with her. "Could you... tell me, perhaps?"

Biemwensé nodded. They did indeed take a good knocking. This was going to be very interesting to piece together, then, and they likely only had tonight to do it before the Whudasha Youth showed up by daybreak.

"What is your name, boy?"

He hesitated, correctly thinking giving his name away would be dangerous.

"You have a yellowskin, a Skopi, and what I'm going to presume to be ibor in your custody, yet I've treated you," she said. "If I were going to harm you, I would have done so already. Besides, you have a Bassai plait in Whudasha and are wearing what are clearly jali guild wrappers. I don't think anyone will really need your name to know who you are."

He sighed in submission. "My name is Danso."

"Rest then, Danso," she said. "Maybe after you've eaten or something, you will remember things. Perhaps I could get you some food? I don't have much of it, but if those children roast that leopard tonight, maybe we can get some meat."

"Leopard?" he asked, alarmed, but she waved it away.

"Part of your long story you might eventually remember."

"I can't eat a leopard," he said. "That's barbaric."

She studied him. Okay, this one was more Bassai than his complexion proclaimed.

"Who are you?" he asked in a voice that was quiet, little.

"Biemwensé, as I said earlier. Or Yaya, if you want."

"Yaya—maa, healer, protector," he said, slowly, as if trying to remember why he knew that. "In Whudan."

She nodded. "Multilingual too, are you?" She motioned toward him. "Idu dress and plait, yet you're Shashi and speak Whudan. These are things that rarely exist in the same body."

He flinched at the word *Shashi*, and she could see why the desert-lander had done the same.

"No, they never do," he said slowly. "I'm a jali novitiate in Bassa. Well, *was* a jali novitiate."

"Before they chased you out?"

His head shot up. "How do you know that?"

"Maybe because I found you alongside three dead hunthands and one of their arrows in your shoulder?"

He looked at his shoulder, as if discovering it anew, and back at her. "Do you know who killed them?"

Biemwensé cocked her head. "My guess is that you people did."

He looked shocked. "How? I've never killed anyone in my life."

"Well, we'll find out soon enough, won't we?" she said. "In the meantime, rest, while I go check on your yellowskin friend." Just saying that word—*yellowskin*—felt off on her tongue. She'd never had to speak of anything referencing islanders with an attribution to living, or existence. This would definitely go down as her most interesting experience before the everlasting darkness took her.

"Thank you," Danso said again. "You have been kind to me."

Biemwensé wondered what life had been for this young man, what sort of people he'd been surrounded with, if kindness was too far-fetched a concept for him to grasp readily.

"There have been only a few people kind to me," Danso said, slowly, as if reading her mind. "And one of them was the only other Shashi person I've ever known. I think it may be a thing of fate, this. You finding us."

"Hmm," Biemwensé said, but she did not think it was a thing of fate at all. She thought it was a thing of mistakes, the kind that never really brought forth anything good. But she went away and let him believe that, because if there was anything she knew about healing, it was that belief was just as good a salve if applied in the right doses.

Zaq

IT TURNED OUT THE Yaya woman was right: Zaq didn't have to go too far before someone found him. All he had done was, after walking far enough in the opposite direction of the house, ask the first person he had come across where he could locate the Whudasha Youth. It had been a small, elderly man with clear desertlander blood in the way his complexion was almost desertlander low-brown but not quite. The man gave Zaq a long look and drew his own conclusions as well.

"You're from the Savanna Belt," he said in Savanna Common.

"No," Zaq replied in Mainland Common. "I'm Bassai."

The man snorted. "Okay," he said in Mainland Common, "if you say so."

"What do you mean, *if you say so*?" Zaq could not leave room for anyone to question his loyalty if he was to retain a chance of being shepherded back unharmed. "I came from the city of Bassa. Therefore, I am Bassai. And so are you, since we are both under the same nation."

"Well, I'm Whudan."

"*Nobody* is from Whudasha." Zaq kissed his teeth, indicating he was not on board with any ideas of secession. "Where do you people learn these things?"

The man shook his head, as if deciding to explain further was a lost cause. "Just go." He pointed in the direction Zaq had been going. "The Whudasha Youth will find you without even looking."

So Zaq went.

The protectorate opened up before him, sprawling. The farther he went, the bigger it got, the more people he saw. It was an odd place, Whudasha. The farther he moved from the east, the flatter the land became, the more visible was the winding edge of the wet sand where the sea, as he'd been told, would soon return. The houses also moved farther inland, so that while in the east he could find homes built into the staggered face of the rocks, almost everything toward Central was built farther and farther away from the cliff.

The people, too, increased in number. After the old man, he first ran into groups that looked like they were returning from work—craftworkers, mostly, from the look of their implements, but also what he thought to be scavengers. He'd heard fellow immigrants tell one or two tales about coastal scavengers and their odd ways—people who dared go into the dry land left by the sea at the day's low tide and scavenge for anything of worth the sea had left behind. He found it distasteful that for a living, people would go out for the day and hope the sea brought something of worth to them. He nodded at the groups when they went past, and they nodded at him non-committally, their eyes unfocused, glazed by dehydration and squalor.

This was what Danso had forced him to abandon his quality life of stability in Bassa for? *This?* Over his dead body.

Later on, Zaq came into what he realised must be a commercial district: The houses were packed tightly together, the pathways were narrow, and people jostled and moved too quickly. He put the cloak of the wrappers Biemwensé had given him over his head to hide his complexion a bit.

Everything was without order. In Bassa, it was always easy to know where one was and where one belonged by simply observing the bodies of those about: complexion, clothes and their colours, hair arches and plaits, and the like. It was what separated Tenth from Second Ward, the guilds from one another, the mainways from the corridors or the markets. Here in Whudasha, though, no two people looked quite the same. Their complexions were neither here nor there and didn't fit squarely into any of the mainland's caste systems; they wore clothing of varying sizes, colours, styles, and qualities; they wore seashells the way Bassai wore gold or coral beads; they wore hairstyles he had never seen in his entire life—some of them even simply let their hair hang down without plaits!

The only thing that tied them together, it seemed, was that every single person clearly had that slight lilt when the sun shone on their skin, that tinge of loosely coiled hair, that told him whatever mainland blood they possessed was only to a level, that every other part of them was made up of something else. Islander, desertlander, both, whatever. Some were even so high-black-like they could be mistaken for pure Bassai, while some were so low-brown-like that they could be mistaken for full desertlanders. This was what made it exactly clear that they were all, one way or another, Shashi—*confused.*

It was chaotic and irregular, and the quickness of it all buzzed around Zaq so that he had to, for a moment, stop and catch his breath, hands on his knees. He had been that way for only a short while when someone tapped his shoulder and said something in a language he didn't understand.

Zaq turned. The young woman standing behind him carried a cutlass, sheathed in leather to a belt on her waist. She was the first person he had met so far who looked exactly half desertlander, half mainlander, so that it was clear she was a prime Shashi.

She was also dressed in a manner different from everyone else. She wore more shell-beads and had one red wrapper tied to her waist alone, not across her whole torso as he had seen happen commonly here, and not multiple wrappers either. Over her torso, instead, she wore a blouse laden with these seashell-beads, as well as on her ankles like Potokin and Yelekuté immigrants, and on her biceps, and in her hair, which was plaited down like a Bassai man's. All of it jingled as she moved from foot to foot, impatient, waiting for his response.

"I don't—" Zaq signalled to his ears and lips. "I speak Mainland Common."

"I said," the woman reiterated in an accented Mainland Common, "are you lost?"

"I'm—I'm sorry," he said. "I was—"

She reached over, impatient, and pushed the cloak off his head to reveal his bald head.

"You are not Whudan," she said. There was no menace in her voice, only disinterest and a flat affect. Her face could've been made of clay, just sitting there, unused. "A desert immigrant from Bassa." She stretched out a hand, the one not tucked into the belt at her waist. "Potokin or Yele-kuté? Let me see your pass from your employer or the local government office that says you can be in Whudasha freely."

"Well, that is just the thing—" Zaq started.

"Do you have your pass or not?"

"I do not—look, I was actually looking for the Whudasha Youth," Zaq said hurriedly. "I was coming to explain my situation."

She studied him for a moment, and her lips turned up. "That so."

"Yes. See, I need to, ehm, turn myself in."

"Because?"

Because, Zaq thought, *this kind of freedom is too expensive.* Because this kind of freedom, the kind Danso sought and was trying to make him seek too, came with a certain kind of privilege that he, Zaq, could not have, because his skin was a kind of shade that did not allow it; because the side of the Soke mountains on which he was born could not afford him.

"Because," Zaq said, exhaling, "I am lost, and I would like help to go back home."

The woman frowned slightly. "And what home is this? Bassa or"—she waved at him—"wherever you come from?"

Home. He'd never lived in Haruna long enough to have one there, and he'd left the little he had in Chugoko in ruins. He had created a home on the mainland and at the DaaHabba household more than he'd ever done in the Savanna Belt. But the DaaHabba household was a place of employment, if he was being truthful with himself. *Home* required some-thing else—a family maybe, but most importantly, a place of belong-ing. He *had* been working fastidiously toward those things, until Danso's antics forced them away from him. Now he had neither, and he wasn't going to find them here. Best to return to the one place he knew and understood, while he still had a chance.

"Bassa," he said. "I would like to return home, to Bassa."

The woman nodded. "Come along, then. You're just right in place and time."

Danso

DANSO'S SHOULDER EXISTED BETWEEN a dull, consistent throb and intermittent bursts of stabbing pain. Biemwensé said the painkilling concoction she had fed him lasted only a few hours, and he was due for another. She handed the pottery bowl of bitter liquid to him and he gulped it down at once and lay down.

He was suddenly completely exhausted, somehow, even though he had just awoken from what Biemwensé had described as the longest she'd ever seen anyone sleep who wasn't dead. He realised now why such a heavy veil of despair hung over him.

He had killed someone, hadn't he? The dead hunthands? It had to be him who did it.

People who have never killed anything, Lilong had said back in the forest, *are the ones who always think killing is easy.*

Now he understood what Lilong had meant. Danso had grown up around a bit of death in Ninth, where murders were rife and trivial. Even though he had not quite been in control of his faculties when he had done the deed, Danso suddenly felt, retrospectively, dead within himself. He lay there, the weight of what he had done to those men sinking into him, sinking him into the ground beneath the bed. He had never even killed a fowl before! Barely had he physically hurt anyone, except for that one time he had struck a classmate in the face, back when the term *Shashi* worked up more rage in him than the mild anger it did now. (It had hurt him more than the other boy, the punch—he learned, later, that striking with a closed fist was a bad idea.)

But *killing*? After he had made Biemwensé painstakingly describe the men in that field, the way their bodies had been mutilated, he felt himself go cold, his mouth turn sour. *Singed to char,* she'd said. When the children had dragged the men, she said, their bones had been broken inside. It made bile want to rise from his throat to his tongue.

And the thing that scared him most? He had done all of *that* with ibor.

He tried to remember what it had felt like, using the power of the red mineral. He remembered picking it up, the feel of the savanna's gamba grass in his hand, but after that only flashes—his body vying for connection to something, *reaching*; his thoughts connecting to something bigger than itself. He remembered being the Skopi—or did he dream that?—and calling on lightning from the sky.

He looked across the room, to where the Skopi hung undead and silent, its back to him, and shivered. He had been excited to discover ibor, to understand what it could do. Now, just the thought of what the mineral was capable of made him recoil. Every fibre of his being rejected the idea of ever getting near the red stone-bone again, told him ibor was *wrong* and *alien* and *horrible* and did not fit into everything he knew and understood about the world.

Right before he drifted back into a little nap, he wondered what version of Danso he would be when he awoke. They said taking a life changed a person, and he clearly would never be the same again, imagining the bodies of those men, charring as they burned. He had already changed so much on this journey, learned so much about worlds he didn't have access to. Where did this new label—*killer*—fit? Was he still Danso, or was he now something else? And if he was, what was that?

⁘——⁘

Danso stayed in bed for an hour, until sundown, gaining strength with each passing moment. He wanted to wait for Lilong to awake so they could go find Zaq, because not only did he owe Zaq an apology, he needed to show him he had his best interests at heart too. But the longer he lay there, the more he realised Lilong might not wake as soon as he'd thought, and he might need to find Zaq all on his own. He sought to move, and Biemwensé said a good way to do that would be to go watch the sunset arrive and the seas return.

"Wear those wrappers," she said, pointing to a heap in the corner. "Don't want nobody troubling you. You should blend in with those more than your Second could."

He dressed slowly, while Biemwensé moved about the house.

"So everyone here—part outlander?" he asked.

She gave a measured glance. "You mean Shashi."

Danso shut his eyes. "I don't like—that word."

"No," Biemwensé said. "You have been taught to not like that word. The word, on its own, is meaningless. Its meaning depends on the mouth from which it comes. The mouths down here, when they call you this word, do not hide blades beneath it, not like the mouths in Bassa."

Danso nodded and finished dressing.

"The hair too," Biemwensé said without looking.

He looked at his plait in a reflective iron frame. Disheveled and completely unrecognisable as the required novitiate plait. He unhooked whatever semblance of it remained and let it fall. It occurred to him that outside of Oduvie—though her hair was dyed and had been done up in arches to look like a Bassai's—he had never seen another Shashi's hair before. Biemwensé's hair wasn't much different—it did not coil quite as tightly as most Bassai, but was not as loose as his. She did nothing to her hair, letting it lie thin and grey and limp. The few ornaments she wore were what he concluded were painted clay pieces.

He observed himself, surprised by how he suddenly looked different, natural. Like a proper Shashi, from the little he could gather of that. Like himself, if he'd given himself a chance.

"There's a tiny cliff a short walk north of here," Biemwensé said. "You stand there and watch the sea return to the bight. Don't wander any farther or I'm not responsible for anything happening to you."

"Thank you."

"You don't want to enjoy it too much," she added, turning her body to look at him. "You don't want to get too comfortable, if you know what is good for you. Before morning light, I am pretty sure word of your presence will have reached the right ears, somehow. You want to decide what you will do before then."

Danso nodded. "And what will you advise that be?"

She snorted. "What any sensible person who looks like you should do. Run."

The cliff was indeed there. Danso went and stood at its edge, which overlooked the Bight of Whudasha. He had never set eyes on something so beautiful. The bight had a magnificence about it: a never-ending expanse of sand that curved and kissed the edges of the world, bottomed out, with the water of low tide gone out for the day. Danso didn't know his mouth was agape until he tasted salt in the air.

This was the closest he had ever been to his maa, he thought, standing over the absence of the great waters. Was it these same waters, which went out at day and returned at night, that took her away? Was this the same place from which she ran? Was she still running?

He looked about and, finding no one, climbed down from the cliff into the vacated seabed of the bight, putting his feet to the wet and slippery stone. He climbed down for over a half hour, almost slipping a time or two. When his feet finally touched the wet sand, he inhaled sharply, wondering if his maa put her feet in the sand too, if she felt the coolness beneath her feet now, too, wherever she was; if she was still alive enough to feel.

Maybe now he understood his daa refusing to tell him anything about her. Just standing here, in the sand on which his ancestors stood, brought an ache to his chest that he had no words to describe. Perhaps this was the same ache his daa felt? He wished greatly that he could say now to his daa: *I have looked upon the great waters on which my people once sailed, wielding the power of a mineral I now possess. I have become the son of the woman you loved.* But then Habba was probably worried to death about his son's whereabouts and might just, above everything, want him back. Danso could appreciate that, but as bittersweet as it was, he didn't see himself returning to Bassa voluntarily for any reason.

Perhaps maa would've understood better, he thought. She once left home in search of answers, too, didn't she? And just like him, she had also been forced to abandon everyone she loved and who loved her because the land chose not to fully accept her. She had left them for a journey of whose ending she was unsure, but with the promise that she might finally stop suffocating, might finally breathe as she was born to breathe. Perhaps he was more his maa's child than he knew.

He heard voices as he stood there, and looked up, back to the cliff. Two children, a boy and a girl, chattered excitedly, pointing at him in an animated fashion. He thought they looked like what his and Esheme's children might've looked like. The boy seemed low-brown like a Yele-kuté, but one could tell something was not quite there. The girl looked somewhere between low-black and high-brown, with hair curls so tight they stood in stark comparison to the boy's loose ones. Whudasha, it seemed, was more nuanced than Danso had initially thought—it was not just a refuge for Shashi, but a place where everything that did not quite fit was given room. He wondered what castes they might've belonged to back in Bassa. He had never thought about what caste a child born to him and Esheme might've fit into. Perhaps Idu, because both parents were Idu, but would they inherit their outcast aspects too? Might they have become just as lost as he was?

Danso realised the children were speaking to him, but he could not understand the language through their gibberish, which was a perfect summation of his current situation. Home, and he couldn't recognise it as much as it couldn't recognise him.

They kept pointing to him and back at the expanse of land at the horizon that was soon going to be the sea when it returned, chattering and jumping, and only when the children were joined by even more children of various sizes and shapes and aspects and complexions, the way people gathered in streets to watch a person gone crazy, that he realised he was the crazy person in this situation. He started his climb back up, noting that the sun had begun a rather quick and silent descent. The children stayed there and chattered some more, some of them urging him on until he was closer to the top, before they scampered away.

He was almost all the way up when he heard the faraway sounds of the waters beginning their return. It was like a trickle from storage pot to calabash, and he stood at the top and listened, drowning in the stories he'd read about the first landers from Ajabo, and trying to reconcile them with Lilong's tales of crossing the violent and unpredictable waters with those dhow vessels powered by ibor.

The sea edged closer after the red-and-orange circle had sunk low over the horizon, after the clouds had offered up their streaks of purple and turquoise to the listless grey of night. Menai and Ashu held little sway here, swallowed by the nothingness of bleak fog above sky and sea, so that it was dark-dark, and nightlight was a thing of dreams.

Finally, the waters came, quiet, returning in a rush of mild tide, clear with a foamy attack so that the sand was still visible beneath them. Then they came violent, green and deep and dark and perplexing, angry at the world. Rolling tides roared and smashed against the cliffs, so that everything that was once dry was drenched, and salt ascended in the air and poised upon lips and caused fingers to itch.

The stories from jali guild said that the reason the sea left the bight every morning and returned at night was that the waters worked for the moon. So they went out and returned after a full day of work. Which made sense if one was headily succumbed to beliefs in the moons, but Danso knew the world worked differently, that the seas went out for a reason and left wet sand in their wake for a reason. If they were so benevolent, working for the moons as the songs exhorted, why did they return with such vehemence, then? Why did they take anything that stood in the way of their return—animals, children—and wash them away until there was not even a trace of their prior existence? Why was their return, their coming home, filled with violence and erasure?

Danso scratched at his knuckles absent-mindedly, watching the bight until it was well and truly dark. Salt water splashed at him every now and then, but he paid it no heed, enamoured by this great mystery. He was pensive for various reasons, but just one of them counted as he stood here and looked out to this nothingness, and it was a question:

What now?

He had aided a fugitive, separated from his intended, abandoned his family and guild, got bitten by hundreds of mosquitoes, been chased by leopards, dipped into supernatural powers, and murdered three whole human beings. If he'd ever had a chance to return to Bassa—perhaps to salvage whatever was left to be salvaged—that opportunity was long gone. Doing so now was as good as suicide. He held a power that *definitely* would be interpreted as dark sorcery, an offence punishable by death if the moon temple decided it was grave enough. And they would, with him having killed two men with it. No one was going to sit him down and have a conversation about his intentions. If he ever set foot in Bassa again, he was going to die, plain and simple.

But then this Biemwensé woman was also telling him he couldn't stay, that he didn't belong in the very land of his ancestors, of his own maa. She was telling him he had to run away from the closest thing to home—*again*— and become a nomad on the mainland, a vagrant with no affiliations. She wanted him to do this with a yellowskin and a desertlander, two people just as foreign to this land as he was, with a possible bounty on their heads.

Danso looked up, at the sea.

Running had always been his dream. He had scratched that itch, and now that dream was over. No more running. He would plant his feet in this land—one that he finally rightfully belonged to.

Whether the Whudasha Youth liked it or not, Whudasha was his home, and he was going to fight for it.

46

Zaq

THE WOMAN TOOK ZAQ through the winding corners of the coastal protectorate's busiest community, what Zaq started to understand was referred to as Whudasha Central. Most of it was, as he had seen, craftworkers—weavers, potters, shoemakers, and the like—and traders of all sorts, including those who seemed to be trading the spoils of scavenging. For quite a while, they didn't come across anything else, just rows upon rows of barter, and not because this was a market at all, but because everyone worked and sold out of the front of their own homes, something that, Zaq mused, would be completely unheard of in Bassa.

He'd put his cloak back on after a few people had given him askance looks earlier, but still, everywhere he went, there were looks of enquiry, especially when people saw him tailing a Whudasha Youth. Now, a growing dread began to spread across his chest. The looks he was being given had changed—they were no longer of enquiry. These were looks of fear, and pity.

It had taken him a while to deduce that that was what the woman was. It should've been clear from the beginning, judging from the air of authority in the way she moved through space. And if not that, then the weapon she wore—no other person they had come across wore any weapon of any sort, which was a far cry from Bassa where some common folk at least were allowed to carry weapons, so long as they were mainlanders or immigrants who worked as Seconds.

Every now and then, they ran into another woman dressed akin to the way his guide was, and she would salute them with a striking fist shake and a proclamation in Whudan that Zaq couldn't understand. His guide would point to him and mention a word, *Kakutan*, and the other person would go *ah*, and then look at him. It would be the same look of pity the others gave him, but just like his guide, with less affect.

They soon left a large chunk of the commune behind, with the houses and commerce getting scantier, until they arrived at a place that was more open land than Zaq had seen since Whudasha East, and suddenly there was the Peace Fence, bordering both sides of a large, massive entryway.

The entryway had two arches, built in the same manner as those that could be seen at the Great Dome in Bassa. It was as high as ten men stacked one on the other, and the structure was decorated all around with etchings and moulded shapes in a myriad of colours. The images and symbols were of people doing things and stories about certain people, and proper inspection told Zaq they were written in High Bassai. He suddenly felt at peace, seeing a familiar slice of home here, even though he could not read High Bassai at all, like most Yelekuté having never been given the opportunity to learn to read or write it.

The woman took him through one of the arches, past a bunch of people standing around, dressed exactly like she was, and into a doorway. The room they entered was hot and in near-darkness, despite the sun of early evening preparing to give way. Zaq squinted. It took him a while, but he got the general lay of the place—there were more Whudasha Youth here, seated, watching him, some with sheathed cutlasses like his guide, some with spears like those of Bassai civic guards but cruder in design. It also took him a while to realise they were all women, and to note that he had not once seen a man who was a Whudasha Youth.

His guide said something in Whudan to the room and mentioned the word *Kakutan* again. Someone nodded in a direction and shouted a name. Another woman looked Zaq over, then went into an adjoining room. Zaq, tired from all the walking—his body had begun to ache severely—made to sit in one of the nearby benches. His guide reached out and gripped him, harder than she had before—her countenance had become frozen since arriving here—and held him up.

"You do not sit when you meet the Supreme Magnanimous," she snapped.

Light came through the doorway, and the woman who had gone in returned with a lamp and announced something in a loud voice. The Youth in the room shot to their feet and held their attention. They shunted away from the doorway, leaving Zaq in the centre of the room with a clear path to whoever was emerging. He gulped, suddenly feeling trapped.

The woman who emerged from the doorway was small, almost half Zaq's height, but with a presence of someone bigger. She came with the air of a woman with a shadow that obscured and with a presence that stifled breath, both of which exactly happened as she walked into the room. Half the women in the room shuffled out instantly; half stayed. The small woman came up to Zaq, her face plain and unmoving, and he could suddenly see why this was such a common thing among the women.

"You will *kneel* in the presence of the Supreme Magnanimous!" Zaq's guide snapped, and pushed him down by his shoulder until he came to his knees. He suddenly felt the urge to weep. He looked up at his guide. *This wasn't what you promised!* he wanted to tell her with his eyes, but she stared straight ahead.

A finger touched his cheek and turned his head about. It was the smaller woman. She pushed his cloak back as his guide had earlier and observed his bald head, then spoke to his guide in Whudan. Her voice was just as small and quiet as she was, but moved about the room and stole attention. His guide stood even straighter and responded at length without once blinking. The smaller woman nodded and looked back at Zaq.

"Welcome to Whudasha, desertlander," she said in clear, crisp Mainland Common. "I am Kakutan, Supreme Magnanimous of the Whudasha Youth, and would like you to state your business."

Zaq gulped. "I—um—"

"Now, little desertlander," Kakutan said, with a wry smile that was not at all pleasant, "I will ask that you be very careful here about the next few words that come out of your mouth. Indina said she found you wandering near Central, but I am pretty certain we do not have a record of you passing through these gates. So." She crossed her arms. "Speak carefully and truthfully."

All of Zaq's confidence disintegrated, washed over him like cold water. *How stupid, Zaq!* What was he thinking? What—that because these were oppressed people too, people halfway just like him, they would see? That because they, too, were smothered and kept under, because they understood what the migrant beads on his ankle meant, they would take absolute pity on him and not be like the men at the local government office, like the Idu and Emuru, and look down on him? What exactly had he been thinking?

"I came to make a report of myself," Zaq said, slowly. "I have lost my way, and I will need help finding my way back."

"Hmm." Kakutan, standing above him in his kneeling position, walked away to sit on a nearby bench. All the women in the room remained standing.

"So let me understand what you're saying," she said. "You *lost* your way from somewhere in Bassa—I'm not even going to ask where—and then you didn't find your way back to the Emperor's Road or *any* of the bushroads, but instead, have somehow appeared right in Whudasha Central?"

Zaq's tongue felt too big in his mouth. Sweat gathered in his armpits and on his top lip, and not just from the heat. What—was he going to tell them that he was a fugitive? The way they sounded, that would not at all go down well.

"Not quite, your...magnanimousness," he said, and everyone snickered.

"Just call me Kakutan." She smiled, and again, it was not a smile of camaraderie. The women in the room showed enough surprise for Zaq to know that he was not, under any circumstances, to call her that.

"I, um, I did not vanish, Supreme Magnanimous," Zaq said. "I lost my way into the Breathing Forest, see—the boundaries are thinning on the Bassai side. So much so that the Breathing Forest is almost no more, and I stumbled into the savanna. I slept in crevices and dodged hyenas for days, until I somehow found myself in an unguarded and easily scalable portion of the Peace Fence—I did not know what it was at the time. I wandered to Central where your... Indina, found me." Zaq gulped. "I mean no harm or trouble, Supreme Magnanimous. I am nothing but a lowly Yelekuté of Bassa."

Kakutan nodded and rose. She gestured toward Indina, who tapped him urgently. "Get up."

Zaq rose. His bones ached.

"Well, obviously I have no manner of verifying if your story is true or false," she said. "So you will be detained until we can do that. If you are telling the truth, we will offer you food and clothing and point you in the right direction. If you are lying..."

She let the sentence hang, and turned away. Zaq opened his mouth to say something, and promptly shut it. But she caught it and turned back.

"Have something to say, desertlander man?"

Zaq shook his head.

She returned her attention to him now, the wry smile wiped off her face, and she was back to that nondescript, unfeeling expression.

"Let me complete that sentence," she said. "If I find out that you are lying, I will take you to the middle of the savanna and tie you there. The lions will start with you first, and then the hyenas when they're done. Vultures will pick off the remains and ants will cart off the rest to their anthills to make their queens fat. The rain will wash away your blood, and the winds will cast your teeth throughout the savanna. Make no mistake—if you lie to me, I will make sure your very existence is served on a platter to all the forces of nature. It will not be a very enjoyable death for you, my desertlander man."

Zaq gulped.

"What is your name?"

"Zaq."

"Zaq, I will ask you again—is there any part of your story you have left out?"

Zaq shook like a leaf. He had never been a good liar. He had always been the kind of person who followed all the rules, did what he was told, believed squarely in dignity and truth. He didn't know how to be this new person, this... *vagabond*. But he had to face it: He couldn't tell her he was a fugitive. He didn't even know yet if he *was* a fugitive. That would just be putting himself in trouble for nothing.

But Kakutan *knew* he was hiding something. She stood there and waited.

"Well?"

"Supreme Magnanimous, if I—"

"Well, be out with it, then!" she said, her voice rising. "I'm not going to spend all day goading you."

"Well, it's just that—"

"What?"

"I wasn't alone."

The room fell silent.

"What do you mean, you were not alone?"

"Well, I—see, I had my charge with me. A young man. We got lost together, but I lost him, too, in the savanna. I don't know where he is. Perhaps he could've found his way over here like I did? I'm worried he could be hurt, see."

"Your charge?" Kakutan said, eyes widening. "Is that—a Bassai person? You're saying there's a Bassai person in Whudasha?"

"I'm saying...perhaps?"

"You're saying *perhaps*." Kakutan sighed. "We will definitely be detaining you until we can sort this mess out. Imagine. A Bassai person in Whudasha! That'll be the end of us. We will lose protectorate status, if this gets out." She pointed at everyone in the room. "You all, I don't want to see anyone here until this whole protectorate has been scoured, and we are certain there is no Bassai here." She hissed, long and hard, and Zaq suddenly regretted offering that information. But it had worked, at least—for now, her attention was on something else.

"Indina," she said, "lock this Second up and join the rest."

She stormed out of the room, followed by the woman carrying a lamp, plunging the room back into darkness as the remaining Youth left them alone. Someone passed Indina something, and she reached for his wrist and placed it. It was heavy iron, cold, and when she went for his other wrist, he realised it was a pair of wrist shackles.

"But why?" he asked, dumbfounded, as she locked them about his wrists and shoved him forward. "Why are you suddenly so harsh? I have been nothing but obedient!"

She said nothing, but pushed him down a dark, winding corridor that was uneven, so that he almost fell a couple of times, unable to see beyond his nose. He heard the whine of a door opening and knew, immediately, that it was a holding stall, because it was the first door he had seen since his arrival.

"Please," he said to the darkness where he thought Indina would be. "I'm starving and have drunk no water in days. Please, help me."

"Oh, I will help you all right," said Indina, her voice low and menacing. "I will help you and…your charge, is it? I know you are hiding something. I will help you remember it."

Zaq froze.

"We have word that there are hunthands camped along the Emperor's Road," Indina said. "They're searching for something only they have knowledge of, and are not allowed to tell. But something tells me you have to do with whatever they're searching for, and you are going to tell it to me, now."

Zaq struggled to breathe, inhaling large gulps as his heart pounded quickly. *What have I done? Dear Danso, forgive me!*

"But first, you will tell me where your charge is," Indina said, and then pushed him. He hit a wall and fell. There was a strike, a spark, a char cloth lit, and then the flame transferred to a torch. He could suddenly see her, standing there in his dank cell, the corridor behind them empty, the fire causing a shadow to fall on her face. Slowly, she pulled the gate closed. It clicked softly.

"No, please," Zaq said. "I don't—I don't know anything." Zaq began to cry. "Oh moons, I am finished! Oh, what have I done!"

Indina smiled, and there was more cold in it than on a harmattan night.

47

Danso

FOOTSTEPS SCRAPED THE ROCKY ground behind Danso. Only a day here, and he had already gained a knowledge of this Yaya woman's walk, and was able to recognise it from afar. She limped from somewhere around the knee, like with a fracture that didn't heal right. He wondered what happened to her, then decided he wasn't going to ask her about it. Too much of her body seemed to be forsaking her at the time of her life when she needed it most, and if experience with his daa's patients taught Danso anything, it was that the sins of the flesh in youth came to roost in the body and spirit in old age. And while he was curious about what those sins might've been for her, he was more grateful that she had survived them to be here in their time of need.

Biemwensé joined him in looking over the cliff, listening to the sea splash against the rocks, eat at the land. When she spoke, it was with a wistful tone.

"It used to be beautiful," she said, so low the angry night breeze could've snatched it away. "The first landers must've enjoyed it in its earliest, purest form. But what we have now is both a broken land and a broken people."

"Do you think they were happy?" Danso asked. "When they came here?"

"They were free," she said. "That's what mattered."

"Until they were not."

"Until they were not," she repeated, then sighed. "That's what you get when you pursue happiness so blindly that you do not appraise the cost."

Danso felt like she was telling him something, perhaps about Zaq, and simply waited for her to spit it out.

"Word will have gone around now," she said. "The children have seen you, and your desertlander, Zaq, must be out in town now. The Whudasha Youth leaders will come around tomorrow and ask about your intentions."

"I do not have any intentions," Danso said. "I just want to be in a place where I don't have to defend my existence every day. I just want to be home."

"This is not your home," Biemwensé said, flatly.

"I'm Shashi," Danso said. "Just like you, just like everyone else here." He kept his eyes on the horizon, where the sea met darkness. "And this is what I will tell them when they come—that this is my home, and I have as much right to remain here as they do. I'm not afraid of a few village youths."

"Protectorate," Biemwensé corrected.

"Sorry?"

"Whudasha is a protectorate, not a village."

"Oh." Danso looked out to the sea.

"Your own people, you say, yet you know so little about us."

"That's not my fault," he said. "I'm Bassai because I had no choice."

"Yet here you are," Biemwensé said. "Running from the city that made you. And that, dear Danso boy, is why this cannot be your home. Because you and your desertlander and yellowskin friends are fugitives, and the Whudasha Youth do not take kindly to fugitives."

Nevertheless, Danso thought. Lilong had been right: His selfishness had caused a lot of trouble. No more. This time, he was going to try to do something that actually helped others, and that included sticking his neck out and insisting on staying. Staying offered the opportunity to protect Zaq and Lilong. He could kill two birds with one stone by righting his errors and keeping them safe.

He and Biemwensé listened to the waves tussle each other.

"They will arrest you if you disagree with them," she said. "They will definitely arrest your companions, that I know. And once they set eyes upon your bat and discover what you did to those hunthands, as well as what you have in your possession..."

She let it hang. Danso realised she was talking about the ibor. She had a funny way of avoiding mentioning it or acknowledging that it existed, even though it was clear she had deduced what it was once she set eyes on the Skopi and the pellets embedded in Lilong's arm. How much she knew was a matter to unpack another day, but for now, she had spirited Lilong and the pouch into hiding, and that action demonstrated sufficient good faith.

"I'm not running," he said with a finality. "Not anymore."

Biemwensé seemed placated. She sighed. "How is your memory?"

"Still lacking."

"Hmm. Perhaps it will return. Sometimes, temporary memory loss is a common side effect of traumatic incidents."

Danso shot her a look. "Are you talking about iborworking?"

She hesitated a moment. "Maybe."

"You know about iborworking?"

"Oh, I know about many things," she said. "I don't need your fancy Bassai education to be aware of what this continent and our world holds. We may be Shashi—we may be looked down upon, but we're not stupid. We hold the histories of our own selves within us, and we do not need to be fed back our own stories to know them. I understand that there are powers beyond us, ibor or otherwise, and I believe them because I have seen what they are capable of. That stone-bone in your yellowskin's pouch, or those embedded in her arms—I don't know how they work. But I know what they mean, and I know what it means for those who have touched such power."

Danso stood rock solid, watching her work her mouth in the darkness, unsure of how much to let on.

"I will not tell the Youth anything," she said. "But the best I can tell you is this: If you can find a way to leave, you must leave. Go away and don't return. That is the only way I can help you. But if you stay, they will take you and your bat and your ibor and, if you're lucky, send you back to Bassa alive."

"And what about the Peace Treaty?"

"And what about it?"

"If I can make my case—if I can give good reason to stay, Bassa cannot harm me, right? Whudasha is covered by the Peace Treaty. If they don't personally hand me over to Bassa, nothing can happen to me or anyone here."

"Yes," Biemwensé said, then said nothing, answering only half the question. Danso had a nagging feeling about why she didn't, that the answer to the second part was too depressing to consider, but he decided he was going to remain hopeful.

"I will at least try," he said, turning away, back to the great and turbulent waters. "I will at least attempt to make a case for my citizenship here. I expect to be found worthy, and my companions deserve a place at my side. Until such a time, we stay put."

Biemwensé nodded. "Fair enough. I admire your courage, actually." She chuckled. "But I pity your careless pride and gross naivety. That is what will get you into trouble, and you are going to die, and it is going to be very funny."

She laughed, hard and loud, leaving Danso bewildered.

"Anyway, come along," she said. "Your woman is close to awaking, and maybe she can talk some sense into your blockhead."

She turned and walked away, and Danso mused and whispered into the wind about what an absolute lunatic the woman was.

48

Lilong

LILONG AWOKE AT LENGTH, and into a body that felt secondhand, borrowed. Someone had touched her while she was under, she knew, invaded her body. Soreness in too many places, the start of healing in some. Her tongue held a taste she didn't recognise. She could feel all of the changes that had happened within her, the foreignness of things she'd been fed, and she was suddenly gripped by panic. Was she in captivity? She looked about her and could recognise nothing, yet at the same time, she wasn't in chains or restrained in any way. Her pouch with the Diwi was also placed next to her. She picked it up and hid it away in her bedclothes.

She lay that way for a while, trying to decipher if she could move or not. A few attempts told her it would be a bit more time before that could happen—her joints seemed to disobey, and her limbs weighed as much as the trunk of a felled palm tree. Her head pounded in heavy drumbeats, and she swore she could hear the sea.

Two people came into the chamber after a moment, and when she saw Danso, she exhaled with relief. Yet the last memory she had before going under returned, and she went cold at the thought of it.

It was him. He had done it. He had used the Diwi again, but this time, to call on lightning.

"Finally!" Danso said, smiling. "I'm so glad you're awake." He reached for her, and she recoiled.

Danso frowned at the response, then motioned to the elderly woman behind him, who looked Shashi too, but in a different way than Danso.

She was so weatherbeaten that it was difficult to determine where exactly she was from.

"This is Biemwensé," Danso said. "She rescued us from the savanna and brought us over the Peace Fence into Whudasha. You're in her house." He said this while staring straight at Lilong, in a way telling her with his eyes what his mouth wasn't saying—*Speak with care.*

But she couldn't quite trust the young man standing in front of her either. She had been sure the Diwi had made a mistake by responding to him. Though she'd been close to unconsciousness and lying in the grass, she remembered what had happened in the savanna. His eyes had flashed red, as had those of the Skopi. The sky might have rumbled or not, she wasn't sure, but when the lightning came down, it did not come with sound, but with smell—something burnt and sharp and ferocious. And it moved jagged and fast, striking the men and the leopard and the field, reverberating across the savanna in a wave that knocked everything out properly, including her.

She had seen malevolence in the eyes of many a person before. She had never seen the kind that made her shiver the way she did now, just thinking about the look in Danso's eyes in that savanna, the sheer *evil* of it.

She knew the conditions for the Diwi's choice now. She had put it together during their time in the savanna. Danso was the first Shashi that she knew of to have ever touched the Diwi. And he had done so while simultaneously in contact with the Skopi. Those had to be the two conditions for red ibor's response: a willing mixed-heritage possessor and a lifeless entity ready to be possessed.

But what if the Diwi required something else—a corruption, a well of misery, a desire to inflict pain? What if the Diwi had not responded to anyone else because it sought exactly that, and had found it in Danso?

"Lilong, are you okay, can you speak?" Danso was saying. He looked to the elderly woman, who was regarding them both with calm. "She is definitely *not* okay."

"I think you may want to pay attention to what she is saying with her silence," Biemwensé said. "I will take a walk and leave you two some time."

She left them in the chamber. Danso looked back at Lilong.

"Are you all right?"

She regarded him, head to toe. He looked ragged, perhaps just as disoriented as she was, the toll of ibor use only just wearing off.

"I have told her nothing, I swear. She saw the Skopi already, and she knows about ibor—"

Lilong held up her hand. "Tell me what happened to you in the savanna."

Danso frowned. "Really? You've only just awoken."

"Tell me."

He settled into the bed beside her, so gently that she did not balk.

"I don't think I can describe it," Danso said. "I had this feeling—like something was calling to me, asking me to reach out and touch it. For a while there I felt weightless, untethered, like I did not have a body to even reach out and touch it. But somehow I did, and there was, like, a... connection." He linked his fingers and unlinked them again. "I felt this *heat* within me, and suddenly I was not... me. I had wings, talons. I felt like I was the sky, a silent thunder, the angry lightning." He sighed. "I blacked out right after that. Everything else I know, it was Biemwensé who told me. She said the hunthands who had tracked and ambushed us—I don't know if you know about them? They died. You and Zaq were lucky because you were not in the line of, well, lightning, I guess. The Skopi too, untouched."

Lilong nodded. It was just as she had expected—he had much too little control over the power than he should have for something so potent and powerful. She was going to have to make a decision about him soon, once she was much stronger and could do what she needed to. But for starters, she would rather die than ever let him near the Diwi again.

"Where is Zaq?" she asked, looking around.

Danso shrugged. "Gone off, I heard." When she frowned, he said: "Yes. Apparently, before we both awoke. Unsurprising, seeing as he actually abandoned us during the journey, while you were unconscious. I may have been at fault for that, though, to be fair. I forced him to come with us, you know."

"But he's your Second," she countered. "Isn't he sworn to you, or something?"

"Employed, not sworn. He's indentured to Bassa, not to me."

"Even then. One doesn't simply betray the confidence of someone who lives under the same roof with them."

Danso went quiet and pensive then. She realised she, too, became conflicted, ashamed. Here she was, thinking about abandoning him for being desirous of new knowledge. Was he perfect? Definitely not. Perhaps a little too naive for her liking. But he had also given up everything multiple times now just to steer her to safety. He didn't even ask for anything in return. Who was she to talk about betrayal of confidence and trust, really?

"Look, I'm sorry," she said, slowly. "In the end, this is all my fault, isn't it? I caused all of this for everyone."

"Not necessarily." He sighed, wistful. "You know, my daa wouldn't tell me much about my maa, but the one thing he wanted me to know was that she never abandoned me." He settled into the bed, crossed his legs. "He wanted me to know that she had no choice. He said that remembering that kept him alive, helped him rationalise hiding me until the hunt for people like me was over." He gazed at the ceiling. "I've always known I was going to leave Bassa one way or another, but it's weird, you know? I hate that city with every fibre of my being—my loudmouth uncles, the performances with Esheme, the repetitive guild duties. Now I miss it. Maybe not miss *it*, but I miss things. The university and its pillars, the musty smell of the manuscripts from the library, my friends from my savings circle. My daa, the smell of his workroom and its herbs. Even that damned lute-harp that I hardly ever played, but that they made me lug to class every other fortnight." He sighed again. "I wonder if I could truly leave it all behind, if I should've stayed and struggled through it like my daa did. I wonder if I should never have abandoned it all." He looked in her eyes. "I wonder if I've made a mistake."

She knew exactly what he meant. Leaving Namge had been hard for her too. She missed her two brothers and one sister, her maa, her daa. She missed her training sessions at the league. She missed going out on the dhows with the fishing troops. She missed riding the tide when it came back in, surfing on flatwood. When she left, she'd known that not only was there a decent chance she wasn't going to return, her return itself wouldn't be seamless, even if she came with the Diwi in hand. Now, the only thing that mattered was that the secret of ibor had to be kept. It was the one thing that had ensured all seven islands remained safe, and it was her duty to ensure that they stayed that way.

"We owe a responsibility to ourselves," she said. "To protect the truth. To protect *our* truth from a world that seeks to make us believe otherwise about ourselves."

She wondered if she was saying this for herself or for Danso. It sounded rather like something out of her daa's mouth, him with his strong advocacy for the islands seeking allies from the continent, his mantra that staying hidden forever was impossible. She was beginning to think like the man now. She still didn't believe they needed allies, but she found herself somewhat agreeing now that hiding forever was impossible. But she knew that the Abenai League, whose sole aim was *protection at any cost*, shared neither sentiment, which was why they saw nothing wrong with doing away with her daa if he was found guilty of conspiring with foreigners.

Here she was now, doing just the same thing that had put her family and her islands in jeopardy in the first place. And with an unhinged Bassai wielding the islands' biggest power at that. *This*, truly, was her duty. Not just to repair her daa's mistake or do the league's bidding. She owed it to herself to save the Diwi and whatever baggage came with it, even if that baggage was Danso. For the sake of what could happen if she didn't.

Outside, crickets had begun to sound. Lilong pushed herself up to a sitting position. Danso tried to help her, but she wouldn't let him. She wanted to be sure she could move when the time came, which it would.

"What you said back then about killing," he said. "I understand now. It's so...cold. I feel like I can never stop shivering." He shivered as he said this. "I never want to feel that way again, ever. So, if I may ask a favour of you—could you be sure to keep that ibor away from me? I don't want anything worse to happen next time."

"There will be no next time," Lilong said, and for a moment she thought it too vehement, but Danso only remained pensive. *Yes, I have to protect him now*, she thought, *but I'm just so tired!* She was tired of staying angry at him, tired of always weighing whether to leave. Perhaps it was time she just made him do whatever she needed to get things done. Starting with once her limbs worked better, when she would take hold of that Diwi and hopefully never have to see him use it again.

"When do we get to leave?" she asked.

"About that," he said, looking sheepish. "There's a slight chance we might not be allowed to stay at all."

"I'm not surprised," Lilong said. "People are the same, regardless of their constitution."

"I should have known," Danso said, and sighed. "I'm going to try to make a case tomorrow."

"For yourself, I presume? If anything, I'm happy to leave with the least possible trouble. There's a better chance they will arrest us and hand us over to the Bassai authorities than agree for anyone to stay here."

"No, we're protected by the Peace Treaty," Danso said. "They won't do that."

"Then the great waters are really punishing me by causing us to cross paths, because your constant choice to cling to wishful hope will have us all killed." Lilong used this new burst of irritation to push herself off the bed. Her knees buckled and she fell to the ground. Danso rushed over to pick her up, but she brushed him away. He stood there, looking sorry and sheepish. She made no move to rise, just sat there on the ground.

"Why do you trust in the good of the world so much?" Lilong asked. "Haven't you been told enough lies?"

"I have." Danso crossed his legs and sat on the floor, facing her. "But I still believe there is freedom to be found in truth. For myself, at least. And I can't find it if I'm always searching for the lie."

He sounded so much like her daa. She wanted to slap him. But she also realised that her mound of distrust toward him had started to melt, like dew in the morning sun. Perhaps she had been too quick to think of him as someone who could easily be corrupted by the kind of power the Diwi held. She would maintain her healthy scepticism, though. Nothing said she couldn't trust *and* distrust him at the same time.

They sat that way for a while, together in silence. Danso reached out and took her hand. She reminded herself not to flinch at the gesture.

"I'm glad you're okay," he said. "I was worried about you."

She nodded. "All I wanted was to do my duty: bring the Diwi home, fix my daa's mistake. I never wanted to hurt anyone."

"I understand," Danso said. "I've always understood. And I want to help you—I *will* help you do that. Let me talk to these people to let us stay, protect us under the Peace Treaty. We can work out our next move from there."

Lilong nodded again, and Danso placed his head on her shoulder. She was stiff at first, unsure of how to respond. Then she eased out a breath and let her head fall on his too, and for the first time in a long time, she felt something akin to camaraderie.

49

Esheme

Esheme was pregnant and she knew it.

She should've known much earlier, when her moonblood did not show up. At first, she had thought it was simply the stress of everything. First the nonsense of her maa simply refusing to wake up—for close to a fortnight now—and then Oboda yet to return with her defected intended. Also, Igan had stayed a few extra days—at no cost—to keep protecting her household but then had abruptly been withdrawn, which left her open to whatever Dọta had planned. Esheme had slept uneasy since, especially as each new day with the red stone-bone brought her no closer to unlocking its properties. In the city, protests turned into riots—sometimes met violently by civic guards, sometimes calmed by the appearance of a councilhand or two—all of which set fires under her apprehension. She had tried reaching out to the coalition again, but Ulobana, who was technically the lead general, had ensured that Esheme never crossed paths with Basuaye again.

The household, too, had begun a slow descent itself, and Satti struggled to keep hold. Half the househands in her employ had become increasingly restless after the standoff with Ariase. Many had found ways to be recalled by the local government office and reassigned, perhaps aided by agents of Dọta, Esheme suspected. Even Habba had been freed to go off on his own for the time being, he and his brothers. He was still required to show up once or twice to check if Nem was awake and leave instructions for her continued care with Satti.

All of this had caused Esheme to do her calculations improperly. The thing that had first raised some alarm was a swelling and slight tenderness in her breasts when she awoke, like they usually did when she had her moonblood, yet without any bleeding. This morning, when she awoke desperately tired, and suddenly everything was wrong—even the air in the room she breathed was *wrong*—she should've known.

It was the morning food that did it. She had stayed in bed, too tired to get out, and instructed Satti to bring her some food. But once the woman entered, and the strong smell of the boiled guineafowl eggs hit her, everything in her stomach jumped into her mouth.

Esheme leapt from the bed and fled to the lavatory, vomiting into the pot. Satti came forward and held back her hair, which she had let down. She retched a few more times without vomit. Satti guided her back into bed, tucked her in, then stood over her, frowning.

"I'm fine, I'm just ill," Esheme said.

"Forgive me, MaaEsheme, but I was not born yesterday," Satti said with a firmness that was the thesis of her demeanour. "This is not illness, and you know it."

Esheme was unsure about why the woman was so brusque. "And what, pray Menai, do you think it is?"

"It is not an illness that resides in you," Satti said, gathering up the food to return to the kitchen. "It is a person."

Satti left the room in a disapproving huff and Esheme waited for her to leave before jumping out of bed, running to the nearest mirror, and lifting up her wrapper to look at her belly this way and that way. It looked perfectly okay, perfectly normal, but suddenly, a fear that she had not known in a while gripped her. Within her, something was brewing, growing, and in time, it was going to become a full-grown thing. Everyone would see, and she would lose the only thing that was currently keeping her alive: the esteem of the people.

If it became common knowledge that she was having a baby at all as someone who was yet to be joined, or worse yet, that she was having a baby by her intended, a Shashi boy who had betrayed the nation? Catastrophe. There was also the little matter of the actual truth coming to light—that she had lain with a Potokin. Catastrophe. If Igharo was

approached by Dọta's people and offered money to break his silence—
and to be honest, he was likelier to break it than not—that would make
defending this pregnancy much harder.

It was a catastrophe any which way this went. If everything else hadn't
already crumbled her life, this was the thing that would do it.

She stood in front of the mirror, observing her belly for longer than
she had ever done in her entire life, deciding that she had to get rid of the
thing growing in it. How soon she could see to it, and how she would do
so, she didn't know. But one thing she did know was that she couldn't
afford to do it immediately, not when Dọta was hovering over her, looking for every little demonstration of weakness.

Something needed to happen *now*.

Esheme ran a hand through her hair, wet and damp from the sweat
of sleep. She was once again going to need help—for a price—from the
coalition.

⟡ ⸺ ⸺ ⟡

It took Esheme a while to circumvent Ulobana's block and secure a visit to
the coalition's headquarters. Once she found her way there, she met only
Igan at the safe house and knew immediately that, in a few moments,
they were going to have sex.

Igan came out wet, bald desertlander-like head shining with water.
The wrapper they had hastily put on midbath clung to their wet body and
accentuated its leanness, its rounder parts. The lazy, relaxed gait Esheme
had witnessed the last time they'd been together was gone, replaced with
a tense, twitchy countenance that caused the muscles in their exposed
arm to stand out. A tiny portion of their wrapper came undone slowly,
revealing the curve of their shoulder, skin smooth and scarless. They
looked at the wrapper and made no move to correct its waywardness.
They didn't bring their gaze back up to meet Esheme's eyes.

"Basuaye isn't here," Igan said, looking away.

Esheme, no stranger to this push-pull, this game of attraction and
words unsaid, nodded. She walked over to the wall ornaments and
touched them gently, lightly. She cast Igan a glance askance as she did so.

"Is there *anyone* here?" she asked.

"Just me," Igan said after a pause.

"Mhmn." She walked over to Igan and fixed the loose knot of their wrapper back on their shoulder, then ran her fingers over their cheek. Igan smelled of the black soap with which they'd bathed, and Esheme felt that, standing so close, she could parse each ingredient by its smell: shea butter, honey, aloe, camwood, palm kernel, cocoa, palm ash, lime. She drank it all in. She wasn't supposed to feel this way right now—her whole life was in turmoil, for moon's sake. Yet it was the stresses themselves that had caused her to become hot-blooded of late, craving pleasure in everything from food to beautiful people like Igan.

Esheme knew the next words out of her mouth would be defining. She was already losing purchase with the coalition, the one avenue through which she could keep her name on the people's tongues—tongues that had kept her alive and her household standing so far. Her last, final path into the coalition was Igan. And Igan was a beautiful, beautiful person who clearly wanted her as much as she wanted them. She could have the best of both worlds, couldn't she?

"Take off your clothes," Esheme said.

Igan stiffened, and the deadly expression of who they were inside, the one that reminded Esheme they were the Left Hand of Darkness, crossed their face. It was instinctive, but then their face softened and reddened slightly.

"Not here." Igan reached out a hand and led Esheme through a corridor, into a small room furnished by someone who clearly loved colour and had tried to fix the dankness of this safe house in their own little way. They untied the remaining knots that held their wrappers together and let them fall to the ground. Their body was just as Esheme had envisioned: smooth, silky, nipples just as alert as hers. She reached out and felt them, gently, and her hand fell in extremely slow motions and stopped between Igan's thighs.

Things moved quickly after that—wrappers away, breaths short, fingers active, tongues between thighs. Esheme grabbed Igan's bald head and cradled it as they moved, and Igan grabbed Esheme's plaited arches and held on for dear life. Together they crumbled like a poorly built house, shaking.

For a long time afterward, Esheme made circles on their chest with her finger, wondering what part of Igan attracted her the most. Was it just the palpable appeal of their body, or how they masked their dedication to commitments with a constant air of casual indifference? Perhaps it was because Igan understood power just as she did, and possessed the physical kind in great amounts that afforded them the flexibility of lowering their barriers whenever they wished, allowing power to sometimes happen to them rather than them always happening to power.

Esheme studied the walls of the room, the touch of colours. This was the handiwork of someone trying to make something better through cosmetic changes, as they were powerless to change the foundation of said thing. This mirrored how Igan felt about the coalition, from what Esheme had gleaned after further conversations before they'd been withdrawn. *Less of a wagon for change, more for economic gain*, was how they'd described it. Igan believed that the change promised was being postponed on purpose, as keeping the coalition running and coming up with new points of conflict invited support and donations from those who railed against Bassai leadership.

Perhaps it was this ability to look her in the eye and speak truth without fear that attracted Esheme the most. Nem aside, Esheme had never had such a person in her life before.

She didn't trust Igan—she didn't really *trust* anyone—but she considered Igan *reliable*. So it was in this spirit that, as they both lay there, she revealed to Igan the conundrum she was facing. She explained Dọta's reason for blackmailing her house and discussed the red stone-bone. She spoke of her fear of dying before she had achieved the feelings of freedom, respect, and acceptance she so badly desired. She wondered about birthing a new life, bringing it into this world to suffer the same fate as her, just as she was struggling to get outside of Nem's shadow. She told them all of it, and for once, she did not fear it would be used against her.

Igan was quiet for a long time, then said, simply: "I'm sorry."

"What for?"

They sat up. "For deceiving you."

Esheme frowned. "Oh?"

"When I was sent to protect you, that wasn't my only task."

"I know," Esheme said. "You were meant to keep an eye on me too."

Igan nodded. "You knew?"

"When the coalition forwent compensation for you to remain as my protection, it became clear."

Igan sighed. "I was supposed to find out what was true about ibor or not, and what you knew about it, especially if your household truly had it in hand. And if possible, to..." They drifted off.

"Kill me?"

"Not necessarily," Igan said. "Just to take hold of it if you did, though I'm not sure I was explicitly forbidden to kill you if it needed to be done."

Esheme ruminated on this. She had never feared Igan in the same way everyone did, the same way Igan never feared her, so she had held her suspicions with a grain of salt. Even after she knew for sure—and even after their confession right now—still she wasn't afraid. It was that sense of dedication Igan possessed, wasn't it? Once they had defended her at that funeral, carried her home with such care, like a child protected, she knew immediately that they would never harm her, and nothing so far had proven her wrong.

"Basuaye ordered this?" Esheme asked.

"Of course not." Igan scoffed at the idea. "Ulobana did. The old man spends his time in hiding and doesn't do too much these days except show up every now and then to add fire to the cause. It is Ulo who has run most things in recent times, even before I joined. She has always skimmed, alongside her pet, Tamino. Ḍota must have approached her after the funeral and offered her a deal." Igan shook their head at the memory. "I didn't find anything to report back, but even if I did, I wouldn't have said anything. I don't believe it was something the true core of the coalition would want."

"What would they want?"

"Honesty. To feel like someone is looking out for their interests."

Esheme looked into Igan's face. "And you? What do you want?"

Igan looked to the ceiling. "Purpose, I guess." They sighed again. "I've been a warrior since I could walk, working for people who want nothing more than to collect and collect, yet offer no value in return. At least not in any manner the nation can use. The coalition does that on some level, but that is insufficient." They looked at Esheme. "After I watched you speak at the funeral, and when I watched you stand up to Ariase, I knew."

"Knew what?"

"That even if I found the stone-bone, I would not report it." They reached out, tentatively, fiddled with a thread loose from one of Esheme's arches, then let go. "I decided that because I believed—I believe—that you would probably do something much greater with it than any First Elder."

Esheme pondered this. "And what if most disagree with that something? What if *you* disagree?"

Igan smiled wryly and leaned away to light a nearby pipe.

"You know why they all don't want you near ibor?" They blew the tobacco smoke into the air. "It's because they all think—no, *fear*—that you're capable of wild, irreversible actions. Actions that could change the very course of history. But I think it is those kinds of actions, in whatever form they may come, that we so pine for. We can't keep doing the same things and expecting different results. Perhaps yours is an idea whose time has come."

Esheme sat with these thoughts. To hear someone else put all her warring emotions into words was equal parts exhilarating—*finally*, someone understood!—but also frustrating because she couldn't see a way out that did not involve walking on a path strewn with nails. Between her failing household, her dying maa, her missing intended, being hunted by a councilhand, and now being spied on by the coalition, when would she ever catch a break?

"I used to feel so much in control, you know?" Esheme said. "I used to know the very next thing I wanted, every time. Now, I feel like *I* am the one being controlled."

Igan blew smoke again. "It's there, within you, and you'll come to it, in due time."

Better not take its sweet time, then, she thought. Dota would stop at nothing to get what he wanted. There was nothing that suggested he wouldn't come for her even if she gave him his ibor, which was why she could never allow him to get his hands on it.

Igan *was* right. Big, irreversible moves. And she knew just where to start.

"I believe that Igharo boy might be a problem if this gets out," Esheme said, deadpan, tapping her belly. She turned to Igan, who adjusted their body to face her, and an understanding passed between them.

"Consider it done," Igan said quietly, then added: "Anytime you need me. Not the coalition, *me.* Just ask."

"I can't pay you," Esheme said. "My household now has less of the means it used to."

"I want nothing you are not already giving," Igan said, fiddling with Esheme's hair again. "For too long, I've been on the outside of things, fighting to get in. You asked what I want. I want to be part of something bigger than what the coalition is ready for. If you truly have what everyone fears you do, then you might just be the only one who can offer me that opportunity."

50

Danso

THE NEXT DAY WAS one of tension, of twitching and anticipation for Danso. He did not sleep properly the night before, spending half of it awake, half of it dreaming of his maa, except she was a yellowskin and she had a face like Lilong's, only older. She kept trying to ask him to *come home, come home*, and he said to her, *I am home, maa*, and she said, *No; no you're not.*

He had woken up bathed in a sweat and dribble, his heart thumping. He wiped his forehead and mouth with the back of his hand and lay there, trying to make sense of it all.

Come home.

Hearing nothing from Zaq or the Whudasha Youth did not make this day any better. Lilong remained bedridden, so Danso couldn't leave for town, and Biemwensé was adamant it was best that they wait for the Whudasha Youth to come to them, because it made for a better neutral ground for the argument he was going to make.

They waited for hours. Nobody came.

"Something is wrong," Biemwensé said, when the sun started to cast evening shadows, and not even Zaq had returned. "If word has not slipped from the mouths of the children to someone by now, at least they should've met with your desertlander."

"How do you know so much about the Whudasha Youth?" Danso asked her. Anticipation had taken such a hold on them that they had now rooted themselves outside her house, facing the sun and the road where anyone coming would approach. Biemwensé leaned on her stick, and Danso stood with her.

Biemwensé massaged the ground with her toe. "I used to be one."

"A Youth?"

She nodded. "I even led them, once."

"Like, a civic guard captain?"

"We call it the Supreme Magnanimous here."

Danso snickered, and Biemwensé shot him a glance.

"It's not funny." Her voice was hard, and there was pain behind it. "They call it the Supreme Magnanimous because your job is to forgive, to not execute whoever tries to take advantage of the freedoms the Peace Treaty has accorded this protectorate. Still, it is a ruthless and heartless existence that mostly involves handing those who are aberrant over to Bassai hunthands or civic guards to have a field day. It was an existence I did not wish to continue. There have been two Supremes after me, both of whom have left for I would daresay the same reasons. The current Supreme is a woman named Kakutan, and for the first time, she seems to be the kind who enjoys the job, and not in a way that's good for people like you."

Danso allowed time for the tension between them to dissipate.

"Is that how you—" Danso motioned in her general direction with his head. "Is that how it happened?"

"Yes," she said. "I got my injuries in the line of duty."

"Animals?"

"Of a sort," she said, and looked away, so that Danso knew she wasn't talking about leopards or lions.

"Hunthands or civic guards?"

She looked back down the road and kept her gaze there.

The sun came low, and with the dark came cold and a thick, blinding coastal fog, like a low-lying cloud that obscured the road and everything within sight, so that Danso could only see his own hands and Biemwensé beside him.

He wondered, then, just as he had many times before, if his maa had seen this once, too. If she had stood here and looked into the white nothingness. Then his thoughts shifted to back home, how he didn't even know if he would return if, by some smidgen of Ashu's luck, he was offered the chance. Yet here, too, wasn't quite home either, was it? The place he had sacrificed everything for, only to get, what, *this*? Waiting outside for people who he'd thought would be sympathetic to his plight to come capture him in the dead of night? It was so radically different from the kind of kinship he'd expected that even his maa had to find him in his dreams and say, *Danso, this smells like cow dung.*

He should've listened to Zaq. Zaq was right: He truly was chasing the wind. He was trying to find something that didn't exist—home wasn't something you *found*, no; home was something you *made*. Maybe what he should've been doing instead was whisking Lilong and himself away under the cover of this blanket of fog. At least he'd be alive long enough to get a chance at *making* this home he sought.

Out of the fog right then, only within two arms' distance of Danso, came voices, and two children emerged, running. They went past him like he wasn't there and collapsed at Biemwensé's feet, catching their breaths and speaking hurriedly in what he'd come to recognise as Whudan. Biemwensé stooped on her stick and cut between their chatter, enquiring. At some point, she seemed to freeze.

"What?" Danso asked. "What is it?"

Biemwensé rose slowly. "They're coming." She whispered to the children, and they nodded and ran inside the house. Then she turned to face the road, planted her stick in the dirt, and leaned on it.

"Now," she said, "let us remind them who owns this land."

51

Kakutan

THE FOG WAS THICK and heavy, but Kakutan didn't need the torches her colleagues held to find Biemwensé's house. Everyone knew where Biemwensé's house was. Kakutan walked up close to the front and was about to clap when she saw the old woman standing there. Next to her stood a young Shashi man—lean, hungry, and looking quite apprehensive. He was exactly as had been described—part Bassai, part something else she wasn't quite sure of, and very much unlike anyone in Whudasha.

"Dehje, Biemwensé," Kakutan said.

"Don't use that nonsense Bassai greeting for me," Biemwensé said. "I'm not Bassai."

Kakutan scoffed and turned to the boy. "We need to ask you some questions."

"You do not speak to him," Biemwensé said. "This is my house. You address me."

"Very well." Kakutan pointed to the young Shashi man. "We have come for him." She pointed to the door. "And the yellowskin woman."

Biemwensé's face did not change. "I don't know what you're talking about."

"They are fugitives from Bassa," Kakutan said. "We have received information that they are on the run after accosting Bassai citizens. The yellowskin herself is accused of murdering the Speaker of the Bassai Nation."

Biemwensé remained silent.

"Do you deny this?" Kakutan asked.

"I have no murderers in my house," Biemwensé said.

"Maybe," Kakutan said. "But you know the law forbids us to harbour fugitives this side of the Peace Fence." She looked at the young Shashi man. "Even if they look like one of our own."

"I *am* one of your own," the young man spat back.

"Keep quiet," Biemwensé growled without looking at him. She kept her eyes on Kakutan. "Is this your business here?"

"Yes."

"Well." Biemwensé adjusted herself on her stick. "I don't know what you're saying, but this boy is a Shashi, as you can see. He is from here, and not a fugitive from Bassa as you say. He has lived here with me for a while. Look, he's even wearing my clothes. So you might want to go back to your informant and probe for further clarity."

"My informant is this young man's Second," Kakutan said. "Surely, you can't mean he's forgotten who his charge is?"

The boy gasped, but Biemwensé looked unbothered.

"We are all Shashi here," she said. "He must be mistaken."

"He knew where your house is. He knows the young man's name."

"And so?" Biemwensé spat. "*Everyone* knows where my house is. It's why you put me here, isn't it? Keep me away from the populace, so I don't pollute them with my ideas of self-sustenance and independence?"

"Your crazy ideas of separation from state?" Kakutan was getting impatient. "Where you don't mind putting us at odds with Bassa and risking us being obliterated and hunted for sport?" Kakutan tut-tutted. "I would've thought from your time as Supreme Magnanimous, and being from a generation closer to the pogroms, you would understand these necessary evils better. But here you are, putting us in this position once again."

"There is no such thing as a necessary evil," Biemwensé said. "There is only evil."

Kakutan was getting tired, and the fog seemed to be thickening. This wasn't the kind of night to stand outside, arguing in the cold.

"Sankofa, come forward."

A big Whudasha Youth appeared from behind her.

"Tell them what Indina told us."

The woman cleared her throat. "It wasn't just the Shashi boy, whom he called Danso, and the yellowskin woman, whom he called Lilong, that came with him, Supreme Magnanimous."

"And what else, moons tell, did he say they came with?"

Sankofa grimaced and said, "A Skopi, Supreme Magnanimous. A lightning bat."

There was a long silence.

"So you believe children's tales now, do you, Kakutan?"

"Not if they come from the mouth of a Bassai Second."

"I don't have such a creature in my house," Biemwensé said.

"And perhaps, if we look and find one?"

"Only if I give my permission," Biemwensé said. "And I do not give it."

"You do not have to," Kakutan said. "We will *take* it, in this case."

"I am a member of the Order of the Whudasha Youth," Biemwensé said. "I have stood in your position and spoken as Supreme Magnanimous like you. In the past, you might have taken liberties and treated me like sand, like the cliffs the seas wash up against and take, take, take from. No more. The law of this land forbids you from entering my house without express permission, and I do not grant it."

Kakutan smiled. "But surely, you know that law does not hold in this instance? You are under suspicion of harbouring a fugitive. An intruder. A *yellowskin*."

"Don't be ridiculous," Biemwensé snapped. "There is no such thing as yellowskins. What do you think this is, tales by nightlight?"

"You will speak with respect to the Supreme Magnanimous," Sankofa said, drawing her cutlass. Kakutan put a hand over Sankofa's and pushed the weapon back into its scabbard.

"I say what there is and isn't." She took a step toward Biemwensé, but only just. "And word has come from Bassa, through the desertlander in our custody, that there in a yellowskin in Whudasha. Now, it is bad enough there is a runaway desertlander and his charge here, and whether they have a Skopi or not is up for debate, but a *yellowskin*? A whole person from the Nameless Islands? The Peace Treaty itself could be revoked if we choose to harbour such people here. And as I am the Whudan charged with ensuring this does not happen, it is my duty to go to all lengths to assure everyone I have handled the situation completely. So I pray you, Biemwensé, one Supreme Magnanimous to another—hand the yellowskin over, or at least let us in to take a look."

The old woman looked, for a moment, like she had broken, like she was going to accede. Then a bold, stormy look came over her face, and she clenched her teeth and said: "No."

Kakutan sighed. So much for diplomacy.

"Take her," she said.

Sankofa moved without hesitation, as did three other Youth. They did not draw until Biemwensé pulled the Shashi boy with a *get behind me*, pushed her weight off her stick, and transferred it into her gripping hand.

"The law also gives me the right to protect my house in the event of an invasion," she said slowly, deadly. "And this is an invasion."

Sankofa drew and charged headlong. Kakutan shook her head. *Foolish.* Every Supreme Magnanimous was selected for being the Whudan who had won the most sparring duels at the time, and Biemwensé had been no different.

Sankofa swung her cutlass and it hit wood, then was smacked out of her grip. Biemwensé's stick came around again, and Sankofa caught a blow to the cheekbone. She fell. There was blood. There might have been some teeth.

Danso pulled back and ran into the house.

"Follow him," Kakutan said to the rest. She plucked a spear from a nearby Youth. "I'll deal with this myself."

Biemwensé

THEY CIRCLED EACH OTHER, the two women, their eyes narrowed. The fog grew thick and fast.

"Stop this, Biemwensé," Kakutan said. "I don't want to harm you."

"Nor I you," Biemwensé said. *But this is my house. I must protect what lies within.*

They came together, spear on stick, iron on wood. They clacked and clacked and separated. She stepped back and balanced herself.

"You're too old for this, you know?" Kakutan twirled the spear and worked her feet through a couple of stances. "Besides, you know this is all for naught. They're getting the boy and girl as we speak."

Assuredly, there were sounds from inside the house—running, crashing into things, yelping, thuds. The fog was too thick to see.

"Not if I get done with you first," Biemwensé said.

They came together again. Kakutan's swings were hard, firm, swift. Biemwensé found herself blocking, blocking, blocking, her grip weakening more than she'd expected. She dodged and ducked and soon knelt in the sharp sand, panting, sweating.

"Why?" Kakutan said, circling her now, like prey, toying with her. She faded in and out of the fog, so that she was visible one moment, invisible the next. Biemwensé followed her voice.

"You do not even know these people," Kakutan was saying. "You owe them nothing. Yet you put your own self at risk on their behalf? They are *intruders*, for moon's sake! What are you trying to prove—that you are better than us? That you are strong, and you can stand up to me—to Bassa?"

Biemwensé rose, slowly. She spat the sand in her mouth away.

"This is my house, my land," she said. "It is you who are the intruder."

She moved, her sight and hearing almost nonexistent at this point. It took her a moment to realise this was what Kakutan was banking on. Too late.

Something came out of the fog and jabbed her in her side. She swung about and hit nothing but air.

"I need you to remember your vows as Supreme Magnanimous, Biemwensé," Kakutan was saying through space and time. "You were once beholden to keeping our motley people of Whudasha safe, just as I am now. This means staying beholden to Bassa, staying behind the fence, staying within the rules. It may not be what we want, but it is what we must do to survive."

Suddenly, Kakutan was there, out of the fog, and she jabbed at Biemwensé's good leg. There was too little time to react. She crumpled into the sand.

Kakutan rushed up and kicked her stick away, then put the sharp edge of the spear to her neck.

"It's over, Biemwensé," she said, and as she did, yells came from inside the house.

There was a screech, a death caw, and a clacking. The Whudasha Youth ran out of the front door. The last Youth who was dragging the yellowskin girl dumped her on the veranda and jumped to join the rest of the group, all of whom now stood behind Kakutan, as if for protection.

Danso emerged from the house, his eyes red and dark like congealed blood. Next to him on the veranda came the Skopi. It looked like quite a normal bat, but if the bat were the size of a Whudan and also dead. Its talons were sizable enough to rip a person's head off with sufficient force applied. Its eyes were as dark and bloodshot as Danso's.

Danso held a red object in his hand. He turned to the group now, and when he opened his mouth, the bat opened its mouth as well, and both spoke in a chorus, yet as if one voice:

"Let them go," they said.

Kakutan, standing over Biemwensé, removed the sharp end of her spear from her neck and pointed it in the direction of man and bat. Biemwensé knew it would take more than sorcery and theatrics to scare this woman, so she was quite unsurprised when the woman poised her body to throw the spear.

"Don't!" the yellowskin girl yelled, maybe at Danso, maybe at Kakutan.

The person who was Danso-not-Danso maybe moved, or didn't. Either way, Biemwensé could tell something was coming before it did.

Lightning descended from above, swift and without sound. All she saw was a flash of silver light, a jagged scar in the air, and then Kakutan's spear was knocked out of her hand. The force of it threw Kakutan onto her buttocks. She gripped her arm in pain.

"Lay down your weapons," that chorus-voice said again, "and let us speak reasonably."

53

Kakutan

THICK FOG CLUNG TO the two groups in front of Biemwensé's house as the Shashi boy—Danso—came out of the daze, gasping. He stumbled and held on to a post for support. He looked in pain.

Kakutan's own arm throbbed. There was pain from her shoulder socket down to her wrist, like someone had driven a rod in and left it there. She gritted her teeth and tried to look stoic. Biemwensé had picked up the yellowskin girl—Lilong, they called her—and taken her over to the veranda, her two ragtag children crowding around them both.

The Skopi remained unmoved.

Kakutan had seen enough dead things in her life to recognise that this bat did not have life in it. And yet, with whatever sorcery this Danso boy had used, something that clearly had to do with that stone, he had called lightning in tandem with the bat, had *spoken* from it. These were things that were only supposed to happen in children's fables, but here they were, standing right in front of her.

Only more reason to ensure they didn't spend one more moment on this land. Their mere presence was a death sentence for all present.

Her Youth still had their weapons laid down as the boy had asked, and Kakutan had not picked hers back up yet. She, like everyone else, waited first for him to speak.

"We do not come to do any harm," Danso said finally, sounding exactly like the jali they said he was. "We seek nothing but solace."

"Is that so?" Kakutan spat sand from her mouth, massaging her shoulder. "You are fugitives from Bassa with an intruder from the outer lands, a bounty on your heads, and hunthands on your heels, and you have just attacked the defenders of this protectorate with your sorcery. Tell me again, boy, how you mean no harm."

"None of us has done anything wrong, whatever we may be accused of," Danso said. "I am an upstanding Bassai citizen and can vouch for that. It is I who have led this woman"—he pointed to Lilong—"and my Second here. I have brought them to the only place on this continent that might be the closest thing to home for me, and for us. And all I ask, now, is that you let us stay here in peace. I promise we bring no harm."

Kakutan looked about at the other Youth, then to Biemwensé and back to Danso. She scoffed. *Surely, he can't be serious?* she thought. The audacity of him to even ask it!

"As a Shashi myself," Danso continued, "my presence here is covered by the rules of this protectorate, including the Peace Treaty. This woman and my Second are under my care, and therefore are covered by whatever laws cover me."

"You are not covered by any laws," Kakutan said, trudging to pick up her spear. "This is not your home. You are not one of us, and you do not belong here, Bassai man." She hoisted the weapon and plunked it in the sand, next to her feet. "You will not be staying in Whudasha for anything longer than the next sunrise. Not while I am alive to see it."

Silence engulfed the groups. The Youth, seeing their leader pick up her weapon, did the same, but no one made any move.

"I have a right to belong here," Danso said.

"No, you don't," Kakutan said. "You are not Whudan, and will never be. And I will not jeopardise the future of a people I have been sworn to protect because some jali novitiate does not know what is what." She spat again. "Do you know what those hunthands will do when they come here and realise we are wilfully harbouring you? Do you know what Bassa is capable of?" She scoffed. "Jali novitiate, and despite all your study of history, you cannot even deduce your fate."

"They will not do anything. We are covered by the Peace Tre—"

"Shut your dirty mouth." Kakutan shook her head. "Stop mentioning the Peace Treaty. It was not written for people like you. You are *not* Whudan."

"We will not go back to Bassa," Danso said. "We just—cannot."

Kakutan nodded. "I can appreciate that. But you cannot stay in Whudasha either. That is not happening."

"Then let them go," Biemwensé said, softly. Everyone turned to look at her, Danso included.

"Let them leave Whudasha unharmed, and no one gets hurt." She rose. "You can be free of guilt, they can be on their way, out of the protectorate, and everyone gets what they want." She stepped forward to Kakutan. "We get them their Second, and I will personally lead them all out of the protectorate."

Kakutan's eyes lingered on the bat for a moment. If this young man chose to stay and wield this thing against them, they stood to lose. Whudasha stood to lose. But letting them leave showed weakness, and it would put Whudasha in Bassa's sights.

No good answers to this, are there? she thought, returning her attention to Biemwensé.

"Where will you go?" she asked.

"Why do you care?"

"I don't." Kakutan looked at the two children kneeling near the yellowskin girl, who looked too weak to travel in the manner required by Biemwensé's suggestion. "And the children?"

"Why not let us worry about ourselves, and you worry about yourself?" Biemwensé did not bat an eye.

A moment passed. The fog thinned just a little bit.

"Fine," Kakutan said at last. "I will give you what you want. But I want you and your sorcery off my land immediately."

"With pleasure," said Biemwensé, and she picked Lilong up.

Biemwensé

On their way to the headquarters, the group went through a residential quarter of Whudasha Central on Biemwensé's advisement, her children Afanfan and Owude leading the way and presenting a shortcut that would take them back quicker and with little chance of running into people at this time of night. The quarter was eerily silent and all of its commerce had folded back into itself, the shopfronts morphing back to the homefronts they once were. There were lanterns in some windows and Biemwensé could see some families inside. On the opposite side of them, the waters roared and bit against the bight at high tide, eating and eating away. Soon, she thought, these houses would be too close to the precipice, and they would have to move inward again, build closer and closer to the Peace Fence. Soon, there might no longer be any land to call Whudasha.

She walked with the children, Afanfan and Owude on either side. Danso went in front of her, next to the Skopi, which bore Lilong on its back as it trudged on all fours, its body moving in ripples. Danso had somehow managed to get the bat to do that without his eyes turning red again, as if there remained tendrils of former connections between them. Biemwensé wondered how this exact symbiosis worked and what fueled and controlled it, and was she the only one who was very much unnerved by it?

Lilong looked uncomfortable there. The girl had recovered quite speedily but was still in no great shape to do anything drastic, and had simply succumbed when Danso suggested it.

Behind her came the Youth group, with Kakutan leading. They were the most unnerved about the bat, and kept quite a distance from the group—far enough to not be within proximity of the bat, but close enough in case the group tried to do anything stupid, like run.

After they had cleared the eastern quarter and made significant progress through Central, Kakutan stepped forward and matched pace with Biemwensé, passing across one of two gourds to her—water. Biemwensé downed it without a word. Fighting for just causes, it turned out, was thirst-making work. Kakutan sipped from her own gourd, which had the strong smell of a spirit. Weybo, Biemwensé guessed.

"Listen," Kakutan said, "I would prefer we start again on a clean slate. Consider this my offer of a truce, one Supreme Magnanimous to another."

Biemwensé wiped her mouth and smacked her lips. "Don't tell me. You need my help now so you want to be friends."

Kakutan scoffed. "You're just too much for your own self, aren't you?"

Biemwensé shrugged. "Well, next time, don't fight someone first, then try to massage their aches after. Nobody is that stupid, you know? Perhaps too much pretend magnanimousness has caused you to lose sight of what normal people are like."

Kakutan sighed. "Fair." She sipped from her gourd. "But I need you, now, to talk to me. Talk to me about what these three are here for. Why are they running? What, perhaps, do they carry, besides that evil bat? Where are they going?"

"Why does it matter? They are leaving your land as you asked."

"It does matter. You know once any Bassai Envoys arrive, which they will soon—we have sent a runner to Bassa with the news, after all—they won't be convinced these three did not pass through this protectorate. They will press, and they will discover we let them through. They will not believe what we have seen here with our own eyes, or at least they will not believe it out of our mouths. We must have a tale to tell them, some sensible reason for us being unable to hold them here. Now, I have only been Supreme Magnanimous for a few seasons, and you much longer than me. Perhaps, if we put our heads together..." She drifted off. "You see how tough this is for me."

"No, I don't think it's tough," Biemwensé said. "You say what has happened: You let them go because they had something much more powerful than you could handle. Something much more powerful than anything Bassa can currently muster."

Kakutan sighed again. "You know that is exactly what I'm avoiding. That would be inviting upon Whudasha everything we have worked to prevent. Bassa has been looking for a reason to break the Peace Treaty for many seasons. This will be the last of us."

"Then may it be so," Biemwensé said. "What is a life if we have to spend it in fear, anyway?"

"So you may say. But some people want to try. Some people want to survive for as long as they can, until a possible path to freedom arrives."

"Maybe that path to freedom has already arrived, have you thought of that? Maybe we must protect these young ones and grant them safe passage today so they can become the ones who enact the change we seek. Maybe that is our duty before we go on our final journeys to the skies."

They walked in silence for a bit. Lilong came down from the bat and managed to walk on her own. Danso remained glued to her side, and they whispered to each other.

"Listen," Kakutan said. "I have some suspicions. That stone object the boy used—I think it might be ibor."

Biemwensé regarded the smaller woman. Tonight was the first time she had ever been in close proximity with the current Supreme Magnanimous. Perhaps Kakutan was a teenager when Biemwensé was Supreme Magnanimous herself. Perhaps Kakutan had even been a part of her Youth then, but Biemwensé had been so caught up in trying to hold together a protectorate built on twigs and twine that she never took the time to look around and know people. Now, somewhere between fighting her and being defeated by the Skopi, Kakutan had decided they shared some sort of sisterly bond through the Youth Order.

Biemwensé, for a very long time, had gotten on just fine on her own. She did not need a *sister*. This did not stop Kakutan from pressing on, though.

"I once helped someone who was seeking this very thing," she continued. "I have walked this path before, led someone out of Whudasha and into the Savanna Belt in search of what that boy may now be holding in his hand."

"And you think they're connected?"

"Perhaps. There is a bounty on their heads for a reason. I believe it has to do with the Speaker's death." She paused. "I believe it is why the yellow-skin is here."

Now *this* Biemwensé perked up at. She was so far away on the eastern edge of the protectorate that she barely stayed on top of news from Bassa, and had only heard about the Speaker's death because her children had been chattering about it. She at once dismissed it as one of those things from Bassa that she did not want to hear, that she had long lost the ability to care for. But if the circumstances surrounding the death of the nation's Speaker were noteworthy, this piece of information was of interest to her.

"Tell me," she said, simply.

"One Supreme Magnanimous to another," Kakutan said, and Biem-wensé almost rolled her eyes. "This is not something you can tell to any soul."

"Why does it matter?" Biemwensé frowned. "Did you do something illegal?"

"I wouldn't say illegal," Kakutan said. "But, you know, when an Idu noble from Bassa asks for your help, with the promise of a returned favour, you do not think twice. That is not an opportunity that comes around very often. It was something I had to do. To be honest, it has weighed on me a long time, and I am glad to be able to confide in some-one else about this, but—" She stopped herself. "You are not going to talk about this with anyone, are you?"

"No. Who was this Idu?"

Kakutan took hold of her arm, slowed their walk so that they opened up a distance between them and the big group, then said:

"The Speaker's daughter. Her name was Oke."

"Was?"

"She went beyond the Pass and has not returned since."

"I see. And what does that have to do with ibor?"

Kakutan resumed walking, looking wistful. "Eh, well, she didn't tell me this explicitly, but I gathered from her random musings at the time that she was leaving Bassa for the desertland in search of ibor, based on information she had gleaned from some arcane manuscript. I don't know if she ever found it, but this yellowskin appearing, the Speaker dying right after, and then this young man speaking and controlling lightning through a lifeless bat? There is too much coincidence there."

Biemwensé digested this information. Kakutan was right—too much was coming to light at the same time for it not to be all interconnected. Perhaps unplanned, but definitely related. But the problem now wasn't who knew what. The problem was who would act on these revelations, and the potential impact of such actions on all of Oon.

"So you helped her go over the Pass?" she asked.

"I didn't help her go over the Pass," Kakutan said quietly. "I helped her go *under* it." When Biemwensé frowned, Kakutan said: "The Dead Mines. There is an abandoned bushroad that goes off the Emperor's Road and leads there, if you know what you're looking for. By helping Oke, I managed to come in contact with a group from the Savanna Belt that she was in coalition with, shored up in a small colony on the other side called Chabo. They call themselves the Gaddo Company, and they apparently have a secret channel within the Dead Mines through which they smuggle various things, including, well, people."

"But the moats."

"I hear they built a bridge. It's a very well-protected and hidden system, see. Even I have never been privy to it—I was only required to deliver Oke-maa to the mines itself. She had a contact who met her there. In return, though, I get one free pass—as many people as I want, whenever I need it."

Biemwensé stopped. "Why are you telling me all this?"

Kakutan shrugged. "I guess..." She sighed. "I guess, I've been thinking that if an Idu was willing to sacrifice herself in that way, if this yellowskin girl and this Bassai boy and that Second all put themselves in harm's way simply to protect this stone-thing, then, well maybe the hand of fate is working here." She paused. "And perhaps you are right."

"Me? About what?"

"Letting them through being the better decision." She paused. "Listen—I have always been a respecter of yours, so I won't lie to you. I am not comfortable either with the way we live under Bassa's thumb and according to the nation's whims. But I cannot afford to be weak, to put the lives of others in jeopardy, because I disagree with Bassa." Kakutan swirled her drink, staring at it intently. "I don't agree with what happened to you, you know? You had given service to this order, and I thought you should've been treated with more honour. Even so, I would've preferred if they punished *you* instead for the accused treason, rather than punish your family—"

"Let me stop you right there," Biemwensé snapped. "Don't you *dare* speak about them. Don't you *dare*."

But even as she said it, the image came again to Biemwensé, of her husband—younger and more agile, then—and her daughter—frail, frightened—being dragged out to the gate at the arch of the Peace Fence, and the stationed Bassai civic guards poking spears at them, shouting directions to the Emperor's Road at them for their enforced journey to Bassa. She had still been imprisoned at the time and wasn't there to see it, but she had gathered the story in whispers around the community and pieced it together for herself.

They never arrived in Bassa. Their bodies were never found.

"I'm sorry, I won't mention them," Kakutan said. "But you must see, surely, that this one-woman fight for independence will get us nowhere? I mean, look at you. You could've been Supreme Magnanimous for much longer. Now you languish on the edge of the protectorate, painting and selling underpriced pottery."

"At least I do not work for oppressors," Biemwensé said. "I can die well, knowing I have made an honest living." She faced the smaller woman. "This continent belongs to all who have set foot on it. Our ancestors came here as much as theirs did. This has *always* been our land, and anything less than complete independence from Bassa's iron hand on the mainland is insufficient."

Kakutan sighed. "I understand. But I have continued to carry out every aspect of my duty with the right amount of alacrity because people depend on me, and I cannot make decisions based solely on how I feel. Still, I need you to remember I am not completely sold to Bassa. I have one eye always turned away, searching for a way out. And if that way out happens to come from this ibor, even if it comes from that evil bat over there, I will not be averse to it."

They walked in some more silence before Kakutan looked to the dark night sky and said: "There is an opportunity hiding somewhere within all of this upheaval. All of these connected incidents are chipping away at the walls that hold us in. All we need is to apply a little pressure at the right place and time. But it requires extreme care, because there are lives at stake." She puffed her cheeks and blew out air. "I just need a sign, is all."

Biemwensé nodded. *Don't we all*, she thought. *Don't we all*.

Oboda

Once Oboda arrived at the gates of the Peace Fence, he did three things.

First, he told the peacekeeping civic guards on the Bassa side of the fence about the runner from Whudasha he had just intercepted on the Emperor's Road. He told them, in slow and clear terms, what the runner had told him about the Yelekuté man the Whudasha Youth had in custody, and how that man was one-third of a hefty bounty he sought, and all they needed to do was to aid him in convincing the Whudasha Youth to release the man to them, and they would get a share when the bounty came. The men did not budge easily, especially since setting foot on the other side of the Peace Fence meant breaking a treaty that had been unbroken for so many seasons, but all Oboda had to do was mention the bounty amount—a hundred gold pieces *per head*—for them to discard their concerns. If there was anything Oboda knew, it was that the only thing that moved men more than the promise of some joy between the thighs was the promise of money or power.

Second, once he had crossed the fence and was immediately blockaded by a host of Whudasha Youth, he calmly explained everything he had just explained to the civic guards, leaving out the part about the bounty, and instead presenting himself as the expected Envoy from Bassa. He had been banking on the fact that whoever had imprisoned Zaq the Second would not have offered complete information to every Whudasha Youth, but he was shocked when one of the Youth asked what had happened to the runner sent to Bassa by their Magnanimous Supreme, because the runner definitely couldn't have gotten to Bassa and back in the time elapsed.

Now, Oboda could not tell her that after extracting all the information he needed from the runner, he had fed the choice parts of the young boy to his leopard and let the rest rot in a bush on the Emperor's Road. (What sensible person would allow such precious information to make its way to the Three-Prong Waystation, to the ears of his competition?) He could not tell her that he was missing three of his hunthands and a leopard, whom he had sent off to cover the savannas in search of the fugitives, and that he was positive that the captured Second had something to do with it. He could not tell her he believed it was his right to capture all three fugitives himself in order to exact the right amount of vengeance and retribution he sought for the disgrace they had brought upon him and the name of the household he worked for.

So Oboda did the third thing, the thing that had not been done in over a hundred seasons: He pulled out his runku and clobbered the speaking Youth over the head. The woman fell, and blood oozed from her head and melded with the Whudan sand.

After that, no one—not even the civic guards, who were Potokin desert immigrants themselves and therefore of the lowest possible civic guard rank—challenged Oboda anymore. So when he asked, yet again, to be taken to their leader and, in tandem, to Zaq, he was obliged.

There was one little problem, though: The Supreme Magnanimous was down in Whudasha East dealing with some matters affiliated with the said fugitives, and had left the Youth who had captured Zaq herself in charge. What luck. They took Oboda to her.

The woman, whose name was Indina, took one look at Oboda and made the right choice not to ask any questions. Instead, she studied him for a long time, then said something that surprised even him.

"I can give you the desertlander now," she said. "*Or*, we could wait for the Supreme Magnanimous to arrive with your other two fugitives in hand—and she will, because the desertlander has given us all the information we need—and then we can have three for the price of one."

"We?" Oboda asked.

"I want a portion of your bounty earnings," she said. "And in return for my help, I would like to be allowed into Bassa."

"I do not have the power to grant your second request."

"But you have the ear of someone who can."

Oboda thought that between his men, the civic guards helping him, and this woman, the bounty was starting to seem very divided, but then he realised he'd be getting all three heads, and three hundred gold pieces was more than enough to go around.

"Fine. I will speak what I can in your favour." He paused. "Your leader will not give them up easily, will she?"

"No," Indina said. "No, she will not."

"And if we offer her a part of the bounty?"

Indina thought for a moment. "I don't think Kakutan cares about money in that way. And seeing as you've already murdered one of our own, well." She shrugged. "You're not in a good position, really."

"So we kill her, then," Oboda said flatly.

Indina looked at him for a long time, then said, slowly, "Yes."

"Good." He rose. "Now, go get the desertlander."

"Now? What for?"

"Because we need an ambush to defeat that yellowskin," he said. "An ambush means surprise. Surprise requires a trap. And a trap is only a trap if there is real bait in it."

56

Lilong

By the time they arrived back at the headquarters of the Whudasha Youth, it was already past midnight and cricket noises had replaced all human noise for the rest of their journey. So Lilong was quite surprised, as they approached the headquarters, to see lights and a growing gathering of people ahead.

Between Biemwensé's herbal potions and the supported trip from the other side of the protectorate, Lilong had regained enough of her strength not only to walk by herself but to do a little bit of ibor on her own. A small group who had seen Danso and his bat do what they did could handle seeing a yellowskin like her. But a larger group without forewarning? There were stories, back in Namge, about the lynchings that followed when desertlanders and mainlanders first set eyes upon stragglers from the archipelago.

She put a cloak over her head and let her wrapper fall to cover her arms, then fell into stride with Danso and whispered: "Cover me."

Before he could respond, she Drew, and changed her complexion, slowly, to that of a Whudan Shashi. In the darkness, no one had quite noticed it happen.

Suddenly the Youth behind them called out something that could've been a warning, and everyone stopped. Kakutan stepped forward, asking, "What is happening?" and everyone looked in that direction and immediately knew something was wrong.

Ahead of them, a crowd of mostly Whudasha Youth and a small

number of citizens had gathered about what looked like a pyre. Under the direction of a turbaned man whose face they couldn't see, but who Lilong guessed was a Bassai Envoy, Bassai hunthands—the Envoy's men, from the look of things—snapped and broke everything wooden within sight, swiftly transforming them into fuel for the pyre. At the centre of the pyre, they had already erected a stake.

But the most disturbing sight was a group of Bassai civic guards, the same ones who were supposed to be on the other side of the Peace Fence, perched in the darkness beside the main road they were expected to be coming through. The men were positioned in such a way that anyone going past would never notice them. In fact, one might even say they were poised for what, increasingly, looked like an ambush.

Kakutan waved everyone to a hiding spot behind a house and asked for their own torches to be put out.

"How did an Envoy get here so fast?" Biemwensé said quietly. Kakutan was speaking to her Youth colleagues in Whudan with an enquiring tone, and Lilong guessed she was asking the same question.

Corralled in the corner were the Whudasha Youth who had perhaps been unlucky to be present upon the Envoy's arrival. They bristled there, relieved of their weapons and incensed at the audacity of what was happening around them, but handicapped by the fact that as long as the person standing in front of them was Bassai and they were not, any wrongful action risked bringing down a host of reactions from Bassa on the whole protectorate. And in the absence of their Supreme Magnanimous, they were devoid of leadership on how exactly to respond to this situation, so they remained agitated on the periphery, shuffling their feet and murmuring their dissent. They were also kept in check by a leopard, which paraded around the growing pyre and snapped at anyone who strayed too close to the Envoy.

Lilong flexed her arms, assessing the situation. Was she strong enough? If it came down to it, could she get herself and Danso out of here in one piece?

A light came on in the house they were squatting behind, and a voice—a woman's—called out a question in Whudan. Sankofa the Youth went and ushered the woman back inside with shushes and snuffed out her lamp with one big hand.

Danso squatted next to Lilong as Kakutan, squatting a few yards ahead, swore aloud in frustration.

"That guy looks—" he started to say, but was cut short by some activity at the pyre. A hunthand dragged a body forward, toward the pile. It didn't take two looks for Lilong to recognise Zaq, though limp and bruised and bloodied, perhaps even unconscious.

"Zaq!" Danso said, hands to his mouth.

The Envoy began to take off his turban in preparation for what Lilong guessed was the burning. He unwrapped his head, slowly, revealing a bald head beneath, coral pieces embedded into his neck.

"Isn't that . . . ?" Danso gulped. "What is Oboda doing here?"

But Lilong was no longer with the group. She was back at the Weary Sojourner Caravansary, staring at the ashes, imagining the scene between her daa and the three hunthands as the housekeep told her the tale, describing the hunthands to her—with this man, Oboda, as their leader.

It came to her again, clearly. The men had been talking to her daa out back, voices raised, which alerted the housekeep. Before he could ask anything, Oboda had silently unclipped a large stick from his belt. The weapon whooshed when he swung it. There was a *crack* of force against bone, like when one snapped a bird's neck before dunking it in boiling water. But her daa had already Drawn and Possessed the closest thing to him—the lamps within the caravansary. Every flame in the room came together and rushed out the window. The housekeep reported going blind, at least for a short moment. The curtains, the chairs, the walls, everything, lit up, ferocious. Someone had pulled her daa's body away from the fire—no one saw who, though Lilong knew it to likely be a skinchanging Abenai warrior out on assignment. Lucky, too, as it was the only way her daa could've been smuggled back home.

Adrenaline burned in Lilong's blood as she rose, slowly. Her body fought what was coming, said, *No, you cannot do this.* She shoved the pain aside. She had been too weak and disoriented to take him on that first time, back when she had just crossed the border. She was not too weak now. And Oboda was right here.

Danso stood, saying something about the Diwi.

"I'm going to kill him," Lilong said to no one in particular, the words out of her mouth like hisses. Her throat tickled as she said it, dry from not speaking the whole day. Time had not only made her voice harsher but also her mind: tougher, angrier.

Yet everyone heard the savagery in her voice and turned, and only then did they really notice how much her complexion had adjusted, how Shashi she now looked, yet how *alien* and *dangerous* she was. Her eyes flashed amber, and her blade, confiscated by the Youth until they were out of Whudasha, rattled in its sheath and flew into her outstretched hand.

There were audible gasps, a sucking of breath. Even Kakutan, usually composed and in command of the power moves within the group, recognised the look in Lilong's eyes and what it meant. She took a moment to gauge her response, before she rose, slowly, and said:

"Wait. I may have a plan."

57

Kakutan

INTO THE LIGHT OF the torches surrounding the pyre, Kakutan stepped forward with a trio of Whudasha Youth, taking care not to look at the Bassai guards who were hiding away. As soon as the group went past them, the men jumped out and blocked them off from behind.

"What's this?" The surprise in her voice was feigned so well even she almost believed it. "Why is our prisoner tied to that stake?" She directed her question toward Indina, who was standing off to the side, away from the corralled Youth.

"Supreme Magnanimous," Oboda said, stepping forward. "I have been waiting." He looked about her. "Where are the rest of the fugitives I was told you would be returning with?"

"What fugitives?" Kakutan asked. "Who are you?"

"I ask the questions," he said, and one of the Bassai civic guards prodded their runku into her back. One of the Youth with Kakutan drew her cutlass, but Kakutan held up her hand.

"I see you are from Bassa," Kakutan said. "Could you perhaps state your business here?"

"I came for my prisoners," Oboda said. "This one here is only one. Where are the rest?"

"What rest? I was only visiting an old friend in Whudasha East. This man is all we have."

"Visiting an old friend." Oboda moved slowly toward her now. "Near the eastern edge of the Peace Fence? Near the savanna? The same savanna where I sent off three of my men and their leopard, and they have yet to return?"

Kakutan grimaced. "Well, I hope you find your men. But if you will please untie that man, we can look at your credentials as a hunt-hand. And if you are who you say you are, you are free to take him away. But mind you, there will still be repercussions for crossing the Peace Fence."

Oboda stopped moving toward her to pause by the pyre. He retrieved a jar of boiled resin from a nearby hunthand and poured it over the wood beneath Zaq. Zaq, still keeled over and lacking consciousness, did not stir or respond to how hot the resin was. Kakutan tensed, and every Youth gathered there bristled and shuffled their feet.

"You should stop this before it's too late," Kakutan said. "You have already committed one violation. You do not want to do this thing you're doing."

"I will give you one last chance," Oboda said, his voice booming. "Bring them forward now, or I will not only burn this man and this whole village to the ground, I will also drag you to Bassa myself and turn you in for treason."

"We are a *protectorate*," Kakutan said, then looked across him, to Indina. "And you. Let me guess—they offered you entry into Bassa? You think this makes you one of them, don't you? You think betraying your own people means acceptance."

"I am only doing what you would do as Supreme Magnanimous," Indina said. "I have pledged my loyalty to Great Bassa, who ensures our continuous survival."

"True," Kakutan said. "You are doing what the Supreme Magnanimous would do, except for selfish reasons and not at all for the survival of the collective."

"Enough," Oboda said. "Where is the light?" Someone passed him a char cloth in a pot from somewhere. "This is your last chance to speak."

"I have said all that needs to be said," Kakutan said.

"So be it, then." He tossed the pot and char cloth toward the resin-laden pyre.

"Now!" Kakutan screamed.

Lilong's blade flew through the air. It shattered the pot into pieces, caught the char cloth in midair, and embedded it into nearby wood.

Then the Youth about Kakutan drew their cutlasses, and the rest of the group stepped out of hiding.

58

Lilong

THINGS DESCENDED INTO CHAOS all at once.

Kakutan and her trio of Youth immediately engaged the civic guards surrounding them. The Youth who emerged from hiding charged for the hunthands. Those who had been corralled without weapons followed their lead, broke free, and joined in the fracas.

That left Lilong with a clear line of sight between her and the big man, Oboda, and she went straight for him without as much as a blink.

Mistake.

He saw her coming, pursed his lips, and gave a sharp whistle. Out of nowhere, a growl, and his leopard bounded forward at speed. It covered ground twice faster than Lilong, and before she could get within a few feet of her man, the leopard leapt and knocked her flat to the ground.

In a heartbeat, it was over her. It might have hesitated a split moment—she wasn't sure—but there was just enough time for the little animal attack survival training she'd received to register: *Don't let it get your face or neck.* And right before it lunged, she grabbed the animal's neck, dug her fingers into its fur-skin, and pushed it back with all her might.

Spittle dripped from the leopard's jaws and into her eyes as it leaned in, its weight like a fallen log, trying for her jugular with each lunge. She held on, her heart beating into her ears. She wanted—*needed*—to call her blade, but she couldn't concentrate enough to do it. The pain in her elbows grew, warning her of this losing battle. *Don't close your eyes—don't close your eyes!* But she had to concentrate!

From nowhere, a *whack*. Something slammed the animal in the head, so hard she felt the force in her hands on its neck. It winced, yelped, and its weight was suddenly gone. Lilong scrambled and wiped her eyes. It had turned its back on her and faced its attacker, lowering for a pounce.

"Go!" Biemwensé said to her, then goaded the leopard: "Come on!" She lured it forward, swinging her stick. "Come on!"

Lilong called for her blade. It flew right into her hand. When she turned back to where Oboda had been standing, he was nowhere to be seen.

Danso was soon next to her, panting. "Are you all right?"

"Where is he?" Lilong found that her voice was a growl. She put her hand into her pouch, pulled out the Diwi, and chucked it at Danso's chest. "Find him with your bat." When Danso frowned at her, she shoved it at him. *"Find him."*

Danso took the stone-bone tentatively, then breathed and closed his eyes.

When he opened them, they were blood-red.

The lightning bat's screech came from somewhere above, and it rose into the night sky with a large beat of sinewy wings. There were gasps and screams as the large animal swooshed overhead, and then even more gasps and screams of awe when people looked and saw Danso's eyes.

The Skopi landed somewhere out of sight and screeched again. Oboda emerged from the direction of the noise, runku in one hand and torch in another, swinging at the bat as it crowded out his escape routes and goaded him back toward the pyre. Then the bat's eyes turned back to dead. Danso came out of the Possession, panting, and fell to the ground.

"Face me!" Lilong shouted to Oboda, who turned and saw her. First he squinted, unable to recognise her in her Whudan complexion. She let the skin slip, let it swing back to her original complexion.

"It's the yellowskin!" someone shouted.

Recognition came over Oboda's expression. A grin spread across his face.

He moved, and before she could Command her blade to take any action, he tossed the torch in his hand onto the resin-laden pyre.

Fire whooshed to life. Zaq, silent since being tied to the stake, began to scream.

Lilong's attention turned to the pyre, and in that moment of distraction, Oboda rushed at her, swinging the runku quicker than she'd thought was possible. She ducked and he swung again, each time the heavy stick making a *whoosh*. Lilong evaded, finding herself unable to concentrate, yet again, enough to offer proper Commands to her blade. She was truly spent, she realised, so much so that her habitual memory was suddenly that little bit out of reach. Each scream from Zaq bit into her attention too, and she had to fight every instinct to tear her focus away from Oboda and turn her head in that direction.

Whoosh.

She tried one Command or the other. Her blade only lurched a few yards and plopped back into the sand.

Whoosh.

"Should've stayed on your side," Oboda said, hemming in. "Should not have come here."

Whoosh. Lilong ducked. She bit her lip to force herself into alertness, into focus, then Commanded again, pushing harder. A pain twisted in her side. She grabbed her rib cage and went down on a knee, just enough time for Oboda's next swing to catch her in the hip.

A jarring vibration rippled through her spine. She hit the ground in pain.

Zaq's screams rang in her ears.

She turned her head. Kakutan and the Youth fought off the hunt-hands and civic guards, and Biemwensé continued to give the leopard the runaround. Danso, who still lay on the ground, reeling from the after-effects of Commanding the bat, met her eyes.

"Zaq," she said, a gasp. "Zaq."

Danso's eyes turned to the pyre and saw his Second burning, the fire beginning to catch at his feet. His yells pierced the air of the early morning. Danso rose painstakingly, fighting the weakness.

Oboda came and stood over her, blocking her view.

"I will bring your body to MaaEsheme," he said. "And I will do it with pleasure."

He lifted his runku.

The air crackled audibly with power. Silver-blue light flashed behind the clouds above, and the sky rumbled in response.

Oboda turned at the same time Lilong did.

Danso, eyes bloodshot red, screamed in unison with the Skopi.

Lightning rained down from above and struck, with pinpoint accuracy, everything within sight that was not Whudan. It struck the leopard that had Biemwensé cornered; it struck each Bassai civic guard that had Kakutan and her Youth outnumbered; it struck every hunthand Oboda had brought with him into the protectorate. It struck them all and set fire to everything it touched.

Danso fell to his knees. Oboda, watching the inferno just as Lilong was, realised Danso had somehow missed him. Perhaps he had been out of sight—he was the only thing that came from Whudasha that was still standing. In that half moment, he saw the opening—Danso weak, vulnerable—and concluded that it was probably the only one he'd ever have.

And Lilong came to that conclusion at the exact same time.

With a last-gasp effort, she Commanded her discarded blade, and it flew into her hand. The pain in her side seared, but she gritted her teeth and rose.

Manually, she flung the blade at him. Her aim was off, and it struck him in the arm, slicing him and bouncing away. He didn't stop, his focus on what he had clearly identified as the greater threat. Lilong ran and jumped on his back, her elbow around his neck. He yanked her off by her hair. The pain from the blow to her hip rang through her body, and her older wounds reared their heads.

Oboda lifted the runku above Danso's head and swung.

Lilong gritted her teeth and did what she had to do.

She Drew the most she had ever had to. She could already feel one or two of the stone-bones embedded in her arm start to disintegrate, the grains pouring down her elbow, succumbing to their depleting power. But she knew she had to make this work.

Danso was the one person who could currently wield the Diwi, the weapon Namge had spent hundreds of seasons trying to protect. If he died, the Diwi could fall apart alongside him, and everything would be lost. *He* was the weapon now. *He* was the priority, the thing that needed protection.

She Possessed Oboda's runku.

Her brain swirled, as power and heat rushed out of her, plucking at every strand in her body. She screamed as she Commanded it. The weapon stopped in midair. She pushed with force, feeling the rough of the wood in her mind, the weight of the blob at the end of the weapon.

Shatter.

The weapon split into many parts in Oboda's hand as she gave the parts their final Command.

Like a set of carved spears, the parts, pointy ends each, reared themselves in the air, gathered force, and plunged into the big desertlander's chest.

Lilong fell as Oboda did. Her senses faded, slowly, as did the noises, the crackle of fire, the smell of burnt things, Zaq's ongoing scream. There were shouts, and there were feet, but for a long time before the black came, all Lilong was trying to do was tell herself that Danso was going to be all right, that the Diwi was going to be all right, that everything was going to be—

59

Lilong

AFTER WHAT SEEMED LIKE eternity, Lilong felt hands pulling her up, out of the darkness. She opened her eyes and they immediately watered from the harsh sting of black smoke, and there was a prevailing smell of roasted meat. Ash floated in the air.

"Shh, you're okay," a voice was saying, from far away, and then it was very close and she recognised it as someone she was supposed to know, but for the life of her, she could not remember who it was.

"You're fine," it said.

For a long time, Lilong did not feel fine. She was supposed to be seeing, but it was all so dark, so uninviting. Her knees didn't work, and she wobbled. Another firm pair of hands joined in supporting her, and a heavy blanket was thrown over her. She tried to think why, wondered if it was to hide her yellow complexion. But soon she was in the dark again anyway, indoors this time, out of the smoke and breathing in better air. She was placed on a bench, her back laid to rest on the wall.

"Well," the person said again, and then she looked properly, and saw it was an old woman, a Whudan. Lilong recognised her, had her name on the tip of her tongue, but her brain seemed to be working at half capacity.

"I can't remember your name," Lilong said.

"Oh?" the woman said, her face wrinkling with concern. "Yaya, remember? Biemwensé." She gestured toward Lilong's head. "Are you okay in there? Tell me, what is your last memory?"

Lilong thought for a moment. "I don't know."

"What is your name?"

She paused. "Lilong."

"Okay," Biemwensé said. "Gah, your ibor is a problem. Short-term memory loss, among other things." She examined Lilong's eyes. "Bloodshot."

Lilong realised she was worried about something, and she dug for it, searching her failing memory until, all at once, the puzzles in her head clicked into place.

"Danso!" The memories came rushing back. She swooned with the wave of it all, and swayed in her seat.

"Easy, easy," Biemwensé said. "You have overspent yourself. This is a thing you do often, isn't it—not giving your body the respect it deserves?"

"I do not overspend myself," she said, as Biemwensé passed her a cala-bash of water to drink. Various people moved through the room at speed, carrying things, calling out for people. There was a person coughing in every corner.

"Are we at a hospice?"

"No." Biemwensé collected the calabash. "We're at the Youth headquarters."

"And Danso?"

"Outside. Took a knocking—overspending, like you. He's probably fine already, though. You, on the other hand..."

Someone went by and did a double take upon spotting Lilong awake.

"Oh," the person said. Lilong peered into the dimness and saw that it was Kakutan.

"And Zaq?" Lilong asked, eyes hopeful.

Both Biemwensé's and Kakutan's heads dropped at the same time, in that manner that told her that there was not even a tiny chance the Second had made it. Something moved in her chest in response, but she parsed it enough to understand what exactly she felt. The constant move-ment was making her dizzy.

"Where is everybody going?" she asked.

"We are leaving," Kakutan said flatly.

"*Leaving?* Leaving where?"

"Leaving Whudasha. Like we should have done all these seasons."

Kakutan crouched and forced some water down the parched lips of a nearby wounded Youth. "It won't take long before Bassa returns with reinforcements. Anyone left here will not live to tell the tale."

"So *everyone* is leaving?"

"Yes."

Biemwensé scoffed then, and Kakutan stopped her task to say, "Oh, so you're not done? If there's something more you want to say to me, say it."

"I still maintain you cannot get a thousand people under a mountain."

"And so we shouldn't try?"

"I'm saying there has to be another way out of this."

"There is no other way. We have harboured fugitives and murdered the Bassai citizens who tried to bring them in. There is no surviving such a thing." She put the calabash down, hard. "I have an opportunity to at least save my people, and moons strike me if I do not take it."

"But a *thousand* people, Kakutan."

"It won't be easy, I agree." Lilong had not seen the Supreme Magnanimous this pensive thus far. She looked like she might cry. "I have no choice but to remain positive here, Biemwensé. These are my people, *our* people. I must maintain optimism for us all. Besides, I consider our numbers a strength, not a weakness."

Biemwensé shook her head. "Fine. But many will still refuse to come. You saw the response at the announcement."

"I will only take the willing, and I believe many are willing to stay alive. I have this one chance and I will use it to get as many people across the border as possible."

Their argument was starting to intensify Lilong's headache, but so was the deep pang of regret rising in her chest. *Leaving? Because of... me?* How could the mere fact of her presence upend a whole community, uproot thousands of people and their lives? And then... Danso. He had barely spent a proper day in the place he'd thought could be home, and it was going to all be over so soon. And now he had lost his Second too! She had to find him fast.

"I'm sorry," she said to Kakutan. "To have brought misfortune upon you in this way."

The two women paused their bickering to stare at her.

"It was bound to happen at some point, regardless of your arrival, wasn't it?" Biemwensé rose. "I have to go see to other things. If you want to find Danso, he is outside."

Both women went off and Lilong thought to seek Danso immediately—she had to secure the Diwi, too—but found she was too tired to even rise. While contemplating her next move, she drifted off from exhaustion. A brief period of darkness, and suddenly, she was waking again to the continuous flow of activity still moving through the room. The injured Youths next to her had been moved. How long had she been asleep?

She tested her powers, nudging to see if she could afford to make her complexion Whudan-like again, which she did after great effort. Then she went out, and was surprised it was very bright outside, close to noon. People scampered about, carrying things. Far off to the side, the remains of the pyre fire oozed smoke still, embers dying. There were at least two or three bodies burnt black by fire or lightning or both, and at least a few dead by some other means. She put a cloak over her head to prevent recognition and tried asking for directions, using signs to describe Danso. She had little success until one Youth who understood Mainland Common but couldn't speak it pointed her in a direction.

When she came upon Danso, he was standing at an overlook where the land tipped down and began to recede into the bight. His Skopi was sprawled a little distance away, unmoving. He was scattering something from a potted vessel into the wind—ashes, it looked like. It took her a moment to understand he was following the Bassai rites, and those ashes were a representation of Zaq—the man himself couldn't have been burned down to ash this quickly. She stood aside a moment and let him finish.

His shoulders drooped as he said the words, punctuated by brief, intermittent scattering of the contents of the vessel. His grief was palpable, so that Lilong herself felt it too, clinging to the salty air. Her feelings about Zaq had been much clearer when the journey began, but became murkier as they went, as she began to understand the complicated relationship he had with his oppressors. As she had learned during their brief chat in the Breathing Forest, there was more to him than just being a Second. She knew, given some time, she might've even come to like him.

No chance of that now.

He didn't deserve this, she thought, bowing her head in imitation of Danso's solemnity. Zaq had been a devoted man: to his charge, preserving his sense of duty to the last possible extent, even when no one would've faulted him for leaving earlier; to his adopted nation, even though it had made sure to keep him under. He was a man devoted to the idea of devotion, unable to separate that which could help him ascend and that which could get him killed.

She shuffled her feet, guilt piling in her chest again. *You're going to be feeling this way for a long time, aren't you, Lilong?* The trail of consequences spawning from the simple acts of crossing the border and returning to Danso's barn was getting longer. Some part of her challenged it—Bassa deserved what they got. Besides, wasn't it really Nem's choices that were forcing her into making hers? And didn't Zaq walk into the hands of the Youth on his own? But another part of her knew it was only deflection. Whether she liked it or not, the truth was that Zaq would never had died if he hadn't come along. He would never have been here if he'd had no reason to be protecting his charge in the first place. And that reason was her, plain and simple.

Danso was quiet now, all done with the rites, but he remained standing there, his head hung low. Lilong shuffled up to him. He noticed her for the first time but returned to gazing into space. They stood there together wordlessly for a while. She slowly turned and embraced him. He returned the embrace.

"I'm sorry," she said. "For Zaq. For everything."

She felt the warm drop of a tear on the back of her shoulder.

"He was still my friend, you know?" Danso said, his voice breaking. "Despite everything, he still cared what happened to me. But I was so blind, so selfish. I brought him to his destruction."

"It wasn't really your fault," Lilong said, knowing it was a lie.

"It was," Danso said. "You know it was."

They remained in each other's arms for a time.

"Do you always feel this way?" Danso asked when they finally pulled away, his voice low and hoarse and contemplative, not at all like the Danso she knew. "Do you always feel this...lost, afterward?" His face twisted, like he was in physical pain.

"Ibor does that to you every time, yes," she said. "The weight it places on your mental consciousness transfers to the physical. It's like your brain has been fried in hot oil, like someone took a mallet to your joints, your teeth. Back home, we follow strict diets to combat the aftereffects on our body."

"No, no." He gripped her hand, tight. "I mean, after you kill something, someone, people, a hope…" He drifted off. "There's a weight. Heavy."

She wasn't sure if he was speaking of the physical murders he had committed in the last two days, or the death of the future of Whudans, whose lives they'd simply doomed by their arrival. Maybe he was talking about his own future, of which Whudasha would never now be a part. The loss of home, of hope—the death of the self. Whichever it was, she understood it, because she had run through this gamut of emotions herself. The weight, whenever she took a life, or now that she'd condemned a people.

"I can't believe that less than a fortnight ago, I was drinking weybo with my friends and cheering them at the mooncrossing festival," Danso was saying. "Today, I am a homeless fugitive and a murderer. I have wielded unspeakable power, learned unspeakable truths about my world. I have killed. I have found myself unwanted among the only people like me on this continent. I have brought death to a man who only ever cared for me, and now I may have done the same to a thousand Whudans." He shut his eyes and opened them. "I didn't quite think this through, did I? I've been so fixated on a quest for my own truth that I didn't consider the consequences. Now I would give anything to return to some normalcy. I would give anything to have Zaq back."

Me too, she thought. Even the part about Zaq. What she would give now to be safe, to be back home, in the warmth and safety of her family, her annoying siblings, the demanding training of the Abenai League.

"You know they're leaving?"

He nodded. "I tried to talk them out of it. They say it's the only way to survive."

"Are they right?"

He thought for a moment. "I'm afraid they are."

She sighed. This was such a far cry from how she'd envisioned her journey would play out. Every single plan so far had ended in disaster for someone. Was it only a matter of time before they met theirs too?

"We must help them," Danso was saying. "At this point, it's the least we can do."

Again, that part of Lilong that said *This is not your fight* reared its head. She had one task: get the Diwi, return home. This was no time for a side quest.

But this is no side quest, is it, Lilong? Danso was bonded to that Diwi now, which meant he was her new responsibility. Somehow, she had to make sure he crossed the border safely. She could figure out what to do with him later, but for now, they had to cross. That look on his face told her there was no way he would abandon these people, which meant she had to go wherever he did. And, to be honest, there was no way her conscience would be settled if she abandoned them too.

Lilong nodded with resignation, a hand on Danso's cheek. "Listen," she said. "We'll be fine, you hear me? We'll cross the border and get through this. Zaq's death is what happens when we're not there to protect each other. So let us live, so that his death is not in vain. Let us cross to safety the same way we started: together."

He looked into her face. "You will . . . come with me?"

"To the border, I will," she said. "The Diwi is bound to you, anyway, so I have no choice. It is my family heirloom. Where it goes, I go, and if it has chosen to go with you, then so be it."

She had absolutely no idea how this was going to work, but it was the right thing to do. Wasn't he a prisoner of the Diwi, in a way? She, like him, was a prisoner of a world that had decided not to make space for people like them. Yes, her one goal was to retrieve the Diwi and save her family from the wrath of the Abenai League and shame in the Ihinyon islands. But part of her also wanted more, didn't it? Part of her wanted to be free of this world's shackles. She had given herself room to let the world in, and it had filled her with feelings and realisations that made her too large, too outsized for the boxes Bassa and Namge and all of Oon wanted to put her in. Now she wanted to be more than just a yellowskin warrior. She wanted her actions to mean something *real*.

"We cross with them," she said, finally. "Then we can take the Diwi back to Ihinyon, together." She paused. "If you want."

Danso's eyes were hopeful. "And then?"

"And then," she said, "we'll decide our fates, on our own terms."

Kakutan and Biemwensé approached them just then. They stepped away from each other quickly, as if caught doing something wrong by their parents. Lilong mentally smacked herself for the reaction.

The women stood looking at the couple without saying anything, until Kakutan put a hand in her wrapper and produced something: two round globulelike objects in a wooden frame.

Danso's eyes widened. "Are those...reading stones?"

"Yes," she said. "I got them from an old lover." She paused, lost in thought. Biemwensé cleared her throat and pursed her lips at Kakutan, who handed the object to Lilong. "Anyway, Biemwensé told me your eyesight becomes something akin to hers when in the sun. We may be journeying for long hours, and since you can do...things, we may need you. And it'll probably be best for everyone if you can see properly."

Lilong put them on. There was a wooden frame around both stones that allowed her to balance the contraption on the bridge of her nose, and twine that allowed her to tie the frame at the back of her head. When she looked up, everything suddenly came into much clearer focus—the details of their faces, the correct colours of their clothes, how far away from her they stood. She found herself gasping in delight. Danso, however, furrowed his brow.

"What?" she asked.

"You look..." He searched for the word. "Alarmed." He made a motion with his fingers and eyes that said her eyes were large.

"Well, I can definitely see better, so." She turned to the women. "Thank you."

"Oh, don't thank us yet," Biemwensé said. "Do something in return for us. We need every protection on this trip, and with what you two can do, you might just be the last living hope for Whudasha."

Lilong and Danso nodded at each other, then together at the women.

"Time to go," Kakutan said, and the two women led the way. Danso retrieved the Diwi from within his wrappers and handed it back to Lilong.

"I think maybe you should hold on to this," he said. "My hope is that we'll never have to use it again before we're done. And perhaps..." He trailed off. "Perhaps, after this is over, it can find attachment with a more deserving person."

Lilong put the Diwi in the pouch around her waist. "Don't be too hard on yourself. You did what you believed was right. This continent failed Zaq, not you. Your only crime was believing in the systems it made." She bit her lip, thoughtful. "And maybe that's not really a crime, you know? The world needs at least one person to harbour a little belief, a little trust in things, or else what a horrible, horrible place it'll be."

Ah, Lilong, she thought right after saying that. *Only a fortnight out of Namge, and you sound like daa already.*

"You think?" His tone was lonesome.

"I do," she said, choosing her words carefully. "I think, maybe, I've been slow to opening myself up to anything different from me. But if anything, this journey has shown me there are good and bad people everywhere. So perhaps, harbouring just a little bit of faith, a little bit of trust, even when you're unsure... maybe that's how we make change."

"Change," he echoed, pensive.

"Yes, change. Like destroying every lie. That's where the power to do so rests, isn't it? And maybe if we keep enough faith with others, together we become powerful enough to force everyone to look, to see the blood buried beneath this land. And true freedom is truth, isn't it?"

He looked into her face. A small smile played about the edges of his lips. Was that admiration in his eyes?

"It is," he said, looking wistful. "And truth is power. And this trio of truth-power-freedom that we seek, we could bring it to everyone too, couldn't we?" Danso locked eyes with hers now. "We may get it for ourselves, but also for others, as much as we can, shouldn't we?"

Lilong cocked her head. Once upon a time, like on the day she got on her daa's kwaga and left her island, her response to this would have been *Absolutely not.* But so much had changed since then, and she saw the world differently now. She was no longer a spectator, hiding behind the screen of the Forest of the Mist, wallowing in anxiety that someone would soon somehow access the archipelago and discover Ihinyon secrets. Now she was a player, already affecting the world, albeit in the wrong ways. Now she was ready to do it the right way. If there was anything a player should do, it was play to the fullest of their ability, and most importantly, play to win, employing everything in their arsenal.

"Yes, I believe we should," she said, and she truly meant it.

60

Esheme

A MESSAGE FROM THE Three-Prong Waystation came by pigeon the next day, and it was not the news Esheme had been expecting.

Oboda had been murdered in Whudasha, the letter, hastily scribbled by a near-illiterate person, said. There had been only one surviving hunthand—the writer of the letter, left behind to keep watch at the waystation just in case the fugitives emerged after. He'd gone on to Whudasha once the waystation had been fully abandoned by other hunthands, and found the death toll to constitute his hunthand group and a bunch of civic guards. Now he was escorting Oboda's body back to the household, as it was the only body not mangled beyond recognition. He had employed someone he met at the Three-Prong Waystation on his way back to help him write this letter and send the message ahead.

Esheme paced and tapped her foot in anticipation, rereading the letter in the midmorning light of the library. The little roll of paper offered further information: Every single Whudan who could possibly tell of what had happened had left—the coastal protectorate had emptied out, perhaps in a bid to escape punishment. Worse yet, it confirmed there was no word on Danso or the yellowskin, yet there was concrete evidence—in the form of the burnt-to-charcoal body of Danso's Second, recognisable only by the migrant beads melted into his ankle—that they had been present in Whudasha at some point.

It was hours before they arrived and brought Oboda's body into the anteroom of the house. Esheme was surprised how overcome with emotion she became. Maybe it was seeing his body tattered like that—shards of wood still sticking out of his chest. He was more her maa's man, but the way he had stood next to her since all of this began, had done all she asked of him—she valued his loyalty and sacrifice now more than ever. From the story the one surviving hunthand eventually told, Oboda had risked everything to do right by her household and bring back what she asked, and for that, she was grateful.

"Leave me," she said to Satti, who had been standing there with her.

Satti left the anteroom without a word. Esheme watched the body, rubbing her stomach with one hand, the other in her wrappers, fingering the piece of red ibor he had brought to her that day in the barn, the day when all of this had begun. His body was going to lie in state for only one day here, after which he'd be burned without pomp or ceremony, simply placed in a furnace overnight. He wouldn't be given a Bassai burial. No hero's ashes scattered from the Soke peak for people who didn't look like the humus, no flight to the skies for them. According to Bassai laws, the ancestors would not be pleased to see people who did not look like them arriving in the skies.

"I know you longed to see this household name become something," she said to the corpse. "If only you'd stayed alive long enough to see it come to pass."

She reached forward and touched his arm, then made to leave.

But something happened, then, like a jerk on her mental consciousness. She felt a heat in her, a startling warming, first in her chest, then most importantly, in her belly.

It was as if the wee infant in her had...awoken.

And then, the red stone-bone in her hand *responded.*

She pulled out the ibor piece and looked at it, surprised. That was the exact feeling her maa had described in the journals! But the red stone-bone couldn't have been doing something, could it?

She looked back at Oboda's body. It had happened when she touched it.

She reached out again, carefully, and touched the body.

Energy flowed into her from the stone, sifting through her body, and settling, again, in that spot in the bottom of her belly, as if it weren't looking for her, but looking for something else nestled there.

She shut her eyes, as her maa's journal had instructed, and let the power take over.

A heady rush of energy surged through her then, body and mind intermixing, chill and heat causing her to shudder.

She fell. For a long time, she could not remember anything. But the one thing she could remember, at least, was seeing the eyes of the corpse open, and beneath those lids, a deep red of lifelessness staring back at her where whites should've been.

· ◇ ⋯ ─────────── ⋯ ◇ ·

Esheme awoke to people shouting. First there was the shouting of people in argument, then that of threatening, of blood about to be spilled. Before she could make sense of it, there was clanging and banging, a good amount of it, and grunts of effort.

She rose from the floor. Why had she fallen? She remembered the feeling in her belly, Oboda's lifeless yet red eyes, *alive*. She looked at the body now, where it lay. It hadn't moved, but the eyes were still open and not red, but simply glassy in death. She remembered clearly the way it had looked, at *her*, the way it had responded to her touch.

She pulled out the stone-bone and balled it in her fist. *How?*

She looked down at her belly. *It can't be, can it?* she thought, and a growing feeling that stood between dread and apprehension rose in her chest, because she knew it was indeed true.

The stone-bone had not responded to her at all. It had responded to the infant within her.

A myriad of questions ran through her mind, a series of *Why* enquiries: Why her? Why this baby? Why the dead? Why this body?

But she didn't have time to answer them, because the door to the room burst open and civic guards marched in. Leading the group was Ariase, Dota's Second. He stepped forward, then aside, and Dota strutted past him into the room.

"Ah," he said, upon sighting the body. "Mourning, I see. Too bad you should've thought of that before you disrespected my office and my name by threatening my Second. I have come here in person now, and either I am leaving with what I have asked for, or you are leaving with me in chains."

Esheme dusted dirt off of her wrappers and stared straight at him, past him, ahead. Her mind was doing something else rather than being afraid: It was concentrating, planning, calculating.

"I have given you sufficient time," he said, tapping his foot in impatience. "Refusal is not an option, you hear me? Because the fallout of such an action is not going to be pleasant for you."

Esheme's focus started to fade, as her grip on the stone-bone tightened, and the stone responded in the way it had earlier, calling to her body again, persistent, asking what she wanted, what she wanted.

Dọta spotted her fist. "Is that it?" he asked. "Is that the stone-bone?"

Esheme's eyes refocused on the man's face, his chubby cheeks and rotund belly, the twinkle in his eyes—the twinkle of someone who knew how to squeeze, to suffocate, who took delight in it. She knew then that there was only one way out, and that way was the start of many to obtain all of the things she wanted now, had always wanted. It was the way things had been obtained for seasons; it was the way Bassa's ancestors had earned their places, the way Dọta himself obtained many things. It was the way her maa had been willing to obtain everything she wanted to.

If she was to have anything—anything at all—she would have to spill blood.

You always know, Igan had said, and in truth, she did. She had always known she would eventually need to go the way of blood.

Esheme stretched her arm forward and opened up her palm. The piece of red ibor lay there in it.

"Here it is," she said. "Come and take it."

Every eye in the room was drawn to the stone-bone, wonder at the realised myth swimming in their pupils, stilled in the presence of something so rare. Dọta, who looked just as enthused, frowned and was about to ask something, then changed his mind mid-mouth-opening and stepped forward to retrieve the piece from her hand.

Esheme shut her eyes then and remembered how to Draw. Energy rushed through her with a vengeance, and she pushed it then into

Oboda's body and Possessed the corpse behind her. Her body shuddered as the ibor did its work: taking, taking, then offering, offering.

There was only one message she needed to give it, and it was clear and ever-present in her forehead.

Kill.

Oboda's eyes turned red, and the body rose with aplomb, without even as much as a bend in the knees or elbows, but like a spirit standing. Before Dọta could as much as look up and be surprised, it moved with impossible speed and reached for the man's neck in a fierce, stonelike grip.

Esheme looked into Dọta's eyes right then, and without blinking, she said: "The fallout of such an action will not be pleasant for you either."

Oboda's wrist snapped, and so did Dọta's neck. A bone poked through his neck and spurted blood onto Esheme's face.

"Sorcery!" someone shouted. The men, eyes bulging, delayed just that little moment between fear and duty before rushing headlong toward her, confused and brainless and blinded, and that was exactly what she needed.

Kill, she Commanded. *Kill them all.*

Oboda's corpse moved swiftly, faster than the eye could see. The men swung weapons at a body that did not have life in it, and caught it many times yet produced no effect. They, on the other hand, came away in many more ways than one: limbs torn, bones broken, eyes gouged, bits of flesh streaming from what remained of them. Blood, slick, carpeted the floor and stained furniture as man after man went down.

Ariase, who had remained in place in shock, moved forward then and reached for a lamp burning on the wall. He turned and made to throw it at the advancing body. Oboda reached forward at the last moment and grabbed his hand, then broke it, slowly, forearm bone jutting out of his elbow. Ariase screamed and fell to his knees. The lamp dropped into the increasing pool of blood.

Esheme walked to the two, barefoot, through the sticky red on the floor. It curdled between her toes and caused them to become slick. But her focus was on Ariase right then, whimpering as he was held in check. She reached for his side and pulled out the golden-hilted knife and scabbard clinging to his belt. She drew the knife and examined it. It was a beautiful piece of weaponry, handcrafted with precision, and with an edge that was made for piercing even bone. It was obvious a craftworker had spent hours honing it.

She liked this knife, Esheme decided. It was like her, like what she was going to be. Beautiful and seemingly harmless, but beneath the pretty golden hilt and scabbard, deadly.

She plunged the knife into Ariase's neck and watched him fall to the ground and squirm until he stopped gurgling and moving and breathing.

Oboda's body, having fulfilled its duty, went promptly into stasis, and stood just as still as all the death about her.

Footsteps. A number of householders and an armed hand or two rushed into the room. Igan and Satti stood at the forefront of them, and when they came upon the sight—of her, of her bloodshot eyes, of the corpse standing erect in stasis, of all the gore before them—they gasped in unison. Someone or two shrieked in alarm. At least one person fainted. Satti herself bent away and retched.

Esheme retrieved the knife from Ariase's neck, wiped it on her wrappers, pushed it into its scabbard, then slowly, before everyone, took off each of her wrappers until all that was left was her undergarment.

"Someone draw me a bath." She walked past them, ibor in one hand and knife in the other, leaving bloodied footprints in her wake.

Esheme

ESHEME COULD TELL HER maa had awoken when she arrived in the room. It was too hot. Nem had always liked her rooms warmer than Esheme could manage, and the hearth was in full blast when she walked in.

Her maa lay in a supine position, almost as if nothing had changed from the last time Esheme was here, when the woman was still as solid as stone. The difference this time was that Nem's piercing black pupils were visible, her eyes open—sharp as the edge of a cutlass, flicking about and taking in everything. Her face and jaw had healed just enough that the lacerations had begun to fill. She was thinner than Esheme had ever seen her, closer to sinew hung on skeleton than a person.

So much changed, Esheme thought. They had contorted into completely different people in the time that had passed. Her maa would never be Nem the fixer again, and Esheme had just gained access to the continent's most powerful item. Both of them had equally murdered one top councilhand. Whatever platform they once stood upon, as fixer-counsel or as maa-daughter, they would now have to completely redesign from scratch.

"Finally," Esheme said, wearing an expression that she thought might look like unbridled joy but was really relief. She sidled up to her maa and embraced the woman, but it felt stilted and laboured, and Esheme was glad to pull away.

Nem blinked, indifferent.

"How are you feeling? Have you been given anything to eat? Water?" She turned to the closed door and yelled, "Satti!"

"I've told Satti I do not want to see anyone," Nem said, calmly. Her words were crusty and hoarse from not having spoken in so long, but that did not dull their slicing action.

"Oh," Esheme said. "Then you just rest. Better for your swift recovery."

"Hmm." Nem kept her eyes roving over Esheme.

Esheme rolled her eyes. "What *now*? You've only just awoken, and you're already *hmm*-ing."

"This is my house," Nem said firmly. "I can *hmm* as much as I want."

"If you say so."

Nem kept her eyes trained on her daughter. "Is there something you wish to tell me? Perhaps, about, say, any recent developments?"

Esheme gritted her teeth. "Satti! That woman wasn't supposed—"

"To tell me?" Nem said. "Have you forgotten who she is really beholden to? You really expect her to refuse me anything I ask of her?"

Esheme sighed. "Fine. What did she tell you? Perhaps I should correct any wrong information."

"No, I have all the facts just fine." Nem struggled to rise, a painstaking and time-consuming effort. Esheme wanted to make a move to help but knew her maa would hate that even more.

Nem drank from a nearby calabash of water. "I think I only require clarity about one thing." Her eyes were soulless pits, sunken from her time under, big bags formed beneath them. "I have heard you did something even I cannot wrap my head around—that the greatest threat to this nation and this household, a threat that even I couldn't subdue, you massacred in cold blood. And while I was informed that Oboda is deceased, I also hear his corpse rose and did the killing at your bidding?"

Esheme waited for Nem to arrive at her destination.

"The red stone-bone," Nem said. "You have somehow found a way to wield it, have you not? I want to know how you did it."

Esheme considered this for a moment. It was Nem herself who had once told her that a secret shared was already half-divulged, that even if it was a secret worth dying for, it was easier for a person to die for not knowing it than for holding back.

"Are you asking me as my maa," Esheme asked, "or as head of this household?"

Nem was quiet for a bit, then said: "What do you think?"

"I think," Esheme said, "I've been waiting for you to wake up and retake the problems you burdened me with. But of course, all of that is pointless now, isn't it?"

"Hmm," Nem said. "I would say you have done a much better job of it than I ever could, anyway."

Esheme chuckled dryly. "I must not be hearing this correctly. You are not complaining about how I have handled things?" She leaned back to regard the woman. "Something in me feels like while you went through the rigors of attempting to balance my proximity to your work with my proximity to the Bassai Ideal, you secretly wished all along that something like this would happen."

Nem stared thoughtfully, as if the thought only crossed her mind now that it had been mentioned.

"I have always wanted a legacy for you that was bigger than mine," she said. "Bigger than this household, if possible. If this is the manifestation of that, I'll take it." She took another sip from the calabash. "You still have not answered my question."

"I don't know how I wielded it," Esheme said, and it was true, to a point. She didn't quite know what the parameters for manipulating the red stone-bone were exactly, and she didn't want to give credence to something she was unsure of.

"Of course you know," Nem said. "Tell me: What did you do differently from what I documented?"

"I'm not sure," Esheme said. "I tried everything you wrote but nothing worked. I just know that Oboda was murdered and his corpse was brought in. I touched it, and the stone-bone responded. That's all."

"Something was different." Nem processed the information. "Did anything change between the last time you tried versus the time it worked?"

"Except for touching the corpse? I doubt it."

"Not even your pregnancy?"

The question took Esheme aback. Then she remembered Nem had already spoken to Satti. She would love a word with that woman later.

"I—um—" Esheme was unsure about how to respond. "You believe my pregnancy has something to do with it?"

"Yes," Nem said without hesitation. "This is not one of the notes I left behind, but the codex did say outlanders have more susceptibility to manipulating the stone-bone than mainlanders do."

"But I'm not an outlander."

"No. But your baby is."

Esheme froze.

"Oh, so you think I did not know about your dalliances with your hairdresser?" She shook her head, as if disappointed. "Listen, my dear, I am your maa. I want the best for you, but I'm not stupid. I know what I did when I was your age. The fires that burn within you have burned in me too. As much as you believe I aim to shackle you, you must realise I understand you more than you know. At the end of it all, my desire is simply one thing: for you to soar."

She cleared her throat before Esheme could formulate a response.

"Now, your baby," she said. "Part desertlander, is it? Interesting. When Oboda brought the ibor pieces from the Savanna Belt, he did so with his bare hands. Yet nothing happened. He did not wield any, and neither responded to him. So it is not the desertlander blood alone, and it is not the mainlander blood alone either. It has to be both."

Esheme gulped, remembering the feeling she'd had when she'd touched the body that first time, the one that had crept up from her belly.

"You're not bonded with the red stone-bone." Nem's tone was loaded with the self-satisfaction of having cracked a seasons-old code. "Your child is."

Esheme paced, hands akimbo. She'd known this, somewhere within her, but had wanted to believe otherwise. Nem voicing it now forced her to face it head-on.

"This poses a problem, doesn't it?" Esheme said.

"How so?"

"For one, I don't want it," she said, pointing to her stomach.

"But you don't have a choice now, do you?"

Esheme raised an eyebrow. "You don't think a Shashi child will raise eyebrows?"

Nem pursed her lips. "You are not paying attention. You are not going to bear that child, because as you continue to wield ibor, it is a matter of time before that child whittles down to nothing, anyway." She watched her daughter pace. "Does that scare you?"

"No," Esheme said, considering it. "I think..." She paused. "I think I'm more concerned that, yet again, whatever power I have to wield is possessed by an extension of me, without which I will be...nothing."

"You can never be nothing," Nem said. "Not anymore." She drank from her calabash again. "No one has figured out any of the things we have just spoken about in this room. It is our duty to ensure it remains that way. I believe fate has smiled upon us that Shashi have not had access all this time, else they would've come to this conclusion earlier. It is our duty to keep it that way." She shook her head. "The power to raise the dead. Imagine what could be done with it."

"Don't start getting grand ideas," Esheme said. "I'm still recovering from all I expended the last time."

"I'm not talking about you," Nem said. "I'm thinking about the only other people we have on this mainland capable of executing what you just did."

Esheme paused her pacing. "The Whudans."

"Imagine it," Nem said. "If, by some stroke of Ashu's luck, they manage to become privy to this information. The natural next step will be to search for the red stone-bone for themselves. And if they ever— again, by some stroke of Ashu's luck—find it, they will be unstoppable." She looked up and saw Esheme's startled expression. "Not your current piece—that can't be used anymore; it is already bonded to your child and will not work for someone else. It may disintegrate if you die. Or maybe once your child dies—this is an extraordinary case, I'm unsure. You're safe, regardless. But only until someone manages to have all of this information *and* somehow gain access to a decent amount of red ibor."

The agreement in the room was made with only a look passed between them. Esheme could *never* let any of this knowledge slip, ever.

"How do you feel when you use it?" Nem asked. "Drained?"

Esheme thought. "Dizzy, sometimes. Some nausea. Pain in my stomach."

"Hmm," Nem said. "You must have stretched yourself, then. Too much at once, or sustained use without rest, and you can have a miscarriage. Who knows what will happen then? Perhaps whenever you feel these things, you should stop."

Esheme sat back down. "I need you to tell me everything you know. No more hiding, no more secrets. Tell me all you did not document in that journal."

Nem spoke slowly. She told Esheme about being hired by Abuso to find his daughter, about the deal with Abuso, hiring Dọta's caravan, Oboda returning with ibor. She told her about the night of the attack, about showing up alone at Abuso's and surprising the whole household, about the smell of burning meat as the house went up in flames from the fires she'd set by wielding grey ibor. She told Esheme about the toll of the ibor on her body. Every now and then, Esheme stopped and asked a question about something, but mostly she just sat and listened. Nem grew weaker and weaker the longer she narrated, but she paused every now and then to drink either water or the throat-calming brew left by her bedside.

When Nem was done, she stared at her legs for a long time and said: "I fear this is the only way I can aid you now—with my words. Once the stories of your actions have propagated, others will start to come for you as Dọta did. Which is why you must move first before they can. You must take the Great Dome."

Esheme took a long look at her maa. What she felt was not quite a bursting pride, but it was close. She had considered her next step to involve removing Ulobana from the coalition in some way, perhaps even taking her place. While she had not considered such an audacious move as taking on the seat of the nation, the moment it came out of Nem's mouth, the idea sank its roots deep into her mind. Every doubt she had ever harboured about being able to face the Upper Council after Dọta's death flew out the window.

"You think I can do it?" she asked.

"Does it matter?" Nem asked. "You have no choice. You have murdered an Upper Councilhand in open daylight. His assets run half the border. Someone will commandeer them, and if that person is wise, they will come after you to ensure that what happened to him never happens to them. If you dispatch said person, the process will repeat itself with a new contender. Cut one head off, four more appear. You will know no peace in this city if you remain anywhere other than on top."

Esheme rose and went to look out between the raffia blinds. A soft breeze blew into the night.

"When this all started out," she said, "I just wanted to be safe. To be free, respected, to not be taken for granted." She turned to look at her maa. "I did not set out to rule a nation."

"Safety is an illusion without control," Nem said. "All those things you desire require one component we don't quite have right now: control. Power, you already possess. But control is what guarantees your safety. Only when we find a way to combine both to our advantage will we be truly safe."

Esheme returned to gazing out the window.

"I never needed to teach you how not to fear," Nem said. "You have always known when not to let fear rule you. For your next move, you must reach into that part of yourself, for it is not for the fainthearted. You have already struck fear into the heart of this nation by demonstrating what happens to those who come against you, from the greatest to the lowliest among them. Now you must ride that wave of fear and claim what is the rightful inheritance of anyone who possesses as much power as you do."

Esheme's heart rate rose.

"You have made an example of the most influential First Elder in the nation," Nem said. "Now, you must knock down every other obstacle, wipe away anything that could challenge or jeopardise your ascendancy. You must clear a path to the one place that matters: the Great Dome."

With that, Nem promptly eased herself back into a supine position and closed her eyes.

Esheme stood there for a long time, processing everything, then left for the library to set a meeting with the coalition.

Esheme

THE NEXT TIME ESHEME met with Basuaye, she decided it was going to be at a public venue. If there was anything the Bassai leadership feared more than the backstabbing within their own selves, it was the possibility of a citywide riot, which had the likelihood of bringing down the whole nation. Now that Esheme's name lay on lips—especially after using her maa's whisperer network to spread news of how she'd handled Dọta and his posse—it was in their best interest to leave her alone whenever she was in public. Greedy and brutish as they were, the ruling group knew a secret truth: Simply because the average Bassai citizen didn't have the courage to carry out a revolt yet did not mean it was wise to set fire to their bottoms and give them reasons to try.

So Esheme chose to meet Basuaye at the Gondola walking bridge on mainway three, as close to the city centre as she could manage. The bridge, at this time of day, was at its least busy. Cart pushers, who used it more than anyone else, had yet to begin their sojourns carting produce from the lower wards to the central market, so it was the few odd walkers that were present, most of them househands off on early errands for water, lugging large waterskins on their backs.

At the bottom of the gully flowed the narrowest section of the Gondola River, after which the bridge was named. It was the only waterway ever to make it through landlocked Bassa, with the Tombolo veering more eastward.

Dressed in large, cloaking wrappers and a headwrap and devoid of all facepaint to avoid recognition, Esheme perched on the bridge and watched the households. Most were from lower households who couldn't afford to hire water carriers to fill household reservoirs, or even have household reservoirs in the first place. They trotted down the bridge and climbed into the gully over which the bridge had been built. The gully was steep, with loose red sand on the sides, so wooden ladders-cum-steps had been built into the sides to aid climbing. The water was clean but as with the increasing water shortages in the desertland, the levels had reduced drastically, which had the knock-on effect of increased pollution by impurities in the sand. In a few seasons, all who drank this water would fall sick and die. But it wasn't like they had a choice, anyway, as they couldn't afford the alternative. The very reason why most people hired water carriers was to get them to go to the portions of the Gondola in the outskirts that had higher levels and less impurities.

Esheme leaned on the side of the bridge and looked out to the city. She inhaled the fresh, misty morning air and wondered why she had never come out here, why it took upheaval in her life to see the sun beyond the clouds. The Gondola was one of the few higher points in the city, and from here she could see the mass of brown thatch roofs and the odd slate roof here and there spread out in a fractal from the city centre. The Soke mountains hunched over everything from here, blocking out the rest of the continent. She stood just for a moment, taking in the grandeur of this seat of power. Power that would, if she took the right steps, soon be hers to hold in her palm, along with the most powerful weapon in all of Oon.

She inhaled deeply and let the cool morning breeze, the calming sound of water, take her. And for a moment, she felt like she was connected to the moon gods themselves, and she forgot about everything she was running from, and everything she was running toward.

"For someone who has just thrown the whole city into jeopardy," a voice said, coldly, "you seem to be enjoying yourself."

Esheme turned to face Basuaye. He looked exactly the same as the last time she'd seen him, perhaps thinner, but he'd always looked frail. Yet there was one notable change: His demeanour was no longer that of a resigned older gentleman. Now he radiated danger, looked like a rabid dog ready to take on whatever stood in front of it. He was currently alone, but Esheme knew it was foolish to think for a moment that he did not have protection in some way.

And just as she thought it, Ulobana and Tamino stepped out of the mist and joined him, their expressions just as icy as his.

"Not here," she said calmly when she spotted them, and walked down the Gondola. She rounded a foot ladder and began to climb down into the gully as the households had done. She came down mindful and slow, thinking about her body. Basuaye was helped down by his generals.

At the stream bank, the households became worked into a frenzy once they spotted Basuaye, gathering about and touching him and his wrappers as if he were Ashu in the flesh, whispering among themselves in mixtures of Mainland Pidgin, indecipherable border pidgins, and Savanna Common. Basuaye changed his demeanour only for a moment to accept their greetings. Esheme watched with curious interest before she led them down the banks and away from the bridge.

"Stop," Ulobana said after a while, her tone sharp-edged. "That's far enough."

"You do realise what you have done, don't you?" Basuaye asked, sitting down on a nearby stone. "You do know that you have soiled the name and purpose of the coalition forever by massacring the most respected First Elder of the nation? Have you no restraint? What were you thinking, doing that?"

Esheme smiled at Ulobana, who stood a good head taller than her. "You would've preferred someone like Dọta alive, wouldn't you? Because all you care about is increasing wealth, isn't it? Tell me, when last did you make an actual attempt to vie for this change you so claim to represent? When last did you truly attempt to take on Bassai leadership?"

"I would speak with care if I were you," Ulobana said. "Perhaps you forget whom you're speaking to."

"You keep forgetting that your voice is your only power here," Esheme said to Basuaye. "Your multitude of followers are the true power behind the coalition, and all it takes for someone to truly prise that power from you is to convince them with another voice better than yours. It is why you have your generals to dissuade others of any such thoughts."

"I'm warning you," Ulobana said. "I am not Igan. I will not be swayed by a pretty face and sweet voice. I will crush your neck right this instant if you don't stop speaking."

Esheme chuckled. "That would make you no different from everyone who wants to have a go at me right now. They do not scare me, and neither do you." She regarded the two generals. "I actually agreed to meet with you because I have a proposition. I plan to march on the Great Dome, and I need the coalition to do so with me."

Ulobana and Basuaye looked at one another, then Ulobana stepped forward again.

"Here is a proposition for you," the woman snarled. "If you even so much as breathe in the general direction of anything concerning the coalition again—and that includes Igan—then consider yourself dead."

"Oh, you misunderstand me," Esheme said. "I wasn't asking."

There was a prolonged silence. Ulobana's hand went to rest on her sheathed sword, and so did Tamino's.

"You know," Basuaye said, "I have always thought you a bit self-important, but I think I was wrong. What you are is greedy and dangerous, willing to kill innocent people to protect your secrets." He pointed to her stomach. "You think co-opting Igan into murdering your Potokin lover is going to keep that hidden forever? Tell me, what better does this make you than our oppressors?"

So he knows, then, she thought. Expected, considering. No worry— she had planned for this. And now, he had even given her more cause to do what she had to do.

"I see this was your plan all along, wasn't it?" She smiled. "You *did* know Ulobana was collecting money from Dota. *You* were playing both sides of the game, not him."

"Revolutions are expensive," Basuaye said. "One does what one has to. Besides, I was doing so in the interest of the nation. Dota promised that if he got his hands on ibor and eventually rose to become emperor, he would do well by the nation."

"So you see?" Esheme said. "You are no better than them, and neither am I. In fact, I do not want to be better, because better does not win." She stepped forward, her hand within her wrappers. "That is what you have always got wrong, Cockroach. Liberty is not offered. It is reclaimed by blood, by the same manner in which it was taken. You remain, just like my maa was, under the illusion that you can reclaim liberty by way of civility and barter. I once was like you, you know? But things have changed, and now it is time to do away with old thinking. It is time to make way for a new guard. And if you choose to stand in that way, then you will have to reap the consequences."

Ulobana and Tamino drew their swords at the same time.

Esheme gripped the stone-bone in her hand and Commanded with less difficulty than the last time. Her eyes flashed red in response.

Out of the shadows and from nowhere in particular, Oboda's corpse appeared, running toward the group at speed, like a log rolling down a hill with unstoppable force.

"Let it be known," Esheme said, "that I gave you a chance."

The two generals were quick, but not quick enough. Before they could get within distance of Esheme, Oboda was there, planting himself between Esheme and the lunging, extended sword of Ulobana. The sword went through his body like ripe plantain, and came out at the other end, stopping just short of Esheme's clavicle. There was enough time for the surprise of it all to register on Ulobana's face before Oboda reached for her sword-bearing arm and broke her wrist with one twist.

She opened her mouth in a voiceless scream, and Oboda put his hand inside her mouth and yanked. Her jaw popped, then hung loose, open wider than any human mouth was allowed to. Then he pulled the sword from his own body, put the blade through her mouth, through her teeth and into her throat, so it came out on the other side. He tossed her jerking body away, into the river.

The other general, Tamino, who had been standing there the whole time, unsure, weighed his options. He decided, at the last moment, that he was going to go down with honour. He shut his eyes in a short prayer, then opened them and advanced, sword poised, swinging and ducking out of the reach of Oboda. But he could only do so once or twice before that swift, large hand caught his blade and used it to pull him in.

He quickly went the way of Ulobana, body sinking slowly into the Gondola.

Through it all, Basuaye sat still. After the two bodies had sunk, he rose, exuding calm, even though he was visibly shaking.

"I am too old to be afraid of death," he said. "There is nothing you can threaten me with."

"You will not die today." She dusted her palms together, satisfied with the outcome of events. "For you, I have other plans."

63

Esheme

Esheme stood before the people and looked over them, row to row.

The core members of the Coalition for New Bassa were, as she had guessed, mostly Emuru mainlanders and Potokin immigrants. They were the ones who could afford to protest with minimal consequences, those who could most move around with marginal scrutiny and weren't completely subject to the whims of civil guards and the ire of the Idu. They were the farmers, craftworkers, traders, artists, aides, even some civic guards. And, for some, if they were lucky enough, they were the Seconds and aides who had been elevated from Yelekuté to Potokin status. Row to row, it was mainlanders and mainlander-adjacents from every possible walk of life, and the only thing that bound them all together was the same thing she was hoping for: a desire for retribution.

They wanted somebody to pay for everything they were going through, and they didn't care who. Esheme was going to give them what they wanted: an enemy.

Basuaye had not taken easy convincing, initially, to divulge the coalition's resources and hand over the reins to her. But once it became clear he no longer held sway as much as he thought he did, especially once Igan showed up and demonstrated allegiance to Esheme, he succumbed. Nothing broke a man like the betrayal of his last general, it seemed.

Setting up this gathering had become easy after that. It was only a matter of getting word to the right people. Esheme made sure to keep everything the same in order not to arouse suspicions—they met in the market square of Fifteenth Ward, where no Idu dared to go, and where the long arms and the searching noses of Bassai leadership did not quite reach.

Pride rose in Esheme's chest and settled in her belly as she stood before them now, Igan at her side. She had never been one for speeches or speaking for too long, even with her counsel training. But that same time as a novitiate in counsel guild had taught her that people didn't see good works or loyalty to the nation as anything worthy of emulation. People only heard words and followed them in the hope that something would happen, especially if those words were repeated over and over until they became truth.

"I have come here at the request of the Cockroach, who is sadly ailing and cannot come to speak before you," she began. "He has asked that, in case this becomes his dying wish, the coalition continue to prosper and proceed with all that he has planned for us. And so I am here to carry forth the mission of the coalition, and bring forth New Bassa and return us to our days of power."

Some brows furrowed at her use of the word *us*, at this foreign person from the inner wards suddenly telling them what to do and believe in. But many others had seen her at the funeral, and all had heard about her feat with Dọta, so no one spoke up in opposition, which was exactly what she was counting on.

"Only a few fortnights ago, we were still a peaceful nation," she began. "Maybe not content, but we had a handle on the state of things. We farmed, sold, and traded in peace. Our borders were still open. We— you, and even I, privileged as I am—were living the best way we could in our dear old imperfect Bassa." She paused. "Then came a yellowskin from the outer lands."

This had its desired effect. The crowd hooted angrily as one, waving hands and crude weaponry of all sorts. Esheme watched them for a moment, then called for calm.

"Yes, invaders from the outer lands came here and murdered our own people. You know when last this happened? Seasons upon seasons ago! No one has dared touch us in all this time, because they know our might and our wealth. They know what would happen if we cease trade or, for the first time in many seasons, raise an army against them.

"But look! Great Bassa is no longer great. The Upper Council have reduced us to a laughingstock, to a nation the people of the outer lands think they can send a single assassin to cripple. And what did our leadership do? Close the borders! Leave us without salt so our food could no longer last in our kitchens. You hunt, but you can't sell your meat. You craft, but you cannot export. You have been starving, and they do not care! We may mourn the deaths of the Speaker and all those who have died in the wake of this yellowskin's rampant rage, but we care even more about the integrity of our nation!"

The crowd howled and hissed.

"We used to call them the Nameless Islands, the place of the yellowskins, because we believed no one lived there, that all islanders and their evil ways were extinct. Well, they are nameless no more. To us, henceforth, they will always have a name: They will always be the mortal enemies of our nation."

"Yes! Yes!" they screamed.

"Go home," Esheme said. "Gather your households. Gather your friends. Gather your neighbours. That day of reckoning you have awaited, the day you have all worked toward, has arrived. The Upper Council meets tomorrow to decide upon things that affect the very fabric of our nation. They meet to decide the fate of our borders. And they meet to decide my fate, simply because I dared defend myself from Bassa's Idu oppression. But on this same day, we, too, decide, to take Bassa back and make it great again."

"Yes!" the crowd chattered. "Yes!"

"I, Esheme the Brave, will take up your mantle and lead your charge to their gates. We will gather on mainway fifteen, and we will take back our nation. They will hear our voices, and if not, then they will smell our fists. But by moons, we will wring it from the hands of those who have misused it so. We will restore the great in Great Bassa!"

Esheme lifted her arms to the crowd's whooping and cheering. She nodded at Igan, surrounded by their own posse, and Igan nodded back, and their posse goaded the crowd even more, rousing a ruckus louder than Bassa had ever heard since the dawning of the Great Wars.

The coalition set forth at dawn. The crowd started as a trickle of people, mainway fifteen filling up with the usual traders and customers and people who came to see the Great Dome but never quite got up close to it. No one paid any attention to the growing numbers of people from the lower wards until it was too late, until suddenly, there were many more people than mainway fifteen had ever seen in a long time, and there were weapons made from the most crude of materials—axes, machetes, shovels, picks, tree branches, fires in pottery.

At the front of the group was Esheme. It was a rare sight to see, for the first time, someone like this—a young woman no older than thirty-seven seasons, small of build, and with nothing of note but her three arches of hair—leading a group of Bassai to do *anything*. It was a statement, one that resonated louder than the thunderclap of feet and chanting and marching to the five iron gates of the Great Dome.

Behind Esheme walked Igan, a coalition member pulling a cart next to them. In it, the dead, mutilated body of Oboda lay supine and unmoving.

As they stood in front of the Great Dome's gates, a large swath of civic guards lined up. Behind them, up at the highest points of the Great Dome, stood others, arrows poised and angled down toward the crowd.

"In the name of the ruling council of Great Bassa," a voice said from somewhere, "I command you to stop!"

Esheme stepped forward and held up a hand. She turned to face her people, and in her loudest voice, she spoke.

"You see this? This is how your voice will always be met with violence, Bassa. This is how your given rights are taken by force, then returned with false benevolence. This is how they slaughter your people!" She turned back to face the Dome. "You fold your hands while we are under attack, while outlander sympathizers in Whudasha attack those who are sworn to this nation. You allow a yellowskin through our borders, allow them to rain death upon us so, to murder our own Speaker." She motioned to the cart where Oboda's body lay. "We die for your cause, and *this* is how you treat our voices? By raining death upon us, too? What difference is there between you and our enemies beyond the border?"

She turned back to the coalition.

"Come now, be wise! Look at me; I, a citizen like you, have spoken in your courts, learned in the university built by the hands of your ancestors. My sweat, my work, my skin is Bassai, and I say, enough. Our leaders have broken the very commandments of our Ideal, and we must take up arms and meet their violence with ours. I say, join me!"

The crowd roared.

"And you, mere moving puppets of Bassai leadership, will you stop us?" she said to the civic guards. "Will you prevent us from claiming what is rightfully ours?"

The civic guards looked at one another, and then a civic guard captain in front stepped forward and said: "Now look here, you little wench—"

Igan shot him in the throat with an arrow.

As the man gargled and fell, the coalition shrieked in a battle cry, and the people rushed at the gates. They poured forward with a vengeance, with the ferocity of generations wronged, the blind fury of a nation scorned.

"Draw!" someone shouted from somewhere, and a rain of arrows fell on them. Igan and their posse crowded around Esheme and the cart bearing Oboda's body, securing her and the cart in a canopy of shields. Arrows thumped into the corpse.

"Protect her!" Igan said. "Abandon the body!"

"No!" Esheme said. "I need that."

A swath of recent joiners abandoned their crude weapons when the next wave of arrows fell, and ran back to their wards.

"Leave them," Esheme said to those about her. "Let them go! When we take our nation back, the brave will rule over the weak."

More people had reached the gates. The civic guards there swung at them, catching a good number, blood splattering in all directions. But more pressed forward. The archers held back their arrows, unable to find aim, and unable to do so without hitting their own men. The new swath of coalition supporters lunged at the men at the gates, striking them down.

"It's working!" Esheme said to Igan, but just then, there were roars, and leopards came bounding out of nowhere. They tore into the crowd, raising dust, causing people to scatter. Some of the coalition force with longer-range weapons goaded them, poked, while others attacked from behind to bring them down. It was an arduous task, made more difficult by more civil guards pouring out of the gates.

Igan led Esheme and the posse away, ducking through a nearby pedestrian gate. They clashed through a line of civic guards there and pressed their way forward, up to the arena. In the middle of the arena, more blood flowed, as those who had made it this far were repelled often and more by the increasing number of civic guards. The coalition took heavy losses.

But all that didn't matter. All Esheme needed was to get to the centre of the Dome, the grand chamber, where the emperor used to sit. She knew that by this time, the Upper Council's meeting would have been interrupted, and they would have been locked in and guarded for safety purposes. She just needed to get close enough to do what she needed to do.

They slipped into the corridors of the Great Dome, the wheels of their cart making loud squeaks. Every civic guard they accosted, Igan brought down with their axe, until they reached the front of the ballroom and found it barricaded and a small army of civic guards stationed there.

Esheme dipped into her wrappers, gripped the red ibor tight, and Possessed Oboda's corpse next to her.

Destroy them, she Commanded.

Oboda rose with a supernatural alacrity and moved with a promptitude that belied death. The men, paralyzed by fear, could not even as much as lift a sword proper before the big man was standing before them. They tried to put on brave faces, brave impressions, but the being standing before them was not a man against whom they could press an advantage of courage. Before they could decide whether to fight or run, half already lay dead, the metallic smell of warm blood stinking up the place, sticking in Esheme's sandals. The remaining half decided it was no use running, so they turned and faced the behemoth of destruction before them, putting forward their most valiant efforts. But they couldn't kill what was already dead, and Oboda seized their weapons and struck them down with a ferocity and focus only something Possessed could. The final two realised what the others didn't: There was no fighting this reckoning. There was only surrendering. So surrender they did, throwing their weapons down. But they also made the mistake of thinking they could run, absolve themselves of the crimes of a system they had enabled. They turned and attempted to flee, only to be struck down by Igan and their posse.

When Oboda was done, his body went back into stasis, stiff and cold. Esheme leaned on a pillar, weak. Her body had responded heavily to this last use, and she struggled with the growing pains in the bottom of her belly, trying not to pass out. She had to see this through.

They burst open the doors into the grand room. It was one of the many empty spaces of the Great Dome, from the time of the twenty-third and last emperor, Nogowu. The infamous Manic Emperor had rebuilt spaces like these in unruffled grandeur as an ode to himself. Every inch was decorated in gold and bronze and copper and coral. Fine woven drapery adorned the walls, something she barely saw anywhere else, and the cushioned stools were intricately carved by the most expert craftworker hands, their bottoms morphing into various sculptures of leopards, elephants, antelopes, and tortoises. Freshly cut hibiscus sat in bronze bowls of water on nearby windowsills, so that the room had an earthy, natural fragrance. The windows themselves overlooked the city, and she could see a good chunk of Bassa's inner wards from here; mainway fifteen's commercial districts, which usually buzzed with chatter and industry, were now filled with smoke and blood and death.

The First Elders of the Upper Council were huddled together in a corner, trying to decide if the approaching group before them was friend or foe. Upon sighting her, two of them whom she remembered from the funeral as the First Miners stepped forward.

"I knew it was you!" one said. "Offspring of that demon woman. I knew nothing good could come out of that household." He looked at the group behind Esheme. "So, what—you've come to kill us?"

Esheme cocked her head. "Not quite. You will answer to the people yourselves." She turned away, then turned back to them. "On second thought, you have just insulted my household. That is unpardonable. So maybe I will show you how *demon* we are."

She motioned with her head in a small movement, and two men

peeled off from Igan's posse and grabbed both First Elders and dragged them from the room. Esheme eyed the rest.

"Come with me if you know what is good for you."

The remaining seven came without fuss, holding on to their mouths when they saw the bloodbath outside the door. In the city square, the fighting raged on. Esheme stood on the rostrum overlooking it, placed for speaking to large crowds gathered there. Over the din of the clacking of weapons and the screams of death, Esheme spoke.

"Defenders of the Great Dome!" she screamed. "Listen! Listen for your future."

The fighting did not stop, the people so engrossed with killing each other and avenging their loved ones stuck behind the Pass. So Esheme did the next sensible thing: She put her hand in her wrappers, pressed the stone, and Commanded Oboda's body to rise.

It had the desired effect. The sight of a corpse coming to life to stand beside their liberator brought those nearest to the rostrum to a halt, followed by those behind them, and behind them, and behind, so that soon, everyone was standing, weapons hanging in midair, eyes locked on them.

Esheme, fighting an oncoming blackout, pulled out the ibor and lifted it high above her head. The red of the stone-bone was stark against her hand like blood in the late-morning light. The people's eyes followed it, and a collective gasp, murmurs, followed.

"By Menai!" someone said. "It is sorcery!"

"No," Esheme refuted in her most trained, projected voice. "It is not sorcery. It is a gift, handed down to us by the moon gods, a gift to our land, for us to use in conquering all that belongs to us as the most blessed land on this continent." She projected even further. "This power is our birthright, our blood. And with it, we will take back our land."

There were little forms of agreement, but a wave of fear swept through the crowd. Esheme stepped forward.

"Have no fear," she continued. "It is not me you should fear, but them." She pointed to the First Elders behind them. "This is how they held you hostage. This is how the people of the outer lands torment us. They hid this gift from you, told you it was a myth even while they sought it for themselves. Yes, even you, defenders of the Great Dome!" She pointed at the civic guards. "We have all been deceived! But now we know the truth. Now we must liberate ourselves—we must take our land back, and with the might of ibor, we will rule the continent once again.

"I say to you now—lay down your weapons. Let us fight each other no longer, but instead fight the one thing that separates us, that pits us against one another. Let us fight a common enemy, and that enemy is them! Let us signal to everyone in this city and beyond that we will not allow attempts on our name to go unpunished."

She squeezed the stone-bone, and Oboda turned and, in one swift motion, drew a nearby cutlass from a fighter in the group and slashed at the First Elders' throats together. The men held their necks and staggered forward. The crowd was dazed. The bodies fell slowly, one by one.

Then someone cheered, and slowly, someone else responded with a cheer, and soon, many people cried their encouragement. Oboda's body, done with its duty, went back into stasis.

Esheme, pride and satisfaction rising in her chest, covertly leaned on Igan for support, and the posse blocked her from view. After she gained some comportment, she stepped up and put her hand out until the crowd quieted down.

"When people think of us," she said, "this is what they should remember. Fear and respect are two sides of the same blade, my people, and they are taken, not offered. This continent must be reminded, every time, that even the slightest errors against us will be met with retaliation. This is how we put our name on that blade. With blood."

By now, even the civic guards roared alongside Bassai civilians, coalition or not.

"And for my last act," Esheme said, "I will now offer you what you really want: vengeance. If you must quench your bloodthirst, then do it with those who have taken you for idiots, who have made you slaves in your own land."

She nodded to Igan, who nodded to their posse, and the men pushed the remaining seven First Elders so that they stumbled down the stairs of the Great Dome, and down to where the people were now gathered.

"Feast," Esheme said, her voice rising. "Feast!"

The people descended upon the First Elders with venom, hacking through them with weapons and blows of every indignation, every hurt. The sight of blood roused something in Esheme's belly, and she held the vomit that came up in her mouth but refused to let it show. She swallowed it back down and stood there and watched.

The people of the coalition who had had their fill turned back to her then, fell to their knees, and put their foreheads to the ground.

"All hail the one who has returned to us our place," they said. "All hail the one who has liberated us. All hail, Esheme the Brave!"

"No," Esheme said. "Esheme the Red Saviour. Esheme the Red... Emperor."

"Esheme the Red Emperor!" more voices chorused, crazed by bloodlust. "Esheme the Red Emperor!"

Esheme thrust her hand into the air, fisted ibor raised high. Igan followed suit beside her, and the men with them too. The whole of Bassa thrust their fists up in the air in honour of the woman who rose from Fourth Ward to remind Bassa of who it was.

the dead mines

64

Danso

THE ROAD TO THE Dead Mines in the foothills of the Soke mountains was just as dead as the place it led to. It was more trail than road, and even in the waning light of day, the brownness and barrenness of it was evident. Much like the dwindling vegetation Danso had seen where the Breathing Forest met the savanna, the road had succumbed to the shorter gamba grass and gained little in any sort of colour that spoke of life, plant or animal. It showed little evidence of having been trod upon recently, except for two lines of pure barrenness that were definitely made by the wheels of some sort of cart or travelwagon.

"I once read they used to move the minerals they found here to Bassa with carts," Danso said to Lilong as she too examined the road before them. Ahead, Biemwensé and Kakutan led the group. "They'd load them up and drive them by ox to the Emperor's Road. That's why we still have all those waystations along it—they were stop-and-rest points for the transporters and the civic guards guarding them. Also points for sorting all the different precious minerals they collected, I believe."

"What kinds of things did they mine?" Lilong asked.

"Anything they could find," Danso said. "Coal, gold, copper, tin." He paused. "But I've learned it only became a mine for those things after they couldn't find what they sought when they first dug it."

"Let me guess," Lilong said. "Ibor?"

Danso nodded. Once the first landers were discovered on the mainland, he explained, and the mainlanders had engaged with them enough to see what they were doing with ibor, the first order of things was to find some ibor for themselves. Alternatively, the history he had been taught as a jali had simply said the mines had been discovered by accident, without spelling out what accident spurred the discovery of the minerals. The only thing the codex and his Elder Jalis were in agreement with was that the mines became *dead* after much pillaging for the purposes of trade with the desertlands.

"How do you know all these things?" Lilong asked.

"I never told you?" Danso said. "The Codex of the Manic Emperor Nogowu, the last emperor of Bassa. I read a good portion of it. And I never forget anything I read."

"Never?"

"Never ever."

"But still it exists all in your head. Why not start a manuscript or something? That way, someone else can learn from what you know. Isn't that what jalis do?"

He hadn't yet told her that her rebuke in the savanna had led him down this path already. But yes, once they crossed the border, he would make a proper manuscript of it all. The Codex of the First Liberated Shashi of Bassa. There was a nice ring to that.

"Speaking of writing down," Danso said, "the codex failed to mention this, so, if I may ask: How does one lay hands on ibor today?"

Lilong looked at him out of the side of her eye. "Why are you asking this?"

"Oh, come on," he said. "We can't still be keeping secrets at this stage? As an Iborworker at this rate, I kind of deserve to know, don't I?"

"I'm not keeping secrets," she said. "And you are not an Iborworker—not yet. Yes, you can do a few tricks with that... *animal*"—she looked up, searching for the Skopi, expectedly flying above them, though it couldn't be sighted in the dusk sky—"but that barely scratches the surface of what it means to be an Iborworker."

"Then perhaps once we get over the border, you'll teach me?"

"Why don't we get there first?" she said. "And for your question, no one knows where ibor comes from. We simply *discover* it."

"Explain."

"Ibor finds us, we don't find it," she said. "We discover it where it wants to be discovered—washed up on the shore, buried in caves. Ibor reveals itself most easily when you do not seek."

"Hmm," Danso said, and they walked in silence. Lilong stopped every now and then to pick up a found artifact—a pebble, half an abandoned shell—to add to the collection she had started since they left Whudasha. *For my younger brother*, she said when Danso asked. *He would want to know what it looked like here.* He'd then given her one of his earrings to add to the collection.

"The Supreme Magnanimous," she said, out of nowhere.

"Kakutan?"

"I don't like her."

"You don't like anybody," Danso said by way of a joke, but she looked at him and didn't laugh. "Oh right, serious face. Well, what about her?"

"She's too…" She seemed to be searching for the right word in High Bassai. "Like when you're on two sides of a thing."

"Diplomatic?"

"Like that," she said. "It's a dangerous thing for a leader of an oppressed people to be like that."

"But she has clearly shown her side by choosing to lead everyone here, don't you think? I believe she truly cares for the safety of her people, even if it sometimes causes her to act in ways we may deem irrational."

"Which is where my point lies. She is irrational."

"Or just unapologetic about her attempt to balance things?" Danso shrugged. "Maybe you're more used to the *there-can-only-be-one* path to resolution. You must like Biemwensé, then. She's more your direct type."

"Yes. Although…"

"What now?"

She thought for a bit. "She's all emotion, all rashness, which can be dangerous. That much willingness to sacrifice everything could sometimes be…questionable."

"Wow," Danso said. "You're like a scavenger for reasons not to trust people."

She regarded him again, then did not speak for another long time, so that Danso had to break the silence by saying:

"So you never agreed to teach me." He paused. "I just don't want to harm anyone. Or myself."

"I don't know enough about red ibor to do so," she said. "I've told you everything I know about why I believe it responded to you alone and not anyone else. All of that is as much as I and my people know for the time being. I believe that's sufficient for now."

Danso found her satisfaction with the status quo odd. "Don't you want to know if there are others who could possibly do this or more? Don't you wonder if we could, with this, somehow effect long-lasting change in the continent—mainland and desert alike?"

"Like, saviours?"

"Well…" Danso shrugged. "I don't know, maybe."

"Your people tried saviours before," Lilong said. "Tried to make good with mainlanders that didn't want them. Look how it worked out. Their demise forms the stem of Ihinyon moral instruction. Returning the Diwi, then learning more about it is sufficient for now. We can't just go barging back into the mainland, looking for something to fix. I'm not going to repeat Ajabo mistakes."

"Even if we've been afforded the power to possibly do so?"

"Even so," she said. "I came here for something, and I have it. I will return home and put this behind us. We can do whatever we want after-ward, but my hope is that it will not involve the Diwi. If anyone comes seeking it, they cannot be allowed to find it, as has been the case for many seasons. The archipelago may need to remain nameless and invis-ible if that's the only way to save itself."

"Then why are we helping these people?" He gestured toward the Whudan caravan. "Why are we starting a journey toward liberation if we cannot finish it?"

Lilong ground her teeth for a long time, processing the question. She took a drink from her waterskin and replaced the stopper slowly.

"You believe you're wise," she said, finally, "but what you are doing yet again is talking a lot without carefully considering the repercussions of your actions." Then she stepped away from him and went on to speak with Biemwensé. Danso smarted at her rebuke and continued on the journey alone.

65

Esheme

THE NEWS ABOUT WHUDASHA did not take long to spread through Bassa. It raged through a populace with the taste of blood and revolt still fresh on their tongues, the weight of uncertainty pressing down on them, so that everyone was lint, ready to burst into flames at the slightest provocation.

People argued openly in the streets and corridors about the legitimacy of anyone on the mainland who wasn't like the humus. They discussed the various punishments to be meted out on discovered and apprehended Whudans for daring to leave their side of the fence and venture into Bassai land, to break a hundreds-of-seasons-long Peace Treaty. *Emboldened by the yellowskin*, many surmised. *Emboldened by Bassa's lack of bite.*

Many called for a crusade to retrieve them, hang them all in the capital square as a statement. Others asked for their beheadings, for their bodies to be burned as reminders of what it meant to go against Bassa's laws. Some asked that they be shepherded to the edges of the moats and shoved in to their deaths.

And most, if not all, asked that the same person who had liberated them from the clutches of the former lax leadership, Esheme the Red Emperor, take the Whudans to task. They asked that she fulfil her promises, that she put the name of the nation on the blade, as promised. With blood.

When the delay extended past the period where swift action was expected—which was not a sufficient length of time at all—then came the spate of attacks on legitimate, long-term immigrants by overzealous, overeager Bassai. Househands, farmhands, stablehands, Seconds even— anyone who was just that little shade over low-black. First there were hidden attacks on Yelekuté in corridors, in unlit corners, in obscured places, in courtyards, when their employers weren't looking. After a while, even Potokin bodies began to be discovered in dark corners of the city in increasing numbers.

In only a matter of a day, the attacks took to the street, occurring in the open. The civic guards were unsure what to do, how to tackle the crime—if it was even a crime. So the ward chiefs and civic guard captains considered an impromptu meeting of themselves, but wondered: Where exactly would they hold such a thing? The Great Dome, which was currently occupied by a usurper? Could they risk asking, perhaps, that she leave? Could they risk pointing out that though she remained unchallenged, that gave her no legitimacy to occupying the mainland's seat of power? Could they put it to her that calling herself the Red Emperor did not, in fact, make her the Red Emperor?

But no one was brave enough to take any action. They had heard the stories. The ones that said she could raise the dead; the ones that said she commanded a great legion of such undead alongside slippery members of the coalition. The ones that said she wasn't even human, that she was Menai come down in the flesh. The ones that said, even before an errant thought could be formed, or an errant word spoken, something once lifeless would arise, and suddenly be there, present, ready to take one to justice of a bloody kind in the name of Esheme the Red Emperor.

It was with great surprise, then, that the oft-forgotten and little recognised Lower Council, the one made up of various guild and local government and ward leaders, received an invitation to the Great Dome, signed *The Red Emperor of Bassa*. They fumed at the elevation of this ragtag, rogue coalition to a group that could summon them, pureborn mainlanders and citizens of the greatest nation in Oon. So they vowed to take their anger to the Great Dome.

Unrest continued in the city throughout the day and night. Attacks on the immigrant castes increased to a point where immigrant employees refused to show up for work. It took such a toll on the city's economics that city criers had to go out and announce the extraordinary impromptu meeting. The Lower Council was going to be in discussion with the current occupiers of the Great Dome on actions concerning Whudasha's desertion and the outlander invasion, among other matters. The criers announced that until any agreements were reached on how said matters would be handled, every immigrant was to return to their place of assignment as required, and anyone caught carrying out unauthorised versions of justice would be dealt with severely—by exile over the border, or if a serious enough crime, by hanging.

That last part drew a gasp from the populace.

"But on whose order and authority?" citizens challenged.

"On the authority of the occupier of the Great Dome, the seat of leadership of Bassa," the city criers responded, the only answer they could give, as had been relayed to them. "Esheme the Red Emperor."

"But we do not have an emperor," some said in response.

"But you will have one if you want one," the criers said, again, as they had been told to. "And how much better that you decide so after you see the work of her hands."

Before the Lower Council arrived at the Great Dome on the day of the meeting, Esheme met with Igan and Nem—her makeshift advisory team—in the same grand room in which she had captured the First Elders. The formerly fresh hibiscus in the room had now wilted from a lack of attention, since most of the domehands had also fled following the capture.

"What is the report from the civic guards at the nearest waystation?" Esheme asked Igan. She had asked that the men who discovered the Whudans gone be retained there to offer further information.

"They have tracked movement toward the mountains," Igan said.

"The border?"

"No." Igan frowned slightly. "Apparently, they are headed for the westernmost aspect of the foot of Soke. Where the Dead Mines used to be."

The Dead Mines. Esheme knew where she had read about that before—her maa's journal. She turned to Nem, who now had a wheelchair for moving about. Nem's face was ashen, and her demeanour sluggish, but she had insisted Satti bring her to the Dome so she could be next to her daughter in a time of trial. Esheme herself had not left the Great Dome since taking it over. There was the fear that she was going to need her strength in these next couple of days, if she was to win over the people of Bassa fully, and not just the coalition. The one thing they wanted, more than anything else, was to see someone punished, whether it was the yellowskin for her crimes, or Whudans for thinking they could leave their parent nation. If Esheme wanted to be fully regarded as their liberator, then she was going to give them what they wanted.

"They are going to try to cross the mountains," Nem said flatly. "Well, not *over* it—they'll be going *under*."

Yes, that was it—the codex, and in tandem her maa's journal, had indeed mentioned the Dead Mines; something about ibor prospecting being once done there, before it became a mine for other minerals. If they were heading there, that meant one thing: There were channels underneath that somehow went above the moat's waters. And if that was the case, then they would be able to get across the Soke mountains without going past the border.

A whole protectorate didn't just pack up and run away. Esheme's instincts told her that if they were so dedicated to crossing the border that they were willing to go underneath the Soke mountains, then they had to be hiding something vital. She could bet it was the very thing she was after, too.

Nem had warned her already: The Shashi were now the greatest possible threats to her new role, even if they themselves didn't know it. Not only were they possibly the only ones who could wield red ibor like she could—especially if the secret of how she could came out—the manner in which she treated their escape could also form the foundation of her acceptance or disapproval by the populace. She had to make sure those Whudans were destroyed once and for all, and this was the perfect opportunity to kill both those birds with one stone.

"We ride out to the Dead Mines," Esheme said, and rose to go meet with the Lower Council.

On her way down the hallways of the Great Dome, she thought about the role of the ward leaders. Who better to pass this sort of message back down to the people than the grassroots leaders, people from their communities whom they trusted? Basuaye, whom she now kept on house arrest in a room in the Great Dome, had once told her, *If you want to plant a seed, you sow it in the soil where it most feels at home.* She was definitely going to use his advice to further her plan, thank him very much.

She would show the leaders and their people what they wanted to see. She would go to the Dead Mines and capture every single Whudan, and if her hunches were right, then she would also bring the yellowskin and Danso to justice in one fell swoop. Poetic justice, it would be, using Oboda to complete the very task for which he had been murdered.

But she needed one last thing if she was to gain the upper hand in that face-off: bait.

"Igan," she said, and Igan—whom she had now named unofficial Second to the emperor—stepped forward. "I have another task for you."

"Who?" Igan asked.

"DaaHabba," Esheme replied, and in her mind, the pieces of her plan slipped perfectly into place.

66

Danso

THE CARAVAN WENT ON its way for a good three days; on the second day they split from the trail and into even more treacherous terrain that undulated and grew harder. The lengthy caravan became even more unwieldy, uncontrollable. People walked astray and fell into holes and became instantly lame and unable to continue. Some collapsed and wouldn't get up. Some became dehydrated and delirious, some were bitten by snakes, and some just got tired of travelling and stopped.

Before this, simple disagreements did half the work of trying to thwart the journey for most. People fought over bread and salt and sugarcane as the resources became less and less. One man dislocated another's jaw for looking at his daughter wrong. The man with the dislocated jaw turned around and went back to Whudasha, cursing. After him, every other random Whudan threw up their hands at the slightest inconvenience and followed in his footsteps.

On the third day, one person got attacked by a mountain lion before Kakutan killed it with an iron bolt. When they had made camp, the Youth skinned the carcass, roasted it over a makeshift spit, and served it back to the community. They tried as much as possible to ensure that not a single person who didn't want to be left behind was—for every devotee rendered immovable, they constructed a makeshift stretcher, or someone gave theirs up, and volunteers pulled them along.

At dusk on that third day, they arrived at the foothills of the Soke mountains, and here, a camp was built and everyone who was unable to press forward was ordered to stay. The resulting number able to cross through in the first instance was less than a hundred. Kakutan decided the most able group would cross first and then return for the others.

It took another few hours to journey from the camp to the entrance to the Dead Mines. They had torches but did not light them, so Kakutan had to squint and try to remember the way from her time helping Oke. At this distance from the border itself, where the actual Soke Pass was situated—a number of hours eastward on foot from the Dead Mines— they were safe from the danger of being heard, but not that of lights being spotted.

It was not difficult to spot the first mine entrance once they arrived, though. The elevation began to rise soon enough, and the darkness fell proper on them as the scraggly mountains rose before them. This far west of the Pass, the Soke mountains were at their highest elevation, so the nation's leadership did not bother with fortifying the mainland side of this portion, focusing instead on the Pass itself—the lowest elevation— and the desert side of the mountain range, where the moats and their few and heavily guarded overland crossing bridges were situated. It was more important to keep outsiders out than to keep citizens in.

The entrances to the Dead Mines were black, lifeless eyes in the sides of the mountain. A number of them were scattered as far as the group could see, of various sizes, piercing the foot of the formations like holes eaten in yams by rats. Some clearly went horizontally into the foot of the mountain, but some went down right away, into the even blacker darkness below ground.

At this point, everyone turned to Kakutan for direction.

"I remember Oke saying they marked the entrances that would get one to the underground bridge," she said to Danso. "Look for the nearest one with a bone and a piece of red cloth tied to it."

The group split, everyone searching for something of the sort in the waning light. After a while, someone whistled, and everyone moved in the direction of the whistle. One of the Youths had found the entrance in question. It was large enough to fit one person at a time, but small enough that if the person turned just the wrong way, they would easily get stuck there.

Kakutan lit a torch and went in first, gingerly.

The mouth of the mine might've been gaping, but its walls hung low and quite narrow, tapering the farther in they went, so that only a child could walk so far in, enough to tell what lay farther inside. Especially since it seemed to dip into darkness, and downward, at some point inside.

"We need someone really small," Kakutan said upon returning. "I was only able to get up to a point before being in danger of getting stuck. Only a person of much reduced size could fit in there going and coming without getting stuck either way."

"The children could go," Biemwensé said, and produced from behind her the two boys Afanfan and Owude.

"Yes, they'll do."

Kakutan offered them instruction the same way she would've to her Youth: brisk, acute commands in Whudan. The boys shook like leaves after, and one of them kept calling *Yaya, Yaya* for Biemwensé. Danso watched as she calmed them, running a hand through their hair. For a while, he imagined her as just a parent, not the former Supreme Magnanimous she was. He would never have considered that those two things could coexist, but it seemed every new thing he learned on this journey challenged something he thought he knew before.

He went and squatted by her, next to the boys.

"I was once like you," he said to them in the little Whudan he knew, in the only way he knew how to. "Afraid. But fear is only for a moment. Courage, in the times when you need it, comes with the doing."

The boys looked at him, perplexed, perhaps surprised that the language they knew and used was forthcoming from the mouth of this foreigner in this butchered manner. So he simply rubbed on their heads afterward. They pulled away.

Kakutan tied a rope to one of the boys, and they went in with the torch after, while everyone waited outside in the chilling dark. The temperature had dropped significantly as it was wont to do in the late days nearing the harmattan season—which was a false nomenclature, as whether harmattan or rainy season, it still rained whenever the rain saw fit, and the air was still usually some level of humid except for a few days in the whole season. It had gotten drier the farther they went toward the

Dead Mines. This close to the Soke mountains, the air was a constant reminder of how much nearer to the desert they were.

The rope tugged in under an hour, and the boys returned, breathing heavily. They rattled off their findings to Kakutan, who relayed them to everyone else in Whudan. Biemwensé translated to Mainland Common for Danso and Lilong.

"The entrance tunnel leads forward and down into a massive cavern," she said. "Deep, but with more tunnel connections in various directions. Kakutan says the desertlander group have placed similar markers to decide what direction to go in order to lead the way and exit on the other side of the mountains."

Kakutan was still speaking. Biemwensé translated.

"At least one of them should connect to the bridge within the moats, so we all must get in there before we move to the next point, just to be sure that nobody gets separated, picks the wrong one, and ends up falling to their death inside the moats."

Kakutan said something with the tone of a question.

"She's saying we will have to go two at a time," Biemwensé said. "She wants to know who is going first."

"I'll go," Lilong said, quickly.

Biemwensé frowned. "Are you saying that because you want to get away from us, or because you really want to go first?"

"I'm going because none of you have left Whudasha before or done anything of this sort," Lilong said. "These kinds of things have been the sum total of my life in the past few weeks."

"I'll go with you," Danso offered.

"No," Lilong said. "You'll just slow me down. I'll go with one of the Youth."

"I have read about these mines," Danso said. "No one here has seen the inside of them, but I know the most about them through my reading. That information could be of use."

"Fair," Biemwensé said, then nodded, and went and whispered something to Kakutan, who looked up at them.

"Fine," Kakutan said in Mainland Common. "You two go first."

67

Danso

THE ENTRANCE TUNNEL TO the cavern was just as the children had described it. Lilong went ahead of Danso, crouching low—at some points, crawling—with the burning torch in front of her. The rope, tied to Danso's waist, was discomforting at first, but the farther in they went, the more he started to feel at home with it, and grateful for it, a connection to the world outside that soon fast receded from memory. He suddenly couldn't even remember what the air outside felt like to breathe, compared to the dust that gathered at his nostrils here.

The temperature rose as they went farther, and drips of sweat came down his face, from his armpit to arms, and down the back of Lilong's calves, the only part of her he could really see. There also seemed to be a bit of moving air, the torch's flame swaying every now and then. Danso flinched each time the flame came too close to Lilong's hair.

The walls were of various colours, moving from the brown of earth to something greenish-yellow, which he attributed to all of the minerals that had been mined here in the past—gold and copper, which formed the two mainstays of the Bassai nation's trade with the north. These mines were completely drained out, though—the new mines were at the more recent mining town Undati, to the west of the border along the same mountain range. There was no hope of luckily finding gold here. It was why it had been abandoned.

"I think I see something," Lilong said.

They had arrived at the point where the tunnel stopped tapering and opened up to a slightly bigger room that could fit two. Lilong dropped down into the space, and Danso did the same beside her. Before them, the tunnel ended abruptly, and a wide makeshift ladder of dubious-looking wood went down a shaft, into the dark.

"Hold the torch over me while I go down," Lilong said.

Danso did as told. She went slowly, testing all of the rungs with her weight until she was sure. Then he came after her, then waited again while she tested the next few rungs. It took a while, and Danso soon stopped counting all of the rungs, as they went deeper and deeper into the heart of the mine.

She stopped when her feet touched ground. Danso came down and stood beside her and waved the torch about.

"We're here," she said.

Between the children's descriptions and Biemwensé's translations, something must have been lost, because that information did not quite prepare them for what they saw. The cavern seemed more assembled than Danso had expected. There were braces on the walls, columns of both earth and iron, holding up various portions of the walls. The space smelled strongly metallic, like rust and neglect. Huge chunks of rock and mounds of earth took up space in several locations, mostly away from all the various openings the children had described. The openings them-selves were like black eyes staring back at them.

"Tell them we're here," Lilong said, collecting the torch from him. A short gust blew at the flame as she did.

Danso loosened the rope about his waist and dragged it, waiting for it to become taut before pulling, the agreed signal. There was a pull from the other direction, which meant they had received the signal, and another duo was coming down.

Another gust of wind—this time, something that seemed more like *breath*—blew past Danso, and the light about him went out.

There was movement, quick, then a thump, and a thud. Danso froze, frantic, darkness thick about him like gravy. Air in the cavern was shallow, so Danso measured his breathing, the alertness of goosebumps breaking out on his skin.

"Do you feel that?" Lilong asked into the dark. "Danso?"

"It's just the Skopi," he said. "It's back."

They relit the torch to find the bat hanging upside-down in a crevice in the corner, silent, in stasis, casting a large and eerie shadow on the wall.

"You should probably hide it, preferably somewhere it won't be easily stumbled upon," Lilong said. "Any odd thing now will spook the Whudans."

Danso led the creature into one of the dark openings. He managed to find a junction in that tunnel and a rock that obscured a crevice, which was in fact like a natural bat's roost. He left it there and returned to the cavern.

It took the whole night for the remainder of the Whudan caravan to be brought to the foot of the mountains and then lowered into the cavern, two by two. In that time, the camp got spooked by the group taking too long to return for them, and half had already turned around and begun a return journey. Then, upon arriving at the foot of the mountains, the group halved again once many Whudans set eyes on the dip into the Dead Mines.

Those who stayed ended up being less than fifty, and all camped within the cavern and fit snugly. Danso, alongside Kakutan, Biemwensé, and Lilong, decided it would be best if they went ahead and mapped out the exact route to the other side of the mountains and border as soon as possible. Kakutan decided that with the number of people poised to cross, it was best to do so before sunup.

They had an hour to collect their wits about them before starting off. In that time, Danso and Lilong hung out in a corner and ate some dry bread and fermented rice wine offered them by one of the Whudans. Someone had an instrument passed down generations of their family—a round-bodied two-stringed fiddle much smaller than the twenty-one-stringed lute most Bassai jalis played. Danso borrowed it and plucked at it absent-mindedly, thinking about melodies that might fit some of the stories he was already considering writing. But as with the lute, he couldn't put anything sensible together. Composing and singing were the only aspects of jalihood that Danso had never been good at.

Lilong, who had been watching him, asked for the fiddle. He passed it to her, amused, but then she held it, twisted a tuning peg or two, played a series of testing notes, and then strummed it a number of times.

"Ehn, okay," Danso said. "Woman of many skills. Why didn't you say you could play?"

"No, it's just…" She paused. For the first time, Danso saw Lilong look bashful.

"Sing us a song, then." He nudged her with his shoulder. She stayed rigid, uneasy. "Come on, then. If we're about to plunge into the unknown, might as well go in with good memories."

So she sang. Her voice wasn't the best Danso had ever heard, but it belied her typical brusqueness and unveiled a side of her he had never seen—sweet, soft. She sang a song Danso had once read about in the library but had never heard sung by Bassa's jalis: a desertland epic about a sorceress who birthed a son covered in hair from head to toe, but powers passed to him from his maa caused him to do great wonders. She kept it short and ended the song early, which Danso knew because the form of such legends usually ended with a litany of deeds by said warrior, which she didn't go into. There was a little scattered applause, among which Danso's was the most enthusiastic, alongside an amused Biemwensé and Kakutan.

"A desertland legend, though?" Danso asked. "I would've thought you'd sing something from home."

She eyed him, passing the instrument back to its owner.

"Right. Still want to keep it quiet." He nudged her again. "Good song, though. You sing much better than I'll ever hope for. Maybe you can help me write some new songs later? In fact, maybe you can actually sing them!"

She scoffed, but he saw her smile when she thought her face was turned away.

They finished up and joined Biemwensé and Kakutan. Biemwensé had been handed, and had changed into, Youth clothing that made her look exactly like one of them—red wrapper tied at the waist and seashell-beaded blouse. She wore a cutlass belted to her waist but kept her stick. Kakutan smeared her face with some black cosmetic and handed it over to them to do the same.

"It's humus," Biemwensé said while smearing hers, when Lilong wrinkled her nose at it. "For treacherous undertakings. To remind you of the earth you return to, no?"

"We don't paint faces where I come from," Lilong said.

"Don't worry," Kakutan said. "You survive, you remove it."

Danso smeared his own face after Lilong. The smell of it reminded him of home, and for a long moment there, he thought about how different this dark, stuffy cavern was from his own bed far, far away in Bassa. Except it was no longer his bed, and he could no longer call it home. He would have to make his own bed now.

Kakutan left Sankofa in charge, and with instructions. Biemwensé bid her children good-bye. Lilong put her hand on Danso's.

"Let's try to stay alive, okay?"

Kakutan identified the tunnel that had the marker of red cloth and bone, and they entered. A few steps in, she asked Danso: "Where's your bat?"

"Hidden."

"Well you should get it, perhaps," she said. "At this point, we don't know what lies before us. Best to lead with everything we have."

Danso

FINDING THEIR WAY DOWN to the bridge over the moats was a testing and treacherous endeavour. The Dead Mines were very much that—dead— and at every turn, there lay the danger of stepping in the wrong place and, if not falling to death themselves, then sending the walls of the caves tumbling down.

Kakutan led the way with a lamp, spotting the next cloth-and-bone combination and instructing everyone on where to place their feet. Danso and Lilong followed pretty easily, and the Skopi flew forward every now and then, upon instruction. Biemwensé, who turned out to be more nimble than her limping had let on, still intermittently needed help here or there, and each took turns aiding her. At some point, Danso asked if she simply wanted to return like the others and wait, and she shushed him.

"I'm not a chicken," she said. "I've been through worse."

Time went by in the caves of the Dead Mines, though quickly or slowly, Danso couldn't tell. There was no way to estimate how far they had gone either, and after a while, all the information he'd gleaned from the codex about the mines became useless—it was just dark end after dark end without distinction and no light in sight.

Then, all at once, came the sound of water, the same kind of sound he had heard while on the coast, only much tamer. The cloth-and-bone markers had dried up, so they simply followed the sound, taking a series of turns, missing their way into a dead end once, before they came upon an opening just like that of the cavern, but much better lit, and were greeted by the gentle but audible rush of water.

In front of them lay the underground bridge, the cavern lit by a series of skylights streaming daylight onto the bridge.

Danso had thought of the bridge as a lengthy overpass, but it was, in truth, short. He had also thought of the moats as massive and wide and taking hours to cross. But it turned out the moat in this part of the mountains was narrower than he'd believed, much different from its size at other portions along the length of the border. It would be impossible to cross still, of course, without the bridge. Danso was surprised that no one but this Gaddo Company had even tried in the first place, considering.

If the moat was narrower than he'd thought, then the moat was even deeper than he'd expected. Its steep walls went down for ages, and Danso could only see dark bottomlessness beyond the foot of the bridge. It was difficult to tell where the water they were hearing was flowing through. The water itself came from the great seas, so there was no doubt there was a fresh and never-ending supply, and complete assurance that if one stepped in the wrong place and fell, there was no hope for rescue.

The bridge itself was sturdy, but in that old and worn way that told one that many people did not cross it often, and in that rotting way that revealed that it had been in this damp and dank air for too long. Made of bamboo frames and wooden planks, it had become green with age but still looked quite trustworthy, which was why Kakutan nodded with assurance when she saw it. That, and of course, the marker of red cloth and bone that stood at the foot of the mainland side of the moat.

They all took a moment to drink it in. Danso was unsure what the others were looking at, but there was no greater feeling than standing there, looking at the one thing that separated his old life from the promise of his new, the past from his future.

Once he crossed that bridge, he was no longer Danso the jali novitiate. He was Danso the Red Iborworker.

"We should probably walk across it," Kakutan said. "See if it's safe for everyone."

"Hmm," Biemwensé agreed, leaning against her stick.

"I just need to mark the last three turns," Kakutan said, pulling out a short blade. "Can't have people go missing when we make this trip. We are out of time as it is." She grabbed a torch. "I will be making this sound." She made a hoot, almost like an owl. It echoed about the cavern. "If you hear it, you know I'm finding the turns. Now, if you hear *this*—" She made a sound like a shrill bird, piercing the cavern. "You know I've missed my way. You will need to come and find me."

She passed by the Skopi, stopped to look at it, shook her head, then disappeared into the opening.

"We should probably spend some time checking this," Lilong said, and stepped onto the bridge. For a moment, Danso thought she had finally made up her mind to leave them, after they had brought her to the edge of her return home. He could see that Biemwensé thought the same, because she tensed. But Lilong only took a few steps before turning back to them.

"Coming?" she asked.

The three stepped onto the bridge gingerly. Again, it was sturdier than it looked, with no sense that it was going to crumble anytime soon. It looked like it could hold all three of them just fine. Danso left the bat in a shadowed crevice, out of sight.

They went slowly, testing plank by plank. Lilong's eyes flashed amber, and her blade ejected and, with the hilt, knocked on and tested each plank's weight before she put her foot on it.

They went this way for a bit, every now and then listening for a hoot from Kakutan. They heard the first hoot without issue, and the second. The third, they waited for, but it did not come.

They were almost midway over the bridge when there was what might've been a shrill, piercing whistle, cut short before it even started. They listened again but heard nothing.

"Do you think—?" Danso started.

"Maybe we misheard," Lilong said. "Or it was a mistake."

Danso looked at the expression on Lilong's face and could see now that Lilong indeed was eager to cross to the other end. Her face was set, determined, like the way she had looked at him that first night at the barn. He could see, now, that she did not, in fact, intend to cross back with them. He realised that once they had arrived at the other side, she was going to leave them behind.

"We are going to go back," he said, and turned around.

Just then, light poured out of the opening, and Kakutan emerged.

But she was not alone. Behind her were a handful of people bearing torches. They resembled civic guards or registered hunthands, but were neither, and instead looked like a special task group. One of them, a low-black person of indeterminate gender with a bald head, had the tip of a long axe resting in the small of Kakutan's back.

Then out of the opening stepped Esheme.

She looked drastically different from the last time he'd seen her that night at the barn. Her hair was now up in five arches rather than her usual three. She looked out of breath, sweaty, maybe even sick. There was a glint of unpredictability in her eye that made her a tad dangerous.

Then those eyes flashed red, and out with her stepped the body of Oboda, as lifeless and dead as it had been on the night he was murdered in Whudasha, except he was now walking of his own accord. In front of Oboda, his dead and rotting hand resting on his neck in a loose but firm grip, was Danso's daa, Habba.

"Nice to see you again," Esheme said, smiling, "dear runaway intended."

Danso

"Daa." The word escaped Danso's lips.

Habba was a bag of bones, a skeleton with skin draped over it, with bruises across various parts of his body. He seemed like he had gone through a special trial of woes that had broken him to the point where he couldn't even speak or look up, his head perpetually bent in submission, his eyes only looking to the ground. He couldn't even look his son in the eye. Something pinched at Danso's chest. Was it fear, or was it shame? Neither answer was better than the other.

"By moons," Biemwensé whispered. "She is a Red Iborworker too."

The person holding on to Kakutan pushed the Supreme Magnanimous to the ground and put a boot on her back, long axe pointed down to the nape of her neck. Oboda did the same, and both prisoners soon knelt in the dust.

Esheme stepped forward, her eyes focused on the three on the bridge, and spoke. Her voice carried over the sound of the moat's waters, and for a moment there, Danso remembered that she was a trained counsel novitiate who had learned to project herself at court.

"My request is simple," she said. "Step forward, slowly, with the red stone-bone in your hand, and I will not lay waste to these two behind me. Do otherwise, and you will lose everything."

Danso found his legs moving before he could even think. His daa raised his head and mouthed something to him, but Oboda's strong hand rested atop his head and pushed it down.

"Let him go!" he found himself saying.

Esheme cocked her head. "If you bring me the ibor first."

Biemwensé and Lilong shuffled behind him, their footsteps unsure. He had taken a few more steps forward before he realised he didn't have the stone-bone, but Lilong did. He turned around to see that, though Biemwensé had begun to follow his lead, Lilong did not move a breath.

"No," Lilong was saying, more to herself than them, her eyes in slits. *"No."*

"Lilong," Danso said, a plea in his voice.

Lilong gazed right at him. "No. I sacrificed everything. I—" She shifted her gaze to Esheme. "This murderer can never lay a hand on this. Never."

Esheme, perhaps seeing the look in Lilong's eyes, smiled. Then she motioned with her chin, and the person with the long axe over Kakutan's head raised it and prepared to swing.

"Wait!" Danso and Biemwensé called out in unison.

The axe hung in midair and remained there.

"The next moment of my time you waste," Esheme said, "that axe comes down."

Danso turned to Lilong then. "Listen! You have to give me the Diwi."

"No." She held firm to the pouch slung across her body.

"Lilong."

"Everything will be lost. Everything we have fought for, that people died for, that my daa—" She swallowed. "No."

"Listen," Danso said, leaning closer to whisper to her. "You have to let me deliver it." He cocked his head, to signal to her. "Let *me* deliver it."

She frowned, trying to understand what he was communicating. Danso had his face set, his heart set, in a way that he hoped told her he knew exactly what he was doing.

"Trust me," he said.

She stared at him a long time, then slowly opened the pouch and produced the stone-bone. When Danso took it, he put a hand over hers, gently, and nodded.

"*Trust* me," he said, holding her eyes.

She nodded and let go.

Danso rose, and out of the side of his mouth, without turning his head, said to Biemwensé: "Follow me, both of you, but slowly. Buy me time."

He put his two hands up and stepped forward.

"Okay," he said, raising his voice to be heard over the distance and the water, shuffling forward. "Okay, I'm coming. Just don't hurt anybody, please."

Esheme scoffed, then folded her arms as he came over the bridge, counting his steps. He measured the closing distance between them, thinking of how much time he needed to buy.

"Esheme," he said, taking a risk. "We can talk about this."

"Keep my name out of your dirty mouth," she snapped, an increasingly dangerous sneer forming in the corner of her lips. "The time for talking is over. You will be brought to justice for what you have done, plain and simple."

"And what have I done?" he asked. "Followed my dreams like you have followed yours? That is my crime?"

"Your crime is betraying your own nation," she said, then paused, hesitant. "Your crime is making me—us—look weak, open to disrespect, to being stepped upon. Your crime is betraying your own intended."

Danso stopped then. "I'm so sorry, Esheme." And to be fair, he truly was. "I'm sorry you got caught in the middle of all this. All I want is to be allowed to seek what I want to. I never meant—"

"Enough!" That dangerous expression flickered on her face again. "You will get justice—by my hand, if I can help it—and it will be as swift as the people want it. You can have your remorse then. Now step forward as I've said, or heads will roll."

Danso sighed, moved forward again, then stopped.

"This thing you want, Esheme, it's dangerous," he said, waving his hand with the stone-bone lackadaisically. His swing crossed the bridge's edge, and he saw the way her expression flickered into one of horror for a moment. "Why don't we settle personal matters separate from things much more dangerous?"

Esheme's eyes narrowed in a nasty and bitter manner, and her lip curled up full when she said:

"I warned you." And her eyes flashed red.

"Stop!" Danso screamed, and put his hand over the edge of the bridge. "Stop, or I drop it."

"Danso!" Lilong was saying from behind him. "What—"

"I *will* drop it," Danso said, coming forward again, slowly. "Let them go, and you can have it." He paused. "You can have me."

"Danso…" Lilong's voice, again. He did not look at her.

"It's me you really want, isn't it? You want your revenge. You want this stone-bone and its power too. Who doesn't? You can have both—you can have all you want—if you just let them go."

"Don't do it, Danso," Habba said weakly, without raising his head. "Don't—" He was cut short by a smack to the mouth. Danso flinched.

"It's okay, daa," he said. "Stay with me."

"I'm sorry," Habba said, spittle dripping from his lips. "I'm so sorry."

"Stay with me, daa. *Stay.*"

Esheme regarded the kneeling man for a moment, then looked back to Danso. Oboda remained in stasis, waiting for her Command. Everyone held their breaths, waiting for her response.

"Where you are mistaken, Danso," she said at last, "is that you think you know me. You have always thought yourself wise, knowledgeable. And somehow, you believe I am still dependent on anyone or anything to get what I want." She stepped forward and put a hand on Habba's hair. "That woman you knew is gone. And this woman—this woman does not take kindly to threats."

She drew a blade out of a nearby hunthand's sheath and plunged it into Habba's shoulder.

Danso and his daa screamed in unison. Habba fell over.

Just then, a blade flew past from behind Danso and headed straight for Esheme. Her eyes flashed red in the last instant, and Oboda stepped in front of her.

Lilong's blade went right through the dead man's chest and lodged there. Oboda, unruffled, pulled it out without difficulty.

Danso found himself Commanding—more out of reflex now than with any specific aim—and out of the darkness came the screech of the Skopi, its wingspan bringing darkness as it swept low over the group. Oboda ducked over Esheme and covered her. The bat grabbed a nearby couple of hunthands and swept down with them, into the darkness of the moat. At the same time, Kakutan shoved the axe over her head, rolled forward, and pitched for the bridge.

Someone shot an arrow at her. She dodged it, and the arrow missed her, went straight ahead, and pierced Danso in the chest.

Danso found himself falling in slow motion, gazing at the fountain of red springing from his chest but failing to comprehend what was happening. Kakutan ran toward him, her face fading, and then she was grabbing his arm and first screaming something in his ear, and then she was dragging him. Another set of arms joined.

Then Lilong was running, past him, toward the group that was now pouring onto the bridge. Kakutan—and someone that he believed was Biemwensé but did not see—was yelling again, but at Lilong, telling her to come back.

Biemwensé broke the tip of the arrow in his chest and yanked the other half from beneath him, and the pain brought him back to life. The whole of his shoulder blade burned, and he was numb from his sternum to the small of his back.

Ahead, Lilong dealt with the hunthands piling onto the bridge, dodging their lunges and swipes, moving with a speed and startlingness Danso had not seen before. The bridge thudded with their movements, creaking dangerously, the narrowness of it forcing Lilong to keep backtracking to deal with the advancing men. She looked behind her every now and then to be sure of her footing. Whenever she looked, he could see her eyes flash amber, Commanding her blade here and there.

She knocked man after man as they came. Then, suddenly, she was standing face-to-face with Oboda. The hulking man charged for her, and Lilong's blade moved in response.

Oboda grabbed her blade and held on tight, the point only an inch from his face. Lilong's eyes flashed harder, but the blade stayed in his hand, never moving. Over on the land side, behind Oboda, Esheme screamed as her eyes burned red, channelling more and more power into the man, guarded by the same person with the axe who had held Kakutan. No matter how much Lilong seemed to will it to stab and stab and stab his body, Oboda kept the knife glued to his hand.

Then the man freed one hand, reached out, and caught Lilong by the neck.

Lilong retched, sputtered, and Danso realised she was trying to say something.

"Go," Lilong sputtered. "Get it—*away.*"

No, Danso thought. *Can't let another person die. Not in my name.*

With all the energy left in his bones, he squeezed the ibor in his hand and Drew. His body whined in response, and he screamed with the pain that came with it. But he held on tight, reached with his mind, and Possessed.

Out of the depths of the moat came the Skopi, wet and black and shiny, screaming the cavern hoarse. Danso Commanded one last time.

Strike.

The long axe came swinging into the air from the land side, thrown with two-handed force. It caught the bat and pinned a wing into its body. The Skopi lost flight and pivoted, falling straight into the bridge.

At the same time, a bright whiteness lit up the cavern as lightning came through the opening above with a crackle and struck the body of Oboda. He dropped Lilong, and she called for her blade in that last instant.

"No!" Danso found himself saying in unison with Kakutan and Biemwensé, as the bat crashed into both people and bridge.

Everything in sight plunged over the edge and into the darkness of the moat. Stones rained down from above, destroying what the first impact had not, and slammed into the bridge.

The bridge first creaked, then groaned long and loud, before it slowly began to tilt away from them and into the moat.

"Move, move, move!" Kakutan yelled, and both women were now dragging him with unbearable force as the elevation grew increasingly steep. Danso yelled as his wound bit harder. He turned to look behind him. The edge, the side that led to freedom, was *nearly* there.

His body had barely touched ground when, with a loud and deafening crash and splash, the bridge collapsed into the moat.

"Lilong," Danso found himself saying. "She's—she was—"

The women were pulling him back, pulling him away from the edge, but he found himself struggling against the pain in his body to look over the edge, into the glaring darkness that was once occupied by the bridge.

Just then, there was a *thud*, the smack of something against wood. Then another thud, and another. Then the gemstone hilt of Lilong's blade appeared, the iron stuck into the wood and bamboo parts of the bridge still connected to their side of the land.

Lilong flopped over the edge, wet and gasping for breath.

The three of them rushed and pulled her over. She collapsed onto her back and coughed up water.

Over at the other edge, Esheme watched them intently. Next to her stood her now axeless guard. Not a single other soul had survived, except for Habba, who was still flopped on the ground next to them both, passed out and bleeding.

Esheme, staring right at Danso, shuffled toward Habba's body, picked up one of the discarded burning torches, touched it to his clothes, and left it there.

"No," Danso whispered, but even as he said it, he knew it was over.

The flames started slowly in one corner, but soon they were everywhere. The man did not move as the flames spread, making way from his clothes to his hands, his legs. The flames took hold of his hair, his face, and soon, every single part of Habba was engulfed in fire. Danso fell to his knees, tears clouding his eyes. Black smoke rose to the roof of the cavern, out of the skylight. Danso called his daa's name over and over and over as he watched the man's final journey to the skies unfold before his very eyes.

I'm sorry, he kept saying, thinking about the man's last words. *I'm sorry, too.*

Things stood like this for a long time. Esheme never stopped glaring across the moat at Danso, and for a moment, Danso thought what he saw was a smile, but she was too far away to tell for sure.

A deep hate, a violent anger surged in him then. He rose and pressed at the stone-bone in his hand, and Drew and waited and waited. It took him a while to realise there was nothing to Possess, nothing to Command.

The Skopi was gone. The bridge was gone. The Whudans were gone. Habba was gone.

Everything they had and knew and loved was gone.

70

Danso

WHEN THE FOUR EMERGED from beneath the Soke mountains and into the early afternoon heat of the Savanna Belt, it was like walking into another continent entirely. Even for Danso and Lilong, who had crossed a semi-savanna on their journey, this was a separate experience in itself. Everything spread before them, a vast, rolling grassland scattered with shrubs and isolated trees. The air was sharp, fiercer, harsher, and the little animals and long-legged birds they ran into scurried across, almost unafraid of human presence. The isolated trees had thick bark, large trunks, shedding leaves. The grass was short and sharp. It was like everything on this side of the mountains was trying to survive, toughening themselves up for the conditions ahead.

And this perhaps dawned on them all the moment they set foot on the land. A weariness Danso did not feel at the bridge overtook him, and he saw the same from his three fellow travellers. Perhaps it was the nothingness that lay before them, the monstrosity of the task ahead of them, and the crippling dread that after getting this far, they did not have what it would take to make it farther.

Danso fell into the grass and lay face up, the sun beating hard on his nose and cheeks and causing them to smart. His chest throbbed, but it was only painful if he didn't move too much. Lilong trudged up to him, stood there for a moment, then lay next to him. Biemwensé and Kakutan, who had led them out and had been ahead, came back and sat with them.

They all sat there, nobody saying a word. Kakutan, the only one who still had a waterskin, produced it, drank from it, and passed it around. Between the bridge and here, each had had time to contemplate their fate, to come to terms with what this meant for them: that they were all, together, forever, fugitives. That everything they had left behind on the other side of those moats was gone. For Kakutan, her people; for Biemwensé, her children; for Danso, everything and everyone he had known and loved, even if the most important of those now lay on the other side of the bridge, a pile of ashes.

Silent tears fell from the corners of Danso's eyes, into his ears, wetting the sharp grass beneath his head. He blinked and blinked, unsure why he was crying. Hadn't he known what he had been doing the moment he decided he was going to help Lilong? Didn't he know the sacrifice he was making on behalf of everyone who was related to him in some way—his daa, his uncles, his friends, his Second, even Esheme? He had reaped what he had sowed, hadn't he? Why was he *crying*?

He wiped his eyes. No. He was done being victim, being the naive young Bassai man whom the world happened to. He was ready now, to happen to the world. He was ready for the work ahead.

He was ready. To become an Iborworker, to become a jali, to become whatever it took.

A hand came over his, and he looked to see Lilong's hand intertwined with his. He turned to look at her. For the first time, he saw her eyes up close, her irises of yellowed strands on brown: tired, scared, hopeful. She smiled, gripped his hand tight and nodded. *We did it*, she was saying, or, *Hang in there*, or, *I'm sorry*, or, *We'll figure it out*, or, *We'll get them*. He gripped her hand and smiled back, and his smile said everything hers did.

The sounds of hooves and riding and someone goading their kwagas came to them just then. The group jerked to attention and sat up together. Lilong swiftly adjusted her complexion to a Whudan's.

Danso shaded his eyes, expecting to perhaps see civic guards or hunthands guarding the border. Instead, the men who rode up to them and quickly surrounded them had their heads wrapped in turbans and their noses covered so that only their eyes showed. The lead man was distinguished from the others in that he wore a large flowing robe, wrappers stitched at the edges to form a bulbous kaftan. He, like the rest, had the desertlander complexion, but none of the tentativeness Danso was used to. Instead, he spoke tersely and quickly in Savanna Common and, without missing a beat, pulled out his blade, a curved sword.

At first Danso did not catch any of the words, and only when the other three pairs of eyes turned to look at him did he realise he was the only one in the group who was multitongued.

He rose, stepped forward, and bowed.

"We come in peace and upon invitation," he said in Savanna Common, putting on his jali voice and enunciating the words the way he had been taught at guild. "We are escapees from Bassa, seeking Chabo."

The man frowned at his probably weird accent, then said, in Savanna Common:

"I said, how did you find the secret passage?"

Danso turned to Kakutan and motioned to one of the bone-and-red-cloth markers she had thought to take along. She passed it to him, and he passed it across to the man, saying: "We were invited. By a former Bassai Idu called Oke."

The man, examining the bone-and-cloth marker in his hand and looking between it and the group, seemed to perk up at the name. He spent some time in that disposition, before a warm smile suddenly broke out on his face.

"Welcome," he said, in surprising but broken Mainland Common. "I am Kubra, general of the Gaddo Company. Come, we take you to Chabo." He stopped, then looked directly at Lilong. "You don't change back." When her mouth went agape, he said, "Yes, we know your kind. We are friends of the seven islands. But we must be careful, because not all in the desertlands are."

Lilong looked sheepish but nodded.

A few men came down and helped Biemwensé up onto one of the kwagas, which were quite big, larger than the average kwagas Danso was used to in Bassa. Kakutan helped herself onto the back of one of the others.

Lilong held him back for a moment. From her waist, she untied the pouch containing the Diwi, which she had retrieved from him after the fracas. She looked at it for a long time, holding it by the strings, before offering it to him.

"I think this belongs to you now," she said, a wry grimace tugging at her mouth, as if it pained her to do this. "I was wrong—it responded to you, and it did so for a reason. I can't argue with the Diwi. Perhaps it believes in you in a way I hope I can come to experience. Maybe I misjudged. Maybe you can do much more good for us all with it."

Danso accepted it slowly. The mineral weighed more than he remembered it.

"I know we lost the Skopi," she said, "but perhaps there are others out there? Or other beasts of ibor? I don't know. But rather than argue, I should be helping you instead. Maybe we can figure it out."

"Don't you want to return this to your league?" Danso asked.

She thought for a moment. "I want to, but I don't believe I can go home just yet." She dusted her hands at the idea. "There will definitely be a bounty on our heads out here too, and there is no way I alone, or both of us, can cross eastward and slip back over the isthmus without being tracked. That will mean leading every hunthand on the continent into the archipelago, and I cannot have that on my hands. We will have to wait around until we can find another way."

"And in the meantime?"

"In the meantime, maybe we put the Diwi to the use it was made for? Especially now that we really need it, when a portion of it lies in the hands of a vindictive monster." She stared off wistfully. "It's what my daa would want."

"And the Abenai League?"

"We'll deal with them when we get there."

Danso sighed. "Even if we still had the Skopi, I don't know what I'll do with this now. I just..." He sighed. "I don't even know if this is what I want. I just wanted to get away from Bassa."

Lilong motioned with her chin to Biemwensé and Kakutan, who were speaking to one another across their separate kwagas. "People risked their lives to help us save this. We cannot let all that be in vain."

"But what if this means things never get better? What if it means we get stuck in Chabo forever?" He looked into her face. "What if it means you never go home?"

She stared off again. "I don't know. All I know is that the time for hiding is over. Maybe it's time to show our true selves to the world." She angled her head. "You of all people know we can't allow that woman to get her way and find us. We will never forgive ourselves for what she'll do with ibor. If a whole new people become choked under her crazed grip, is that a victory compared to saving an archipelago no one can find anyway?"

Danso nodded. She was right. If there was anything Danso knew about Esheme, it was that she would never stop hunting them. She would also ensure that every single person associated with them, especially the Whudans, was punished. Anyone who objected would join the list. In no time, the whole of the mainland—and maybe even the whole continent—would feel the heat of her appetite for malice. Especially as she could now raise the dead with such a powerful mineral.

He and Lilong were the only two people on the continent with the ability—and the willingness—to do something about it. They could hide, for now, but they could not hide forever.

"So what now?" he asked.

"We regroup," Lilong said. "Gather resources. Maybe even find ibor. I'm willing to bet someone somewhere on this continent knows some tales, and there's likely to be a little truth in at least one of them. But first, we must get to safety, away from the reach of everything your intended touches. I'm not thrilled about following this company into hiding in some obscure colony, but it's the only option we currently have."

With that, she turned him and led him to the nearest kwaga. Its rider reached down and hoisted Danso onto its back. Danso winced at the pain in his chest. Another rider did the same for Lilong. She looked across at Danso and nodded at him. *We did it*, her nod said, and, *Hang in there*, and, *I'm sorry*, and, *We'll figure it out*, and, *We'll get them*. He nodded back.

With *hyaahs* and the click of tongues, they turned their backs to the Soke mountains and cantered off into a new adventure.

Epilogue

Esheme

THERE WAS NO FESTIVAL at the next mooncrossing. The night before had lain still, peak nightlight passing over Bassa for the first time without a gathering. Still, there was celebration in the streets and in homes, partly muted. The Whudans had been recaptured, hadn't they? Sure, the intruder and some accomplices had escaped, but justice would be served on those captured, wouldn't it? There would be a bounty on the heads of the escapees, even in the outer lands, and they would forever walk Oon uneasy. It was a message to everyone that Bassa was willing to do whatever it took—including sacrificing their own—to retain the mainland's crown.

Perhaps, for the first time in a long time, people were hopeful for Bassa's ascendancy, were glad the old order was gone. There were those who were unsure about the new order to come, but they comforted themselves with the belief and hope that it would not be like the last.

The sun that morning rose on a new Bassa, as the city prepared for a coronation.

The Priests of the Moon Temple, the man Ilobi and the woman Ebose, came forward, before the huge crowd gathered in the courtyard of the Great Dome. For the first time in many seasons, all five gates into the Great Dome had been thrown open, and every single citizen, caste be damned, had been invited. Fear of the people was a thing that no longer drove the occupiers of the Great Dome. For the first time in a long time, the fear was in the hearts of those who gathered, and no one dared go past where they were not meant to.

Esheme stepped forward onto the rostrum, the very same one on which she had captured the Great Dome. The crowd grew and spilled over into mainway fifteen, and people craned to catch a glimpse of their new ruler. She knelt, and let the new regalia of all-red fall over her.

She had asked Nem what she should wear for court dress, and Nem recalled Nogowu's description of his own dress from the codex: a large skirt of the finest velveteen wrappers, wrapped from breast to feet; a top made from an intricate interweaving of stringed coral; a high collar of interchanging bronze and copper rings, so high she could feel the cold of it beneath her chin now. Fashionable, still, Esheme thought. Perhaps the Manic Emperor had not *just* been manic after all, perhaps more intellectual beneath all of his sociopathic and murderous tendencies.

The two priests came forward and settled the crown on her head, between her newly plaited and oiled arches. Seven arches, the highest in the land. Seven: the sacred number of the gods, of wiping clean. Seven for a new beginning, a new nation.

The crown, which had been saved in the Great Dome's own archives, had remained the exact same: copper scaffolding, gold and bronze accents, strung coral dangling down the sides. The leopard head at the top, in gold, had been designed during the Leopard Emperor's time and remained unaltered since then. Perched atop Esheme's head now, one ridged portion of the arrangement tickled her scalp. She had only made slight alterations to it—only for more curves and less heft. A small shape change, too: at the very crest of the headpiece, two tiny pieces of stone-bone stood proud, lodged in the eyes of the leopard.

Of course she had shattered the red stone-bone into a great many pieces. *Who keeps their most dangerous weapon all together in one place?* Nem had asked. They buried the disparate pieces in various places only Nem and Esheme knew, to be unearthed when the red piece in her crown was used up and turned to dust.

When Esheme emerged in her regalia, the crowd in the courtyard of the Great Dome rose and responded. Most did so with roaring, exalting full praise to the new emperor. Some did so with whispers beneath their breaths.

She adjusted the crown daintily and wondered how she looked, wishing for a reflective surface in which to regard herself. Her wrappers where exactly so, just as she'd wanted them. And the crown—she knew what it looked like, at least. She had stood watch as its lesser parts were hewn. She'd had them repaint it red, not just to camouflage the ibor that stood atop it, but so that the people, every time they looked upon her from head to toe, remembered death.

She, too, was doomed to always see death. According to the court's sworn physicians, the heartbeat of the infant in her belly had become too faint. Esheme knew her last battle had been the catalyst, and that it was only a matter of time before the child would become cold, lifeless, and she would have to pass its remains. She could feel the time coming already—soon. What would happen after that—whether she would lose ibor or not, how she would hold on to her crown—she didn't know. At night, she sat up, thinking about this trade she was making, knowing that as long as she had this stone-bone and the power it commanded, she was free to do anything she wanted, but only as long as there was also a Shashi child in her belly. A child she must always have, but never bear.

She lifted her chin, drinking in the veneration of her people. An unfair trade, this child, but perhaps a necessary sacrifice. It wasn't the only necessary sacrifice either. As long as Danso lived, for instance, there would always be the risk of someone who thought he could contest her ascendancy. It was no good thing that the embodiment of defiance against her, who had disgraced her *twice*, continued to live. The fact that he held the only other known piece of ibor in the lands on both sides of the Soke mountains made his existence even more dangerous.

She would hunt him until the edge where the desertland met sea, if that was what it took.

Esheme adjusted the crown again, stood straight-backed. She wondered about the weight of the crown. Its physical weight, to start, which she decided she would need to whittle down some more, at least so that it didn't make turning her neck a task. The shape and form of the head-piece she would keep, retaining ease of recognition, a quick reminder of the older days and a promise to the people that their glory would return. The weight of that promise, though, that she would be the one to deliver it? That, she would figure out as she went along. Right now, her priority was keeping them believing in her sovereignty.

She was the Twenty-Fourth Emperor of Great Bassa, The Red Emperor, Emperor Esheme. Everyone standing there knew it, respected it, believed in it, feared it. And for those who didn't, she would very soon ensure that they were forced to.

She would be emperor over every edge of the continent touched by Menai's and Ashu's light, if it killed her. And both gods willing, she was going to be alive for a long, long time to come.

The story continues in...

WARRIOR OF THE WIND

Coming in 2022!

Acknowledgments

To bring a book to life, it truly does take a village, and my village consists of the following folks and more, including all those I have forgotten to mention because I am, sadly, human.

—Eddie Schneider, my able agent, for your overwhelming patience guiding this noob, through the waters of publishing and otherwise. My gratitude extends to all the folks at the JABberwocky Literary Agency, for your indelible support.

—Nivia Evans, my amiable editor at Orbit. I've often joked that I've been blessed by the gods of editors, and you're just another reason that is completely true. It is really an honour to work with such a star. Major thanks to Rachel Goldstein, Tiana Coven, and Amy J. Schneider for your additional careful notes in helping me shape this book for the better.

—Dan Dos Santos, for the dope cover art, and Lauren Panepinto, for the just-as-dope cover design.

—The rest of the team at Orbit US and UK, for all your support in getting this book to where it needs to be.

—My biggest cheerleaders since I began this writing journey: Tade Thompson and Sarah Ladipo Manyika. Thank you for your encouragement, for your push, and for not giving up on me.

—The MFA in Creative Writing classes of '19 to '22 at the University of Arizona. A large part of the writer I am today is made up of a little piece of each of you. Special shouts to Lucia, Emma, Katerina, Kim, Logan, Matt, Gabe, Emi, Hea-Ream, Lucy, Raquel, Sami, Joi, Brian, Natalie, Sophia, Margo. Also big-ups to present and former faculty Julie

Iromuanya, Manuel Muñoz, Kate Bernheimer, Chris Cokinos, Bojan Louis, Alison Deming, Ander Monson, Farid Matuk, Aurelie Sheehan.

—My partner, Dami, for putting up with all my excesses during the writing of this book, and for all your support and succour at every other time.

—My parents, Prof. M. O. and Prof. F. I. Okungbowa, first of their names, without whom this book would not exist in the first place.

—My siblings: Ehi, Wema, Osarumen, Mike. For being sounding boards for all my tales.

—My non-writer friends, especially those who know almost nothing about my author alter ego but offer it the respect it deserves upon discovery: you are appreciated. Special shouts to Chukwudi Jarrett, Chisom Ojukwu, Ifeanyi Onwuka, Amy Takabori and Chris Griffin, Laura Werthmann.

—My writing comrades who know where the shoe pinches: Rafeeat Aliyu, Ehigbor Shultz, Nandi Taylor, K. Tempest Bradford, Nicky Drayden. Also, those who have offered a welcoming embrace to the SFF writing community and have been advocates of my work one way or another: Tochi Onyebuchi, Rebecca Roanhorse, Martha Wells, Chuck Wendig, Dan Wells, Christina Orlando, Kwame Mbalia, Khaalidah Muhammad-Ali, Patrice Caldwell, S. A. Chakraborty. Thank you.

—Everyone who has offered a platform for me and my work to speak and grow: thank you. Special shouts to Jacey Bedford and the 2017 Milford SF Writers committee, Rebecca Schwarz and the board of the Turkey City Writing Workshop, Malik Toms and the Virginia G. Piper Center for Creative Writing at ASU, and the three musketeers of the *Just Keep Writing* podcast: Wil, Marshall, and Nick.

—Every member of Suyi's Street Squad: my deepest gratitude for all you have done to promote this book by word of mouth. Big thanks to Lara, Moustapha, Yemisi, Joshua, Oghenechovwe, Bezi, Seyi, Chinelo, Caleb.

—Every reader and fan out there who has engaged with my work and helped others find it one way or another: I appreciate you. You are the reason I do what I do.

extras

orbit

meet the author

Photo Credit: Manuel Ruiz

SUYI DAVIES OKUNGBOWA is the author of *Son of the Storm*, first in The Nameless Republic epic fantasy trilogy, and the godpunk novel *David Mogo, Godhunter*. His shorter works have appeared internationally in periodicals like *Tor.com*, *Lightspeed*, *Nightmare*, *Strange Horizons*, and *Fireside*, and anthologies like *The Year's Best Science Fiction and Fantasy*, *A World of Horror*, and *People of Colo(u)r Destroy Science Fiction*. He lives between Lagos, Nigeria, and Tucson, Arizona, earning his MFA and teaching writing at the University of Arizona. He tweets at IAmSuyiDavies and is @suyidavies on Instagram. Learn more at suyidavies.com.

Find out more about Suyi Davies Okungbowa and other Orbit authors by registering for the free monthly newsletter at orbitbooks.net.

interview

What was the first book that made you fall in love with the fantasy genre?

The fantastic has generally been woven into a lot of stories I grew up with—from speaking tortoises to ghost stories to next-door neighbours who could fly. Most of the stories by Nigerian and other African authors I read growing up had elements of fantasy in them—*Wizard of the Crow* by Ngũgĩ wa Thiong'o, *The Bottled Leopard* by Chukwuemeka Ike, *The Rape of Shavi* and *Kehinde*, both by Buchi Emecheta, etc. But these were unfairly classified as "African literature" back then, so I never quite considered them fantasy. The first "fantasy" novel I loved—according to mainstream understanding back then—was *Silverhand* by Morgan Llywelyn and Michael Scott. Afterward, I started seeking more fantastic stories with protagonists familiar to me, and I happened upon Nnedi Okorafor's *Who Fears Death*. It was after reading that book that I realised fantasy could feature folks like me. That was when I decided, "Yeah, this is my jam."

Your first novel, **David Mogo, Godhunter,** *was a standalone. What was it like transitioning to writing a trilogy? Did it change your creative process? If so, in what ways?*

I think it got me to deeply consider story as something that happens to a particular people in a particular place at a particular time. With *David Mogo*, the story world was woven tightly around the characters. But with The Nameless Republic trilogy,

I began to think about pasts, presents, and futures of the continent of Oon, and how the characters in, say, *Son of the Storm* were just a drop in that ocean. I think what that did for me was get me to consider how each character thinks of themselves in relation to this bigger world: where they fit in it, and what they could do to impact the small slice of it around them.

Where did the initial idea for Son of the Storm *come from and how did the story begin to take shape?*

I grew up in Benin City, Nigeria, a city born of the ancient Benin Empire that, in its heyday around the fifteenth century, spanned a huge chunk of today's southern and western Nigeria. Growing up, I'd hear snippets of myths and fables from back then, references to legends in old ballads sung by elderly musicians. But when I looked in books, I barely saw anything more than a passing mention of its legendary artifacts, or only discussions of the kingdom's invasion by the British. I became interested in what it might've looked like before all of that, how vibrant it must've been. In 2016, that interest inspired me to start putting together what would eventually become *Son of the Storm*.

I love epic fantasy, so I've always wanted to write a fantasy story that's epic in a way I recognise, that's markedly distinct when compared to the traditional, expected, Tolkien-esque forms. Benin's best parts were a good starting point for me, but I also ended up studying other great African empires—Mali, Ghana, Dahomey, the Senegambia, Egypt. I spread my wings and drew from every possible corner.

I'm also a fan of non-warrior characters. I know epic fantasy is filled with weapon-wielding heroes, but I've always wanted more stories of those who have to employ skills other than combat to solve their problems. Scholars, fixers, activists, courtiers, etc. I consider myself someone who solves my own problems via non-traditional approaches, and I wanted characters like that to get their day in the light too.

extras

What was the most challenging moment of writing* Son of the Storm*?

Writing the middle third of the book. That's the part where characters have made all the decisions and now have to grapple with the consequences. Also, by this time, you've thrown every flashy new exciting thing you can into the story, and unless you want a *deus ex machina*, you have to start asking serious questions about what characters *really* want and where this story *really* ends up (news flash: almost never where you think, haha). I had to go back and forth often to reconsider every character's position or choices, and make some radical moves I hoped would pay off. It was a tough time in the real world too, what with tons of crazy happening in everyday life. I spent more time in this stage than I've ever spent with any other story, but it was worth it, because when the final part of the book eventually came around, it was a cruise.

The continent of Oon is incredibly well developed and hints at rich histories waiting to be explored. What was your approach to creating the various cultures and ethnic groups? Did you do any specific research to build the world?

Only as much as I needed to borrow from the real world. At the inception, whenever I was back at my parents' in Benin City, I'd be knee-deep in their mold-infested books in storage for anything that spoke about the old Benin Empire, especially its legends and the dynamics of everyday living in the old city. I found a few materials, locally produced. The library and special collections at the University of Arizona were great resources too, to the point that I ended up making only two purchases for my personal library: *A History of West Africa, 1000–1800* by Basil Davidson (with F. K. Buah and J. F. A. Ajayi) and *Africa's Great Civilizations*, a PBS documentary by Henry Louis Gates, Jr.

Oon is not any of these kingdoms or histories, though, so I really had to think about what I wanted Oon itself to be. I considered how the sociology of a people is deeply rooted in

the physicality of their environments, and how the spiritual—
or a people's interpretations of it—helps bind those together. I
considered how all of this shapes a collective psyche, and the
circumstances that forge outliers. What makes sense to these
people, to their ancestors, and who tells these stories? It was, and
continues to be, a very fascinating and exhilarating experience,
I'll tell you that.

**The characters in Son of the Storm *are vibrant and compel-
ling. If you had to pick, who would you say is your favorite?
Who did you find the most difficult to write?***

My favourite would be a toss-up between Biemwensé and Danso's triplet uncles. I love me some no-nonsense elderly African
aunties and uncles. And when they come in packs, ooh boy.
With Biemwensé, I like that I get to explore her outside of the
main characters, and in forthcoming books, she's likely going to
play a larger role in Oon's future than I—and she—anticipated.
The triplet uncles might be making a comeback too, so fingers
crossed there.

The most challenging to write would probably be Lilong? She
holds a lot of anger and distrust for something she has only ever
known through stories. After inheriting a ton of secondhand
generational trauma, she suddenly realises history and reality are
much messier. I often had to think about where she stood at each
moment in the novel, as she oscillated between aiding a people she should otherwise hate versus berating her own people's
reductive approach to history and security. In the next book, she
really begins to commandeer the course of her life. I'm looking
forward to charting that experience.

**Finally, *without giving too much away, could you give us a hint
of what happens in the next novel,* Warrior of the Wind?**

More. More Oon, more magic, more beasts, more quests. We
get to see the remaining ibor minerals in action. We get to see
Danso try to make sense of a world outside Bassa, Lilong try to

return home, and Esheme grapple with her newfound role, as well as exciting new folks who aid as well as antagonise them in these choices. We get to see more cities and locales outside Bassa, everything from the Nameless Islands to the desertlands to the hinterland protectorates and the delta swamps. And of course, if not a lightning bat, at least more beasts with an eye— or nostril—on ibor. It's going to be a joyride, I can promise you that!

if you enjoyed
SON OF THE STORM

look out for

THE BONE SHARD DAUGHTER

The Drowning Empire: Book One

by

Andrea Stewart

The emperor's reign has lasted for decades, his mastery of bone shard magic powering the animallike constructs that maintain law and order. But now his rule is failing, and revolution is sweeping across the Empire's many islands.

Lin is the emperor's daughter and spends her days trapped in a palace of locked doors and dark secrets. When her father refuses to recognize her as heir to the throne, she vows to prove her worth by mastering the forbidden art of bone shard magic.

Yet such power carries a great cost, and when the revolution reaches the gates of the palace, Lin must decide how far she is willing to go to claim her birthright—and save her people.

1

Lin

Imperial Island

Father told me I'm broken.

He didn't speak this disappointment when I answered his question. But he said it with narrowed eyes, the way he sucked on his already hollow cheeks, the way the left side of his lips twitched a little bit down, the movement almost hidden by his beard.

He taught me how to read a person's thoughts on their face. And he knew that I knew how to read these signs. So between us, it was as though he had spoken out loud.

The question: "Who was your closest childhood friend?"

My answer: "I don't know."

I could run as quickly as the sparrow flies, I was as skilled with an abacus as the Empire's best accountants, and I could name all the known islands in the time it took for tea to finish steeping. But I could not remember my past before the sickness. Sometimes I thought I never would – that the girl from before was lost to me.

Father's chair creaked as he shifted, and he let out a long breath. In his fingers he held a brass key, which he tapped on the table's surface. "How can I trust you with my secrets? How can I trust you as my heir if you do not know who you are?"

I knew who I was. I was Lin. I was the Emperor's daughter. I shouted the words in my head, but I didn't say them. Unlike my father, I kept my face neutral, my thoughts hidden. Sometimes he liked it when I stood up for myself, but this was not one of those times. It never was, when it came to my past.

I did my best not to stare at the key.

"Ask me another question," I said. The wind lashed at the shutters, bringing with it the salt-seaweed smell of the ocean. The breeze licked at my neck, and I suppressed a shiver. I kept his gaze, hoping he saw the steel in my soul and not the fear. I could taste the scent of rebellion on the winds as clearly as I could the fish fermentation vats. It was that obvious, that thick. I could set things right, if only I had the means. If only he'd let me prove it.

Tap.

"Very well," Father said. The teak pillars behind him framed his withered countenance, making him look more like a foreboding portrait than a man. "You're afraid of sea serpents. Why?"

"I was bit by one when I was a child," I said.

He studied my face. I held my breath. I stopped holding my breath. I twined my fingers together and then forced them to relax. If I were a mountain, he would be following the taproots of cloud junipers, chipping away the stone, searching for the white, chalky core.

And finding it.

"Don't lie to me, girl," he snarled. "Don't make guesses. You may be my flesh and blood, but I can name my foster son to the crown. It doesn't have to be you."

I wished I did remember. Was there a time when this man stroked my hair and kissed my forehead? Had he loved me before I'd forgotten, when I'd been whole and unbroken? I wished there was someone I could ask. Or at least, someone who could give me answers. "Forgive me." I bowed my head. My black hair formed a curtain over my eyes, and I stole a glance at the key.

Most of the doors in the palace were locked. He hobbled from room to room, using his bone shard magic to create miracles. A magic I needed if I was to rule. I'd earned six keys. My father's foster, Bayan, had seven. Sometimes it felt as if my entire life was a test.

"Fine," Father said. He eased back into his chair. "You may go."

I rose to leave, but hesitated. "When will you teach me your bone shard magic?" I didn't wait for his response. "You say you can name Bayan as your heir, but you haven't. I am still your heir, and I need to know how to control the constructs. I'm twenty-three, and you—" I stopped, because I didn't know how old he was. There were liver spots on the backs of his hands, and his hair was steely gray. I didn't know how much longer he would live. All I could imagine was a future where he died and left me with no knowledge. No way to protect the Empire from the Alanga. No memories of a father who cared.

He coughed, muffling the sound with his sleeve. His gaze flicked to the key, and his voice went soft. "When you are a whole person," he said.

I didn't understand him. But I recognized the vulnerability. "Please," I said, "what if I am never a whole person?"

He looked at me, and the sadness in his gaze scraped at my heart like teeth. I had five years of memories; before that was a fog. I'd lost something precious; if only I knew what it was. "Father, I—"

A knock sounded at the door, and he was cold as stone once more.

Bayan slipped inside without waiting for a response, and I wanted to curse him. He hunched his shoulders as he walked, his footfalls silent. If he were anyone else, I'd think his step hesitant. But Bayan had the look of a cat about him – deliberate, predatory. He wore a leather apron over his tunic, and blood stained his hands.

"I've completed the modification," Bayan said. "You asked me to see you right away when I'd finished."

A construct hobbled behind him, tiny hooves clicking against the floor. It looked like a deer, except for the fangs protruding from its mouth and the curling monkey's tail. Two small wings sprouted from its shoulders, blood staining the fur around them.

Father turned in his chair and placed a hand on the creature's back. It looked up at him with wide, wet eyes. "Sloppy," he said. "How many shards did you use to embed the follow command?"

"Two," Bayan said. "One to get the construct to follow me, and another to get it to stop."

"It should be one," Father said. "It goes where you do unless you tell it not to. The language is in the first book I gave you." He seized one of the wings and pulled it. When he let it go, it settled slowly back at the construct's side. "Your construction, however, is excellent."

Bayan's eyes slid to the side, and I held his gaze. Neither of us looked away. Always a competition. Bayan's irises were blacker even than mine, and when his lip curled, it only accentuated the full curve of his mouth. I supposed he was prettier than I would ever be, but I was convinced I was smarter, and that's what really mattered. Bayan never cared to hide his feelings. He carried his contempt for me like a child's favorite seashell.

"Try again with a new construct," Father said, and Bayan broke his gaze from mine. Ah, I'd won this small contest.

Father reached his fingers into the beast. I held my breath. I'd only seen him do this twice. Twice I could remember, at least. The creature only blinked placidly as Father's hand disappeared to the wrist. And then he pulled away and the construct froze, still as a statue. In his hand were two small shards of bone.

No blood stained his fingers. He dropped the bones into Bayan's hand. "Now go. Both of you."

I was quicker to the door than Bayan, who I suspected was hoping for more than just harsh words. But I was used to harsh words, and I'd things to do. I slipped out the door and held it for Bayan to pass so he needn't bloody the door with his hands. Father prized cleanliness.

Bayan glared at me as he passed, the breeze in his wake smelling of copper and incense. Bayan was just the son of a small isle's governor, lucky enough to have caught Father's eye and to be taken in as a foster. He'd brought the sickness with him, some exotic disease Imperial didn't know. I was told I got sick with it soon after he arrived, and recovered a little while after Bayan did. But he hadn't lost as much of his memory as I had, and he'd gotten some of it back.

As soon as he disappeared around the corner, I whirled and ran for the end of the hallway. The shutters threatened to blow against the walls when I unlatched them. The tile roofs looked like the slopes of mountains. I stepped outside and shut the window.

The world opened up before me. From atop the roof, I could see the city and the harbor. I could even see the boats in the ocean fishing for squid, their lanterns shining in the distance like earthbound stars. The wind tugged at my tunic, finding its way beneath the cloth, biting at my skin.

I had to be quick. By now, the construct servant would have removed the body of the deer. I half-ran, half-skidded down the slope of the roof toward the side of the palace where my father's bedroom was. He never brought his chain of keys into the questioning room. He didn't bring his construct guards with him. I'd read the small signs on his face. He might bark at me and scold me, but when we were alone – he feared me.

The tiles clicked below my feet. On the ramparts of the palace walls, shadows lurked – more constructs. Their instructions were simple. Watch for intruders. Sound an alarm. None of them paid me any mind, no matter that I wasn't where I was supposed to be. I wasn't an intruder.

The Construct of Bureaucracy would now be handing over the reports. I'd watched him sorting them earlier in the day, hairy lips fumbling over his teeth as he read them silently. There would be quite a lot. Shipments delayed due to skirmishes, the Ioph Carn stealing and smuggling witstone, citizens shirking their duty to the Empire.

I swung onto my father's balcony. The door to his room was cracked open. The room was usually empty, but this time it was not. A growl emanated from within. I froze. A black nose nudged into the space between door and wall, widening the gap. Yellow eyes peered at me and tufted ears flicked back. Claws scraped against wood as the creature strode toward me. Bing Tai, one of my father's oldest constructs. Gray speckled his jowls, but he had all his teeth. Each incisor was as long as my thumb.

His lip curled, the hackles on his back standing on end. He was a creature of nightmares, an amalgamation of large predators, with black, shaggy fur that faded into the darkness. He took another step closer.

Maybe it wasn't Bayan that was stupid; maybe I was the stupid one. Maybe this was how Father would find me after his tea – torn to bloody pieces on his balcony. It was too far to the ground, and I was too short to reach the roof gutters. The only way out from these rooms was into the hallway. "Bing Tai," I said, and my voice was steadier than I felt. "It is me, Lin."

I could almost feel my father's two commands battling in the construct's head. One: protect my rooms. Two: protect my family. Which command was stronger? I'd bet on the second one, but now I wasn't so sure.

I held my ground and tried not to let my fear show. I shoved my hand toward Bing Tai's nose. He could see me, he could hear me, perhaps he needed to smell me.

He *could* choose to taste me, though I did my best not to think about that.

His wet, cold nose touched my fingers, a growl still deep in his throat. I was not Bayan, who wrestled with the constructs like they were his brothers. I could not forget what they were. My throat constricted until I could barely breathe, my chest tight and painful.

And then Bing Tai settled on his haunches, his ears pricking, his lips covering his teeth. "Good Bing Tai," I said. My voice trembled. I had to hurry.

Grief lay heavy in the room, thick as the dust on what used to be my mother's wardrobe. Her jewelry on the dresser lay untouched; her slippers still awaited her next to the bed. What bothered me more than the questions my father asked me, than not knowing if he loved and cared for me as a child, was not remembering my mother.

I'd heard the remaining servants whispering. He burned all her portraits on the day she died. He forbade mention of her name. He put all her handmaidens to the sword. He guarded the memories of her jealously, as if he was the only one allowed to have them.

Focus.

I didn't know where he kept the copies he distributed to Bayan and me. He always pulled these from his sash pocket, and I didn't dare try to filch them from there. But the original chain of keys lay on the bed. So many doors. So many keys. I didn't know which was which, so I selected one at random – a golden key with a jade piece in the bow – and pocketed it.

I escaped into the hallway and wedged a thin piece of wood between door and frame so the door didn't latch. Now the tea would be steeping. Father would be reading through the reports, asking questions. I hoped they would keep him occupied.

My feet scuffed against the floorboards as I ran. The grand hallways of the palace were empty, lamplight glinting off the red-painted beams above. In the entryway, teak pillars rose from floor to ceiling, framing the faded mural on the second-floor wall. I took the steps down to the palace doors two at a time. Each step felt like a miniature betrayal.

I could have waited, one part of my mind told me. I could have been obedient; I could have done my best to answer my father's questions, to heal my memories. But the other part of my mind was cold and sharp. It cut through the guilt to find a hard truth. I could never be what he wanted if I did not take what I wanted. I hadn't been able to remember, no matter how hard I'd tried. He'd not left me with any other choice than to show him I was worthy in a different way.

I slipped through the palace doors and into the silent yard. The front gates were closed, but I was small and strong, and if Father wouldn't teach me his magic, well, there were other things I'd taught myself in the times he was locked in a secret room with Bayan. Like climbing.

The walls were clean but in disrepair. The plaster had broken away in places, leaving the stone beneath exposed. It was easy enough to climb. The monkey-shaped construct atop the wall just glanced at me before turning its limpid gaze back to the city. A thrill rushed through me when I touched down on the other side.

I'd been into the city on foot before – *I must have* – but for me, it was like the first time. The streets stank of fish and hot oil, and the remnants of dinners cooked and eaten. The stones beneath my slippers were dark and slippery with washwater. Pots clanged and a breeze carried the sound of lilting, subdued voices. The first two storefronts I saw were closed, wooden shutters locked shut.

Too late? I'd seen the blacksmith's storefront from the palace walls, and this was what first gave me the idea. I held my breath as I dashed down a narrow alley.

He was there. He was pulling the door closed, a pack slung over one shoulder.

"Wait," I said. "Please, just one more order."

"We're closed," he huffed out. "Come back tomorrow."

I stifled the desperation clawing up my throat. "I'll pay you twice your regular price if you can start it tonight. Just one key copy."

He looked at me then, and his gaze trailed over my embroidered silk tunic. His lips pressed together. He was thinking about lying about how much he charged. But then he just sighed. "Two silver. One is my regular price." He was a good man, fair.

Relief flooded me as I dug the coins from my sash pocket and pressed them into his calloused palm. "Here. I need it quickly."

Wrong thing to say. Annoyance flashed across his face. But he still opened the door again and let me into his shop. The man was built like an iron – broad and squat. His shoulders seemed to take up half the space. Metal tools hung from the walls and ceiling. He picked up his tinderbox and re-lit the lamps. And then he turned back to face me. "It won't be ready until tomorrow morning at the earliest."

"But do you need to keep the key?"

He shook his head. "I can make a mold of it tonight. The key will be ready tomorrow."

I wished there weren't so many chances to turn back, so many chances for my courage to falter. I forced myself to drop my father's key into the blacksmith's hand. The man took it and turned, fishing a block of clay from a stone trough. He pressed the key into it. And then he froze, his breath stopping in his throat.

I moved for the key before I could think. I saw what he did as soon as I took one step closer. At the base of the bow, just before the stem, was the tiny figure of a phoenix embossed into the metal.

When the blacksmith looked at me, his face was as round and pale as the moon. "Who are you? What are you doing with one of the Emperor's keys?"

I should have grabbed the key and run. I was swifter than he was. I could snatch it away and be gone before he took his next breath. All he'd have left was a story – one that no one would believe.

But if I did, I wouldn't have my key copy. I wouldn't have any more answers. I'd be stuck where I was at the start of the day, my memory a haze, the answers I gave Father always inadequate. Always just out of reach. Always broken. And this man – he was a good man. Father taught me the kind of thing to say to good men.

I chose my words carefully. "Do you have any children?"

A measure of color came back into his face. "Two." He answered. His brows knit together as he wondered if he should have responded.

"I am Lin," I said, laying myself bare. "I am the Emperor's heir. He hasn't been the same since my mother's death. He isolates himself, he keeps few servants, he does not meet with the island governors. Rebellion is brewing. Already the Shardless Few have taken Khalute. They'll seek to expand their hold. And there are the Alanga. Some may not believe they're coming back, but my family has kept them from returning.

"Do you want soldiers marching in the streets? Do you want war on your doorstep?" I touched his shoulder gently, and he did not flinch. "On your children's doorstep?"

He reached reflexively behind his right ear for the scar each citizen had. The place where a shard of bone was removed and taken for the Emperor's vault.

"Is my shard powering a construct?" he asked.

"I don't know," I said. I don't know, I don't know – there was so *little* that I did know. "But if I get into my father's vault, I will look for yours and I will bring it back to you. I can't promise you anything. I wish I could. But I will try."

He licked his lips. "My children?"

"I can see what I can do." It was all I could say. No one was exempt from the islands' Tithing Festivals.

Sweat shone on his forehead. "I'll do it."

Father would be setting the reports aside now. He would take up his cup of tea and sip from it, looking out the window at the lights of the city below. Sweat prickled between my shoulder-blades. I needed to get the key back before he discovered me.

I watched through a haze as the blacksmith finished making the mold. When he handed the key back, I turned to run.

"Lin," he said.

I stopped.

"My name is Numeen. The year of my ritual was 1508. We need an Emperor who cares about us."

What could I say to that? So I just ran. Out the door, down the alleyway, back to climbing the wall. Now Father would be finishing up his tea, his fingers wrapped around the still-warm cup. A stone came loose beneath my fingertips. I let it fall to the ground. The *crack* made me cringe.

He'd be putting his cup down, he'd be looking at the city. How long did he look at the city? The climb down was faster than the climb up. I couldn't smell the city anymore. All I could smell was my own breath. The walls of the outer buildings passed in a blur as I ran to the palace – the servants' quarters, the Hall of Everlasting Peace, the Hall of Earthly Wisdom, the wall surrounding the palace garden. Everything was cold and dark, empty.

I took the servants' entrance into the palace, bounding up the stairs two at a time. The narrow passageway opened into the main hallway. The main hallway wrapped around the palace's second floor, and my father's bedroom was nearly on the other side from the servants' entrance. I wished my legs were longer. I wished my mind were stronger.

Floorboards squeaked beneath my feet as I ran, the noise making me wince. At last, I made it back and slipped into my father's room. Bing Tai lay on the rug at the foot of the bed, stretched out like an old cat. I had to reach over him to get to the chain of keys. He smelled musty, like a mix between a bear construct and a closet full of moth-ridden clothes.

It took three tries for me to hook the key back onto the chain. My fingers felt like eels – flailing and slippery.

I knelt to retrieve the door wedge on my way out, my breath ragged in my throat. The brightness of the light in the hallway made me blink. I'd have to find my way into the city tomorrow to retrieve the new key. But it was done, the wedge for the door safely in my sash pocket. I let out the breath I hadn't known I'd been holding.

"Lin."

Bayan. My limbs felt made of stone. What had he seen? I turned to face him – his brow was furrowed, his hands clasped behind his back. I willed my heart to calm, my face to blankness.

"What are you doing outside the Emperor's room?"

if you enjoyed
SON OF THE STORM

look out for

THE JASMINE THRONE

The Burning Kingdoms:
Book One

by

Tasha Suri

*Imprisoned by her tyrannical brother, Malini spends her days
in isolation in the Hirana: an ancient temple that was once the
source of the powerful, magical deathless waters—but is now
little more than a decaying ruin.*

*Priya is a maidservant, one among several who make
the treacherous journey to the top of the Hirana every
night to clean Malini's chambers. She is happy to be
an anonymous drudge, so long as it keeps anyone from
guessing the dangerous secret she hides.*

*But when Malini accidentally bears witness to Priya's true nature,
their destinies become irrevocably tangled. One is a vengeful princess
seeking to claim a throne. The other is a priestess seeking to find her
family. Together, they will change the fate of an empire.*

1

PRIYA

Someone important must have been killed in the night.

Priya was sure of it the minute she heard the thud of hooves on the road behind her. She stepped to the roadside as a group of guards clad in Parijati white and gold raced past her on their horses, their sabers clinking against their embossed belts. She drew her pallu over her face—partly because they would expect such a gesture of respect from a common woman, and partly to avoid the risk that one of them would recognize her—and watched them through the gap between her fingers and the cloth.

When they were out of sight, she didn't run. But she did start walking very, very fast. The sky was already transforming from milky gray to the pearly blue of dawn, and she still had a long way to go.

The Old Bazaar was on the outskirts of the city. It was far enough from the regent's mahal that Priya had a vague hope it wouldn't have been shut yet. And today, she was lucky. As she arrived, breathless, sweat dampening the back of her blouse, she could see that the streets were still seething with people: parents tugging along small children; traders carrying large sacks of flour or rice on their heads; gaunt beggars, skirting the edges of the market with their alms bowls in hand; and women like Priya, plain ordinary women in even plainer saris, stubbornly shoving their way through the crowd in search of stalls with fresh vegetables and reasonable prices.

If anything, there seemed to be even *more* people at the bazaar than usual—and there was a distinct sour note of panic in the air.

News of the patrols had clearly passed from household to household with its usual speed.

People were afraid.

Three months ago, an important Parijati merchant had been murdered in his bed, his throat slit, his body dumped in front of the temple of the mothers of flame just before the dawn prayers. For an entire two weeks after that, the regent's men had patrolled the streets on foot and on horseback, beating or arresting Ahiranyi suspected of rebellious activity and destroying any market stalls that had tried to remain open in defiance of the regent's strict orders.

The Parijatdvipan merchants had refused to supply Hiranaprastha with rice and grain in the weeks that followed. Ahiranyi had starved.

Now it looked as though it was happening again. It was natural for people to remember and fear; remember, and scramble to buy what supplies they could before the markets were forcibly closed once more.

Priya wondered who had been murdered this time, listening for any names as she dove into the mass of people, toward the green banner on staves in the distance that marked the apothecary's stall. She passed tables groaning under stacks of vegetables and sweet fruit, bolts of silky cloth and gracefully carved idols of the yaksa for family shrines, vats of golden oil and ghee. Even in the faint early-morning light, the market was vibrant with color and noise.

The press of people grew more painful.

She was nearly to the stall, caught in a sea of heaving, sweating bodies, when a man behind her cursed and pushed her out of the way. He shoved her hard with his full body weight, his palm heavy on her arm, unbalancing her entirely. Three people around her were knocked back. In the sudden release of pressure, she tumbled down onto the ground, feet skidding in the wet soil.

The bazaar was open to the air, and the dirt had been churned into a froth by feet and carts and the night's monsoon rainfall. She felt the wetness seep in through her sari, from hem to thigh, soaking through draped cotton to the petticoat underneath. The man who had shoved her stumbled into her; if she hadn't snatched her calf swiftly back, the pressure of his boot on her leg would have been agonizing. He glanced down at her—blank, dismissive, a faint sneer to his mouth—and looked away again.

Her mind went quiet.

In the silence, a single voice whispered, *You could make him regret that.*

There were gaps in Priya's childhood memories, spaces big enough to stick a fist through. But whenever pain was inflicted on her—the humiliation of a blow, a man's careless shove, a fellow servant's cruel laughter—she felt the knowledge of how to cause equal suffering unfurl in her mind. Ghostly whispers, in her brother's patient voice.

This is how you pinch a nerve hard enough to break a handhold. This is how you snap a bone. This is how you gouge an eye. Watch carefully, Priya. Just like this.

This is how you stab someone through the heart.

She carried a knife at her waist. It was a very good knife, practical, with a plain sheath and hilt, and she kept its edge finely honed for kitchen work. With nothing but her little knife and a careful slide of her finger and thumb, she could leave the insides of anything—vegetables, unskinned meat, fruits newly harvested from the regent's orchard—swiftly bared, the outer rind a smooth, coiled husk in her palm.

She looked back up at the man and carefully let the thought of her knife drift away. She unclenched her trembling fingers.

You're lucky, she thought, *that I am not what I was raised to be.*

The crowd behind her and in front of her was growing thicker. Priya couldn't even see the green banner of the apothecary's stall any longer. She rocked back on the balls of her feet, then rose swiftly. Without looking at the man again, she angled herself and slipped between two strangers in front of her, putting her small stature to good use and shoving her way to the front of the throng. A judicious application of her elbows and knees and some wriggling finally brought her near enough to the stall to see the apothecary's face, puckered with sweat and irritation.

The stall was a mess, vials turned on their sides, clay pots upended. The apothecary was packing away his wares as fast as he could. Behind her, around her, she could hear the rumbling noise of the crowd grow more tense.

"Please," she said loudly. "Uncle, *please*. If you've got any beads of sacred wood to spare, I'll buy them from you."

A stranger to her left snorted audibly. "You think he's got any left? Brother, if you do, I'll pay double whatever she offers."

"My grandmother's sick," a girl shouted, three people deep behind them. "So if you could help me out, uncle—"

Priya felt the wood of the stall begin to peel beneath the hard pressure of her nails.

"Please," she said, her voice pitched low to cut across the din.

But the apothecary's attention was raised toward the back of the crowd. Priya didn't have to turn her own head to know he'd caught sight of the white-and-gold uniforms of the regent's men, finally here to close the bazaar.

"I'm closed up," he shouted out. "There's nothing more for any of you. Get lost!" He slammed his hand down, then shoved the last of his wares away with a shake of his head.

The crowd began to disperse slowly. A few people stayed, still pleading for the apothecary's aid, but Priya didn't join them. She knew she would get nothing here.

She turned and threaded her way back out of the crowd, stopping only to buy a small bag of kachoris from a tired-eyed vendor. Her sodden petticoat stuck heavily to her legs. She plucked the cloth, pulling it from her thighs, and strode in the opposite direction of the soldiers.

On the farthest edge of the market, where the last of the stalls and well-trod ground met the main road leading to open farmland and scattered villages beyond, was a dumping ground. The locals had built a brick wall around it, but that did nothing to contain the stench of it. Food sellers threw their stale oil and decayed produce here, and sometimes discarded any cooked food that couldn't be sold.

When Priya had been much younger she'd known this place well. She'd known exactly the nausea and euphoria that finding something near rotten but *edible* could send spiraling through a starving body. Even now, her stomach lurched strangely at the sight of the heap, the familiar, thick stench of it rising around her.

Today, there were six figures huddled against its walls in the meager shade. Five young boys and a girl of about fifteen—older than the rest.

Knowledge was shared between the children who lived alone in the city, the ones who drifted from market to market, sleeping on the verandas of kinder households. They whispered to each other the best spots for begging for alms or collecting scraps. They passed word of which stallholders would give them food out of pity, and which would beat them with a stick sooner than offer even an ounce of charity.

They told each other about Priya, too.

If you go to the Old Bazaar on the first morning after rest day, a maid will come and give you sacred wood, if you need it. She won't ask you for coin or favors. She'll just help. No, she really will. She won't ask for anything at all.

The girl looked up at Priya. Her left eyelid was speckled with faint motes of green, like algae on still water. She wore a thread around her throat, a single bead of wood strung upon it.

"Soldiers are out," the girl said by way of greeting. A few of the boys shifted restlessly, looking over her shoulder at the tumult of the market. Some wore shawls to hide the rot on their necks and arms—the veins of green, the budding of new roots under skin.

"They are. All over the city," Priya agreed.

"Did a merchant get his head chopped off again?"

Priya shook her head. "I know as much as you do."

The girl looked from Priya's face down to Priya's muddied sari, her hands empty apart from the sack of kachoris. There was a question in her gaze.

"I couldn't get any beads today," Priya confirmed. She watched the girl's expression crumple, though she valiantly tried to control it. Sympathy would do her no good, so Priya offered the pastries out instead. "You should go now. You don't want to get caught by the guards."

The children snatched the kachoris up, a few muttering their thanks, and scattered. The girl rubbed the bead at her throat with her knuckles as she went. Priya knew it would be cold under her hand—empty of magic.

If the girl didn't get hold of more sacred wood soon, then the next time Priya saw her, the left side of her face would likely be as green-dusted as her eyelid.

You can't save them all, she reminded herself. *You're no one. This is all you can do. This, and no more.*

Priya turned back to leave—and saw that one boy had hung back, waiting patiently for her to notice him. He was the kind of small that suggested malnourishment; his bones too sharp, his head too large for a body that hadn't yet grown to match it. He had his shawl over his hair, but she could still see his dark curls, and the deep green leaves growing between them. He'd wrapped his hands up in cloth.

"Do you really have nothing, ma'am?" he asked hesitantly.

"Really," Priya said. "If I had any sacred wood, I'd have given it to you."

"I thought maybe you lied," he said. "I thought, maybe you haven't got enough for more than one person, and you didn't want to make anyone feel bad. But there's only me now. So you can help me."

"I really am sorry," Priya said. She could hear yelling and footsteps echoing from the market, the crash of wood as stalls were closed up.

The boy looked like he was mustering up his courage. And sure enough, after a moment, he squared his shoulders and said, "If you can't get me any sacred wood, then can you get me a job?"

She blinked at him, surprised.

"I—I'm just a maidservant," she said. "I'm sorry, little brother, but—"

"You must work in a nice house, if you can help strays like us," he said quickly. "A big house with money to spare. Maybe your masters need a boy who works hard and doesn't make much trouble? That could be me."

"Most households won't take a boy who has the rot, no matter how hardworking he is," she pointed out gently, trying to lessen the blow of her words.

"I know," he said. His jaw was set, stubborn. "But I'm still asking."

Smart boy. She couldn't blame him for taking the chance. She was clearly soft enough to spend her own coin on sacred wood to help the rot-riven. Why wouldn't he push her for more?

"I'll do anything anyone needs me to do," he insisted. "Ma'am, I can clean latrines. I can cut wood. I can work land. My family is—they were—farmers. I'm not afraid of hard work."

"You haven't got anyone?" she asked. "None of the others look out for you?" She gestured in the vague direction the other children had vanished.

"I'm alone," he said simply. Then: *"Please."*

A few people drifted past them, carefully skirting the boy. His wrapped hands, the shawl over his head—both revealed his rot-riven status just as well as anything they hid would have.

"Call me Priya," she said. "Not ma'am."

"Priya," he repeated obediently.

"You say you can work," she said. She looked at his hands. "How bad are they?"

"Not that bad."

"Show me," she said. "Give me your wrist."

"You don't mind touching me?" he asked. There was a slight waver of hesitation in his voice.

"Rot can't pass between people," she said. "Unless I pluck one of those leaves from your hair and eat it, I think I'll be fine."

That brought a smile to his face. There for a blink, like a flash of sun through parting clouds, then gone. He deftly unwrapped

480

one of his hands. She took hold of his wrist and raised it up to the light.

There was a little bud, growing up under the skin.

It was pressing against the flesh of his fingertip, his finger a too-small shell for the thing trying to unfurl. She looked at the tracery of green visible through the thin skin at the back of his hand, the fine lace of it. The bud had deep roots.

She swallowed. Ah. Deep roots, deep rot. If he already had leaves in his hair, green spidering through his blood, she couldn't imagine that he had long left.

"Come with me," she said, and tugged him by the wrist, making him follow her. She walked along the road, eventually joining the flow of the crowd leaving the market behind.

"Where are we going?" he asked. He didn't try to pull away from her.

"I'm going to get you some sacred wood," she said determinedly, putting all thoughts of murders and soldiers and the work she needed to do out of her mind. She released him and strode ahead. He ran to keep up with her, dragging his dirty shawl tight around his thin frame. "And after that, we'll see what to do with you."

The grandest of the city's pleasure houses lined the edges of the river. It was early enough in the day that they were utterly quiet, their pink lanterns unlit. But they would be busy later. The brothels were always left well alone by the regent's men. Even in the height of the last boiling summer, before the monsoon had cracked the heat in two, when the rebel sympathizers had been singing anti-imperialist songs and a noble lord's chariot had been cornered and burned on the street directly outside his own haveli—the brothels had kept their lamps lit.

Too many of the pleasure houses belonged to highborn nobles for the regent to close them. Too many were patronized by visiting merchants and nobility from Parijatdvipa's other city-states—a source of income no one seemed to want to do without.

To the rest of Parijatdvipa, Ahiranya was a den of vice, good for pleasure and little else. It carried its bitter history, its status as the losing side of an ancient war, like a yoke. They called it a backward place, rife with political violence, and, in more recent years, with the rot: the strange disease that twisted plants and crops and infected the men and women who worked the fields and forests with flowers that sprouted through the skin and leaves that pushed through their eyes. As the rot grew, other sources of income in Ahiranya had dwindled. And unrest had surged and swelled until Priya feared it too would crack, with all the fury of a storm.

As Priya and the boy walked on, the pleasure houses grew less grand. Soon, there were no pleasure houses at all. Around her were cramped homes, small shops. Ahead of her lay the edge of the forest. Even in the morning light, it was shadowed, the trees a silent barrier of green.

Priya had never met anyone born and raised outside Ahiranya who was not disturbed by the quiet of the forest. She'd known maids raised in Alor or even neighboring Srugna who avoided the place entirely. "There should be noise," they'd mutter. "Birdsong. Or insects. It isn't natural."

But the heavy quiet was comforting to Priya. She was Ahiranyi to the bone. She liked the silence of it, broken only by the scuff of her own feet against the ground.

"Wait for me here," she told the boy. "I won't be long."

He nodded without saying a word. He was staring out at the forest when she left him, a faint breeze rustling the leaves of his hair.

Priya slipped down a narrow street where the ground was uneven with hidden tree roots, the dirt rising and falling in mounds beneath her feet. Ahead of her was a single dwelling. Beneath its pillared veranda crouched an older man.

He raised his head as she approached. At first he seemed to look right through her, as though he'd been expecting someone else entirely. Then his gaze focused. His eyes narrowed in recognition.

"You," he said.

"Gautam." She tilted her head in a gesture of respect. "How are you?"

"Busy," he said shortly. "Why are you here?"

"I need sacred wood. Just one bead."

"Should have gone to the bazaar, then," he said evenly. "I've supplied plenty of apothecaries. They can deal with you."

"I tried the Old Bazaar. No one has anything."

"If they don't, why do you think I will?"

Oh, come on now, she thought, irritated. But she said nothing. She waited until his nostrils flared as he huffed and rose up from the veranda, turning to the beaded curtain of the doorway. Tucked in the back of his tunic was a heavy hand sickle.

"Fine. Come in, then. The sooner we do this, the sooner you leave."

She drew the purse from her blouse before climbing up the steps and entering after him.

He led her to his workroom and bid her to stand by the table at its center. Cloth sacks lined the corners of the room. Small stoppered bottles—innumerable salves and tinctures and herbs harvested from the forest itself—sat in tidy rows on shelves. The air smelled of earth and damp.

He took her entire purse from her, opened the drawstring, and adjusted its weight in his palm. Then he clucked, tongue against teeth, and dropped it onto the table.

"This isn't enough."

"You—of course it's enough," Priya said. "That's all the money I have."

"That doesn't magically make it enough."

"That's what it cost me at the bazaar last time—"

"But you couldn't get anything at the bazaar," said Gautam. "And had you been able to, he would have charged you more. Supply is low, demand is high." He frowned at her sourly. "You think it's easy harvesting sacred wood?"

"Not at all," Priya said. *Be pleasant,* she reminded herself. *You need his help.*

"Last month I sent in four woodcutters. They came out after two days, thinking they'd been in there *two hours.* Between—that," he said, gesturing in the direction of the forest, "and the regent flinging his thugs all over the fucking city for who knows what reason, you think it's easy work?"

"No," Priya said. "I'm sorry."

But he wasn't done quite yet.

"I'm still waiting for the men I sent this week to come back," he went on. His fingers were tapping on the table's surface—a fast, irritated rhythm. "Who knows when that will be? I have plenty of reason to get the best price for the supplies I have. So I'll have a proper payment from you, girl, or you'll get nothing."

Before he could continue, she lifted her hand. She had a few bracelets on her wrists. Two were good-quality metal. She slipped them off, placing them on the table before him, alongside the purse.

"The money and these," she said. "That's all I have."

She thought he'd refuse her, just out of spite. But instead, he scooped up the bangles and the coin and pocketed them.

"That'll do. Now watch," he said. "I'll show you a trick."

He threw a cloth package down on the table. It was tied with a rope. He drew it open with one swift tug, letting the cloth fall to the sides.

Priya flinched back.

Inside lay the severed branch of a young tree. The bark had split, pale wood opening up into a red-brown wound. The sap that oozed from its surface was the color and consistency of blood.

"This came from the path leading to the grove my men usually harvest," he said. "They wanted to show me why they couldn't fulfill the regular quota. Rot as far as the eye could see, they told me." His own eyes were hooded. "You can look closer if you want."

"No, thank you," Priya said tightly.

"Sure?"

"You should burn it," she said. She was doing her best not to breathe the scent of it in too deeply. It had a stench like meat.

He snorted. "It has its uses." He walked away from her, rooting through his shelves. After a moment, he returned with another cloth-wrapped item, this one only as large as a fingertip. He unwrapped it, careful to keep from touching what it held. Priya could feel the heat rising from the wood within: a strange, pulsing warmth that rolled off its surface with the steadiness of a sunbeam.

Sacred wood.

She watched as Gautam held the shard close to the rot-struck branch, as the lesion on the branch paled, the redness fading. The stench of it eased a little, and Priya breathed gratefully.

"There," he said. "Now you know it is fresh. You'll get plenty of use from it."

"Thank you. That was a useful demonstration." She tried not to let her impatience show. What did he want—awe? Tears of gratitude? She had no time for any of it. "You should still burn the branch. If you touch it by mistake..."

"I know how to handle the rot. I send men into the forest every day," he said dismissively. "And what do you do? Sweep floors? I don't need your advice."

He thrust the shard of sacred wood out to her. "Take this. And leave."

She bit her tongue and held out her hand, the long end of her sari drawn over her palm. She rewrapped the sliver of wood up carefully, once, twice, tightening the fabric, tying it off with a neat knot. Gautam watched her.

"Whoever you're buying this for, the rot is still going to kill them," he said, when she was done. "This branch will die even if I wrap it in a whole shell of sacred wood. It will just die slower. My professional opinion for you, at no extra cost." He threw the cloth back over the infected branch with one careless flick of his fingers. "So don't come back here and waste your money again. I'll show you out."

He shepherded her to the door. She pushed through the beaded curtain, greedily inhaling the clean air, untainted by the smell of decay.

At the edge of the veranda there was a shrine alcove carved into the wall. Inside it were three idols sculpted from plain wood, with lustrous black eyes and hair of vines. Before them were three tiny clay lamps lit with cloth wicks set in pools of oil. Sacred numbers.

She remembered how perfectly she'd once been able to fit her whole body into that alcove. She'd slept in it one night, curled up tight. She'd been as small as the orphan boy, once.

"Do you still let beggars shelter on your veranda when it rains?" Priya asked, turning to look at Gautam where he stood, barring the entryway.

"Beggars are bad for business," he said. "And the ones I see these days don't have brothers I owe favors to. Are you leaving or not?"

Just the threat of pain can break someone. She briefly met Gautam's eyes. Something impatient and malicious lurked there. *A knife, used right, never has to draw blood.*

But ah, Priya didn't have it in her to even threaten this old bully. She stepped back.

What a big void there was, between the knowledge within her and the person she appeared to be, bowing her head in respect to a petty man who still saw her as a street beggar who'd risen too far, and hated her for it.

"Thank you, Gautam," she said. "I'll try not to trouble you again."

She'd have to carve the wood herself. She couldn't give the shard as it was to the boy. A whole shard of sacred wood held against skin—it would burn. But better that it burn her. She had no gloves, so she would have to work carefully, with her little knife and a piece of cloth to hold the worst of the pain at bay. Even now, she could feel the heat of the shard against her skin, soaking through the fabric that bound it.

The boy was waiting where she'd left him. He looked even smaller in the shadow of the forest, even more alone. He turned to watch her as she approached, his eyes wary, and a touch uncertain, as if he hadn't been sure of her return.

Her heart twisted a little. Meeting Gautam had brought her closer to the bones of her past than she'd been in a long, long time. She felt the tug of her frayed memories like a physical ache.

Her brother. Pain. The smell of smoke.

Don't look, Pri. Don't look. Just show me the way.

Show me—

No. There was no point remembering that.

It was only sensible, she told herself, to help him. She didn't want the image of him, standing before her, to haunt her. She didn't want to remember a starving child, abandoned and alone, roots growing through his hands, and think, *I left him to die. He asked me for help, and I left him.*

"You're in luck," she said lightly. "I work in the regent's mahal. And his wife has a very gentle heart when it comes to orphans. I should know. She took me in. She'll let you work for her if I ask nicely. I'm sure of it."

His eyes went wide, so much hope in his face that it was almost painful to look at him. So Priya made a point of looking away. The sky was bright, the air overly warm. She needed to get back.

"What's your name?" she asked.

"Rukh," he said. "My name is Rukh."

Follow us:

/orbitbooksUS

/orbitbooks

/orbitbooks

Join our mailing list
to receive alerts on our
latest releases and deals.

orbitbooks.net

Enter our monthly
giveaway for the chance
to win some epic prizes.

orbitloot.com